BLISSFUL MAGIC

"I think I love you, Seneca," Emily said quietly. "No, don't say anything, just kiss me. I'll go in the morning, I promise I will. But let me have one more night in your arms."

He wanted that, too. He wanted, just for a while, to hold her close and lose himself in her sweetness. But, love? She was so naive, so vulnerable. He hated to be the one to disillusion her. And yet he couldn't let her leave.

"Emily, we have to talk."

"No. No talking." Out of a sense of fear and desperation she clung to him. "I don't want to talk anymore."

She slipped the buttons of his shirt open and ran her fingers over the hard masculine contours of his chest. Her head began to spin from the sensation of her flesh against his, but the feelings surging through her body were too compellingly sweet to deny. She wanted to drown in them.

He closed his eyes and groaned in delicious agony. How could he stop her, how could he put an end to the blissful magic of her shy loving? Instead of pushing her away as his brain commanded, his hands pulled her closer, holding her captive so she couldn't escape even if she tried . . . .

HEARTFIRE ROMANCES

MIDNIGHT ENCHANTMENT

JEANNE E. HANSEN

ZEBRA BOOKS
KENSINGTON PUBLISHING CORP.

ZEBRA BOOKS

are published by

Kensington Publishing Corp.
475 Park Avenue South
New York, NY 10016

First printing: February, 1990

Printed in the United States of America

With grateful thanks to my Aunt Helen for digging through the archives of the Franklin Library for historical documents on the waterways and underground railways of Pennsylvania and New York.

Chapter 1

Emily Harcourt watched as from far away as her fingers twisted the white fabric of her gloves in her lap. She still couldn't quite believe the tragic events that had led her to be sitting in her attorney's office while he droned on about her Uncle Joe's will. Uncle Joe. A single tear escaped and fell onto her wrist. She touched that one tear then deliberately blinked the rest away. She had promised herself she wouldn't give in to her grief today. The time had come to put her tears away and get her life in order. Uncle Joe would have wanted that. Her father, who had died only two months earlier, would have expected it of her. Little Peter, he . . . Another tear. Little Peter, her young cousin, also dead, would have been dreadfully upset at her continuing depression. But how was one to shake loose of its hold when constantly reminded of the awful losses that had caused it?

Thomas Stevens stopped reading and looked up. She had drifted away again. Going over the last will and testament of Joseph Harcourt was useless just yet. Maybe in a few weeks, when she regained a balance in her life . . . A great wave of sympathy for the lovely young woman seated beside his desk swept over him. He'd known about her for years, but only recently had he met her, and she was every bit as angelic as Joe had claimed. She was as close to an angel as a mortal could

7

imagine.

Her features were exquisite, like those painted so delicately on the finest porcelain doll. Her hair, a pale silvery blonde, usually fell in abundant curls down her back. It was confined today beneath her black hat. Thomas didn't like her in black. No woman as fair should have to wear black. She should be in blue, in a dress the color of her cornflower blue eyes. Oh, that he were forty years younger . . .

"Emily, dear, let me get you a cup of tea," he offered.

"No," she replied, turning shimmery eyes up to meet his. "I'm all right. Really, I am."

"You mustn't go on grieving. You're young and beautiful, and it's time to look after yourself. You've looked after your father for years, then became as close to a mother to Peter as any woman could have been. Don't you want a family of your own?"

"They were my family," she reminded him gently.

"A husband, a baby . . ."

She nodded. "Of course, but . . ."

"I know. Always someone else has needed you."

"We had planned such an exciting summer. Uncle Joe was going to take us traveling. We were going to New York City and on down to Philadelphia and Washington. Peter was so interested in politics. He wanted to be a senator, you know."

"That's why he was working as a page while Congress is in session?"

"He wanted to learn everything. If only he hadn't . . ."

"Now, now. None of that. There was absolutely nothing you could have done to prevent their deaths. They were simply in the wrong place at the wrong time, and got in the way of some very nasty men who killed them."

"They were murdered."

He nodded. "Yes, murdered . . . killed." She'd made that comment on a couple of occasions. He wondered why. "But you could not have stopped it."

He didn't believe her. She could see that. She meant murdered. Intentionally murdered. She supposed she could have pressed the matter, but she said no more. No one believed her, not even Paddie McMurdie, Joe's closest friend, the policeman who'd come to tell her of her awful loss. She heard his voice just then in the outer office. He would be flirting with Mrs. Beam, Mr. Stevens's secretary. Paddie was born flirting. He'd die with an outrageous wink at death. He had been her salvation over the past two weeks, taking her home to be comforted by his wife. Margaret had held her as she wept; Margaret had fed her and cared for her, had calmed her when her bad dreams started. Margaret believed her. But Paddie . . .

"Now, lass," Paddie had said, "who'd be wantin' to hurt Joe Harcourt and a lad like Petie. You're mistakin', lamb. 'Twas no more than bad luck. Just a couple cutthroats out to find a fat purse."

She had tried to explain what she and Peter had overheard the day before, but it was all a muddle in her mind, and her words came out in a confused jumble of nonsense.

Tom Stevens thought to try one more time. "Emily, do you understand what I've said this morning?"

She looked up into his troubled hazel eyes and gave a small negligent shrug. "Uncle Joe left everything to me."

"Except for the ten percent that Mr. Petrie owns in the mill, and . . ."

Paddie's fist rapped on the door and he walked in. Thomas Stevens gave up. The rest would have to wait. He stood and greeted Paddie.

"McMurdie. Good to see you."

"How's my girl today?" he beamed, giving Emily's shoulders a hug while his eyes met those of her attorney.

"She . . ." Thomas began, then shook his head. "She needs a few weeks yet. We'll talk again then. I do think

9

it best if she not return to the house just yet. If you and Maggie could see your way to keep her with you until . . ."

"Aye, 'tis a treat to have her. Maggie loves the company. And you, Miss Emily, me heart, what of you? Will you let ol' Paddie take care of you?" He turned the power of his rosy-cheeked grin on her.

Her spirits lifted as they always did when he teased her into a grin of her own, even if hers was still a bit wobbly.

"I'd like that, if you're sure you don't mind. I don't want to impose. Mr. Stevens," she said, extending her hand, "thank you very much. You've been patient. I know I . . . well, my mind is . . ."

"Never mind, Miss Harcourt. We'll discuss business later. There's no need to rush, certainly. I suppose Petrie can't bungle things too much in a few weeks."

Emily caught the uncertain glance that Thomas Stevens and Paddie McMurdie exchanged. She opened her mouth to ask what it was they had against Petrie, but Stevens forestalled her.

"You leave business to me for now. You are to concentrate only on yourself. Pamper yourself. Buy a new wardrobe. Visit your friends or family. You have two aunts in North Carolina, don't you?"

"Yes, sir, only we aren't very close. I don't think . . ."

"It's time to get on with your life."

"We'll see she does that," Paddie answered robustly.

They meant well, she thought as she walked down the narrow stairs with Paddie, but they were wrong. She needed to get her mind off herself and her troubles.

Paddie's thoughts were running along the same vein. Emily had never in her life been a self-serving girl. It was unlikely she'd become one now. What she really needed was to get involved with something or someone who needed her again.

That evening he asked Margaret what she thought of

Emily working at the hospital.

"The hospital? What for?"

"She'd be busy, distracted, useful."

"She'd be surrounded by sick people who might indeed need her help but who would remind her every minute of every day of her father. And if there were sick children, would she not see in her mind the broken and bleeding body of young Peter?"

Paddie sighed. "Aye, I hadn't thought of all that."

"But the idea is a good one, Paddie, me dear. Only you've the wrong place and the wrong people. She needs life, health, and energy around her. And maybe a good fight to get her blood moving again."

"A fight?"

"Maybe fight is the wrong word. A struggle, then."

"Lass, you've lost me."

"Think, Paddie. Who did you say you had a beer with yesterday? Who said he had a new shipment coming in that he wished he had help for. And she'd be away from all reminders of Joe and Peter."

"Whoa, now. I'm not letting Emily anywhere near that man. She's an innocent girl."

"Paddie, he's not that bad."

"Lord knows he's one of my best friends, and in some ways he's a fine man, but frankly, I wouldn't trust him with Emily. He's a different man now, a hard man. There's no telling what he'd do."

"Don't you think the same man is still there under that cynical bitterness. They could help each other. She's what he needs to restore his faith in women."

"And what if he destroys her? He could, you know. It's too risky."

"She's a woman, Paddie, not a little girl. She's twenty. The only reason she isn't married with children of her own is her father's illness. Isn't it time she started to live? Isn't it time for her to learn what being a woman is all about?"

"Not at his hands. I won't have it. He's a womanizer;

11

he drinks too much; he gets into brawls for the hell of it. He's a reprobate. No. Absolutely not."

And that was the end of it until much later that night when Emily's piercing screams tore them from the arms of sleep. They both jumped up, threw on robes, and raced for her room. They found her sitting up in bed in the dark, shaking with the sobs that wracked her young body.

"Emily," Paddie groaned, his heart breaking for her pain. "Darlin', don't." He sat beside her and pulled her trembling body into his arms. "Hush, now. I'm here. It's all right."

"Paddie, they were deliberately murdered," she cried between sobs. "I know it, I know it. Peter and I heard them talking. They saw us. They started to walk toward us and they were very angry. We left. They watched us go."

"Shh. It was a nightmare, sweetheart. It wasn't real, just a dream." He looked up and met the worried eyes of his wife.

"No, please listen to me. It happened. It did. Please believe me. They're going to kill me, too."

"Paddie McMurdie," Margaret said sternly, "it's time for you to listen to the girl. You hear her out, I'll make some hot milk and honey. Go on, Emily. Tell him what you told me. And don't interrupt her," she warned her husband on her way out the door.

"All right, now, what is all this about?"

"The day before they were killed, I took the buggy over to pick Peter up at work. I was late, and he wasn't waiting on the steps, so I went in to look for him. I found him, but as we were leaving again we heard several men talking. They sounded very upset and angry. We stopped, just for a few seconds. Peter wanted to listen. They were discussing abolition and Peter's very keen on that. I couldn't get him away without causing a commotion."

"Can you remember what you heard?" Paddie asked,

wondering if there could be something to her story. It was no secret — the volatile controversy over abolition.

"Erie. I remember hearing that name. And something like Shalata. Not that, but something like it. It sounded Indian."

"Erie? And what was that again?"

"I can't remember exactly. Sha-shagua? Something like that."

"Chautauqua?"

"Yes, it could have been that. Chautauqua. Lady Chautauqua."

"And that's all?"

"I didn't listen that intently, but Peter said they were talking about getting rid of the source of the problem. He thought they were going to send someone to kill some man."

"Honey, those men use those terms rather loosely. They could have been discussing any of a hundred bills up for vote."

"But when they saw us they came after us. They tried to stop us."

"Perhaps they thought you were spying for the opposition."

"Would they kill someone for that?"

"I hardly think so."

"But they did. They killed Peter, and Joe, because Uncle Joe was with him. It was supposed to be me who died with Peter. I usually take him to work."

"Ah, so that's what this is about. You feel guilty because you're still alive."

"No. But if I'd told Uncle Joe what we heard . . . I forgot all about it, you see."

"Do you really think it would have made a difference?" He smiled sadly.

"I keep thinking someone is watching me."

That sobered him. "You've seen someone following you?"

"No, it's mostly a feeling, but it leaves me cold and

scared. And these dreams. It's always Peter, and he's trying to warn me. And then they have him, and no matter how fast I run I can't catch up. And then he's there on the ground, bleeding . . ." She caught a ragged breath. "And then they're chasing me."

Her tears began again, and Paddie calmed her and hushed her words. "Don't fret anymore, princess. I'm going to take care of everything."

"Then you believe me?" she asked, turning big pathetic eyes up to his.

Whether he did or not, whether there was truth to what she said or pure imagination was irrelevant. He had to act as if what she said was fact. For her safety and for his own peace of mind.

Margaret returned with a tray of hot cocoa, reading the expression on Paddie's face at a glance. She'd reached him. He was concerned at last.

Paddie pressed the mug into Emily's hands and waited until she'd finished her drink. He swung around and sat facing her, taking both her hands in his.

"How would you like to get away for a while. Do you think you're up to a short trip? Just for a few weeks?"

"A few weeks? But . . ."

"I have a friend, his name is Seneca, and he makes a cargo run across the canal every once in a while. He's due to leave in a couple days."

"But I couldn't do that, with just a . . . a stranger. A man."

"He's involved in a rather tricky business. I have to warn you. There could be some risk, but nothing Seneca couldn't handle. He's a pretty tough character. And you'd be away from here and whoever is frightening you. And I'd be free to check into things."

"What kind of business? Illegal?"

"Well, truth to tell, aye. 'Tis illegal, but 'tis the right thing to do as well."

"Seneca says the law he's breaking needs to be broken, and should never have been voted in. Tell her,

14

Paddie. She needs to know."

"He's helping slaves into Canada. He has a young couple coming into town any day now, and she's due to have her baby. You'd be a big help to him. He doesn't know what to do with a newborn babe. Or, heaven forbid, how to birth one."

"Can I think about it?"

"Aye. It's sure we're not to be forcin' you into this. You think on it. I'll talk to Seneca tomorrow. Get some sleep now."

She lay in the dark and tried to imagine a young couple with a new baby. What would they have endured already simply to get to Albany? How would this man Seneca get them to Canada? What would happen to them if they got caught?

After a night of restless speculation it felt good to get back to mundane activities. Emily found peace and security in walking through the open market with Margaret, selecting fruits and vegetables and a cut of meat for their evening meal and chatting pleasantly with sympathetic friends and neighbors. She tried not to think of the decision she would soon have to make, to leave the place she'd called home for the past months since her only parent's death. Of course it wasn't forever. She could return to Albany in a few weeks and start her life anew. By then Paddie would have put a stop to whoever was following her. And she'd be better emotionally, too, she was sure. How patient the McMurdie's had been with her.

The paper bag in her arms jerked, and at the same time a glass jar of honey exploded in a stall beside her.

"Get back," Margaret screamed, jerking Emily behind the heavy wood of the produce wagon.

"What is it? What happened?" Emily cried.

"Someone just shot at you!"

Paddie slammed his empty beer mug onto the bar

and rounded on Seneca Prescott. "I've never asked anything of our friendship before, but I have to ask this."

"Don't push me. I said no. No it is. I'm not nurse-maiding some useless female who's going to cry and bellyache all the way to Rochester and back. Sorry, pal. I'll have troubles enough this trip. Some other time."

"Seneca, listen. She's not like that."

"You just said she's a wreck, cries all the time, has nightmares."

"Good lord, man, she's just lost her uncle and cousin. All that on top of just losing her own father. But it's not just that. She's convinced someone's trying to kill her."

"Now that tears it. Not only is she grief-stricken, she's paranoid, as well. Come on, Paddie. Don't put me in the position of having to damage our friendship."

"I'm askin' it, Seneca. I'll beg, if you make me."

Seneca rubbed his temples with the thumb and fingers of one hand. If he didn't relax he'd get one of his headaches again. He pushed his dark hair back from his forehead and straightened to his full height.

Paddie stood taller too. Not a small man himself, he still stood half a head shy of Seneca's six foot two. Nor did he have the brawn Seneca had acquired from working the docks. Paddie squared his shoulders.

"She'll be able to help you. She's a good cook, she's good with children. She knows nursin'."

"McMurdie! Hell, man, I've looked all over for you," one of his fellow officers exclaimed, striding up to the bar and handing a letter over to him. "Message from your wife. She said it was urgent. Beer, George. How ya doin', Prescott?" Seneca didn't answer.

Paddie read the short note, then handed it to Seneca. "Seems I misjudged her. Someone *is* trying to kill her."

Seneca's jaws worked as he scanned the note, making the long scar down the side of his face undulate. He hated this. Mac had no right to put him in such a spot.

The last thing he needed was to get involved with another oversensitive, even hysterical, female.

"A whiskey, George," he said and crumpled the note. He turned to Mac. "You're a copper. Can't you stop this, man?"

"Until last night I thought she was imagining all of it. I haven't had time. Seneca, can't you make room for her? With her gone I can work faster. Otherwise I'll feel I have to stay by her side. You don't seem to realize that bullet came within inches of killing not only Emily but Maggie, too. Please."

Seneca sighed in resignation. "All right, Mac, but you owe me. I'll leave early in the morning."

Back at the house Margaret packed a small trunk for Emily while Emily packed a hamper of food. Maggie looked at the row of dark gowns—black, gray, deep blue, mourning clothes—and knew they would irritate a man like Seneca. She shoved them to the side of the closet and chose instead to pack several of Emily's pretty dresses along with more servicable day dresses and skirts and blouses.

She was closing the lid when Emily came in to help. "All done? I feel badly about taking your food."

"Nonsense. I can get more tomorrow. Something smells good. Supper, I hope. I'm starved. Come, help me get this out by the front door."

"I hear Paddie now. Does he have to work again tonight?"

"Yes. All this week. It's his turn," she answered acceptingly.

"Don't you worry about him?"

"Of course. But he's happy. I wouldn't have him any other way. And he's careful. He's a good policeman."

Paddie burst into the house with his usual booming greeting, demanding hugs from both his wife and Emily.

"It's all set," he said. "He's agreed." He looked a little sheepishly at Emily then. "I did sort of promise him

17

you'd help with the cookin' and his . . . passengers, lass."

"I would have done so anyway," she said, feeling suddenly apprehensive and not a little sad. "I shall miss you both."

"Aye. We'll miss you, too. But 'tis only for one trip. You'll be home before you know it."

"Sure," Maggie agreed. "Think of it as a vacation. A holiday."

Their evening meal was interrupted by the clang of the fire bell, and Paddie went to give assistance. The ladies cleaned the kitchen and took their tea to the parlor, where Emily asked about the man who would be taking her across the length of the state the next morning.

"Seneca Prescott. Well, he comes from . . ."

A crack sounded and the window behind them shattered. The cup in Emily's hand came apart and emptied its contents in her lap.

"Get down," Maggie barked, turning down the light and lifting the globed lamp to the floor to protect it from another bullet. "Get over in the corner," she ordered, crawling to the broom closet. She drew out a long shotgun and loaded it.

"What are you doing?" Emily demanded. "You're not planning on going out there?"

"No, but I'm going to make them think twice about coming in here." She went to the window, aimed the gun into the air, and fired. The rumble rattled the china in the sideboard. She reloaded.

"Come on, you scourge of the earth," she yelled out the shattered window. "Give me a target to shoot at."

Emily gasped. Was this the same woman she'd lived with for two weeks?

Maggie saw her stunned expression and chuckled. "You don't think they would have heeded me if I'd pleaded in a docile voice for them to go away, do you? There are times in life when anger is permitted. There

18

are even times when violence is necessary. You must learn to accept that. And one more thing you must remember, sometimes anger and violence cover up a sore spirit."

Another shot sailed through the window and chipped a piece of stone from the fireplace.

"We have to do something," Emily said. "If we stay here, we're ducks in a pond."

"Unlock the back door, we'll cross over to Maple Road and try to get to the river. Our only hope is to get to Seneca. Paddie could be anywhere."

Margaret caught a flash of movement across the street in the bushes and she fired the shotgun. Unfortunately, by the time the shot reached that far it would be a harmless dispersion of pellets that might sting, but little else. She dropped the weapon and dashed out the back, pulling Emily with her.

"Stay in the shadows and keep close to me. We have a hill to slide down here."

They ran east along Maple. Voices followed, cursing them, as at least two men thrashed their way down the hill behind them. Another shot rang out and Maggie groaned and grabbed her shoulder.

"Oh, Lord, you're hit," Emily cried. "This is my nightmare all over again, only worse."

"It's not bad. Keep going."

They ran through the back streets of town directly toward the docks. Emily kept her eye on Margaret, saw the patch of red spread down her arm, saw her falter and sway. She wrapped a supporting arm around her and led her down an alley between two large warehouses. They ducked inside one and found a dark corner. Emily lowered Maggie to a crate and checked her shoulder.

"It's just a graze," Margaret objected shakily.

"Maybe, but you're in shock. You'll have to rest a while. Let me bind this wound, then I'll go for help."

"You go, I'll take care of myself. Go. Seneca's boat is

called *Prescott's Wake*. Find him."

Emily hesitated at the door, then flung herself out and ran. She'd gone two blocks before they spotted her again. A shot rent the air and whistled past her ear.

"This way," said a voice, and a hand grabbed her arm and swung her into an alley and around a corner through a door.

Emily jerked free and looked at her assailant, a tall, thin Negro girl with features that were arrestingly exotic.

"Come," the girl said. "You'll be safe."

"I can't. I have to find a man named Seneca. Or a boat called *Prescott's Wake*."

"Seneca," she repeated, her attention caught. "What do you want with him?" she asked cautiously.

"Oh, please, if you know where he is, tell me. I've left my friend back in the Greenleaf Building. She's been shot and she needs help. I must find Seneca."

"And these men who are shootin' at you?"

"They're trying to kill me, but that doesn't matter now. I have to get help to Maggie."

"You will stay here. I will go to find Senena and bring him here to you. You will stay?"

"All right, only please hurry."

"If you go from here, they will find you," the Negress warned just before she disappeared among the stacks of crates.

Emily hugged her arms to herself. Only enough light entered from the high windows to cause grotesque shadows to bob around her from her own movements. She crept slowly down the aisles between the mountains of wooden boxes. The Negress had left, not by the front door but by a second. Emily wanted to know where it was.

She never found another exit, so she returned to the place where she had been instructed to remain and sat down to wait. She had no timepiece to measure the passing of the minutes, but it seemed to her that she'd been there far too long. She was worried about Margaret. And what did she know of the Negro girl? Nothing at all, save that she'd hid her from her would-be killers. One more minute, and then she'd leave to get help for Margaret.

Voices and footsteps sounded. A light appeared at the window. She pushed herself farther into the darkness. The door rattled, clicked, and opened.

"You take that side. I'll look here. And if you find her, I want her before you kill her. I'm gonna take me a piece of that hair as a trophy."

Her hands tightened on the short piece of two-by-four she'd found earlier as the horrible man passed within a yard of her. He caught a whiff of her and turned, his beady eyes pinning her to the spot.

"Well, well. If she ain't right here."

Emily swung her arms in a wide arc, slamming her club against the side of his head. He staggered back and she bolted for the door, but she ran into a solid wall of man. The man twisted the club out of her hand and tossed it aside.

"Jay, you okay?" her captor called.

Jay grumbled, something that sounded distinctly like a promise of doom, and Emily fought for her life. She twisted, kicked, scratched, and bit until the man slapped her across the face and grabbed a handful of hair. He wrenched her head back so far she thought her neck would snap.

"Hey, Jay. I got her and she's a real wildcat. Real pretty, too. Hurry up, pal."

"Your . . . *pal* won't be joining you," came a deep growling voice. "I strongly suggest you let the lady go and get yourself out of here before I twist your head off."

Emily's spirits rose. Someone had come to help her.

"You come near me, I'll kill her. I swear I will."

The giant, for that's what he looked like to Emily, stepped out of the shadows into the dim light. Emily's stomach clenched. This man was going to save her? He looked more menacing than her killers.

"Well, well. Calvin Zandee," the giant drawled. "Who hired you to do his dirty work this time? Too bad you took the job. It's going to cost you."

The man holding her tightened his grip on Emily's ribs and jerked back on her head. "I'll kill her, I swear it."

"Please," Emily cried in a strangled whisper.

The giant shrugged. "Go ahead. She's nothing to me. It's you I want."

Suddenly she was propelled forward with a sharp shove between her shoulder blades. She gasped as she stumbled and started to fall. The giant scooped her up as if she weighed nothing and he lifted her into his arms.

So instantly had she been thrust away from one man and into the arms of another that she didn't know what had happened to her. All she knew was that she had to get away. Away from this dark place and this frightening man.

"Let me go. Please. I need to go." She pushed against him, but he was like iron.

"You better stay right here, angel, or the bad man will get you again."

"Won't he get away?" she asked to distract him. She jerked back against his hold.

He laughed and tightened his grip, his white teeth showing through his crooked grin. "Lijah will get him outside."

"Lijah?"

"Elijah, actually. A friend. He should be back by now."

"Listen, please. I have a friend who is in trouble. She's hurt."

His black eyes narrowed as his brows drew together. He studied her intently, her hair, her face, the curve of her breasts that had been exposed when her dress was

22

torn. She felt totally exposed, vulnerable, afraid.

"The other man," she asked. "Is . . . is he . . ."

"He's dead."

"Oh, God, no. Did I . . ."

"Would you rather be dead yourself?"

"No, but . . ."

"Don't worry, angel, you didn't kill him. I did that for you."

His cold and careless manner frightened her. "Please, please, let me go." Terror set in at his implacable refusal. She began to fight him in earnest.

"Settle down and stop thrashing about now."

"Let go of me. Help! Help me!" she screamed.

"Enough, I say," he barked, shaking her.

"No. I want out of here. Let me go. Help!"

"Dammit," he cursed at one blow that connected with his nose, and when she wouldn't quit fighting him he lifted her off her feet completely and trapped her hands behind her back.

He tugged her hair to lift her face to his. "Stop it, now. Do you hear me." She made herself calm down, knowing she would never get away from this man unless he decided to release her.

"Please, mister, don't hurt me," she pleaded.

Seneca cursed again. He should have stuck to his guns and told Mac to get someone else. Now here he was, stuck with her for weeks. Well, he might as well make the most of it. She certainly was beautiful. A lot like Belinda, actually, with those big, expressive blue eyes and her flaxen hair. His body's instinctive response reminded him how much he'd always been attracted to that particular combination.

Emily, too, felt his response and panicked. "No, don't, please."

She watched, unable to escape, as his mouth lowered to hers. She tried to move her head aside, but his grip on her hair tightened. Her heart was pounding so hard she felt it in her skin. She could taste her own fear. She waited for his cruel mouth to assault hers, she waited to feel his hot fetid breath on her lips. She closed her eyes and prayed for it to be over quickly.

The first touch against her tightened lips was like the kiss of a butterfly. And his warm breath carried the faint scent of peppermint. Again his lips brushed against hers, and her eyes flew open to meet the dark glitter of his gaze.

"Open your mouth."

"No, I . . ."

Again his mouth met hers, coaxing, persuading, until she felt her lips relax on their own and soften beneath his mastery. Of course it was because he had taken her by surprise. Otherwise . . .

"Open your mouth, angel," he murmured against her mouth and ran his tongue along her lower lip.

She gasped at the sensation of it, and he took advantage of her momentary surprise and plunged his tongue deep into her mouth.

She'd been kissed before. She was twenty years old. But she'd never been kissed like this. The shock of it stabbed through her, setting her nerves to tingling. A slow insidious warmth crept through her limbs, sapping her strength. A sensation not unlike floating in a dream left her melting against him, surrendering to his lips and mouth.

A low moan came from deep in her throat. His grip tightened, his arms molded her body to his. She felt his masculine parts stir against her, and she tensed in sudden fear, all warmth running out of her and leaving her in the cold.

He lifted his head and looked down at her. Quite suddenly he thrust her away from him, holding her at arms length, scowling fiercely.

"You're a virgin, aren't you. A goddamn virgin," he demanded.

"I . . . ah . . ." How did one answer that?

"Aren't you?" He shook her. "Answer me."

"What if I am? Is it a crime?" Her sudden spurt of indignation died a short death at his murderous scowl.

"Damn him. Why me? Why you? Why now?"

"What?" He was mad, she thought. Stark raving mad.

Chapter 2

He took her by the arm and led her roughly to the door. As he reached for the latch, the door exploded inward. She found herself suddenly sitting in an undignified heap on the floor, and the man, whose name she didn't even know, was fighting off two other men.

She watched, horrified, as fists connected with faces and other parts. A particularly nasty blow to one man's stomach doubled him over, another to his jaw sent him careening into the crates. He melted onto the floor. The other man drew a wicked looking knife from his boot, and he and her rescuer were circling each other warily.

And just where was this Elijah he spoke of? She scrambled on her hands and knees to the corner where one of her attackers had thrown her club. She picked it up and stood waiting for a chance to help. So the two men who attacked her had brought an accomplice with them. They must really want her dead. She looked from the villain holding the knife to the unconscious man on the floor, and for the first time she noticed that neither of them had been her earlier assailant. These were two different men altogether.

A quick slice through the air had her rescuer jumping backward, but not before his leather vest suffered extensive damage.

"Here," she yelled at him, and in the second he took

to glance her way, she tossed him the chunk of wood.

In one deft movement he snatched the club out of the air and swung it in an arc that caught the treacherous knife. Both knife and board went flying off to skate under a stack of crates. Weaponless, the attacker turned and fled out the door. She didn't blame him. Not many men would be a match for her black-haired, black-eyed giant. Not hand-to-hand and alone.

So why was she waiting around?

She picked up her skirts and followed the coward out the door, running for all she was worth. But she wasn't worth much. She hadn't reached the end of the alley before his arm clamped around her waist and lifted her off her feet.

"Not so fast, angel. I'm not through with you yet."

"Help!" she screamed, but only once, then she was pinned to his side with one large hand clamped over her mouth.

With her dignity in tatters she was ignominiously hauled down the dock, made to endure raucous and scandalous jeers from drunks and not-so-drunk onlookers, and dumped in a dark room in the back of a dumpy boat.

The minute she hit the bunk she shot back up. "You filthy swine. Is this what I get for helping you?"

"Helping me?"

Ooh, he was an insensitive cad. She kicked his shin and bolted out the door. Once again she was swept off her feet, but she had only begun to fight. She planted her feet against the outside wall of the cabin and kicked. He staggered backward, taking her along with him. Before he fell, he managed to see she got to her feet. She watched as he landed hard on the deck. She dared to meet his gaze and saw unholy anger glittering there. He untangled his foot from the coils of rope that had tripped him and rose to his feet. She backed away.

"I won't let you hurt me."

"You won't . . ." he sputtered. The little termagant.

She'd be dead or worse but for him. Didn't she realize that? By rights he ought to turn her over his knee and thrash the daylights out of her.

"Get back in that room," he ordered menacingly.

She laughed, a high, hysterical sound. Did he think her stupid. "Stay away from me, you beast."

His face tightened and darkened at the insult, and he started toward her.

She backed up farther, holding her hands up in front of her as if she could will him to stop. Her fear seemed to trigger more anger.

"Dammit, I said get in there. Now!"

Out of pure instinct to survive she turned to run, but she banged her knee in her flight and realized, as her momentum took her forward into empty space, that she'd turned the wrong way. She pitched over the side of the boat and into the icy black waters of the Hudson River.

She screamed, and before she knew it water was flooding into her mouth, nose, ears. Blackness was all around. No matter how hard she kicked and thrashed she couldn't reach the surface. Something was holding her down.

Her lungs burned with the need to breathe until she could no longer resist. And then cold water swam through her lungs, seemingly into her veins, and she quit fighting. She was drowning and she knew it, but it wasn't at all as frightening as she'd sometimes imagined it would be. It was pleasant, actually. Floating. Like she felt in his arms when he was kissing her.

Those same arms were around her now, pulling her upward. They squeezed hard, harder still, again and again, until she was coughing and sputtering, grabbing for support in the freezing water.

"Be still, you idiot girl, or I'll be forced to knock you out. Here's the ladder. Pull yourself into the boat, if you think you can manage to do even that right."

She got up two rungs but had to stop, seized by a fit

28

of coughing. Not only that, but she had to further embarrass herself by emptying the contents of her stomach.

"God help me," he grumbled as he pried her fingers from the ladder she was gripping for her life and hoisted them both aboard.

He lifted her trembling body into his arms and strode across the deck to the room at the rear. He set her on her feet and proceeded to divest her of her sodden garments.

His hands were gentle and warm, and even though his words were harsh, his eyes held sympathy. Pity, maybe. It was too much. She broke down and began to cry and cough and sob.

"Lord," he grumbled, pulling her nearly naked body into his embrace. "Hush now. You're going to be fine." He soothed her with a calming touch and tender words. After a while her sobs ceased and she chanced to look up.

"I'm sorry. I . . . I'm all right now."

He lit a lamp, then continued to undress her, ignoring her protests that she could do it herself. His hands were firm on her shoulders as he turned her to face him and then held her arms away from her naked, shivering body.

"You're very beautiful." Oblivious to her mortification, his eyes roamed over her full breasts, her narrow waist, the gentle curve of hips and thighs. "So very beautiful."

Terrified, she pulled away. He let her go, watching her arms instinctively cover her breasts. He drew a flannel shirt from his bureau and buttoned her into it. He wrapped a towel around her dripping hair then took her chin in his hand and turned her angel's face to his.

"Is dying really preferable to being in my unseemly company?"

His voice was hard and cynical, but his eyes, in one

unguarded second, betrayed his inner disillusionment and pain. It was then she saw the jagged scar that ran down the side of his face near his hairline and along his jaw.

She gasped, horrified, not at the scar, but at whatever disaster had caused it, and that he should think she . . .

"Ugly," he sneered and gave a sardonic chuckle. "Isn't it? But not as bad as this."

With that he tore off his wet shirt to reveal another scar, much worse, that disfigured the skin from shoulder to elbow. He didn't stop there, even as she shrank back from the angry glitter in his eyes. He removed the rest of his clothes as well. His thigh bore the same kind of scar. That's as far as she'd let her eyes go. She turned away.

He threw his wet clothes onto the pile hers already made and turned away in disgust to draw on dry trousers and a clean flannel shirt. She was trembling when he turned back to her. He cussed and poured her a drink of whiskey.

"You're in shock. Drink this."

Her eyes flew to his. Shock? "Oh, my stars, I have to go. My friend . . . she needs help . . . she . . ."

"Is fine. I wondered when you'd think of her."

"What?" she demanded, suddenly irate. "You're the one who prevented me . . ."

"There was no need. Your little slave girl took care of her."

"My slave what? I have no . . . Oh, you mean that pretty Negro? But I don't know who she is. What if she doesn't find Maggie? What if . . ."

"I said your friend is fine. Believe it or not," he barked impatiently.

"You don't mind if I see for myself." She got up and started for the door. The room began to spin.

"Sit down. You're in worse shape than she was."

"She'll be worried."

"How do you think she'd have felt if you'd succeeded in drowning yourself?"

"I wasn't trying to . . . Good heavens, is that what you thought? I thought *you* were holding me down. I couldn't get up."

"You silly twit. You got yourself stuck under the boat. I had the devil's own time finding you. You scared the hell out of me, woman."

"Do you always cuss so much?"

"What if I do? It's nothing to you. Drink that. All of it."

She did. It hit her throat and stomach like a ball of fire, but it also spread warmth through her chilled body. She closed her eyes and relaxed.

"Better?" He wrapped her in a warm blanket.

"Yes, thanks. Much better. I really wasn't trying to drown myself."

He sat beside her and removed the towel from her head. He began to brush out the tangles from her pale hair. It felt heavenly to her. She felt heavenly. She took another drink from her glass.

"You ran right over the edge of the boat," he reminded her, the corner of his lips twitching at the sight she had made.

She looked up and shrugged. "Mistake. I ran the wrong way. I'm not very good with directions. I'm always getting turned around."

"Humm," he murmured. "There. I think that's it. Get into bed now. I'll tuck you in."

"I can't stay here," she protested drowsily. "Really, I have to leave on a trip in the morning."

"I'll wake you early. Your clothes should be dry by then. Did you forget your wet clothes?" He chuckled at her sleepy nod and her sheepish grin. She could be charming, he realized.

"Could I have one more drink?"

He poured her a little and held it to her lips. "Do you drink often?"

31

"Never. It's rather nice." She finished the whiskey and lay down. "Thanks for saving my life. Twice over. I should go home." Her voice sounded muzzy to her own ears. Her eyes were so heavy. "Maggie might need me. Maggie's hurt, you know. You said she was fine?"

"So she is. Your little friend found her husband for her. She's in good hands now."

"Oh. She'll be worried. We have to find Seneca. He's her friend. She likes him."

"Seneca?" he asked. "What do you know about this Seneca?"

"Nothing. I'm going away with him." That didn't sound quite right, but she hadn't the strength to fix it.

"You're going away with a man you don't know anything about?"

"Paddie said it was all right. Paddie knows him; he said it was the best thing to do right now. You'd like Paddie."

"Yeah," he said wryly. "Go to sleep, angel."

He paused at the door and looked back. She was already asleep. He snatched up the whiskey bottle and left, locking her in. Damn Paddie McMurdie! Some bewitching, flaxen-haired goddess was the very last thing he needed in his life. He turned the bottle up and let the whiskey scorch his throat, but it couldn't obliterate the image of her round, full breasts, or her tear-filled blue eyes, or her soft parted lips.

He sat down and pulled on his discarded shoes and socks with abrupt and jerky movements. He slung a jacket over his shoulder, grabbed up his wallet, and strode down the rickety gangplank. It wasn't too late. Camille might still be at the Boar's Head. She'd take his mind off *her*. He didn't want to think about *her*. He didn't want to be feeling what he was feeling.

He met Elijah a couple blocks away. "Everything all set?" he asked his friend.

Elijah nodded. "Dey be here afore dawn. She borned her wee babe, so you don't hafta worry yo'sef none 'bout dat, boss, sir."

"Well, that's one sweet mercy."

Elijah's brows furrowed curiously. "Sir?"

"We have another passenger. She's already on board," Seneca said. "Locked in. Keep her there."

"Mac's friend? She's goin' up the ribber?"

"I couldn't change his mind and I'm not sure I should. Someone is trying to kill her. By the way, did you catch that other man?"

"No, boss, sir. I los' him. I got back in time to see him hightailin' up de hill."

"Damn. Sorry, not your fault."

"Did you know him?"

"Cal Zandee, and McMurdie has a lead on where he holes up. If anyone can nab him, Paddie can. Oh, I had a visit from two of Ryker's men."

"Dat dere man mus' be gettin' mighty sore at you of late. You take five o' his studs already dis year. You be wise to keep a eye open dis trip."

"Yeah, well, I'm going out for a spell. Watch the boat, will you? I don't think anyone will disturb you, but you never know."

Elijah turned and continued toward the boat. He was a tall man, as tall as Seneca, and solid. He hadn't always been. When Seneca found him he'd been chained to the whipping post for days for trying to escape. He was barely alive. But, as he learned later, his wife and son had made it away from their plantation. Elijah's owner was livid about it and Elijah was made to pay. It took Seneca two weeks to convince the man to sell him Elijah and two more to get Elijah back to health. Elijah agreed to work for three years in exchange for his freedom. He had almost completed that now, but he was still a very unhappy man. In nearly three years he had been unable to find his wife and son.

The Boar's Head was teeming with bodies. Seneca ordered a bottle of whiskey and elbowed his way through the rowdy throng in the smoky room to a vacant corner table.

"What's with you, Prescott? You sick or something?" one of the regulars called. "Come on over and join the game. We got an open chair."

Seneca smiled grimly. By damn, he would. He didn't come in here to brood. He came in here to forget. And forget he would.

"Don't mind if I do," he said. "Anyone seen Camille?"

"Oh, she'll be back shortly," laughed another man, one he didn't much care for. "She was askin' about you, too. You got a thing going with her? Lucky man. The rest of us gotta pay."

"Maybe she needs a man who can do a man's job now and again. Now shut up and deal the cards, O'Rourke."

O'Rourke laughed. "Oo-eee. Just trying to be friendly, that's all."

"That kind of friendly will get your knees broke," he replied in a quiet but deadly tone. "Who I choose for company and why ain't none of your goddamned business. Got it?"

"Okay, okay."

"Seneca," a voluptous redhead trilled, gliding up to his table and perching on his knee. "I wondered where you were."

O'Rourke leaned over and tucked a ten-dollar bill down her low-cut gown. "Now you're mine for the next hour," he said, pulling her from Seneca's lap and imprisoning her on his. His hands roamed her bosom openly and squeezed her fullness.

"Take your money, O'Rourke," she said, swatting his hand away from her breasts. "I choose my customers, not the other way around." She made to stand, but O'Rourke wouldn't let her.

"O'Rourke," she warned.

"You'll like me, honey. I can do you just as good as Prescott."

"Bill," she called to the bartender. "Where's Mo?"

"Never mind Mo," Seneca growled. "I can bounce him out on his square head as good as Mo can."

That was all it took for O'Rourke, already on the outside of half a bottle of whiskey, to fly across the table at Seneca.

Adrenalin raced into Seneca's blood. This was what he needed. Every month or so a good brawl broke out at the Boar's Head. Time was ripe for another, and so was he.

By the time someone yelled that the cops were coming, ten men were at each others' throats. Tables had been overturned, chairs broken, glasses smashed. The new mirror behind the bar had shattered again. Seneca sent O'Rourke through the new multipaned window just as the police arrived.

Camille grabbed his belt and pulled him out of the fracas and into the back hallway. She led him out the back door and up the back steps of the neighboring hotel to her room.

"You fool. One of these days they'll throw you in jail," she upbraided him.

"So who the hell cares," he muttered, splashing cold water on his bruised face.

"I do," she replied, sliding her arms around his waist and downward. "I'd get very, very lonely."

"Not likely," he said sardonically, turning and pulling her into his arms. He covered her crimson lips with his.

She was experienced and she was good, but she didn't smell like wildflowers, she didn't taste of honey, she wasn't the right shape in his arms, she didn't make his blood sing in his veins.

He kissed her harder.

Across from the boat Bekka sat, huddled down with her knees close to her chest. She was wrapped snugly in her wool shawl. Her head leaned against the window frame, the moonlight falling on her smooth, dark skin, her slanted black eyes, her exotic high cheekbones, her finely chiseled nose and mouth.

She had an unusual beauty all her own, a mixture of her African, French, and Polynesian ancestry. She could see it staring back at her from the glass. Had her mother been left on her island home she would have been a queen by now. Bekka would have been a princess. But her mother had been stolen away in the night. Six months later, having been sold into slavery, she died in childbirth. Bekka had been raised by the family cook on a plantation in Georgia.

She stood, looked one more time at the boat that held her heart, and sadly turned away. She had work to do, a train to catch. She shouldn't be here watching, she knew. It was risky. She might be caught, and then her charges would be without assistance. But the high attic window afforded a clear view of the boat, and Elijah. One last look.

A tall shadowy figure moved into view. Seneca was back. Elijah would be outside no more until dawn, when Roger Timary brought the young couple out of hiding. By then she must be far away. It had been good to see him again. Just watching his solid sleek body as he moved around the deck, coiling ropes, setting things to right, had made her feel closer to him. How she missed him.

"Back so soon, bossman, sir?"

Seneca didn't answer at first, only scowled as he kicked off his shoes and pulled a blanket around his shoulders. He made himself comfortable on the bunk below Elijah.

"I told you not to call me that," he grumbled. "Any

trouble after I left?"

"No, siree, Massa Prescott, sir."

"Cut it out, dammit. I'm in no mood."

"Tell me about this girl then. Why does Mac think she's in danger? Who wants her dead, and why?"

"He has no idea. But apparently she was supposed to die when her young cousin did, instead of her uncle. She's been in a bit of a state about it lately. Or so he said." She hadn't appeared to be too torn by grief when she fought him. His shin still hurt.

"Hmm," Elijah murmured in the dark cabin. "Losing two loved ones at the same time might do that to a person. What's she look like? Pretty?"

"You mean you didn't peek to see for yourself?"

"No, siree, bossman, sir. I is a gentlemen, fru and fru."

"Yeah, like hell. Go to sleep."

Chapter 3

The voices hadn't awakened her, even now she had to strain to hear the whispers outside her door. Something else. Movement? The boat was rocking some, not much. Not enough to have disturbed her sleep. She heard it again, the cry of a baby. A very new baby, by the sound of its angry wail.

She stood up and immediately remembered how the giant had peeled her clothes from her and wrapped his shirt around her. And not only that, he'd undressed right in front of her and she hadn't looked away. Her cheeks burned at the memory. How was she to face him again?

She sat back down, pulling a blanket over her bare knees. Her clothes were nowhere in sight. She could go back to bed and wait until morning, but what better chance to get help than now. Whoever was on board would surely take pity on her.

Taking courage at the thought, she stood again, made a skirt of sorts with the blanket, and ran a brush through her hair. Taking a deep breath she strode to the door and turned the knob. Locked. He'd locked her in like some . . . prisoner. It was enough to put her over the top. She pounded with both fists on the panel.

"Let me out of here, you beastly devil. Open this door, do you hear me."

On and on she screamed, beating until her fists were

bruised. He wasn't getting away with this. Somehow she'd get off this horrid boat and back to Paddie and Margaret. Paddie would see that he paid for treating her so contemptibly.

The door swung inward so suddenly that she had to jump away to keep from getting her toes pinched. The giant stood there, scowling furiously. She found that her courage had been much more substantial when the door had been between them.

"Are you finished with your childish tantrum yet?" he growled, looking every bit as angry as she was herself.

"I will be as soon as I'm off this boat. I'm leaving, and if you try to stop me I'll scream and make enough commotion to bring the entire port to my rescue."

He slammed the door behind him and took her by the shoulders. "Now you listen to me, you wretched brat . . ."

"Let me go. You have no right to treat me this way."

"Some would say different, since I saved your hide not once but twice. Some would say you at least owe me a debt of gratitude. I claim that debt, and I expect you to pay it. Is that clear?"

"Then throw me back in the river, hold me down. I'd rather you had let me die than have to endure being defiled by the likes of you."

His fingers bit into her tender flesh as he pulled her hard against him. "You're very brave for such a fragile thing. I could break you with one hand."

She winced as his fingers tightened painfully. "Brute. Does hurting women make you feel more like a man?"

His mouth hit hers hard and fast, before she had any chance to evade him. This kiss, unlike the others, hurt. It hurt not only her lips, but for some strange reason, it hurt her feelings. Had she provoked him intentionally so that he'd kiss her again, like he had before? Had she wanted to be held gently? Had she needed his reassurance? She had to admit that he was the first one she thought of when she woke up. And her heart had performed rather queerly. Until she'd found herself locked in.

A salty tear touched his lips and he thrust her away, glaring at her when her fingertips went to her sore mouth.

"Never mind the waterworks. Your feminine wiles are wasted on me. I'm not impressed by tears. They simply confirm what a spoiled child you are. You ask for it, then try to make me feel . . ."

Oh, he was beastly. She hated him. But she dried her eyes and faced him squarely. "I want to go home."

"Sorry. This will be your home for a while."

"I can't stay here. Please. Last night you said I could leave this morning."

"I believe I said your clothes wouldn't be dry until morning. You assumed . . ."

"You can't keep me here."

"Angel, I can do whatever the hell I want. Don't ever forget that. And for God's sake don't look like that."

"Like what? How am I supposed to look? And stop cussing at me."

He let her go and ran his fingers through his hair. He rubbed his temples.

"Have you a headache or is it a hangover?"

He ignored that. "Look, angel, can we reach a truce. Temporarily? You said you were going somewhere with some man you don't even know. Well, can't you go with me? I'm going upriver too. I need some help."

"You have the gall, after the way you treated me?"

"And how is that?" he asked quietly.

"Well, you . . . this room . . . you . . ."

"All I did was help you." He shrugged. "So maybe I stole a kiss, but you can be very enticing, and when you're not that, you can be most exasperating."

"No one has ever called me exasperating before." She turned away. "Nor enticing."

"You must have been living in a convent," he said,

40

shaking his head. "Do we have a truce. Will you help me?"

"But that man is expecting me. Paddie will be frantic if I just disappear. I suppose I could send a message to him."

"No, I'm afraid you can't do that. You don't want to risk alerting those killers to where you are. Why not let me take care of it. Where does this Paddie live? Who is he?"

"He's a policeman. Paddie McMurdie. How long must I stay with you?"

"Could I ask for a week? At the most. If you want to leave after that I won't try to stop you."

"Leave? Where will I be in a week? It's easy to say I can leave, if you intend to take me somewhere where I can't."

"I'll see you are delivered to your doorstep. How is that?"

"Well, I . . . I guess . . ." She was being shanghaied. She should walk off this boat now. What would Paddie think of her for even considering such an arrangement. But hadn't Paddie said she needed a change, a vacation, something to do with her life? Yes, he'd arranged a trip for her, but she was reluctant to find herself with yet another stranger. This one she was at least used to. And she had to admit he made her feel alive as no one else had ever done. Her behavior with him had been appalling, he had every right to call her a spoiled child, but he brought all her strongest emotions to life, even against her will. He seemed able to strip her of her civilized self-restraint.

"How 'bout it, angel? Will you help me?"

"What is it you want me to do?"

Before he could explain, a knock sounded at the door. The door opened and a very tall Negro entered. Tall and muscular. He twisted his hat in his hands nervously and bobbed his head at the giant.

"Bossman, sir, dat dere woman, she be sicker and

sicker. Burnin' up, she is."

"Thank you, Elijah. We'll see to her presently. That will be all."

"Yes, sir, bossman, sir."

"Do you think you can help this young woman?" the giant asked. "Will you come with me?"

"I'll have to see her. Who is she?"

Dark eyes studied her intently. "She's a young woman who foolishly ran off and got herself in a mess of trouble. I'm simply seeing that she ends up where she belongs."

Emily frowned, wondering at the niggling feeling that she was overlooking something. "All right. I'll see what I can do. But I want one concession. I reserve the right to leave whenever I choose. I don't want you locking me in again." She squared her shoulders, lifted her chin stubbornly. "I mean that." She took a step forward and immediately tripped on the edge of the blanket.

Strong arms caught her up and steadied her. But they didn't release her again. She looked up into his deep, dark eyes, feeling that curious curl of excitement spiral through her again.

"Damn," he cussed. "Too tempting."

She watched his head lower and she couldn't move. And when his lips slanted across hers and his tongue demanded entrance, she didn't resist. It was impossible to resist when she had no strength in her limbs. Sweet, sweet lassitude.

He groaned, his arms crushing her into his body, then just as ferociously he set her apart from him. "God, did you have to be so innocent? You don't even know what you're doing."

His anger was a splash of cold water. "Well, don't kiss me, then. Nobody asked you to."

"Didn't you?" His supercilious grin fueled her anger again.

"No, and let me make it plain that I'm agreeing to help you in return for some time away, some protection until Paddie McMurdie can track down my assailants, but I will not provide . . . *other* entertainment."

"Who asked you to? When I want a woman, I don't want her fresh out of the cradle. I prefer a little experience."

"Why you big . . . . I'm not submitting myself to this treatment. Get out of my way."

His arm blocked the door and held it shut. "Where are you going?"

"Home."

"We have an agreement. I'm holding you to it. There's a young girl in the forward cabin who needs your help badly. I'm afraid I must insist."

"So all those polite arguments to convince me to stay were just so much garbage."

He opened the door and motioned for her to precede him. "Please don't make a fuss. I would hate to muffle you and tie you to the bed."

"You'd do that, wouldn't you? I was right about you all along." She brushed past him, nose in the air.

"And what does that mean?"

"Oh, never mind." She meant it to irritate and was pleased to see the scowl darken his brow.

The young girl lay on the bunk, murmuring incoherently in the grip of fever. To the side sat a young man, holding a small, unhappy bundle. Beside him stood Elijah. Her gaze rested on him. Something in his eyes caught her attention, an intelligence, an alertness that was at odds with his humble, slump-shouldered stance.

She pulled her eyes away from him and sat down beside the girl. The giant, whoever he was, hadn't mentioned that the couple were Negroes. He had said he was taking them to where they belonged. Was he one of the slave hunters Paddie had spoken of? She looked from the young girl to the giant. After getting this far, would she be returned to bondage, punished, maybe even killed? And for what, a fee? Money?

"Can you help her?" the giant asked.

Help her? Of course, he wouldn't get anything for her if she died. Poor little thing.

"I need to be alone with her."

"No."

"Look, whoever you are. You asked me to help. I need to examine her. She just gave birth. Do I make myself clear?"

"Come wif me," Elijah said to the young father, leading him out. The giant remained, looking uncertain. She glared at him, unflinching, until he finally left. Suddenly she didn't care what his name was. He had no right to play so loose with other people's lives. No right at all.

It required only minutes to ascertain the source of the fever. The young girl woke up, and Emily gave her water to drink and bathed her face and arms to help bring down the fever.

"How are you feeling?"

"My baby, where's my baby? Where am I? Where is Simon?"

"Shh. Relax. I'm here to help you. And your baby's fine, apart from being hungry. I'll see to him in a few minutes. It is a boy, isn't it?

"Yes. Simon is so proud. Then I got fever."

"Don't worry, it happens. I know a physician who will get some medicine to us when he knows what we need it for."

"No, you must not. I don't wanna be the cause o' Simon gettin' caught. Please, Missy, please. Have mercy."

"Don't fret, now. I'll see you reach a safe place."

"Ain't no safe place, ceptin' Canadie now. That's why we's goin' there."

"Canada?" She could be right, what with the recent passage of the Fugitive Slave Law. Well, then Canada it would be.

A bizarre thought struck her as she suddenly realized what it was that had been prodding at her memory. Could the giant be Seneca? Paddie had mentioned escaped slaves, a young girl about to give birth. But surely he would have told her who he was, if that was the case. Why keep his name from her? Why pretend he didn't know Paddie McMurdie? And he had said he was going to return the slaves. No, this man couldn't be Seneca. Paddie wouldn't have anything to do with slavers. But it was possible this couple was originally supposed to go with Seneca, but had been somehow diverted.

"Are you supposed to meet a man named Seneca?" she asked the girl. "Was he going to take you across the Erie Canal?"

The girl's eyes grew enormous. She shrunk away from Emily.

"What is it?" Emily asked.

"Dis boat, dis ain't his?"

Emily shook her head. "I don't know. I'm sort of trapped here myself. But I have a plan. When I leave you, I'll send Simon in, and you explain my plan to him. You must convince him to believe me. I don't know what these people told him already, but I'm not taking any chances with your lives. We're getting out of here to a place where you will be safe." Her face hardened. "I don't intend to see you enslaved again. I can get you to this man Seneca. I can make everything right, but you have to do what I say."

Emily joined the men. She took the baby and sent Simon in to his wife. The baby was wet and fretful. She bathed him and found a clean diaper and blanket. He settled down some, but he was a poor, hungry little mite. She cooed and cuddled, trying to soothe him. She looked up to see two pairs of eyes watching her antics.

"I need some supplies. Immediately."

The giant found her a paper and stub of a pencil, and she made a list. A long one.

"What is your name?" she asked, poised to write.

"Why? What difference does that make?"

"I'd like to mention it to the doctor to introduce you, so he'll cooperate."

"I can introduce myself."

"May I know your name then, for myself," she demanded irritably.

"Since you haven't introduced yourself, I don't see why I should."

Which told her clearly he wasn't Seneca. Paddie said Seneca agreed to take her. Seneca would already know her name. She handed him the list.

"As you wish. It's of little interest to me anyway. 'Hey, you' will do as well as anything else."

With a quirk of his lips, Seneca read the list. "Bottle, milk?" he asked, his grin disappearing. "Why can't she . . . you know?"

She looked down at the baby. "In a few days. Right now she has a rather painful problem. I need these things. And you might consider doing me a favor and stopping by McMurdie's to pick up my trunk. And check on Margaret."

Elijah looked at Seneca and back at the girl. This was promising to be an interesting trip. He couldn't have found anyone, if he had searched for a year, who more closely resembled his fiancée. His former fiancée, he corrected himself. Such a coincidence had to be pure chance. Yes, things might just hot up some on this trip.

"I go, Massa bossman, sir," he offered.

"I don't know. They might be out looking for these two, and her. I'd better make this trip. I don't want to take any unnecessary chances."

Emily watched him stride away, wishing in the back corners of heart that things could have been different. She turned and found Elijah's watchful dark eyes on her. She blushed and turned away.

"If you'd like, you could get some sleep. I'll sit up

46

with Mara."

"Yes'm, missy bosslady," he said, bobbing a bow as he backed uncertainly away.

"Elijah, I'm Emily. I'm no one's boss, least of all yours. Please don't call me that."

"Yes'm," he murmured watchfully.

"Oh, for heaven sakes. Go to bed. He turned away, but she called him back. "Do you belong to that . . . man?"

"Yes'm. He haves my papers." That was no lie.

"What's his name?"

"Massa bossman," Elijah said cagily.

She gave up on that. "Elijah, don't you ever think of being free? Wouldn't you like that?"

Elijah looked down and scuffed his toe, wondering what was going round in her head. "Massa needs me, missy."

"Well," she said, making her way toward the fore cabin. "I'm going to sit with Mara. I'll try to keep the baby quiet so you can sleep."

Elijah closed the door, waited a few minutes until Emily was in the other cabin, then took up his watch on deck, hiding himself among the crates in the center of the keelboat. He didn't know what was afoot, but he knew something was. He hoped Seneca wouldn't be too long. He wasn't anxious to step in and play the tough guy with Miss Emily. From all he'd heard, he guessed she had a fairly short fuse.

But who could blame her? Seneca could be a brutal man to deal with when he was in one of his intractable moods. And this ridiculous game he was playing, keeping his identity from her, was going to backfire. It was only a matter of time.

After twenty minutes had passed, Emily let herself out of the forward cabin and tiptoed to the aft cabin. She stood for some time, listening at the door.

Elijah remained motionless, watching, waiting. She had exchanged her blanket for a pair of trousers, his trousers, tied at her waist with a rope. Her telltale hair had been knotted up and covered with a dark bandana.

When she heard no sound inside the cabin where she thought Elijah was sleeping she returned, motioned for Simon to bring his family, and led them toward the gangplank.

Emily wanted to go back for Elijah, he deserved freedom as well, but she doubted his desire to achieve it. His loyalty to his master was more important to him than escaping. She couldn't risk it. Simon and Mara were going to have their chance. Paddie would be able to see that they reached Seneca and that Mara received the help she needed.

She stepped onto the wobbly boards and reached back to help Mara, who was still weak from fever. But it was not Mara whom she faced, it was Elijah.

"They're staying here, Miss Harcourt."

"Elijah," she said breathlessly. Gone was the meek subservient posture, the downtrodden slave man. Here stood over six feet of pure male muscle and brawn — tall, proud, and determined.

"Come back aboard now, miss. You don't want to find yourself in any more trouble." His rich voice rang with authority. His heavy accent was gone, as was his colloquial manner of speech. A disguise, she realized. But why?

"We're leaving, Elijah," she returned reasonably, hoping her calmness and firmness would persuade him that she was as determined as he. "Mara needs help. I can get her that help. Surely you aren't going to stop me. These are your people. You can't really mean to take them back to the sort of life they had before. Well, I don't intend to let you. Simon, bring Mara and the baby."

Elijah said nothing, simply motioned them back into their cabin. They studied his impressive stature, his steady eye, his resolve, and they did as he said, leaving Emily on her own.

"Fine, but you won't get away with this. I'm going straight to Paddie McMurdie. He'll stop you. You'll see."

She turned and bolted down the gangplank, blind with anger and disappointment. She couldn't think of nasty enough names for men like Elijah and whoever the other one was. How sorely tired she was of people who thought they could play God with others' lives.

"Whatever happened to the milk of human kindness? Why am I surrounded by uncivilized Goths who only want to murder, rape, pillage, and plunder? Excuse me," she muttered, bumping into someone in her headlong dash down the dock.

The man stepped in front of her again, blocking her path. And again a third time.

"I said, excuse me. Now let me pass." She was in no mood for this, another male who felt he had the right to bother her.

She glared upward then, into the laughing eyes of the giant. He set a basket down and swung her trunk off his shoulder.

"Are all those angry words for me?"

Flop went her stomach. She'd never seen him laugh before. It quite transformed his face.

"Here, carry the basket. It was nice of you to come meet me."

"Come meet . . . You're quite mistaken," she said, mindlessly taking the basket he handed her. "I'm leaving. I'm going to the police and tell them what you're going to do with those slaves. You won't get away with this."

She looked down at the basket, shoved it into his arms, and ran.

"Why you little snake. You'll do no such thing." He plunked the basket on the trunk and went after her. Without the hindrance of all those skirts, she was fleet of foot.

He caught her just as a pair of policemen came down

49

a side street and dismounted from their horses to patrol the riverfront boardwalk. She would have screamed but for the hand that clapped over her mouth. He pulled her into the dark shadows.

"Make any noise at all, you viper, and I'll make you sorry you were born."

She wiggled against him in an attempt to free herself, a token attempt, but she already knew from past experience that until he chose to release her she was stuck. She waited, consternation welling up within her as the policemen passed by and walked on down the wharf and out of sight. Again she was alone with a very angry man. He released her, pinning her with black glittering eyes. She was afraid to stay but equally afraid to try another escape.

"Oh, for pity sakes, get back to the boat. I'm not going to hurt you."

"Why can't I leave. If I promise to be quiet about . . ?"

"No. I'm afraid I have little or no confidence in your promises. Let's go. Mara needs your help."

She let him lead her back down the boardwalk. Why not? It was futile to fight him, but he'd be sorry. She didn't plan to be pleasant about this, and at the first decent opportunity, she'd get Simon's family away and to safety. He'd see she was no manner of woman to be pushed around.

Emily bathed Mara again and ministered to her needs while Simon fed his son from the bottle the doctor had sent along with the other supplies and medications. Soon the young family, fed and cared for, was sound asleep, the baby with Mara in the lower bunk, Simon up top.

Exhausted, Emily sat down on the floor beside the bunks and leaned her head back. Quiet, blissful quiet. The lock clicked, she looked up, her heart jumping oddly to see the giant in the doorway.

"Come," he said quietly.

She followed him out. "What is it?"

"You need some sleep too. Elijah will watch over them. That's his cabin."

"But . . . " She trailed along as he pulled her across the flat deck, around the crates and barrels, to his cabin.

"Hush. I'm tired too. I could do with a little shut-eye before morning. So, please, don't let's have a fuss." He pulled her into the little room and closed and locked the door.

She looked at the bed she'd slept in earlier, but it seemed much smaller now. And no haven of rest.

"I'm not going to let you . . ."

"I didn't ask," he said mockingly.

"Some men don't," she shot back pointedly. "Some just take and never mind what the woman thinks."

"And some women ask for it."

"And some men can't stand to think they're just lustful, selfish animals, so they blame their lack of self-discipline on the women."

"By God, you . . ." His whole presence vibrated with anger. He took a steadying breath and a long swallow from the whiskey bottle on his bureau.

"And you're a lousy drunk," she accused.

He turned and laughed, his lips twisting sardonically. "It won't work. I know what you're doing, but you may as well forget it. I'm not letting you go. Now get in that bed before I put you there myself, because if I lay my hands on you, as angry as I am, I may lose control."

"Brute," she muttered, but knew better than to anger him further. She kicked off her wet shoes and tucked herself under the blankets as close to the wall as she could get. How in the world did he think she was going to get any rest? He was crazy.

She was crazy, absolutely crazy, or he simply had the wrong woman. He kicked off his shoes, unbuttoned his shirt, and shrugged out of it. *A sweet, gentle young woman, bereaved, beside herself with guilt and remorse, who'd be no trouble at all, who'd do all she could to help someone out, whose quiet manner would bring peace and tranquillity to his soul.* Right, McMurdie.

He lay down and pulled the blankets over his chest. He folded one arm under his head and stared at the ceiling. Now what? Sleep? With her cowering in abject terror against the wall?

"Emily," he said huskily, using her name for the first time. Emily.

She turned over. Her eyes met his, trailed down the scar on the side of his face to the worse scar that swept across his shoulder and down his upper arm. She was curious, but not repulsed as he had once suggested.

"It's cold tonight. Could you come out of your corner and snuggle?"

"You won't . . ."

"I couldn't."

"Are you sure?"

He let out a frustrated sigh.

"All right," she said quickly, wanting to preserve their momentary truce. "Only I've never snuggled before."

A tender smile spread across his face, and he traced the winged shape of her brows with one finger, and in a mere second had quite mesmerized her.

Before she knew it, he had pulled her close, so close her cheek was a breath away from his shoulder. Her fingers came up and touched the scar. He flinched and pulled slightly away, but she only spread her fingers out more firmly and planted a little kiss there.

"It must have been very painful. I'm sorry for that."

"You're not sickened?"

She turned big blue eyes to meet his. "Should I be? Will you be sickened at the sight of your wife's scars after she bears your children?"

He jerked away so fast her head bounced on the pillow. He leaned over her, staring down into her face, angry again.

"I'm sorry, I . . . I shouldn't have said that," she

stammered. "Goodness, you probably already have a wife. And children. I didn't mean . . . it's just that . . ."

"As it happens, I have neither. But why would you think I'd feel that way about childbirth."

"I don't know," she defended herself quickly, trying to diffuse his temper. "You seem to think scars are . . . are . . ."

"Ugly?"

"See?"

"It's not me. It's not . . . everyone. It's women who feel . . ."

"Does your mother think you are sickening?"

"Of course not, but . . ."

"Just us other women, hmm?" she teased.

"Look, let's forget it, okay? Just believe me, I know what I'm talking about." He lay back down.

"Slam go the doors to his mind," she muttered to herself.

"Yeah, well, so what? Mind your own damn business."

What an ungrateful oaf. "My own *damn* business is not on *this boat*." With that she turned away and snuggled up to the wall again.

He rolled to the edge with his broad back turned to her, and yanked until he had enough of the blanket to cover him. Which left her exposed to the cold night air.

Gritting her teeth, she yanked them back. But they were his blankets, as he soon demonstrated by practically rolling himself up in them.

She glared at him, trying to squash the giggle she felt bubbling up within herself. It was wasted effort.

He jerked upward again and scowled at her as the bunk continued to jiggle with her silent laughter. She guessed he must not have realized how much blanket he took, for his eyes widened when he saw her coverless side of the bed.

"That tears it," he grumbled, lifting her and turning her to lie with her back to the curve of his front. He

53

packed them both in, wrapping her in the added warmth of his arms. "Now, if you don't mind . . ."

One last giggle escaped. "Okay, okay," she cried when he stiffened. "Good night." She yawned, shifting to get more comfortable, unaware of the immediate impact her movements had upon his body.

"For Chrissake, be still."

"You know, one of these days, you'll swear like that in a thunder storm and get your comeuppance."

"Then I'll keep you glued to my side. God wouldn't dare strike down such a paragon of virtue. *Now go to sleep.*"

She gave up. She'd never get in the last word with him. She closed her eyes, weaving her fingers through his. Curiously, she felt his heart thud heavily against her back. Her lips curled into a satisfied smile. Just why she should be smiling she did not fully understand.

Chapter 4

Emily forced her eyes open. This time it was motion that woke her. And voices. She jumped up and peeked out the high window. Albany was slowly slipping away. They were out in the middle of the river.

She jumped down and started for the door. She had to get off. She couldn't go. She had responsibilities, for heaven sake.

But she didn't, she realized on a piercing stab of grief. No one was waiting for her to cook breakfast. No one needed her love or her care. When would the awful ache of loss end. When would she stop expecting to see Peter come bounding through a door. She sucked in a ragged breath.

So she might as well go along with the giant. He said he needed her. She brushed her hair and started for the door when she saw her small trunk beside the bureau. Quickly she tore off the man's clothes she was wearing and dressed in a navy skirt and pale blue blouse. No black, she noticed, had been packed for her. Margaret apparently didn't hold to mourning clothes for uncles and cousins. Or for fathers who'd been dead for months. Clean stockings and dry shoes felt wonderful between her feet and the cold floor. She found a blue ribbon and tied her hair back from her face.

The small cookstove outside the cabin was lit. A small stream of smoke swirled from the stovepipe that had been cleverly attached to the cabin by wrought iron braces. On the back plate was a steaming kettle.

"I didn't know if you'd want coffee or tea," said a deep voice behind her, making her jump.

"Oh, don't do that," she cried, spinning around to pin him with a scowl.

"Wrong side of the bed?"

"As there is only one, that can hardly be the case."

"Must be me, then," he concluded with a twisted grin.

"Now isn't that just like you," she huffed, plunking her fists on her hips, "to assume you have enough importance in my life to be able to upset me."

He held up his hands and backed away. She felt like a shrew. A bad-tempered harridan.

"Wait. I'm sorry. Sometimes I wake up thinking of my little cousin. It makes me sad and . . . and angry. He was such a bright boy. He would have made such a contribution to life. I didn't mean to snap at you."

"Well then," he said. He stepped near and took her shoulders in his hands. "Good morning, Emily."

"Good morning, . . ." What was his blasted name anyway?

"As you're up, you might consider warming the baby's milk. He'll be hungry soon, and I'd like to let Simon and Mara get some rest. Simon hasn't slept for days, and Mara, well, the more rest she can get the sooner she'll be back on her feet. Could you do that? I got fresh milk this morning. It's in the ice chest."

"Ice chest?"

"Come, I'll show you where everything is kept. We don't usually keep this much food on hand when just Elijah and I travel. We generally find restaurants along the canal. But with all of us . . . Here's the milk. I already washed the baby bottle."

She gave him an impish grin. "Wow. You'll make a great father some day."

Suddenly, from him or from her, or from both of

them, or from nowhere, came such a sizzling current of electricity that the air between them seemed to hum and vibrate. She stepped back, her wide eyes caught in his narrowed gaze.

"Is that an invitation?"

Her cheeks burned, not because her careless comment was so inappropriate but because her thoughts had conjured up quite by themselves the vision of his tall, naked body. And her own, standing brazenly before him. And he, blast his hide, knew it.

He threw back his head and laughed. "Well I'll be damned."

She turned away. "No doubt." She snatched the bottle from him, filled it with milk, and returned to the stove. She poured some of the boiling water into a smaller pan and set the bottle in it to warm.

She was sure now that she hated him. He was loathesome, daring to laugh at her just because she found him mildly attractive. Well, he could just go whistle.

By the time she'd fed and bathed the baby and had him tucked back into bed, it had turned eight. She set out to prepare breakfast—bacon, eggs, coffee, and thick chunks of yeasty bread that Margaret had packed in the wicker hamper.

"So you can cook," her Goliath said when he and Elijah sat down to eat.

"Very good, miss," Elijah said hurriedly, throwing his friend a reproving scowl.

"Thank you," she muttered, not ready yet to forgive either one of them. "Where are we going, if I may presume to ask?" She brought the coffee pot from the stove to refill their mugs.

"We're going inland. We're about to enter the canal now." He looked up and waved to a group of men fishing along the bank.

"The canal? The Erie Canal?"

"Ho, Prescott, get yourself married, did ya?" one of the men yelled out across the water.

"Not me," he answered.

"She's a stunner, Seneca, my boy. You better grab her up."

The giant waved him off and continued eating, but his eyes glanced up to meet Elijah's. Elijah didn't move a muscle.

"Seneca?" she asked in deadly quiet. "Senaca?" This louder. "You're . . ." Rage swelled up until her throat was choked. Not another word would come, but her breath whistled between her clenched teeth.

Seneca jumped up and carefully removed the hot coffee pot from her tightly clenched hand, placing it back on the stove.

"Emily, I . . ."

Her name on his lips did it. "All this time! I've been out of my mind with worry over Maggie . . ."

"I told you she . . ."

"Shut up! I've been frightened out of my wits, pushed around, held prisoner against my will, nearly drowned, mauled by someone who thinks he . . ."

"Easy now," he warned.

"I'm not finished. Someone who thinks he can do whatever he wants without consequence, some pig-headed, self-centered bully."

"Now just a damn minute."

"Who has a mouth like a drunken sailor. Have you any idea what I almost did. Those people in there . . ."

"Keep your voice down," he warned.

"I almost took them away from here," she rasped. "I almost ruined everything because of your imbecilic games."

"You didn't almost anything," he barked back, defensively. "Do you honestly believe you ever had either the chance or the ability to foil my plans. Don't be so ridiculous."

She glared up at him, a mass of confused emotions. "I could have. I almost did. I nearly got away."

"Only because Elijah saw me coming did he let your

foot touch the dock. Those three in there," he hissed in a hoarse whisper, "are going to freedom. You, I regret to say, are my *duty*, and as such, you will, if necessary, become my *prisoner*."

"Never. I'm getting off this boat. You won't know when it happens, or where, but you'll look for me and I'll be gone." She looked at Elijah and back at Seneca. "And neither of you can stop me." Deceitful cads, both of them.

"Emily," Seneca cajoled, changing tack. "Be reasonable." He reached out a hand to brush back the hair that had blown across her face.

"Don't touch me," she spat. "Ever again. Do you hear me."

"Oh, I hear you," he growled, grabbing her and pulling her hard against him. "But you need to learn one thing right now. Never, never tell me what I can or cannot do." His kiss was swift and thorough, sweeping aside her resistance like so much chaff in the wind.

"That-a-way, Seneca!" yelled an onlooker as they were towed into the lock.

Seneca raised his head and laughed, waving to the man. Emily was mortified. Tears of anger, frustration, and just plain hurt filled her eyes. She pulled out of his arms and fled to the privacy of the cabin.

Seneca's grin disappeared and his mouth tightened. He rubbed his lower lip with the knuckle of his thumb, staring at the closed door. He looked at Elijah, shook his head, and resumed his meal.

"Learn your winnin' ways at you mama's knee, did ya, bossman, sir?" he quipped.

"Hell, what do you know?"

"Well, now," Elijah said, leaning back against a crate, sipping at his coffee. "I know a song is wasted on a deaf man, I know a blind man will never see a golden rainbow. And I know a flower bud will never bloom once it's been crushed."

Seneca's cup never reached his lips. He stared at his

friend, then stared at the cabin door.

"I'll take some food to our passengers and see that they get settled in below before we reach the toll station."

Seneca watched him load up a plate with food, grab the coffee pot, and stroll up the deck. To anyone watching he was going to his room to enjoy a meal in peace. They had learned that most folks along the canal were quick to look the other way when slaves came through. Though they, themselves, might not take to breaking the law, they saw no reason to interfere if someone else was brave enough to chance it. It was the commissioners you had to watch for. And they could be anywhere.

"Hey, Seneca," one of his friends called to him. "I hear we might be in for a storm."

"Hey, Sam, thanks. I'll keep an eye out."

"You do that, boy."

"Catch anything yet?"

"Catfish. Git your pole in."

"I just might. Have a good day, Sam."

Seneca went forward and rapped on Elijah's door. He opened it and poked his head in. "We have commissioners up ahead. Get them below as soon as you can."

He went back to his own cabin and knocked. "Emily, I need to talk to you. May I please come in?"

She opened the door and faced him, knowing her eyes were probably red, but not caring. "Yes, what is it?"

"I . . . ah . . . oh, hell. Hey, I'm sorry. I didn't mean any of that stuff. Okay?"

She responded readily with a tentative smile. "I know. I'm sorry too. I hardly know myself anymore."

"About Mara and Simon," he said, shifting from one foot to the other. "Did you really mean it about turning them in to the police?"

"What?"

"You said last night that . . ."

"Yes, but I meant you. I thought you were going to

sell them back to their former . . . masters. You said you were taking them back home."

"When? I said I was taking them where they belonged." He chucked her chin when she scowled. "To freedom, silly. To Canada."

"You didn't say that," she accused.

"I didn't know you any more than you knew me. I had to be careful. Emily, we're coming to a toll station. They'll search the boat."

"What will you do?" she asked, alarmed.

"Don't worry. Mara and Simon will hide in the usual place, but I can't risk the baby. There'll be loud noises, the boat will bang and bump against the pilings. If he cries, the game is up."

"So what do we do?"

"We pretend he's ours. You take him. Keep him covered and quiet. Be a fussy mother and don't let anyone near him. It'll work."

"What if we're caught?"

"They take Simon and Mara and the baby back to some hellhole until they learn who they belong to, then they sell them back. And they fine me a thousand dollars that will go in God only knows whose pocket."

"But that's incredible, unthinkable. Inhuman."

"These slave commissioners are inhuman. They don't care for anything but the money they'll get. Come on, let's get ready for them."

"Where will Simon and Mara be?"

"These first two crates are false. They're built over a compartment below in the hull of the boat, accessible from Elijah's cabin. You wouldn't see it unless you knew what to look for. We've fooled them for three years."

"What if they want to search the crates?"

"We let them. They are filled a foot or so down from the top with actual cargo. This trip it's bolts of fabric for my mother. She's redecorating."

Mara was feeling better. Her fever had broken and

61

her discomfort was somewhat alleviated by the hot and cold compresses the doctor had ordered. Very reluctantly she gave up her bed and followed Simon into the lower chamber. And more reluctantly she handed over her child to Emily.

"It won't be for long," Seneca assured her. "But whatever you hear above, *whatever* happens with this boat, you be quiet and stay here. I'm warning you because they will lift the boat completely out of the water on a platform to weigh it. The boat may tilt, cargo could shift, but it's all pretty routine. Just noisy."

"We be quiet. You don't worry," Simon said bravely.

"The boat will be searched. Don't be afraid if you hear voices, and even some hammering, should they want to open some crates."

"It's time," Elijah said. "We are coming into Troy. We must get topside or they might get suspicious."

Emily took the baby back to her cabin and arranged their food hamper to look like a tiny crib. She laid out a few baby garments and flannel blankets for affect. Then she changed the baby, fixed a spare bottle, set some diapers to soak outside in a pail of water and lye soap. She was as ready as possible.

She wrapped the infant in a blanket and let Seneca guide her from the boat. They walked along the path as their boat was towed into a weighlock, the water lowered, the boat hoisted on a cradle, then floated back into the canal.

Ahead of them the craft was docked. Elijah went aboard, setting to order the shifted cargo. Two men approached him and produced a document, a permit to search. Elijah shook his head, directing them to Seneca.

Emily felt herself tense. "Relax," Seneca said, smiling down into her face. "I'll take care of it."

"You Prescott?" a burly, bearded man asked.

"And good day to you, too," Seneca replied sarcastically. "Yes, I'm Prescott."

"We got a permit to search all boats for escaped slaves."

"All or just mine?"

"We suspect you might be carrying other than cargo this trip."

The baby began to fuss. Emily rocked him against her shoulder. "Must you? Charles is waiting to be fed." She left it at that and watched the men look from the baby to her bosom.

"New baby?" the tall thin man with the thick black moustache asked.

She didn't like his eyes. They looked mean. Cold and mean. "As a matter of fact, yes. If it's any of your business. Or are you into selling babies of every . . ."

"Darling, don't get yourself upset. It isn't good for you," Seneca reproved gently. "There's a bench over there. Take Charles and wait for me there."

"Yes, dear."

"Maybe I should have a look at the baby," the tall one said.

"You will pardon me if I refuse," Emily huffed, "but until you can also produce a document from a reputable physician attesting to the fact that you do not carry tuberculosis or any other communicable diseases," she added distastefully, "I won't permit you to *breathe* near my Charles. Excuse me."

Seneca chuckled and shook his head, watching her fondly. "She's been that way since the little mite was placed in her arms. If I as much as sneeze, I'm banned from his presence."

He turned and, realizing who was beside him, cleared his face of expression. "Yes, well, inasmuch as you have gone to all the trouble of ferreting out a judge or sheriff who would issue you such a permit, you may as well have a look. You have exactly one minute, after which my friend and I shall bodily throw you into the canal. And I assure you we can—and will."

Two minutes later they were on their way down the

canal, leaving two disgruntled slave hunters on the shore.

"That won't be the end of them," Elijah warned. "Someone's tipped them off."

"You mean they'll follow us?" Emily asked.

"Possibly," Seneca said, squeezing her shoulder. "Depends on how much they want these two."

"Three," Elijah reminded him. "The baby's worth a handsome price."

"You're quite a little actress," Seneca said dryly. "I was convinced you were holding my son, Charles."

She flushed self-consciously. "It was the first thing that popped into my head. Sorry."

"No need to be. I was proud of you. I didn't think you'd . . . I wasn't sure you'd help us."

She looked away. "I see. So I'm still not to be trusted. Excuse me. I'll put the baby in his bed."

"Hey, I didn't mean anything . . ."

"Leave her alone. I expect she'll get used to your outspoken ways in time. I'll bring Simon and Mara out. Why don't you see to the hayburners and the boy. Get your mind off the lady."

"I guess you're right."

Emily was fixing lunch when Elijah came by with an empty baby bottle. She took it to wash and refill.

"Where's Seneca," she asked idly.

"Back with the hoggee."

"I beg your pardon," she said, laughing.

"Missy, you're a canawller now. You gotta learn the language. The hoggee is the young man who leads the horses or mules, hayburners, down the towpath. Seneca tows a small barge behind us for the second team and the second hoggee. They take six hour shifts. We have a fine team — two brothers, Cob and Benjie. Seneca hires them for the year."

"I wondered about that. Who feeds them? Should I be making more?"

"No, they stay to themselves, do for themselves and

their mules. They prefer it that way. So does Seneca. He's free then to go about his business without curious eyes."

"Would they betray him?"

"I do not think. Seneca pays well and he pays every trip, unlike most who pay at the end of the season. And definitely not like some who fail to pay at all. These boys know a good deal when they have it. Still, if someone came by with a roll of bills, they might be tempted to pass on a bit of information here and there. What they don't know, they can't tell."

"What is he doing now?"

"Checking the hookup, seeing that there is ample grain and hay, making sure the hut is supplied with blankets, and staying out of your way."

"My way? Why would he care about that now? It didn't bother him before."

"When he was hiding in anonymity? Yes, perhaps you are right. Now I think you make him feel nervous."

Her brow creased in skepticism. "Now you're teasing me."

While she prepared their meal, Elijah perched on a crate and watched. "No, I do not tease."

"Where were you born. You have an unusual accent. Very musical, actually."

"I was brought to this country fifteen years ago from the West Indies. I was overseer on a large sugar plantation until I angered the bossman. Then I was sold."

"Do you really belong to Seneca?"

"I have indentured myself to him to pay back the price he gave for my release."

"Did he ask that of you?"

"I ask it of him. It is fair."

"Why do you act like a slave in public?"

"We have found that it causes less curiosity."

"Here's the baby's milk. How is Mara feeling?"

"She's much better. She says she will feed her baby by herself tomorrow."

"That's good. I'll take her a hot bath after lunch. Another day of bedrest won't hurt her."

"I shall leave you to your chores then. Seneca is returning. Do not be too harsh with him," he admonished with a wink.

She laughed. Seneca stopped in his tracks and watched her animated face. She had a beautiful laugh. She had a beautiful face. She took his breath away. He damned Paddie McMurdie all over again.

She saw him and gave him a shy smile. "Lunch will be ready soon, if you want to wash up," she said.

His gut twisted into knots, and anger, hot and unreasonable, rose inside him. "None for me. I'm not hungry."

"You really should eat something."

"Don't mother me," he barked.

Such a hothead. She tried teasing. "Yes, I can see you're past the short pants."

He grumbled something and went into the cabin.

"Oh, Seneca," she called. "How much of that fabric does your mother require?"

"Why?" he asked, stepping into the doorway. He'd taken off his shirt.

Speechless, she stopped slicing the bread and stared. He had an arrogant nose, and his too-stubborn jaw needed shaving. His black hair had just enough curl in it to prevent it from looking shaggy. His body was as darkly tanned as his face, telling her his recent concession to shirts was on her behalf. His chest . . .

"Enjoying the show?" he baited.

Her eyes swept once more across the firmly muscled shoulders and arms, down the chest and flat abdomen that sported a sprinkling of black curls. Even the long scars he bore couldn't detract from his overall beauty and supreme aura of masculinity.

"Yes, actually." She lowered her eyes and continued with the bread. "You're a very attractive man, as I'm sure you already know."

"Are you flirting with me, Miss Harcourt?"

"You mean am I going to bat my eyes at you and sashay around your deck? No, I won't inflict that on you."

He began to relax and leaned against the door frame. "It might be fun to watch."

"No doubt, since I'd make a fool of myself."

"You're not schooled in the fine art of mild social flirtation."

"Hardly. I've lived my life entirely with men. I've learned to be more direct."

"Now that sounds interesting."

She clucked her tongue at him and rolled her eyes. "You know what I mean."

"No mother?"

"She died when I was three. I don't remember her."

"Do you look like her?"

"I'm told I do."

"Why haven't you married? A beautiful girl like yourself."

She looked up to see if he was mocking her. He appeared to be quite serious.

"My father had a stroke when I was fifteen. He needed constant care."

"So you stayed with him."

"Do you think I should have left him? He had no one else."

"What about this uncle who was just killed?"

"Uncle Joe was my father's cousin. We never knew him very well. Besides, he was here in Albany. We were in Virginia."

"Virginia? You're a Southerner?"

"If you consider twenty miles outside of Williamsburg as the South."

"You've no other family?"

"Two aunts, but they turned their backs on us. Papa made the mistake of criticizing their way of life."

"Don't tell me. They own slaves," he said.

"Yes. Are you any hungrier now?"

"I could get around one of those sandwiches and a cup of coffee. Let me wash up."

Miles away a young girl gathered her party together and hid them in a shack outside Utica. It was in this town they must change to another train, a train that would take them far north to the border. Here they would meet another guide. Bekka would return to Albany.

"Stay here until I return with your passes."

"Couldn't one of us go for some food? We's awful hungry."

"I'll go," one young man said.

"No. You will all stay," Bekka ordered.

"You ain't got the right to say who goes and who stays. We got to New York widout you," he retorted belligerently.

"That may be so, but you are with me now and you will do as I say."

"And if we don't?"

"You're free to do as you choose, Virgil, but if you leave this place and endanger everyone else, don't come back."

He was clearly annoyed. With everyone and everything. "Dis ain't like I thought it'd be like."

"What did you think? Folks'd welcome you with lovin' arms?"

"Always hidin', always hungry, always runnin'. It's worse'n what we left."

"It may get worse yet. Stay here." She left them before she lost her temper. Always there was one who nursed some wild fantasy about life outside of bondage. But usually, thank God, they were ready to endure a little hardship for ultimate freedom. They were eager to take responsibility for their own lives. Unlike Virgil, they didn't expect someone else to feed and shelter them. Virgil didn't have the dream yet.

Unfortunately, the Virgils were a threat to the rest.

She made her way in the shadows to the big house up on the hill. She had no idea who lived there or which of the occupants was helping the slaves. She found the back door, gave three knocks followed by three more, then waited.

The door opened. All she was to do then was hold up the number of passes she required for the train. She held up five fingers. The door closed and she waited. Some minutes later she was handed a flour sack of food and five passes. The door closed before she had the chance to offer her thanks.

She found her way back to the little group. She was hungry too, but she gave up her portion so they would each have a little more. She'd eat at the safe house later, after she got this group on the train.

She leaned back against the trunk of a tree and looked at the shape of the night clouds outlined by the silver-gold of the moon. Even in the clouds she searched for his face.

She held her necklace in her hand and prayed with her heart that she'd see her son again. The clouds shifted and swam on her tears. He'd been only five. Just a baby. How could she have lost him? How could she have been so blindly stupid? How could God have permitted it?

She could see his laughing face clearly in her mind. His five-year-old face. How would she know him now, three years later? He'd have lost his baby teeth by now. He'd be taller. Yes, his father was very tall.

"Oh, Elijah," she whispered. "How can I make it up to you. You suffered so much so your son would live free, and I lost him. I lost him. How can I ever face you again?"

And that was her problem. She couldn't.

Chapter 5

"I believe I must consider rerouting them," Elijah said that night. He was sitting with Seneca and Emily on the flat roof of the rear cabin, enjoying the cool of the evening, the moonlight on the water, the night sounds of life along the water's edge.

"You're really concerned," Seneca acknowledged.

"They know we have them."

"How could they?" Emily asked quietly. "They searched the boat."

"They will have expected us to have put them off before the weighlock and to have picked them up again after."

"Have they been following us, then?"

"It's hard to say," Seneca answered.

"Where would you take them?" she asked Elijah.

"I have several options. They are expected to meet a man in Rome, but I could divert them before that in Utica. I've heard of a woman who works between New York and the railroad spur in Utica. She might be able to arrange transportation north."

"Do you know her?"

"No. They call her the Princess, but I've never met her."

"Oh, like they call Harriet Tubman Moses."

"Exactly. You know of Miss Tubman?"

"My little cousin was very interested in abolition. He

read everything he could find about Miss Tubman, then talked endlessly about what he read. But how does it work, the Underground Railroad? He could never quite put it all together."

"That's its secret. They're all different. Change is essential. Once a routine is established it's doomed."

"Then how . . ."

"I'm not convinced you should be telling any of this," Seneca said.

"Why not?" Emily asked defensively. "Are you still afraid I'll go to the police?"

"No," he answered condescendingly, angered at her quick and erroneous conclusion. "But life is uncertain, at best. If you were captured and threatened with violence, might you not exchange pain for information? If you don't know . . ." He shrugged.

"You think I'd betray hundreds of people just to save myself?"

"Wouldn't you? I don't think any of us knows what he would or wouldn't do under certain conditions."

"I assure you, I'm stronger than that."

"And what if you were forced to watch Mara being whipped and beaten, tortured. What then?"

"Come on. People wouldn't go to such lengths," she scoffed.

Seneca and Elijah exchanged looks. "Oh, I assure *you* they would. Slavery is crucial to the South. Their economy is based on free labor, and they won't give up their rights to own slaves without a fight. Every slave who escapes is a threat to their way of life, and if the slaves aren't stopped and made an example of, even more will run off."

"The Negro is considered a step below human," Elijah explained. "How do you think it looks when an inferior being outsmarts his owner? It is a personal affront. So we're not only talking about a life of being waited on for every little thing, but about greed, power, pride, and stubborn, blind conviction that retribution

71

is their due."

"How do your aunts treat their slaves?" Seneca asked.

"I never spent any time with them. We weren't exactly welcome in their homes."

Emily was the first to admit that she was out of touch with current events. Until she went to live with Joe and Peter she had confined herself pretty much to the house, to caring for her father. He hadn't wanted to hear the newspapers read to him. He said they unsettled him. She spent hours each day reading to him from his favorite novels. After that she had the cooking, cleaning, laundry, and gardening to keep her busy. She had no regrets about her labors of love for her father, but she realized now how much her life had been restricted. Peter, with his unceasing curiosity, his unquenchable thirst for knowledge, had shown her a little of the world she had been cut off from, and now here was another view, through other more worldly eyes than Peter's.

"You look a little bewildered," Seneca remarked, watching her expressions.

"She's a butterfly, man," Elijah said.

Emily's surprise showed. "A butterfly?" She liked to hear Elijah talk when he was relaxed and not thinking about his speech. He sounded aristocratic, with a British touch to his words.

"A butterfly just emerged from a long winter in a snug and safe cocoon. And here you are, glittery and colorful and ready to live, only you find yourself in a world where you cannot recognize the safe meadow from the one where the falcon lives."

"Elijah," she said, surprised. "That was very nice. I think."

He chuckled. "I meant it in the kindest way." He pulled out a pocket watch and checked the hour. "Good timing, this. We've a lock ahead, and it's time to change teams. I'll sound the bell."

He jumped down. Emily turned to look at Seneca. "I like him," she said.

"He's quite the philosopher today," Seneca remarked, looking out over the dark water of the canal. He shifted and rested his elbows on his updrawn knees.

Silence stretched between them, growing more and more tense as they each sought for something to say. It shouldn't be so hard.

Emily sighed. "You don't like me, do you?"

His dark gaze snapped around. "Don't be silly. I like you fine."

"Then you resent liking me."

"Are you reading my mind now?"

"No. I didn't mean that."

"Then kindly stop telling me what I'm thinking."

"Then why don't *you* tell me what you're thinking. It might help me to understand why you're such a sorehead whenever I'm around. What have I ever done to you?"

He swore. "I don't need this." His hand went to his forehead, then he seemed to snap. He turned toward her and took her chin in his hand.

"All right, I'll tell you. You think you've learned to be direct. Let's see if you have."

His grip was tight, though not painful, but his piercing black eyes made her instinctively grab his wrist for fear he would hurt her. "Seneca," she began.

"Maybe I do resent you. I know I could gladly strangle Paddie McMurdie for throwing us together like this."

"What? Why? Because I might betray . . ."

"No," he snapped. "Would you please quit saying that."

"Then what? I just don't understand."

He was very quick. One minute they were sitting up facing each other, the next she was pinned down by one strong leg and a pair of wide shoulders.

"Maybe you'll understand this."

73

His lips, when they met hers, were not brutal or punishing, as she'd expected, but gentle and persuasive, which was more devastating in a far different way. He coaxed her lips apart; he tempted her to meet him in his passion.

His fingers caressed her face, her neck, teased the upper curves of her breasts until she found herself clutching at his shoulders, caught in a whirlwind of sensations.

"Beautiful Emily, so sweet," he murmured against her hungry lips.

"Seneca," she whispered in a haze of desire.

His lips trailed warm kisses across her cheek to the delicate curve of her ear. "You make me crazy," he whispered and brushed the sensitive side of her neck with his lips. Her head went instinctively to the side, allowing him the access he sought, and he groaned deep in his throat and took his liberty there.

The buttons on her blouse were undone, the material pushed to the side, and his lips burned across the swells of her breast. His hand lifted and molded the softness of one mound, and through the fine linen of her camisole his lips and teeth closed over the swollen peak.

She gave a whimper of surprise at the nearly painful pleasure he was giving her. She held on to him, surrendering her young and untutored body to his care, giving freedom to the pleasure coursing through her veins.

A bell clanged as Elijah alerted the lockkeep of their approach. Seneca jumped and pulled away, looking down into her bemused face. He, too, was dazed. Carefully he folded her blouse back into place, covering that which he had uncovered.

"Do you begin to understand now? No man, sane or otherwise, should be expected to share such a small space with someone like you and keep his hands to himself. Yet I'm expected to do just that. For weeks."

She rolled away, sat up, and fastened the buttons of her blouse. Of all he'd ever done, this hurt the worst.

"Is that supposed to be a compliment, that you . . . that you want me? Being wanted like this, grudgingly and resentfully, for that's what it is, is an insult. I trusted your kisses, I believed that you meant what you were doing—what *we* were doing. And all the time you were teaching me a lesson."

She climbed down the ladder and looked back up at him sitting there with his head in his hands. "I may be unschooled in this sort of thing, but I am not stupid. I can understand English. Just tell me if you want me to hide away like Mara and Simon. I can stay out of sight."

"And what will get you out of my head?" he asked.

She glared at him. Was she to do it all? "I won't need a repeat of your lesson. You used a cruel and degrading way of doing it, but you made your point."

A minute later she was trouncing out of Seneca's cabin, carrying a blanket and a pillow. She let herself into the forward cabin. Let him make of that what he would. She wasn't staying where she was not wanted. And at the first opportunity she was getting off this tub.

Sometime later that night she woke up. Mara was asleep, the baby tucked in his basket by her head. Simon was snoring softly. She sat up and looked around, wondering what had awakened her. Elijah was leaning up also from his pallet on the floor.

She pushed her hair out of her face. "Did you call me?" she whispered.

He shook his head and nodded at the door. "It's Seneca."

"He called me?"

"No. It's one of his headaches."

"A hangover?" she asked cynically.

"A migraine, I'd say."

"Does he get them often?" She understood headaches

75

well enough. Her father had suffered them.

"No, not often. But when they come, they are bad. Shall I go to him, or will you?"

"I don't think he'd want me near him," she said, letting her hurt show.

"I think you are mistaken. He wants you very much, but he is also very much afraid."

"Of what? Of what Paddie might say?"

"Do you sincerely think Seneca would care what Paddie might do? He is afraid of you, of being hurt again."

"Again?"

"Yes. He is afraid to believe in love again. It is not you he despises but a memory. Go to him. He needs your comfort."

She needed no more encouragement to believe what her foolish heart longed to believe. She slung her blanket over her shoulders and quietly let herself out of the cabin.

"Thank you, Elijah," she whispered.

She found him leaning over the railing, holding his head in his hands. He was naked but for a pair of ragged-edged trousers that were cut off at the knees. She came up behind him and covered his shoulders with her blanket.

"Seneca?"

He lifted his head, obviously in great pain. "Go back to bed."

"No. I can help you. Will you let me?"

"You can't do anything. No one can. Please."

"This time you lose, Seneca. Give in gracefully. I'm staying by your side until the pain is gone, so don't argue. You'll only make your headache worse. Now come back to bed."

"I'm in too much pain to argue," he groaned.

"I know you are, or you surely would," she agreed, leading him back to his bunk. "Close your eyes for a minute and try to relax. I'm going to make you some

76

special tea that my father found helpful."

"Your father had headaches?"

"Yes."

"He died of a stroke," he said, coming to his own conclusion.

"Yes, and there are some who suffer severely with migraine headaches until they reach a very healthy old age, and some who never have a headache and suffer stroke in the prime of life. Now quit thinking and relax."

She returned shortly with a steaming mug of her specially concocted tea and helped him lift his head to sip it.

"Awful."

"I know. Drink it."

"You're poisoning me."

"Of course. Would I pass up such a golden opportunity? Drink up like a good little boy," she added motheringly.

"A witch and her brew."

"Now roll over so I can work my magic."

She knew better than to touch the muscles of his legs or buttocks as she would have done with her father. Instead she began at his waist and worked her way up the tensed and knotted muscles of his back, kneading and soothing until she felt him relax beneath her fingers. She did the same with his arms and across the taut muscles of his shoulders. All the time she worked, she hummed soft melodies.

She had him roll to his back and she knelt above his head and coaxed the tension from his neck and scalp. Her arms and hands ached from her labors, but his forehead had relaxed and his jaw was slack. His pain had receded. Now only sleep could heal.

She smoothed his hair back from his forehead, reluctant to leave him just yet. His coal black hair curled around her fingers like a soft caress. With her thumbs she worked along his brow to behind his ears, then across the bridge of his nose and down his jawline. She closed her eyes and, like a sculptor, memorized the planes and angles of his face. He might never again be so passive under her hands.

She bent over and dropped a kiss on his forehead. "Sleep now, my handsome giant," she whispered, thinking him already asleep.

"Stay with me," he murmured groggily.

"Lie still. I'll put out the light."

Careful not to disturb him, she crawled over him. She pulled the blankets over them and snuggled close to his side. He didn't move, and soon was breathing deeply and evenly.

Emily closed her eyes and let her tensions drain from her. "He is afraid of you," Elijah had said. She thought about that and what it could mean. It certainly explained his attitude. And he *did* say she was making him crazy. Her spirits lifted.

On the other hand, another part of her mind admonished her, if he were leery enough of love he could walk away from it completely. And from her. And she could end up the one hurt. So she would have to see that that didn't happen. She'd just have to teach him that he was safe in loving her. Because if she didn't, she was in big trouble.

Emily let Seneca sleep the next morning, knowing he'd need his rest to dispel the lingering effects of both the headache and the tea she'd made for him. She fed Elijah and their passengers and heated water for baths and laundry.

"We're beginning to resemble a shantyboat," Elijah said when she'd laid out the baby blankets and diapers to dry on top of the crates and barrels.

"Babies require a great deal of extra work," she said.

"Yes, I remember."

"You do?" she said, laughing because he sounded so

experienced.

"Indeed. I too have a son somewhere."

"Really? I didn't know you were . . ." She bit her lip, reluctant to blunder her way into an embarrassing situation.

"Married? Yes, I have a wife. A very beautiful wife. And a son who is almost eight by now. At least, I hope I do. I haven't seen them for three years."

Emily wrung out the last flannel blanket and spread it over a crate. "There, all done. What shall I do with the water?"

"I'll take care of it when we change teams. We try to keep the canal clean. We have an unwritten code, those of us who care."

"It's really quite amazing, not at all what I expected."

Elijah picked up his guitar and motioned her to join him on the forward deck. "Sit with me for a few minutes. We get busy up ahead."

A bench ran the length of the front of the cabin. Elijah sat down and propped up his feet on the front railing. He strummed the strings, tuning them.

"I visualized the canal as a creek. A river. I didn't expect it to be so . . . constructed."

"Yes, it is not a natural waterway."

"How deep is it?"

"Six or seven feet, and sixty or seventy feet across. It narrows, of course, where it crosses over another waterway."

"It's like I imagined the ancient Roman aqueducts to have been. It is strange to float in a stone trough that is actually elevated over another river. How is the water level maintained?"

"From feeder lines along the canal."

"Tell me about your wife. Why haven't you seen her?"

"Ah, Bekka. Such an exotic woman," he bragged.

"Where is she?"

"I don't know. For three years I have searched for her

and my son, Tyler." He shook his head. "It is a big world. We had a dream to one day be free and to help others reach freedom. And so I travel routes where I think she might be doing that."

"Are you sure she was not captured and returned?"

"My sources tell me she is not there."

"That must be very disheartening."

"The uncertainty, yes. It would be far better to know, one way or another, if she is alive or not."

"Where did you meet her?"

"I did not meet her. I watched her grow up. She was ten when I was brought to the plantation. She used to tag along with me when I worked. When she turned twelve she was put to work in the big house as the upstairs maid.

"It was to me she ran when the massa ordered her to come to his room one night. She was fifteen, and scared to death. I would not let her become his private mistress. I took her as my own. The overseer found us together. We were both punished, but the Massa left her alone after that. Sorry, I should not speak of such things to a lady."

"I asked."

"Our marriage was arranged. We were to 'breed' more slaves. That is the way of it, you see."

"Only you decided to escape."

"Yes. The overseer, a very evil-minded man, took an interest in my lovely wife. He was not as fussy as the owner when it came to sharing."

"I'm glad you escaped."

"I did not. We would most certainly have been caught, but I hid my wife and my small son and I led the search party away from them. They escaped, but I was returned and punished."

"What happened to you?"

"I was given to the overseer to punish. Both of them, the master and the overseer, wanted their pound of flesh for what I took from them. And so I was chained to the whipping post.

"I cannot remember much after the fourth day. I do remember looking into eyes that were blacker than my own. I remember someone coming out at night and giving me water, bread, and cheese. The next I remember I was lying in the back of a wagon while the man with the black eyes bathed my body and treated me with soothing ointment. I thought I was going to die. So did he for a while. But he hired a room in town, brought in a doctor, stayed by my side through the worst of my delirium. Finally I passed the critical point, as the doctor said. It took two weeks to get on my feet again. By then I knew the kind of man who was my new master. I would have done anything he asked."

"What did he ask of you?"

"He asked me to help him prevent others from suffering as I did. That was not a request I could refuse, even though it meant I should lose time in finding my family. When he handed me my papers, I was actually disappointed. I wanted to pay him back in some way for all he'd done. I wanted to remain his friend. To stay with him."

"So you indentured yourself."

"We have had a profitable association."

"Would you never want to return to the West Indies, then?"

"No. That is all a lifetime ago now." He strummed a minor chord. "Follow de drinkin' gourd; follow de drinkin' gourd . . ." he sang in deep mellow tones.

They traveled for some time in the quiet of the deep woods, the only boat in sight, with Elijah singing softly and Emily letting the peace and music carry her thoughts away. Finally they came to a dock, then another amid a group of shacks.

"Time to get to work," Elijah said, nodding toward the next corner they were approaching. Emily watched, entranced, as a series of stairstep locks came into view.

"My stars, we're going up that?"

"Why don't you get the baby and walk round this one. I'll have to hide Simon and Mara."

"Are we there already?" came Seneca's voice from behind them. "Damn, what time is it?"

"Ten o'clock, bossman."

He scraped his hand against his dark stubble of a beard. "Good God, what did you give me?" he scowled at Emily. "You drugged me."

"Good morning, Seneca," she said in answer. "Feeling better, I see. I'll tend to our guests, if you'll excuse me."

"You might warn them that we have several of these in the next stretch of the canal," Elijah said. "Until we get through the mountains. They should be prepared to move quickly."

"I'll tell them, And Elijah, you sing beautifully."

She left. Seneca watched her go. Elijah watched Seneca.

"Headache gone?" he asked.

"Yes. Whatever she gave me, it did the trick. I feel as good as new, except for needing a shave. Looks like we'll be stuck in line here for a few minutes. I'm going for a swim."

"You might consider offering a gracious thanks to her when you get presentable. I'm sure your mama taught you how. "

"Yes, Daddy," he said facetiously.

Emily returned to the deck as Seneca was shaving. A towel was slung around his neck, but he hadn't dried his shoulders or back. Drops of water sparkled against his tanned skin in the morning sun.

She walked back and forth, rocking the baby gently in her arms, but she found her gaze going time and again to his tight buttocks, the long flexed muscles of his thighs that stretched the fabric of his trousers. She found her eyes straying to his slim hips and his broad tapered back, to the fragment of his face she could see in the mirror above his wash basin. Finally he rinsed his razor and splashed his face.

"Do you like what you see?" he taunted, catching her eye in the mirror.

Some defiant imp inside her refused to let him see how embarrassed she was at being caught staring.

"If you insist on parading around without a shirt I guess I'll look."

He dried his face and shoulders and combed his fingers through his hair. He picked up his shirt and walked toward her. "I want to thank you properly for last night."

She watched him shrug into his shirt and tuck the tails in his pants. She swallowed dryly. "That's okay. I'm glad I could help."

"How did you just happen to have what you needed?"

"I always carried some powders with me when Papa was alive. I still had some in a purse that Maggie packed for me. It was pure chance."

"The massage had nothing to do with chance," he said. "You've the hands of an angel. And the face." *And the body.*

She gave him a quizzical smile. "Why, thank you, Seneca."

"And about last night, I didn't mean to hurt you. And I wasn't trying to teach you a lesson."

"You weren't?"

"I'm trying to tell you that there are times I find you quite irresistible."

"Oh."

"Just *oh?*"

"And yesterday was one of those times?"

"Sitting up there, you looked as if you'd come down from the heavens on a moonbeam. I know I don't have the right to kiss you, but sometimes the need to do so is more than I can withstand."

"And then you get angry with me."

"And with myself."

"I see." The baby squirmed, and she realized she was holding him too tightly.

Seneca took hold of her elbow to steady her as they were towed into the first lock. The boat bumped to a stop.

"I can't believe we're going up this thing," she said, looking at the high wooden gates that marched up the hill, separating the individual locks.

"We'll walk up the steps. That way you'll be able to see how the water levels are changed and how the gates are opened and closed."

Once they were off the boat, Seneca took charge of the baby, cradling the tiny bundle in the crook of his elbow while he held Emily's arm with his other hand.

Elijah stayed with the boat, more to insure that no attempt was made to jump aboard and search for Simon and Mara than for any other reason.

"Has he decided yet what he'll do at Utica?" she asked.

"Unless he sees someone following us or hears that we have comissioners on the canal, he'll stick to the original plan."

"What if those men are around but you don't know it?"

"These folks know who comes up and down their part of the canal. All strangers are noted. You'll see, next time you come by here, they'll call you by name."

The hoggees pulled the boat and barge into the dockside and exchanged teams at the top of the locks, giving them a few more minutes to stretch their legs on dry ground. Still holding the baby, Seneca walked over to a few of his friends to chat. He motioned to Emily to join him and introduced her as his cousin who was going to visit his mother. The baby began to cry, and Emily took him, excusing herself to go back

"Beautiful woman," Henry said, watching her depart. "Cousin, you say?"

"That's what I said," Seneca replied, meeting his old friend's speculative gaze.

Old Henry nodded, looking at the sky. "Fair weather ahead, I think, unless a stray cloud creeps over the hills."

"Thanks, pal."

"Catch ya on the way back, eh?"

Seneca withdrew a pouch of tobaco from his pocket and handed it to Henry. "Found some of your favorite chaw. Enjoy it."

"Hey, thanks," Henry called as Seneca returned to the boat. "That's mighty decent of you."

Emily heard just enough of the exchange to arouse her curiosity. "What was decent of you? Have you been hiding a benevolent nature from me all this time?"

His lips twisted in exasperation. He jumped aboard. "You make me sound like a real ogre."

"You have had your moments, cousin dear."

"Ah, about that. It was either my cousin or my wife. I thought you'd much prefer being my cousin."

Her stomach did a crazy flip-flop, and she turned away in case her face revealed what errant thoughts had just run through her mind. To be his wife. But of course, it was crazy. He practically hated her. He had to exert himself to be civil to her.

She tucked the baby into his basket and carried him into Elijah's cabin, where Mara would expect to find him once they were on their way again. She was strangely reluctant to go back on deck with Seneca. If he sensed what she was thinking, he'd throw her in the canal.

"You coward," she rebuked herself aloud. And fool. He would guess she was falling in love with him if she weren't careful. If he guessed that he would make her life a misery. He was a long, long way from trusting in that most bewildering of emotions again. She must go on as usual.

Supper. She'd put on a kettle of stew. That would keep her busy for a little while. She stepped out of the cabin and walked right into him.

"Oh," she gasped, stumbling over his feet.

He caught her and steadied her in his arms. She looked up into his dark eyes, then, afraid he'd see how his touch was affecting her, looked quickly away.

That was when she saw them, standing in the trees on the opposite side of the canal. Two of them. One was tall, bald, with a long mustache, the other was the man who had attacked her in the warehouse. She was sure of it, even at that distance. Her skin turned cold and clammy.

"Seneca, behind you. They've followed me. They're here."

"What's wrong?" he asked at the same time. "You're as white . . . What did you say?"

"Two men . . ."

Seneca spun around. "Where?"

"They're gone now. They were there," she said urgently when he looked askance at her.

"I didn't see anyone."

"I did. One of them was the one who . . ."

"Emily, calm down. No one knows you're here. You've imagined it."

"I know what I saw."

"Two men walking through the woods," he said patronizingly. "You don't have to make up stories to get into my arms. I'll be glad to . . ."

"Why you . . ." She slapped his hands away and stepped back. "Of all the arrogant, egocentric ideas." She rubbed her arms as if to rid herself of his touch. "Whatever gave you the ridiculous notion that I or any woman would go to such lengths for the dubious pleasure of being manhandled by you?"

He had the audacity to laugh at her.

Chapter 6

During the day, Seneca and Elijah spelled each other at the tiller bar. Curiosity grew in Emily until she had to go back and ask her questions.

"It manipulates the rudder," Seneca answered. "On straighter sections of the canal we lock it in place, but through the mountains we have to navigate or else the towlines would pull us into the bank."

"What if one boat wants to go faster than the one ahead of it?"

"We raise the towlines on poles and pass the other boat and its lines. Sometimes it's a problem, especially if lines get fouled. Watch. Here comes a hoodle-dasher from the other direction. His boats and mules will stay to the outside and raise the lines, we'll go under on the inside. It works the same way when two boats are going the same direction."

"Seneca, what is a hoodle-dasher?"

"It's one bullhead, or freighter like us, usually loaded, towing a couple empty bullheads behind it. One team pulls the whole string. It's efficient, but a damn nuisance to get past. See, Elijah's ready with the poles to shove them away if they crowd us. And that's Blackjack Blue at the tiller. He always takes his half right out of the goddamn middle. Hold the tiller a minute."

"Seneca, I can't . . ."

He pulled her fingers over the heavy wood handle, then raced to the stern where Elijah stood. She held on and concentrated on keeping the bar in the same place it had been when he left.

"You bungling bastard," Seneca yelled out to the other captain. "Who taught you how to navigate? Get the hell over." He too grabbed a long pole and prepared to guide the crafts apart.

"Give ground, Prescott," Blackjack called. "I got a corner to make."

"No way. Hire some steermen for your empties you skinflint. I'm not running aground just to save you two bits."

"Give ground, I say, or I'll ram this thing down your throat."

"Better do it," Elijah warned. "Tangle with him on dry land, not when innocent people could be hurt."

"That fat-bellied bastard. I'll break his arm next time I see him. Emily, hard to port."

"What?" she screeched. Port?

"Turn right, to your right."

Right. She thought hard and fast to make sure she got it correct, then shoved the tiller to her right as hard as she could.

She watched, dismayed, as the front of the boat did just the opposite of what she'd expected and veered directly into the path of the oncoming freighter.

Seneca swore, gripped the pole, and prepared for the inevitable collision.

Suddenly the freighter dived for the opposite bank. "You goddamn son-of-a-bitchin' halfbreed. I'll nail your hide to the wall for this," Blackjack cussed.

Emily realized her error and pulled hard on the tiller, swinging it to the opposite side. The boats passed within inches of each other, and the two captains filled the air with foul obscenities that made her cheeks and the tips of her ears burn. And some of it was directed at her.

She looked back as they passed, only to see the hoodle-dasher scrape to a stop against the high rock wall on the south side of the canal. The three boats slewed sideways into each other. The lines pulled taut, and one of the horses shied and slipped off the towpath and into the canal, taking the other two horses with it.

"Oh, my stars," she gaped.

"Emily, for Chrissake, look where you're going," Seneca yelled, grabbing the tiller and swinging them about just as they would have run aground on the other side.

Elijah was bent over double with laughter.

"Are you trying to kill us all, women? I said to turn right," Seneca fired at her, getting the back on course.

"I turned it right. It went left. How was I to know it's backward? And don't yell at me. You had no business making me do that in the first place, just so you could see which of you could swear the dirtiest."

"That wasn't why."

"Yes it was. Don't add lying to your long list of sins."

"My long list. Keeping track of them, are you?"

"And never, *never*, ask me to steer this thing again. I'll clean your blasted boat and I'll wash your clothes and cook your meals, but . . ."

"While I'm captain, you'll do exactly what I tell you to do, including steering this blasted boat. Do I make myself clear?"

"I will not," she defied him, turning her back to flounce away.

He swung her back around. "You little hellcat. I ought to—"

"Take your hands off me!" They were both out of

control and she knew it, but she couldn't stop. Since running into Seneca she had lost her calm, her reserve, her ever-present restraint. He set her emotions off like no one else had ever done, and she didn't know what to do with the flood of feelings he aroused.

Seneca did. He kissed her until she grew weak from fighting him and began to cling to his broad shoulders. Only when Elijah came to take over the tiller did Seneca release her.

"Sorry to interrupt," Elijah said, still smirking, "but we have locks ahead."

Emily turned away in a huff and went forward to warn Mara and Simon. Seneca watched her go, shaking his head in consternation.

"There are times I'd like to strangle her."

"And then there are other times," Elijah said, laughing. "Give up, man, you love her."

Seneca scowled. "What the hell kind of nonsense is that? She's just an aggravating female, no more, no less."

"Um-hmm."

"Oh, what the hell do I waste my time talking to you for?"

Once through the mountain pass the locks became fewer and farther apart. The canal stretched out over gently rolling hills. In the towns that had grown up along the canal, the bridges over the famed waterway were fairly high. Out in the countryside, where the canal bisected farmlands, the access or occupation bridges, though crafted beautifully of natural stone, were only seven or eight feet above the canal. This presented no problem except when Emily took her chair up onto the roof of the cabin to sit and read or to enjoy the scenery. Elijah's "low bridge" always made her laugh, even as it reminded her to get down.

They were a few miles outside of Utica when Seneca joined her, plunking a wooden chair beside hers and hoisting himself up to the rooftop.

He leaned back, his hands folded behind his head, his long legs stretched out in front of him. The sunlight turned his hair a blue-black, as dark as a raven's wing.

"This is the life, isn't it?" He looked over at her as she laid her book aside.

"It's beautiful. I envy you."

"Has it been good for you—helped you to forget?"

"Yes. Although I still think of Uncle Joe and Peter the pain is not so devastating. I often find myself thinking I must tell Peter about this or that."

"That's natural. It will pass with time, and you'll remember them and smile eventually."

"Have you ever lost anyone close to you?"

He turned away. "Yes. Though not in the same way." He pulled his legs in and sat forward as if to leave.

"Don't go," she said rashly, laying her hand on his arm.

He looked from her fingers to her eyes, and she felt his gaze all the way down to her toes.

"I won't pry. I didn't mean to make you uncomfortable."

"God, you are the most capricious creature. One minute you bite off my head, the next you're actually seeking my company. I don't ever know what to expect from you."

"I'm not fickle-minded, if that's what you're suggesting. I just never hold a grudge. Actually, I never used to get angry."

"So Paddie told me. He said you were the mildest of young ladies, the quintessence of gentility."

"Oh my, I haven't exactly been that, have I?"

"Not hardly." He gave her a sidelong look and chuckled.

She bristled. "It's not altogether my fault. You pro-

91

voke me. And I think you do it intentionally."

"Oh, yeah? Why in hell would I want to do that?"

"Because you like me and you don't want to. And stop cussing."

"Why should I? How I talk is my business."

"Because it's uncouth and vulgar."

"So am I."

"You try very hard to be, and sometimes you succeed. But I don't think you were always that way."

"How would you know?"

"Intuition." He said another vulgar word. "All right, nothing weird or witchy, but I see refinement in your movements, in the way you lift a spoon or smooth the front of your shirt collar. Even your flannel shirts. At some time you've dressed in white silk shirts and tailored suits, and have been very comfortable in them."

"Is that wishful thinking? Are you hoping I have money? Getting ideas of attaching yourself to the coattails of my success?"

Her chin rose and her eyes flashed disdainfully. "As it happens, I have money sufficient for all my needs. Yours holds no interest for me."

"Yeah? Maybe I should go after you for your money. How much do you have?"

"Don't be gauche."

"Sometimes life is gauche, Emily."

The canal at Utica opened up into a basin that held boats of all kinds. Several packets were docked near the hotels, long boats that carried passengers who were canawlling through the state. Bullheads were being loaded and unloaded, and dozens of shanties lined the south harbor of the basin, where a floating community had been established by gypsielike families.

A wiry old man approached them toting a bundle

of straw. Emily recognized him by his whisks of straw as one of those hired to patrol the canal and search for leaks or weak spots in the walls. A towpath walker inspected a ten-mile section of the canal daily. If he discovered even a tiny whirl in the water that might erode the fiber of the canal, his duty was to wade in and plug the leak with straw and notify the "hurry-up" boats to come fix it. This towpath walker carried a string of muskrat hides over his shoulder.

"Ho, Evers," Seneca hailed. "Got some skins, eh?"

"Yeah, I did that. They'll fetch a decent reward. How doin', boy? I hear tell we have storm warnings today. You best take care."

"Really?" Seneca straightened, his black eyes scanning the docks. "Thanks, Evers. I'll be sure to do that."

"It's a beautiful day," Emily said, handing him the ropes he asked for. "Will it really storm?"

"He isn't referring to the weather, Emily," he said quietly, his dark gaze meeting her quizzical blue eyes. "Make certain they are tucked away downstairs, angel, and send Elijah to me. We may have to alter our plans."

"You mean . . ."

"Stormy weather."

Seneca sent the hoggees after grain and hay and left Elijah to guard the boat. He took Emily with him to town. He handed her some bills and sent her after food supplies. He planned to scout the bars.

"A saloon?" she moaned when he told her his plans. "Seneca, you have to give up this awful thirst for liquor. It does you no good."

"Don't lecture me. The best places for learning what we need to know are the saloons."

"Oh, Seneca. Don't fool yourself."

"Just finish up your shopping and get back to the boat."

Emily wandered in and out of the little shops along

the main street that bordered the canal. She purchased her foodstuffs at the grocer and had them delivered to the boat. She stopped at the pharmacy and bought some creams for her hands and face and another small jar for Mara to use with the baby. She found a few other toiletries that she thought Mara would appreciate. And she asked the druggist to replenish her supply of powders for Seneca's headaches.

Seneca was waiting for her when she returned with her packages. "I was about to come looking for you." He lifted her aboard the boat.

"Afraid I'd abscond with your money?"

He chuckled, deciding against telling her the real reason—that two strangers had been seen in town who resembled the men Emily had described.

"Afraid some handsome stranger would come along and abscond with my little angel."

"You mean there's more than one of you?"

"But I kidnapped you first, so you're mine."

"Here I thought Paddie McMurdie had arranged for you to take care of me." She threw him an insouciant grin.

"Paddie McMurdie has no part in this any longer." Not since that first kiss. And as for keeping her safe, well Paddie knew him. Paddie knew what was likely to happen. And getting likelier by the day. "The minute I saw you, your fate was sealed."

"That all sounds very ominous," she joked. "Am I in danger?"

"You could be," he said, his voice losing its lightness, growing instead quite solemn. "Yes, I think maybe you are."

She was caught in the glittering depths of his eyes, spellbound by the naked emotion she saw, the need, the desire. Her own body turned warm, her blood rolling heavily through her veins. Her waist, where his hands held her, burned, her breasts, brushing against his chest, swelled and ached. Her breath came in short gasps. She closed her eyes at the pleasurable yearnings of her body and murmured his name.

His hands tightened and he shook her. "For pity sake woman," he growled. "What are you doing to me?"

Her eyes blinked open, looking into the anger of his. "What now?"

"This is hardly the time or place to look . . . like that. Elijah," he yelled, "let's get out of here."

Her cheeks burned at his rebuff. She took her parcels to her cabin. He was right, of course he was. She sat down on the bed and covered her hot face with her cool hands. She had forgotten there was anyone else around. What was happening to her? Suddenly she was a complete stranger to herself, entertaining thoughts that had never bothered her before, releasing emotions and desires she had always kept in check and now had no idea how to control.

Were these overwhelming feelings natural or a backlash from being confined when she should have been learning gradually what being a woman was all about?

She put away her toiletries and put Mara's gifts aside for later. She took off her hat, her good dress, and the layers of petticoats and folded them into her trunk. She replaced them with her dark skirt and a fresh blouse the shade of lilacs in the springtime.

She found Seneca at the tiller. "I'm sorry, Seneca, for making a scene. I was frightfully . . . gauche."

He laughed. "You're forgiven, angel. But let me warn you never to look at me like that at any time when we are alone." His eyes traveled from her full lips to the front of her lace-trimmed blouse. "In fact, it might be very wise to continue to sleep in the other cabin. When Simon and his family leave us, I'll move in with Elijah. I can't be alone with you, Emily. See that I am not."

The afternoon moved by languidly as they floated down the canal. How much different this was, she thought, than some torturously bumpy trip overland by wagon.

Emily had put a piece of venison that one of the lockkeeps had sold to them in a deep iron kettle with a variety of vegetables and had set it on the wood-burning stove to cook. The aroma was tantalizing, and she realized that she had been hungrier in the last days than she'd been in weeks.

Seneca left his post and came to examine the pot. "Smells wonderful." He took off his shirt, picked up a broom, and began to sweep the deck. Emily didn't offer to help; instead she sat on the back railing with Elijah as he manned the tiller for his shift.

"Do you ever go faster?" she asked him.

"Can't," he said. He locked off the tiller and picked up his guitar. "Unless you want to pay a fine. Fast speeds cause turbulence that washes against the sides of the canal. It weakens the structures, especially where the canal is constructed of wood. Legal limit is four miles an hour. Faster will earn you a ten-dollar fine."

As they did often of late, Emily's eyes followed Seneca as he moved about the boat. He began rearranging cargo, as he had some to deliver and some to load at their next stop in Rome. She watched the play of muscles along his bare arms and back. He was tanned to a dark golden brown that contrasted like night against day to her creamy pale skin. Even the shinier skin of his long scars was tanned.

"How did he get those scars, Elijah?"

Elijah stopped playing and looked at her for a long moment. He strummed a chord and began to pluck out a tune.

"Do they bother you?"

"Only in that they bother him. They're from a burn," she guessed. "Except the one on his face. That

96

was a bad cut."

"Maybe you should ask him. It would do him good to talk about it."

"He thinks they're repulsive. He flinches whenever I touch them."

"That is a natural reaction from him, since he meets with it in others so often. He did not always have scars. He can remember when he did not, and he can see the difference they make in how some people react to him."

"You mean women? When he found you did he have them?"

"His shoulder and arm were still bandaged, but the stitches had been removed from the side of his face. He was in pain, physically and emotionally. Perhaps that is why he felt such compassion for me."

"I love him, Elijah." *There, she had said it.*

"I know you do. Give him time, girl."

She smiled. "Yes. There is no hurry, is there? And all I have now is time."

Elijah glanced sideways at her as he continued to play, seeing the love and longing etched clearly on her face. His gaze moved to Seneca, who picked up his shirt and mopped his face and neck. Now here was a match that could work. That other one wouldn't have been caught dead on a freighter with a runaway slave family and a man who insisted on going about shirtless. She wouldn't have cared for a fugitive's baby, washed clothes, cooked all the meals. That one would have gone into hysterics at the thought of cleaning a catfish. And she'd have crumbled under the sharp tongue and cynical attitude that was Seneca's way these days.

Not Emily. She was a tough lady, even though she looked like a fragile china doll. The problem would not be with her so much as with Seneca and his bitterness. Emily looked too much like Belinda for Seneca to separate them in his mind as yet. Seneca was going to require Emily to prove herself time and time again before he would commit himself to any relationship with her, and all for something she had had no part in. He hoped she was tough enough to endure it.

"Elijah, were there two strangers in town today?"

"Strangers? Why?"

"One of Seneca's friends mentioned stormy weather. If the slave hunters are around, will they attack us on the canal? Do they have the authority to stop us?"

"That's a difficult question to answer. They do not have authority to disrupt our lives. If they shot at us they could be arrested. At the same time, ironically, the law is on their side with regard to the slaves. If they did attack us and force us to stop, and if they did then produce the slaves, we would be the ones to suffer the consequences."

"That doesn't seem fair."

Elijah gave a sardonic chuckle.

"But surely something can be done to repeal these laws."

"My dear girl, have you not heard of the 'irrepressible conflict between opposing and enduring forces?' It is the term that lost Seward the presidential nomination."

"That sounds very final, as if we have no hope of changing things."

"None through peaceable means. There were others who didn't like the sound of it either. Still, all attempts at compromise have been in vain."

"So what will happen? Will this go on and on?"

"So innocent you are. We will eventually solve this problem as we solve most others."

"You mean a battle? In Congress?"

"We can only pray it will stop at Congress. Already rumor is spreading that some of the Southern states wish to break away from the Union and form a coalition of their own."

"Yes, I heard that, but it's just talk. No state would want that."

"Does not the Constitution guarantee liberty and equality to all? Either it is adopted and enforced by all or it is thrown out by all, which then puts the freedom of everyone at risk. The North won't relinquish the Constitution."

"And the South won't relinquish the right to hold slaves."

"Irrepressible conflict. It is not a situation where a compromise can be reached. One side must, of necessity, forfeit."

"You're saying we'll go to war with our own countrymen?"

"More than that. Do you not live in the North and your kinsmen in the South?"

"Family against family," she said bleakly and shivered. "Must it be so?"

"I am a Negro. You are a woman. We are powerless. We can only watch and see what a small group of white men will decide for our future."

She began to get a sense of the awful futility, the frustration and anger that such oppression and injustice could stir in the breast. What man had the right to hold such power over another?

"How do you bear it? You must have so much anger and resentment in your heart."

"Yes, at times, but never when I can look upon a face as lovely as yours."

She blushed. "Now you're teasing me."

He laughed aloud. Part of her charm was her lack of awareness about her appearance. He felt sympathy for poor Seneca, who had never been blind to a woman's attributes and who had to look upon Emily's womanly beauty and her innocent eyes and burn. No wonder he was so irrascible.

They reached Rome by evening and tied up at the

docks. Seneca supervised the unloading of the cargo that was destined for that town and helped load a pallet of special hardwoods for a furniture maker in Syracuse.

"Don't bother with the stove, Emily. We'll be eating at a restaurant tonight. So get prettied up."

"A restaurant? I can't remember the last time I had a meal I didn't cook. How long do I have?"

"I have to clean up too. I'll give you half an hour."

"What will happen with Simon and Mara?"

"Elijah will see to them. He's better at this than anyone I know. Did you say good-bye? They won't be here when we return."

Emily nodded. "This afternoon. They will be all right, won't they? I'd hate to think that after all they've been through . . ."

"Elijah will deliver them directly into the hands of the next guide. Nothing will happen to them."

"What if those men are around? The comissioners?"

"You worry too much. Concern yourself with getting into your best dress. Uh-uh, no more talk. Go on, now."

Emily felt like a princess on the arm of her tall and strikingly handsome escort. She had not been mistaken. He was very much at home in his white shirt and dark suit, and his manners were impeccable. He might be her black-eyed giant, her pirate, but he was also quite the most arrestingly handsome man she'd ever seen.

He took her to an inn owned and operated by a young couple who had immigrated to the United States from England. From the number of patrons seated in the dining room, the couple appeared to be doing very well in Rome, New York.

The couple, the Dugans, came to greet Seneca

personally and escorted them to a table beside the large stone fireplace. A low fire burned, crackling and snapping, taking the chill out of the evening air.

The Dugans were a warm and cordial couple, but Emily couldn't help but feel she had in some way shocked them. Mrs. Dugan kept glancing at her with a curious expression on her face. Perhaps she had offended them by traveling unescorted with Seneca and Elijah. But that was certainly not something she had had much control over. She would feel bad about it, though, if she were to lose the respect of Seneca's friends. She made a mental note to ask Seneca about it.

"This is lovely," Emily offered, glancing around the dining room at the exposed beams, the brass candle-holders, rich-hued paintings.

"Thank you. Seneca helped us put it together. He knew just where to find all these accessories. We're very proud of it."

Emily met Seneca's gaze, her brows lifting curiously. "Truly? I'm impressed at your artistic talent. How long have you been in business?" she asked Mr. Dugan.

"Four years now. Do you live in Rome?" Mr. Dugan's question answered one of hers. They didn't know she was canawlling with Seneca.

"Oh, no. I'm from Albany."

Mrs. Dugan's curiosity was piqued. "You met Seneca in Albany then?"

"Well, you could say that."

"Emily's going with me because we needed a woman's touch with some of our cargo."

"Ah," Mrs. Dugan replied knowingly. "Are you going on to Rochester then? You'll enjoy Seneca's family. Especially his sister."

"You have a sister?" she asked, turning surprised eyes to Seneca.

"The bane of my existence."

"What's her name?"

"Marianne. She just turned eighteen."

"Any brothers?" So much she didn't know about him.

"Nope. Just Marianne and me. And Mother and Dad."

"Will I really be going to your home?" she asked.

"To my parents' home. Of course. Where else would you go?"

"I don't want to impose. I'm a stranger."

"You'll be a stranger for a minute, and then Marianne will talk your ear off. Do *not* worry about my family."

"Speaking of families," Mark Dugan said, "Alicia is going to have a baby. Our first," he explained to Emily.

"That's wonderful news," Seneca boomed, standing to shake Mark's hand. "Congratulations." He placed a kiss on Alicia's cheek.

"Yes," Emily agreed. "That's wonderful. I'm very happy for you."

"We've waited a long time," Alicia said.

"Then it is a double blessing."

Seneca ordered their meal, and when his friends had gone he picked up Emily's hand and traced the lengths of her fingers. He was in a strange mood that she couldn't fully understand.

"You're very beautiful tonight."

She withdrew her hand, blushing. "Seneca, don't. I can't handle you when you're being nice."

"Am I really so terrible?"

"No, you're not terrible at all, except when you're being absolutely horrid."

"I probably deserved that." He chuckled and ran his fingers through his hair. His flawless style was undone, but he looked more like the man she knew—and loved. Less contained, more reckless, with that mysterious air of danger. Her heart gave a kick in her breast, sending liquid heat rushing through her veins.

"What are you thinking, Emily?"

"Oh, nothing."

"Coward."

She laughed self-consciously. "Perhaps. But at the moment strategic retreat seems the best move."

He smiled, but his eyes lit with a dark fire of desire. She knew she was right to keep her thoughts to herself. If he knew just how he affected her he'd take advantage of the knowledge to seduce her. She could see it in his eyes. And she wasn't at all sure she could resist him.

But where would that put her? Living as his mistress? Always wondering if he still resented her? Or maybe watching him grow to hate her because he'd feel responsible for taking her innocence.

"You did warn me to be wary," she said, glancing up at him.

"And so you should."

Their meal was beautifully prepared, and they ate with relish after their very plain fare on the boat. They talked easily together, although the tension of awareness still stretched and hummed between them.

She spoke of her life before her father's death, of her brief time with Joe and Peter. She listened as he told of his family, of his work on the canal. She learned that he also ran a freight line up and down the Hudson River from New York to Albany, and several oceangoing freighters up and down the coast from New York to New Orleans.

"Do you miss going to sea when you're back here? *Prescott's Wake* must seem like a child's toy on a little stream compared to an oceangoing vessel."

"Oh, but I love it. It's restful after the hectic pace of normal business. Actually, I look forward to these trips. I come as often as I can manage it."

"It's nice that you get to see your family regularly.

I bet they love having you come to visit."

"You missed all that, didn't you? You never had a normal family life, with brothers and sisters, or a mother, for that matter. Why did your father never remarry?"

"I don't know. I would have liked that. He never did, that's all." She shrugged and glanced away. Her eye caught movement at the window across the room. She focused on the face outside—narrow eyes, a long nose, bushy mustache, a bald head.

"Seneca, that's him," she cried, pointing at the window. "That's the man."

Seneca jerked around in time to see a flash of movement. "Stay here," he ordered, jumping up and making his way out the door.

He saw a man dodge a couple other men, shoving them out of the way. By the time Seneca reached the side street where the man had turned the corner he could see no trace of anyone. The man had simply disappeared.

When he returned to the restaurant, Emily was waiting for him at the door. "Did you catch him? Did you even see him?"

He looked from her to the door, and frowned thoughtfully. "It could be someone looking for me," he said. "Some very powerful men are more than a little irritated with me lately." He smoothed her hair with the back of his knuckles. "Try not to worry. I won't let them hurt you."

He paid for their meal, bid the Dugans goodnight, and escorted Emily down the sidewalk toward the canal. She snuggled into his side as they walked, seeking the comfort and reassurance of his arm around her shoulders. She told herself over and over that she had nothing to fear. Seneca was beside her.

Seneca looked down at her golden head, at the frown that marred her smooth forehead. His eyes darted ahead, to the right and left. He glanced behind them. He'd promised to protect her, but what if by coming with him, she had leaped from her own troubles right into his. Ryker's men were as mean as they got. They wouldn't care who got between them and their target. The thought of Emily taking a bullet meant for him left him cold clear through.

Chapter 7

Emily slept alone in Seneca's bunk that night while Seneca shared Elijah's cabin. So it was to dark and lonely surroundings she awoke when her nightmare returned to torment her.

She didn't know she had screamed until Seneca burst into her room. All she knew was that she was scared and confused and alone. When his arms came around her she released the torrent of tears that had been dammed up inside her for weeks.

He held her as she sobbed, feeling her body tremble in his arms. He pressed her face to his chest, smoothing her tumbled hair back from her drenched cheeks.

"Shh. I'm here. It's all right, angel. Nothing can hurt you with me beside you."

"Oh Seneca," she wept, "it was so awful."

"Can you talk about it? It might help to stop the dreams."

"I don't know. I thought they had stopped. Why won't they just leave me alone."

At first he thought she meant her dreams, and then he realized she meant the men who were supposedly trying to kill her. He lay down and pulled her close, covering them both with the blankets. He stroked her hair in calming rhythmic motions.

"Now start from the beginning. Paddie told me

only bits and pieces, and he didn't even believe what he said. Not until Maggie was shot. Forgive me, but I too thought you were being paranoid. Now I think I need to know the whole story."

"You believe me now?"

"I don't know yet, but you aren't the sort of woman to get hysterical over things that go bump in the night. Start at the beginning."

And so she did. "I came to live with Joe and Peter two months ago. I had to sell our home to pay Papa's bills and to bury him. Uncle Joe was the only family member who came to the funeral. He came all the way from Albany, and my aunts couldn't cross one county. He took me home with him. I don't know what I would have done if he hadn't."

"Which naturally makes you feel guilty because they died," he said.

She went on. "Peter was a page, a messenger in the State Senate. He had only two weeks to go before summer recess. I usually took him to work in the mornings and collected him in the afternoon in time for his lessons with his tutor. He didn't go to public school. His teachers said he excelled beyond children much older than him. They all thought he should be tutored since the older children would resent and possibly react badly to his precociousness. That suited Peter fine since he could then spend his days in Congress. I wish you could have known him."

"He sounds like a remarkable little boy. One we should have protected at all cost."

"I went to collect him as usual that afternoon. He was a very punctual child, always coming out the door as I drove up to the steps. I never had to wait. He wasn't there that day, and I became concerned and went inside to look for him.

"He was coming down the corridor, but the minute he saw me, he motioned me to follow him. I didn't know what he wanted, but I went with him. He stopped outside one of the lounges and nudged the door open. I tried to pull him away, I knew he shouldn't be eavesdropping."

"Did you hear what the men inside were discussing?"

"Some of it. It didn't make much sense to me. Anyway, they must have heard us or perhaps they saw Peter. The next thing I knew Peter was pulling me along as we ran out of the building. I looked back once and saw the men standing in the hallway. Two of them came after us. They were very angry.

"I asked Peter what it was all about as we drove home. He said he needed to think about it some more and check on what had been discussed that day in session, but he thought it was a plot to overthrow one of the candidates or discredit the president. I can't remember, Seneca. I was upset that he'd do such a thing as spy on a private conversation."

"I believe that somewhere in the back of your mind you know what was said. You know why Peter stayed to listen. You know why those men were so angry. That knowledge is what is causing these nightmares. But go on."

"The next day Joe drove Peter to work. He was going to a business meeting with his lawyer, Mr. Stevens. They passed the back corner and turned down the side street toward the front of the building. As far as the police can tell, two men were waiting there. They shot them both, and the mare as well. Two different guns were used. They took Uncle Joe's money, but a thief would hardly leave his watch or the gold stickpin he'd worn that day."

"Emily, you have to remember what they said, and what Peter said. It could be extremely important. Can you try to do that? Anything you remember, you come tell me right away."

"I'll try."

"But not tonight. Close your eyes now. You're exhausted."

"Will you stay with me?"

"Right here. Go to sleep, angel."

Seneca lay for a long while thinking about her story. The papers had printed only that her uncle had been killed and robbed and that her cousin had unfortunately gotten in the way. Emily's version was quite different, and in a strange way it made much more sense. But what an unconscionable waste that a young boy with Peter's potential should be cut down before his life had begun.

"The rules is the same as they always was," Charlie Perkins declared before the assembled crowd early the next morning. "You depart at ten-minute intervals, your times will be clocked at two intermediate points, and finally at the finish line. The man to make the trip to each check point closest to the times listed on your race forms will win that leg. Overall best time wins the race and the five hundred dollars.

"Along the way you are required to scavenge six items. At the first check point you must present a red rose and a live fish taken from the canal. The biggest fish is worth a thirty-second adjustment either way to your final score. At point two you must present a charcoal rubbing of the face of a tombstone and a yellow iris. Paper and charcoal are being distributed now. At the finish line you are to turn over a lady's corset and a cat."

"This is exciting," Emily exclaimed, bouncing on her toes. "Can we find all those things?"

"If we want to win," Seneca answered indulgently. "You don't happen to have a corset in that trunk, do you?"

"Golly, I don't know what Maggie packed. I haven't gone through it all. But I never wear them."

"So I noticed."

"Oh."

"Seneca Prescott," Charlie bellowed, "place three. Depart in twenty minutes. I warn you not to leave the docks, you guys. Anyone trying to buy any of your six items before departure will be disqualified. Jimbo Bellamy, place four."

"Let's get aboard. Elijah will be waiting. We're both going to be busy plotting our strategy, so you'll have to be our fisherman."

"I've never fished. Oh, Seneca, don't depend on me. I'd feel horrid if I let you down."

He steered her quickly through the crowd, pulling her, pushing her, hurrying her so that she was practically running. "Then don't. There's no trick to catching a fish. Ho, Elijah," he yelled, nearing the boat. "We're third out this year."

"Right, man. Sure beats seventh like last year."

"You do this every year?"

"Twice a year. If we're here. This year we arranged to be here. This race is Elijah's favorite part of the trip."

"Yours too?" she guessed.

"We've won two years running. Elijah's saving up the money to start a business when he gets his family back."

"Do you think he will?"

Seneca turned his head slowly and cocked a brow. "What anyone thinks is unimportant to Elijah. He won't stop looking until he finds them. Or their graves."

"I wish we could help."

"Do you ever *not* wish you could help? You helped your father, your uncle, Paddie, Mara. Now you want to add Elijah."

110

She grinned self-consciously. "I like to keep busy."

"You can get busy, then, catchin' us a fish."

He stopped, looked around, then took a jogging detour up the bank between the towpath and the town. He turned over a big stone, giving a whoop of delight. He returned with four very large and wriggly worms.

"A present for you, Miss Emily."

"Ugh. I'll allow you to hold them for me. They look quite comfortable in your hand."

"Coward," he said, jumping into the boat.

"Too true. Hello, Elijah," she said, taking his hand as he helped her board the boat. "This is going to be so much fun."

"If I may make a suggestion," Seneca said, scrounging around for a tin can to put the worms in, "we're going to be doing some running about in and out of the boat, so it might be more convenient for you to get into a pair of trousers again."

"Trousers? Me? I haven't got any."

"I think you'll find a pair on the bed. My sister left them on board when she went with us last time. They should fit."

"Does she like the canal?"

"She's a hoyden, a tomboy barely grown into womanhood."

"I suppose she could catch your fish for you."

"You're not going to let Marianne beat you? I thought you had more spirit than that."

"Oh, fiddlesticks, I'm not a child you can dare into doing what you want," she said, throwing him a scornful scowl.

"Then you won't catch my fish?"

"I didn't say that. All right, I'll put on your trousers and I'll *try* to catch your fish. But please don't yell at me if I botch it."

"Emily," he reproved dramatically. "Would I do that?"

"Huh."

"Prescott, five minutes. Pull your boat up."

"Here we go. Man the tiller, I'll shove off."

Twenty minutes later they had been weighed and clocked and were on their way. When Emily returned to deck, wearing Marianne's trousers and not too sure she should be seen in public considering how alluringly they clung to the feminine curves of her thighs and hips and derriere, Elijah and Seneca had their heads together over a large chart. Without attracting their attention she found a fishing pole, baited the hook with one of the worms Seneca had unearthed, and tossed the line over the side. She pulled up her knees, hoping to hide what the trousers revealed. She sat by herself for no more than ten minutes before her line jerked. She pulled up on it sharply as she'd seen Peter do when she went with him to the river. And then she screamed for Seneca. Whatever she had hooked fought like the very devil.

"Take this," she blurted, thrusting the end of the jumping pole into his midsection.

"Jeez, what did you hook? Elijah, come see this. I think she got Methuselah."

"What's Methuselah?"

"A granddaddy of a catfish. So far all we've had is a rumor that he's here. Get the net. I can't bring this monster in on this line."

"Hold up, Cob," Elijah hollered. "We got us Ol' Granddad here." When the boat slowed and came to a standstill in the water, Elijah slipped over the side with the net. Up to his chest in water, he waded back toward the splashing fish.

"Hurry. He's going to break this damn line."

"Just hold him steady. If I scare him he'll take off for sure."

"Benjie," Seneca called to the other hoggee, "Get in there with Elijah and help. Run that bastard into

112

his net."

Obeying, Benjie took a splashing jump into the canal. Elijah made a quick dive with the net outstretched in his hand. At the same time the pole in Seneca's hands whipped backwards, singing in the air.

"Goddamn it, we lost the son-of-a-bitch."

"No! Elijah's got him," Emily cried.

"Ouch, you wily bastard," Elijah swore uncharacteristically as the fish thrashed in the net with his razor sharp fins extended. "I can't hold him, man."

Seneca went over the side in a clean dive from the deck of the boat, surfacing beside Elijah. Benjie paddled back to his raft, helpless since he was still short enough to have to tread water. But he stood at the edge and cheered the two men on as they wrestled the monster from the six-foot deep.

Emily looked at the discarded pole, at the jar of worms, at the two men cussing and thrashing in the water. What had she done? She didn't know whether to laugh or hide. They were losing minute after minute. Seneca would be furious with her. The fish, still tangled in the net, sailed over the side of the boat and landed at her feet. She gasped and jumped up onto the nearest crate. The thing was nearly three feet long with mean eyes and long whiskers extending from his jowls. She didn't trust it for a minute. It could take her foot in one bite. Her bare foot.

Elijah and Seneca hoisted themselves into the boat, careful to keep a respectful distance from the flopping fish. They were both bright-eyed and laughing from the exhilaration of battle.

"Go, Cob. We have time to make up. Let 'em out," Seneca called.

"Yes, sir," Cob replied. He jumped onto the back of one of the horses and urged the pair on. As the boat gained speed, skimming the surface, he let the horses take them faster and faster.

"I'll gladly pay the fine today." Emily had climbed over the cargo to stand on deck on the other side with the men. Seneca swung her up in the air then gave her a resounding kiss. "That might have been beginner's luck," he said, "but I'll take it. You've earned your fare today."

"You're not angry, then?"

"Hell, no. Every man along the canal wants this fish. We got him."

"Don't forget he has to be alive," Elijah reminded him.

"Don't worry. Catfish can breathe for hours outside the water. But you're right. We need to get him back in. As soon as he's been weighed, I'm going to turn him loose."

"Get that extra piece of rope," Elijah said to Emily. "We'll make a stringer line and tow the rascal behind us."

The men braved the beast and cut him free from the netting, careful to wear heavy leather gloves to protect their hands from the fins. Seneca threaded the rope through his mouth and out the gill while Elijah held him still. Together they held him up to show Cob and Benjie, then slowly lowered him into the water, securing the end of the line to a mooring cleat.

"Now for the rose," Seneca said, rubbing his hands together.

"Why a rose?"

"Who knows. The 'long level' between Rome and Syracuse has no locks, nothing to prevent boaters from speeding right along. No one pays any mind to what he passes along the way, including me. Now, to make up for ignoring our surroundings, we have to try and remember where the flowers are and who has cats, for heaven sakes."

"What if you can't find one of the items?"

"We forfeit points."

"Surely by now you know where everything is."

"Except that for each race the contest changes. Last trip we were given treasure maps. We had to actually dig for clues that led us to a fake treasure."

"Who organizes it?"

"Merchants in Rome and Syracuse. It's part of their spring and fall celebrations. We'll attend a town festival in Syracuse tonight."

"Then we have to find a cemetary, right? What better place to find flowers and also do the chalk rubbing. Now think. Have you ever seen one? Or a church steeple? Where there's a church, there is generally a cemetery."

"A church. Yes. Elijah, stop when we get to that old stone building."

"The one that's falling down. It's nothing but rubble. You don't even know if it was a church."

"Sure it was. Can you think of another place along this stretch where we're likely to find a gravestone."

"There's that little village near Oneida. But that's too late. Okay. You might be right."

"If that doesn't pan out, we'll try that valley to the north. There has to be a farmhouse up there. That will be where the first two boats will stop. I'd bet on it. And if so, they will pick all the flowers in sight just to spite us."

"Should we increase our speed then? By the markers, I'd say we are almost caught up to where we should be."

"Keep this pace a bit farther. We'll lose time at the church."

Elijah shook his head, not at all convinced that Seneca was doing the right thing. But whether or not he was, Seneca was happy. His face hadn't sported such a genuine smile since . . . well, since a very long time. And Emily was more relaxed as

115

well, not as tense and on edge, no longer expecting Seneca to yell at her or kiss her. Perhaps they were beginning to understand each other and themselves at last.

The crumbling stone building might indeed have been a church, but neither Seneca nor Emily could find anything to prove it was.

"Elijah will be happy to know he was right again," Seneca allowed, climbing over rubble and stone.

"Don't be hasty," Emily said. "If it was a church the cemetery would have been nearby. Let's look around before we give up."

"We're running a race here, Emily. We don't have time to waste on a walk through the woods."

His condescending tone annoyed her again, but she bit her tongue and brushed past him. She knew she was right. The subtle scent of flowers wafted on the breeze, almost unnoticeable.

She ran down a little hill and found her flowers. "Seneca. Come quickly."

She had a small assortment picked into a bouquet by the time Seneca reached her, gold and pale irises and wild roses included. She looked up and laughed.

"Shall we pick them all?" she asked with devilment in her voice.

He chuckled. "No need. No one else will find this place. No one else has you along."

Beneath one of the overgrown rose bushes they found a small headstone. Emily laid the paper against the face of it and rubbed the charcoal gently over the paper until the name of a woman, Edwina Connelly, came into view. "Born 1808, Died 1825," the stone said.

"Seneca, look. She was only seventeen years old. Do you suppose she died a violent death, as Peter did?"

He put an arm around her shoulders and gave

her a hug. "We'll never know. Come on, don't make yourself unhappy. Elijah will be pleased with us."

Hand in hand, they sprinted up the rise and down the long meadow to the canal. As they approached, they could see Elijah pacing up and down the length of the boat.

Laughing and waving the rolled-up paper in one hand and the flowers in the other, she was lifted and swung over the railing into the boat.

"Ah, you were successful, then. Good, good," Elijah said, beaming. He signaled Cob from the tiller, and the boy led the team out, pulling the boat faster and faster.

Emily found a glass canning jar, filled it with water, arranged the flowers in it, and placed it atop the icebox. She stood back to admire her work.

Changing out of his wet shoes and socks, Seneca, admired Emily, his gaze going from her windblown hair, her sun-kissed face, her feminine lacy blouse and the womanly shape it concealed. Downward his gaze moved to the slender waist and the gentle flare of hips.

He expelled his breath slowly and jerked on dry socks and his high boots. Whatever had possessed him to give her those pants? It was a crazy idea, but at the time all he'd thought of was how Marianne had loved to get into them so she could be free to run the race with him, to jump in and out of the boat, to race from one destination to another in search of some prize, all without hindrance of skirts. He had wanted Emily to enjoy that freedom too. He hadn't counted on the disastrous effect she would have on him in the very same clothes.

With his pocket watch in hand and his canal charts before him, Seneca took them into the first time station only two seconds behind the alloted time. He surrendered the red rose to the official, or rather to his robust wife, and he and Elijah hauled in the fish.

"Ye gods, you got Granddaddy Methuselah," the official said. "I thought he weren't real. You always hear talk, but then, whoever believes fish stories."

"We'd like him to be turned loose after he's weighed," Seneca said.

"Hell's bells, man, don't you want the others to see 'im? Why don't I tie him here at the landing. As soon as the last boat checks in, I'll cut him loose. He won't come to no harm at my hands."

"Well, I guess, if . . ."

"I'd like to think he's still out there for me to catch. Put up much of a fight?"

Emily laughed. "It took both of them to wrestle him aboard. It was quite a sight."

"Emily," Seneca protested. "A man likes to maintain the illusion of power and prowess. Especially over a fish."

The boat ahead of them was still at the landing, and the man who captained her strolled over. "Damn, boy. I never seen a man with so much luck as you. I got a beauty myself, a four pounder, but he don't begin to match this one."

"If I'm to tell the whole truth, I have to give Emily credit. She hooked him. Elijah and I just fought him into the boat."

Cap'n John chuckled and spat a stream of tobacco juice into the bushes. "There's a fish with an eye for a lovely gal. I'd a jumped on her line too." He laughed heartily at his own joke.

"We're going to free him when all the other racers have seen him," Emily said, grinning. She was beginning to relax around the raw humor and the unrestrained manner of the canal people.

"Well, ain't that mighty decent. Now we've proved he exists, everyone will want a chance to catch him."

"Two minutes, Cap'n John," the official, Mr. Potts, reminded him.

Emily sat on a weathered plank bench Mr. Potts had built for fishing. Mrs. Potts sat beside her, bringing her a tall glass of sweet lemonade.

"It ain't often we see a woman with Mr. Prescott. " 'Cept that young rascal of a sister. I can't help being curious. Are you kin?"

Emily hesitated, uncertain as to whether she should stick to Seneca's story or tell the truth. Lying was so difficult for her. Lies got stuck in her throat, and showed in her eyes.

"Actually, I am just a friend. I haven't known Seneca for long at all. I was living with friends of his after my uncle and my young cousin were murdered. The men who killed them came after me. My friends thought I should get away, so they arranged for Seneca to bring me on this trip."

Mrs. Potts' mouth hung open. "Someone tried to kill you, a pretty girl like you?"

"Yes, ma'am. I know it isn't proper for me to be traveling alone with a man, or two men, but I . . ."

Mrs. Potts clucked her tongue. "Horsefeathers. It ain't proper to get killed either, if you can help it. And I don't know no one I'd trust more to keep me safe than Seneca Prescott."

Emily smiled and nodded. "That's what my friends said. And so here I am. And do you know something else? I'm having the time of my life. I love the canal."

"Ah, yeah. You got the fever already. It happens that way."

"What are you two gossiping about?" Seneca asked, coming to stand beside the bench. He propped one foot up and leaned on his knee.

"We ain't gossiping, Mr. Prescott. Just havin' a woman-to-woman chat. I don't get so many ladies by here that I can afford to let one like Emily get away."

Emily didn't feel like a lady in her pants, but

then Mrs. Potts was wearing trousers also. "Is the fish all right?"

"Yes. Caleb used a smaller rope, so Methuselah will suffer less for his day in captivity. Such concern over a fish," he teased gently.

She tossed him a quelling look. "He's not just a fish, he's a legend."

Another boat came into the landing just as Cap'n John took his bullhead out again, and a big burly man jumped ashore, yelling his greeting to Potts and Elijah.

"Where's that dad-blasted boss of yours," he said to Elijah. Elijah grunted a response and nodded at Seneca.

"Dammit. He's coming over here," Seneca said. "Emily, I hope . . ."

"Well, well, well, who do we have here?" the man said, eyeing Emily openly. "She kin of yours, woman?" he asked Mrs. Potts. "Or is she your latest mistress?" he jeered at Seneca. "How about I take her with me on this next leg?"

Seneca's fist connected with the man's whiskered jaw before Emily knew what had happened. The man fell to the rough planks and howled in rage.

"You son-of-a-bitch. I'll break your friggin' neck."

Emily jumped to her feet, but Mrs. Potts pulled her back to the bench. "Stay out of it, girl. You can't stop it. These two been fightin' like this for years."

"Who is he?"

"Jimbo. He's not a bad sort. A lot like Seneca, if you wanna know the truth."

Emily's eyes moved from one man to the other as they swung at each other. "They'll kill each other," she said in alarm. She turned to find Elijah. Surely he would help. But Elijah was deep in conversation with Potts, totally ignoring the murderous brawl on the landing.

Seneca took a powerful blow to his jaw and sprawled backward on the rough turf beside the landing. Jimbo launched himself after Seneca, coming down hard on top of him. Together they rolled and wrestled until they tumbled over the edge into the canal.

"Lord in heaven," Emily said. "Can't anyone help?"

Mrs. Potts stood. "He'd hate you for trying. Brawling is a way of life along the canal. These men love it."

"They're crazy."

"Ah, yeah," she agreed. "Come along. You have to leave in a few minutes. I want to show you something."

She led Emily up the hill to her home, a modest but carefully cared for house set back from the canal. Potts ran a landing for the canawllers, a place to buy supplies, to get help if necessary. He was one of the officials whose responsibility it was to maintain the canal.

Mrs. Potts opened the door to a small shed beside the house. Light from outside fell on a whole passel of kittens, all fighting and frolicking together.

Emily's eyes lit up. "Oh, they're precious." She knelt down, and immediately the kittens climbed into her lap.

"Sorry about that," Mrs. Potts said, sitting down beside Emily. "I play with them, so they like people."

Emily picked up the one who held back, a furry little gray one with enormous yellow eyes.

"You don't have much of a chance, do you, mite?" she crooned, lifting the tiny creature to her face. She received a lick from a very scratchy tongue.

"I promised one to Seneca's sister. Could you take one to her? That one, maybe?"

121

Emily frowned, remembering the contest. "Mrs. Potts, you do know we're to find a cat on this scavenger hunt."

Mrs. Potts nodded. "I know. I also know that it's okay for anyone along the canal to help the racers, if they ask."

"Really? I can take the kitten then and I won't jeapordize the race?"

"Not at all. Once you left Rome all restrictions were lifted. I wouldn't be surprised at all if someone tried to rob you along the way."

"Have you an old corset, then?" she asked.

Mrs. Potts laughed. "I had one hangin' on the line just a minute ago. Let's see if one of those men snatched it yet." The corset was gone.

"You tuck that kitten out of sight. I don't want just anyone takin' them so they can drown 'em later."

Emily heard Elijah calling for her. She hid the kitten inside her blouse and turned to thank Mrs. Potts.

"This one won't be drowned. Marianne will love it, and if she doesn't, I will."

"I knew that, girl. Go along now. Seneca will need some tender loving care, no doubt. Damn fool men."

Mrs. Potts watched Seneca's boat leave. She waved to Emily, a satisfied gleam in her eye.

"What's she been telling you?" Seneca asked, coming to stand beside her. He dabbed at his bruised eye with a cool, wet cloth.

"What a damn fool you are," she answered, waving back.

"What the hell's wiggling around in your shirt?" he exclaimed, catching sight of the lump at her waist.

Emily turned and looked at him, taking stock of his black eye, his bruised and battered face, his

122

scraped and bleeding knuckles, his sopping wet clothes.

"What was that all about?" she demanded, hands on her hips.

"You heard him. I was defending your honor. What is that?"

"A kitten." She turned away and unbuttoned her blouse to retrieve her new pet. "It's for Marianne."

"A kitten? You cheated. We could lose the race now."

"I did not cheat. Mrs. Potts said that once . . ."

"Mrs. Potts is an official's wife."

". . . we left Rome, all . . ."

"I'll be disqualified."

". . . restrictions were off. Did you steal her corset?"

"That's different. That's legal."

"Oh, Seneca. Come on little Muffin. I'll get you some milk."

"Muffin? What kind of name if that for a cat? And button your blouse."

"A cat," Elijah said, laughing when he saw the tiny furry creature in her hands. "What a scavenger you are."

"Wait a minute. I'm the one who suggested we stop at that pile of rocks," Seneca objected.

Emily handed Seneca the kitten, buttoned her blouse again, then reached up to pat his bruised cheek. "Of course you are, dear." She took the kitten back and gave it a snuggle under her chin. "Why don't you get out of those wet clothes? They aren't helping your disposition."

"My disposition is fine," he grumbled, watching her cuddle the kitten, envying the little creature.

How could he want to protect her virtue one minute, and the next want to obliterate it?

Chapter 8

Emily made a pot of strong tea for the two men seated on the edge of the rear cabin roof. Seneca took the tray from her, set it aside, and lifted her up to join them.

Elijah was tracking their progress on the chart, noting the mile markers as they passed them and gauging the boat's speed. With no more need to stop along the way, they could relax and enjoy the long level.

"Where did you take Mara and Simon?" she asked Elijah when he had satisfied himself that they were on time.

He leaned back on his elbows, stretching out his long legs. "There is a man, a Quaker, outside of town who will house them until he is convinced that the way is clear. He will then put them together with another man who will go with them the rest of the way into Canada."

"Will you ever know what happens to them in Canada?"

"No. There are a few people who prefer to take their fugitives the entire way themselves. Our network of people prefer to operate differently. It can be heartbreaking to become emotionally attached to people you must turn loose and never see again."

"Yes. I can understand that. I keep thinking about Mara. She's so young."

"Have you remembered any more about your cousin?" Seneca asked.

"I did overhear two names, Erie and Chautauqua. I mentioned that to Paddie. Did he tell you?"

"No. Erie and Chautauqua." His brows drew together thoughtfully. "We won't be that far from Erie. Maybe we should go there."

"What do you think it means?"

"I couldn't guess. Like Peter, I'd have to learn what was being discussed that day to see if it might shed some light on those names. Can you describe the men you saw?"

"They looked like all the politicians. Both wore dark suits and had dark hair, bearded. One was portly, though, while the other was thin."

"What about their voices? You said they called out to you."

She shook her head. "I can't recall. It's all so fuzzy."

"Don't worry about it," he said, seeing her distress. "It will come to you in time."

"What if I don't remember and someone else dies because of me."

"You say that as if you blame yourself for Peter's and your uncle's deaths."

She smiled ruefully. "I know. With my mind I can admit I couldn't have prevented any of what happened. But in my heart I still wonder."

"You must think of it in a different way, then," Elijah said. "If you had been with Peter, you and your small cousin would certainly be dead. But then, so would your uncle, for he would know nothing of the men you saw and would not have known, as you did, to be suspicious. You may not have done it consciously, but you protected yourself after your family was killed. Did you not?"

She thought about that. She had stayed in her room, reluctant to go out, to see anyone. She had been afraid, more so because no one believed her. She had protected herself. But Joe wouldn't have done that. And those men would have assumed that Peter told Joe what he had overheard.

"You think they would have killed him anyway."

"Most assuredly."

"I was terrified to leave the house for weeks."

"With good cause," Seneca said. "I think I'll risk a telegram to Paddie and have him dig up some information for us. We'll get to the bottom of this eventually."

He looked out over the countryside, a patchwork of tilled ground, some already showing vivid green growth. He thought about what she'd told him. Erie. Chautauqua. Both were names he was familiar with, both could have any of a dozen meanings. What had she stumbled into that had taken her only family from her and threatened her own life? He also knew politicians. Most were careful enough not to be overheard, but then they were generally so convinced of their own importance, they wouldn't care if someone did hear their opinions. Especially a young woman who had no political clout. Perhaps it wasn't a politician at all.

Whatever it was she overheard, whatever she knew but didn't realize she knew, was something she could use against these men. Something they would suffer for if it became known. But what? And who where they?

"More tea?" Emily asked.

"Thanks." He ran a finger down her satin cheek as she refilled his mug, surprised at the violence he felt capable of doing to any man who threatened her safety or threatened to take her from him.

Hell, look what he'd done to Jimbo just for spouting off in his usual brash way. Jimbo wouldn't hurt anyone. He was all hot air. But just the thought of Jimbo with Emily sent a red rage shooting through him. He was not sure he liked the way he was reacting to her.

They arrived at their next official point five seconds early, so they simply slowed the boat so that they were clocked in at exactly the right time.

"Congratulations, Seneca. You're still in first place," Tom Flynn, the official, said. "Hardly see how you can lose this one, what with that fish you brought in. Couldn't believe it when the runner arrived with the results from the last leg."

"We still have three hours to go. Anything could happen."

"Yeah, yeah, could at that." he agreed. "You got fifteen minutes. Why don't you go up to the tavern and wet your whistle? Rosie may have a pot of tea ready for your cousin," he said, nodding to Emily.

"Who . . ." Emily began.

"Thanks, Flynn," Seneca said, taking Emily's arm and pulling her away. "Keep quiet, angel, and walk. Elijah."

"Gotcha, bossman, sir." Elijah turned away and walked off.

The tavern, like the other establishments on either side of it, was built right beside the towpath. Seneca opened the tavern door and guided Emily inside. He took her to a little table in the corner and left her there to go after something to drink.

She looked around at the collection of men, most of whom where eyeing her. She spotted Cap'n John at the bar. He slapped the man beside him on the shoulder, and they both stood up and left. Cap'n

John turned at the door and gave her a broad wink.

"Seneca, I'd rather go back to the boat," she said when he returned, uncomfortable suddenly.

"I know. This is hardly the place for a beautiful woman."

"It isn't that. That man outside called me your cousin. You only said that to the slavers."

"Which means they've been here."

"Or still are. I left the kitten in the cabin. What if they go . . ."

"They won't. Elijah will . . ."

A sudden excited murmur ran through the crowd, then they were all scraping back chairs and getting up. With their beers in hand, they rushed for the door.

"Hey, Seneca, you better get out here. Those slave commissioners are havin' a go at your man Elijah."

Seneca and Emily both raced to the scene of the fight. "Stay here," Seneca ordered her as he elbowed his way to the center of the circle.

"Now we got us a fight," one of the spectators called out. "I'll bet two bucks on Seneca and his man."

"I'll take that," another answered, and so it went.

Disgusted with the lot of them, Emily made her way around the crowd to the landing by the boats. Elijah may have had good reason for the fight, but as far as she could see, they all enjoyed it much too much.

Cap'n John's boat was already gone, Jimbo was tying up at the landing, being briefed by the official who was hard pressed to keep his mind on business with a brawl going on behind him.

"You had better make ready to leave, Benjie. Mr. Prescott and Elijah have their hands full at the moment," she told the young hoggee.

"Yes, ma'am."

"We'll be leaving whether they're back or not," she said. "They can swim all the way to Syracuse for all I care. It might do them both good."

Benjie looked from Emily to the crowd of rowdy men, uncertain exactly what to do.

"Just be ready," she said, seeing that he took her teasing seriously.

"Well, well, look who we got here," drawled a gravelly voice behind her. She spun around, knowing before she did that she'd see the bald-headed man.

"Grab her and let's get the hell out of here," his friend said.

She backed away. "Benjie, get Seneca. Quick," she cried. "Who are you? What do you want from me?"

"I think I better just do her here and now. She's led us clean across the state." He pulled a long, wicked-looking knife from a sheath at his waist and came at her.

She screamed. At the same time a huge dog launched itself into the air and clamped its powerful jaws around her attacker's arm. The knife flew from his hand into the water.

"Smokey, heel," commanded a gruff voice. The dog released the man immediately and disappeared.

Emily's attacker threw her a venomous glare, a promise of retribution, then, holding his bleeding arm, he turned and fled. Emily spun around to see who owned the dog. At the end of the landing, kneeling to give his dog a scratch, was Jimbo.

Seneca and Elijah shoved their way through the mob, followed by Benjie. "What is it?" Seneca demanded, seeing her standing all alone by the boat.

Tears came and she ran into his arms. "They were here," she cried. "They nearly killed me."

"Who? Where are they?"

"There were men here," Benjie said, looking around to see if he could see them. "Two of them. One had no hair."

"Are you all right?" Seneca demanded, holding her away from him.

She sniffed and wiped her eyes, fighting to get control of herself. She hated being weak. She let the anger come then, to blot out the terror.

"I'm fine, thanks to Jimbo and his dog."

"Jimbo?" Seneca's head snapped around, and he faced the same man he'd fought earlier that day.

Emily watched the two men. They both stood proud and tall. Seneca nodded in recognition and in a sort of thanks. Jimbo gave an acknowledging shrug. She waited for something else, but both men turned away.

She jumped aboard the boat and came back with one of her yellow irises. She walked down the landing and stopped behind the man and his dog.

"Jimbo?" She didn't know how else to address him. He turned abruptly, obviously surprised that she'd approach him after what he'd said about her. She held out the flower. Very slowly he stood up.

"You might already have one."

"No, I don't. Are you sure?"

"Your dog saved my life. That man would have killed me. His knife is now in the canal."

"Prescott, one minute," the official called out.

Jimbo took the flower and nodded. "I didn't see the knife. I thought to save you from their advances, to make amends for my own thoughtless comment."

"You did much more than that, and you have my gratitude. Thank you."

He jammed his hands into his pockets and nodded self-consciously. "You're welcome, I'm sure. If

I'd a known they was planning to hurt you, I'd a let Smokey tear his throat out. You . . . ah . . . you better go." He glanced down the landing and rubbed his jaw. "Seneca's waiting for you, and I don't relish gettin' him furious again today."

"Don't worry. He hasn't got another fight in him."

"You wouldn't consider saving me a dance this evening, would you?" he ventured courageously.

"Why, I just might. But only one," she added. "He gets angry with me, too."

"Emily," Seneca yelled impatiently.

She rolled her eyes heavenward. "Good-bye, and thanks again."

Seneca expended a considerable amount of energy in the next couple hours ignoring her. At first she was furious with him, then she realized that he was just plain jealous because she'd given Jimbo a flower. And for him to be jealous, he had to be a little bit in love with her.

She also noticed that for all his attempts to appear indifferent to her, his eyes rested on her with marked regularity.

Victory looked to be in the bag. Seneca checked all the tow lines and the lines that secured the hoggees' barge to the bullhead. All were secure and in good repair. All gear was stowed, the boat in shipshape, condition. He sat down to treat his leather boots with oil.

He looked up at Emily, who was playing with her kitten again. She glanced up and met his gaze with a tentative smile. He looked back down at the boot he was cleaning.

"You haven't had a word for her in over two hours, man," Elijah remarked. "Why the silent treatment?"

"I'm not deliberately trying to be rude to her, but I have to stay away from her. She was beginning to get under my skin. And fool that I am, I thought she was different."

"Different? Different from Belinda, you mean. But she is."

"Not so very."

"Sorry, man. I don't see what you're referring to."

"Jimbo," he hissed. "Jimbo's who I'm talking about. You saw her. I went through hell with one woman who couldn't make up her mind about who she wanted. I thought the best way to avoid that in the future was to steer clear of any serious relationship. And so I did. And will again."

"All this because she gave the man a flower? It was her way of saying thanks."

"I'd already done that."

"You weren't the one facing a ten-inch blade."

Seneca gave a disbelieving snort. "I saw no such knife. In fact, I saw no one but Jimbo. Look, it really doesn't matter. The point is I was reminded of a time in my life I never care to repeat. I was reminded of the fickle nature of women. I was reminded of the vow I made to myself never to repeat such a mistake. I don't want Emily to be hurt either, so it would be best if we both understood how things are."

"I see. Well, if that is how it must be, then it must be." He stood and looked down at his friend, then back at Emily. "You have been given a beautiful second chance. It is a shame you are determined to throw her away."

"You aren't listening, my friend. I don't want a second chance."

"As you wish. You won't take offense, I trust, if I enjoy her delightful company?"

"By all means, you must suit yourself," he answered shortly.

Elijah entertained Emily with songs and stories of

his life and work as a slave. He encouraged her to believe in Seneca even though he was acting like a cad at the moment. Elijah refused to believe that Seneca could turn his back on a life with a woman as sweet and as lovely as Emily. Seneca was a family-oriented man, much as he tried to be a loner. Elijah was wagering on the return of Seneca's good sense, knowing that if he bet wrong, both Seneca and Emily would be badly hurt.

The people of Syracuse lined the canal for a mile outside of town, waving and cheering as each of the canawllers came toward the finish line. The banner that stretched across the water was in sight when the trouble began.

A timber raft came into view. Seneca shouted a warning to Elijah, then got the long poles ready.

"What is it?" Emily asked.

"Hopefully, nothing. It's a timber raft. Loggers tie their logs into rafts and float six or eight rafts at a time down the canal."

"Can it be a problem?"

"Only if the lines break."

"But there's no chance of that, is there?"

"Probably not, but we're on an inside curve here, which means we have to pole the logs out of our path. If you ask me, they ought to be outlawed."

"We're going to lose time here unless you give us a hand, Emily," Seneca said when she and Elijah joined him at the side railing. "If you could be our steerman?"

"Oh, please. You know what happened last time."

"But you know how to do it now. You won't have any problems. Unless, of course, you prefer to let Jimbo win."

She drew a sharp breath and turned away. He was a monster. No matter what Elijah said, she wasn't putting up with his foul moods and accusations. "All right." She swung around to face him. "I'll steer your boat for you, and as soon as you win your blasted race, I'm going back to Albany. I'll catch a ride with someone going that way. There is no need for you to concern yourself with me ever again."

"Hey now, wait a minute, folks," Elijah interceded. "Let's not overreact here."

"I promised to deliver the kitten to Marianne. Would you be good enough to see she gets it, Elijah?" She turned and walked back to the tiller and perched on the rear railing. She kept her eyes straight ahead, ignoring the two men who, by turns, swung around to watch her.

She didn't know what she was feeling—a mixture of anger, disappointment, fear, pain. He had no right to accuse her, and no reason. So to do so, he must really *want* to be angry with her. It hurt that he thought so little of her. It also angered her. And she was disappointed that their time together was over. And, if she were honest with herself, she was afraid of being on her own. But she was not staying when he so obviously wanted her gone. He could just go jump in the canal.

No sooner had that unkind thought crossed her mind than the tow line from the passing log raft slipped from the hoggee's pole and dropped, catching her across the shoulders. She grabbed it and tried to get out from under it, but it tightened, pinning her to the rail. And then it very slowly pulled her over the back and into the water.

Unfortunately, when she fell over backwards, her hip caught the tiller bar, pulling it sharply to the side.

She splashed into the water. When she surfaced it was to see the boat swing ever so slightly to the left and collide with the third raft of logs. It didn't hit with any real force, only enough to snap the ropes holding the raft together. As their hoggee kept going, oblivious to the havoc he'd caused, the raft broke up, spilling the long logs into the canal right in front of *Prescott's Wake*. Just before she lost her footing on the slick bottom and sank beneath the surface, she heard them all turning the air blue with cuss words.

It was at that same moment that she realized the hoggees' barge was upon her. She prepared herself for that collision, but it never happened. Instead Cob was in the water at her side, pulling her back to her feet. Taller than Benjie, he was able to stand and support her.

The barge with the two extra horses was still behind them. Cob had cut the towrope. She leaned her head on his shoulder.

"I'm sorry, miss. I saw it all happen, but I couldn't do nothing to stop it."

"At least you didn't run me down."

"No, miss. I cut the ropes right away. I'll walk you to the shore, then I have to get these horses up to the landing. Sorry I can't stay with you."

"Ah, that's okay. I'm fine." She waded ashore and turned to give Cob a smile of thanks. Dripping wet, she began her walk to the landing. Several men had seen what happened to her and they offered assistance, but she refused, more embarrassed than anything else. Embarrassed and cold. The evening air was still brisk.

She had gone several hundred feet when Cap'n John met her. He shook his head and clucked over her. "Never seen the likes before. Here."

He wrapped his coat around her shoulders and pulled her to his side. "That damn Bull Renegal ought to be made to pay for this. He has no business hiring kids that young to tow a thing like this.

135

The boy never looked back once. I'm going to lodge a complaint, you can bet on it."

"Oh, please, not on my account."

"No? You could have been hung, your neck snapped, drowned in five feet of water, girl. You want that to happen to someone else?"

"Well, maybe you should say something. Maybe the boys could be given a few lessons before they're hired."

"Not a bad idea, missy."

Walking beside Cap'n John, she watched the men work frantically to clear the waterway. She was already on the landing when Seneca clocked in two minutes and forty two seconds late. Even the bonus for catching the biggest fish wouldn't make up that much time. He was furious and couldn't help apologizing over and over to Elijah for the fact that the money was lost.

"One simple little assignment and she couldn't do even that right," he exploded, running his fingers through his hair. Or worse, he thought. She could have deliberately steered into the raft so her friend Jimbo could win instead.

"You're wrong," Elijah said. "I can see what you're thinking and she wouldn't do that. You can't blame her for this."

Seneca looked back at the boat and scowled. "Where is she then? If she's so blameless, why can't she face us?"

"Is she in the cabin?"

"How the hell should I know. I haven't seen her. Where else would she be?"

"I haven't seen her either. Not since we hit the raft. You don't . . ."

Emily heard them, so did Cap'n John. "Don't mind them, lass. He don't mean none of that."

"I guess I better go face him then. He can be so

136

impossible." She knew she was blushing, humiliated that Cap'n John should see how things were between her and Seneca.

"He can at that, but you'll see. He's a nice guy, really."

"Emily," Seneca called, striding back to the boat. He jumped aboard. "Emily, stop your childish games and come out of there." He checked both cabins before he realized that she was not on board his boat.

"She isn't here," he said almost to himself. He looked at Elijah then searched the dock area.

"Seneca! Did ya lose this little package," Cap'n John called. He led her to Seneca, who immediately took her shoulders and shook her.

"Where were you? What happened?"

It was a stupid question and it made her furious. "Take your hands off me. I'm shaking enough as it is." Every time she touched that tiller something disastrous happened. And she'd had enough of his strong-arm tactics.

She shook herself free. "Thanks for your coat, Cap'n John. I hope I didn't get it too awfully wet." She handed it back, and turned immediately toward the boat. She'd got as far as the cabin door when Seneca jumped aboard.

"Just a minute," he demanded.

She turned to face him squarely, her fists planted on her hips. She was a sight, her dripping hair plastered against her face, her blouse molded to her bosom. Her eyes flashed angrily, lighting up her face. God, but he wanted her. He reached for her.

She batted his hands away. "Leave me alone."

His lips twitched in anger. Deliberately he took hold of her shoulders again. "You lost us the race. I hope you're pleased with yourself."

"I lost . . ." In one motion she freed herself and

137

swung her arm. Her palm connected loudly with his face, hurting her hand more than his tough jaw. Wisely, though, she stepped away from the fury in his eyes. She didn't know what had gotten into her. Never had she lost her temper as she did with Seneca. And in front of all his friends who were even now jeering and laughing at him.

"I'm sorry," she said lamely, turning her face away from his cold eyes.

"Sorry?" he growled. "Sorry? No one is more sorry than I am. I should have listened to my gut instincts and left you in that warehouse in Albany."

Hot tears sprang to her eyes and she felt her chin wobble. The fact that he could make her cry made her temper rise.

"Boy, oh boy, you . . . you sure are . . ." she stammered. "Well, why did . . . why didn't . . . I wish . . ."

She was in his arms then, and his mouth was on hers in a gentle and loving kiss. His arms held her, warmed her, comforted her. His deep voice murmuring her name dispelled her hurt and her anger. His lips coaxed hers open and his tongue invaded her mouth, his gentleness turning to passion. She melted. For some reason she always melted when she was in his arms. She melted and turned to warm, thick honey.

Her arms wound round his neck, her fingers tangling in his thick black hair, holding his mouth to hers. She surrendered to the sweet lassitude invading her body, to the desire unfurling deep within her.

In a quick jerky motion he pulled back from her, keeping her at arm's length.

She was disoriented for a second or two, but it didn't take her long to read the smug satisfaction on his face. He turned to the cheering crowd and waved.

So his kiss had been her punishment for slapping him in public. Her cheeks burned with humiliation and her heart broke. She looked at the crowd of laughing men and met Elijah's solemn gaze. He shrugged and shook his head in disgust.

Elijah might not know what to do with Seneca, but Emily did. And it was extremely just, since she was wet to the bone too. She turned and glared at his smirking face. Then she launched herself at him, shoving her shoulder into his ribs, pushing until he toppled over the side and into the water. She watched him go under, then turned, ignoring the laughing crowd, and locked herself in the cabin.

Chapter 9

Elijah drained his mug of beer and tried again to reach Seneca. "I ask one thing of you. Before you say anything more to hurt *her*, consider how *you* will feel when you learn you've been wrong."

"I told you before that I have no intention of hurting her."

"Um. Just remember the old saying, 'The road to Hell is paved . . .'"

"All right, Elijah, you have my word. I'll be the epitome of gentlemanly courtesy. Now go on your way and don't worry about us."

"Seneca, I'd never delay you like this if it were not important. And I would not leave you alone with her. But this is a chance to find Bekka. I can't walk away from it."

"I understand. We're in no rush. We'll hang around until you get back. And quit fussing over me. In fact, I'd appreciate it if you'd go now. The sooner you leave, the sooner you'll return." And the sooner there'd be an end to his nagging. Seneca ordered a refill. He was drinking whiskey.

Elijah stood up, hesitated, then turned away. Nothing would be gained by irritating him. He'd simmer down eventually, if he didn't get roaring drunk first. Elijah put on his coat and adjusted his hat.

Seneca turned his head, watching his friend. "You have your papers?"

"I have them."

Elijah wore the latest of fashions with remarkable élan. Quite a commanding figure he made, standing tall and proud by the door. But all the style in the world wouldn't save him from chains or the cat o' nine if he were caught without proof of his freedom.

"Good luck, Elijah. I hope you find something this time."

Seneca finished his drink then ordered a bottle to take back to the boat. The street outside was still alive with a handfull of late partiers making their own music, but the musicians had retired, the booths had been taken down, the fireworks were over, the townspeople in for the night.

Remembering how Emily had danced and laughed and enjoyed herself with Cap'n John, Jimbo, the two boys, and a number of other eager gentlemen from town, Seneca jerked the cork from the bottle and tilted it to his lips.

Well, that was just fine with him. It's what he wanted anyway. He certainly didn't want her hanging on *his* arm all evening, did he? So why the hostility, the jealousy. Yes, jealousy, he admitted reluctantly. Why couldn't he put her out of his mind? Why was his stomach churning? And why did her face always pop into his mind's eye when he thought about finding himself a willing woman for a little evening diversion? She was ruining his life and he didn't like it. And why in hell couldn't he get drunk tonight?

Emily had dozed for a couple hours, then blinked wide awake again, troubled by the memory of Seneca's harsh accusations and his continued silence. As

141

far as he was concerned, she'd given the race to Jimbo. She'd tried several times during the festivities to break through his icy reserve, but each time she'd approached him he'd turned to one of the ladies and asked her to dance with him. It didn't take a genius to understand a snub like that. She got out of bed and pulled her trunk from the corner. No use lying in bed and going over it all again. All her thinking before hadn't helped, it wouldn't now.

She arranged the clothes remaining in her trunk and began to pack the articles she'd left out or stored in one of the spare dresser drawers. There was no reason to postpone the inevitable, not since it would only worsen an already strained atmosphere. The best thing to do was return to Paddie. Cap'n John had offered her a ride when he returned in four days. She would stay in the hotel until then.

She heard Seneca return. He banged into something outside and swore his usual oath. She couldn't keep from smiling, nor could she help the tears that blurred her vision. Maybe he'd find out he missed her. Perhaps he'd look her up in Albany. She found it difficult to give up her hopes that he'd grow to love her as much as she loved him.

Elijah said that Seneca wasn't fighting her as much as he was fighting a memory. That didn't help much, since she didn't know anything about that memory. At least Elijah could have given her that much ammunition to fight with. As it was, she was helpless. She'd tried every reasonable approach she could to span the gap between them. He preferred the gap.

Her door swung open and smashed into the side of the bureau. Startled out of her thoughts, she whirled around. He stood in the doorway—big,

142

dark, half drunk, and when he saw what she was doing, furious.

"I think it would be best if I take a room at the hotel," she said into the long and uncomfortable silence. "I have enough money to take care of myself until I can get back home. Cap'n John agreed to let me go with him."

"Why not Jimbo? Surely he owes you a ride."

"I'm certain he'd agree, but it was Cap'n John I asked." She turned back to her packing.

"You've been crying."

"You're imagining things."

"Couldn't you sleep?"

"I woke up when you slammed your way aboard."

"Hmm. Sorry about that." He held out the bottle and the two glasses he'd brought with him. "How about sharing a drink with me?"

"Haven't you had enough yet?" she asked.

"I don't think so. I can still see you and Jimbo together."

She turned to glare at him in all her righteous indignation. "Really? Jealous?"

He ignored that and poured two glasses of whiskey. "Come, sit down," he invited, sliding back on the bunk and holding her glass out to her.

"I don't drink."

"You did once before," he reminded her. "Don't be so stuffy. Or are you afraid to drink with me?"

"Afraid?" She snorted inelegantly. "There is a difference between fear and intelligent caution."

"You don't trust me? Or is it yourself you don't trust?"

She flung her neatly folded blouses into the trunk and turned. "What is it with you?" When she looked at him he was looking back with such a mischievous challenge in his grin that she couldn't let him get away with it. "All right. One drink. And

143

then you leave."

"It's my cabin."

"Fine. Then I'll leave."

"After your drink. Bottoms up." He drained his glass and gave a shudder as the liquid burned its way to his stomach. Immediately he refilled his glass.

Emily took a small sip. "Really, Seneca, you shouldn't drink so much."

"You're preaching again. Don't drink, don't cuss, don't fight. *Really*, Emily, you're such a prude. Don't try to reform me."

"Some reformer. Here I am sitting on *your* bed, drinking 'demon rum.' "

"That's because I'm the better reformer. I'm trying my best to make you more . . . human."

"I'm quite human, I assure you." She drank another swallow, this one going down much more easily. She leaned back, pulling her knees up and covering her bare feet with the edge of the blanket.

"Did you have a good time tonight?"

She shrugged negligently. "It was okay. I did want to dance with you," she said before she could check the thought.

"Yeah? Why?" he asked tauntingly.

"Can't imagine now. A moment of insanity, I guess."

He grinned crookedly and refilled her glass. "Don't worry about it. It hits us all at some time or another."

"Were you in love once too?" she asked, not realizing until the words were out how much her question revealed. But he didn't seem to hear what she hadn't said.

"In love?" he repeated bitterly. "Is there such a thing? Or is it an illusion meant for a man's destruction?"

"Oh . . . What did she do to you?"

Absently he rubbed the scar running down the side of his face. "Nothing. Forget it."

"How did you get your scars?"

He scowled at her. "Why the hell would you ask about that? Have you got some sick sense of curiosity?"

She reached up and laid her hand along the side of his face. "How?" she persisted, meeting the black light of his gaze.

He took a shuddering breath, shrugged away from her hand, and took another swallow.

"A fire."

"What happened?"

"I don't talk about it," he growled. "I never talk about it."

"Talk about it now."

He frowned at her obliquely. "What the hell is it to you?"

"Perhaps a great deal. I have the feeling I'm paying for your past miseries."

"That's nonsense."

"Then tell me. Or are you afraid if you do, you'll see I'm right?"

"Damn you."

"Yes, I'm sure you do." She finished her drink and tossed the glass toward the foot of the bed so he wouldn't be tempted to refill it for her. She moved boldly closer and took his glass and the bottle from his hands.

"I'm not finished with that."

"You can have it later. I'm cold, Seneca."

"Emily, for Pete sake. I'm drunk enough already to be a danger to you. Don't play games."

"Put your arms around me and talk to me." She pressed her lips to the silvery scar at the base of his chin, running her lips up to the angry line by his

145

ear. "What fire?"

His arms tightened and a strangled moan came from deep in his throat. "God, Emily." He pulled a blanket free and put it around her shoulders, setting her apart from him. "Just sit there, okay?"

"Okay," she said submissively, watching him struggle for his composure. She knew she was playing a dangerous game, much as she might want to deny it, but she couldn't seem to care. Maybe he had reformed her to his ways before she could reform him to hers, but she wanted this last night to remember. She wanted to be in his arms again, to be transported by his kisses to that sensual world of pleasure she'd only briefly tasted before. She wanted him to talk, to take down that wall, to cross over and reach for her. She wanted to drive him beyond that ironclad control he exercised so frequently with her.

"Who was she?" she asked.

"We were to be married in a month. Three weeks, actually. I'd taken her to visit her grandmother. We were to spend the weekend with her as she was confined to bed and wouldn't be able to attend our wedding. She wanted to see Belinda in her wedding dress. And she wanted to meet me.

"I never learned how it happened, but I woke up choking on smoke. I rushed into the hall to find the whole downstairs filled with flames. Belinda and her grandmother were both upstairs.

"I raced through the parlor to the stairs. The runner was already on fire and I had to beat it out with a pillow from the sofa before I could get up. All the time I fought to reach her, I screamed her name to wake her up.

"Well, she finally woke up and went into hysterics. I can understand her being afraid, hell, I was, too. But she went crazy. I tried to calm her down, but she screamed for me to get her out, get her out, don't let her burn. I tried to explain that I had to help her grandmother first, that Belinda would be all right if she stayed close beside me, that we'd get out.

"I had picked up the old lady and was carrying her toward the stairs. I called to Belinda to follow me but she just froze. She wouldn't move. She slumped to her knees in a blind panic, crying out that she was going to die, going to burn to death, that I was letting her die to save a woman already half dead.

"I didn't know what to do. How could I choose? I gambled on time. I ran down the stairs with the old lady and laid her on the grass away from the house. Then I went back for Belinda. As I went in the front door the chandelier fell."

He rubbed the scar that ran down the side of his face. "I was stunned for a minute. I didn't know what had happened. Then Belinda's screams reached me, and I bolted back up the stairs. There were flames everywhere. That house was like paper. I swore then that I'd never live in a house that was not made of brick or stone.

"Walls were collapsing by the time I reached Belinda. I picked her up. She was totally out of control, kicking, screaming, fighting even me.

"The stairs were impassible by then. I found a window, and using bed linens, lowered her to the ground. A dozen men had arrived by that time, and I could hear the fire wagons coming. Two of the men took Belinda and led her away. Then the floor under my feet seemed to explode upward and flames were everywhere. I tied off the sheets and slid out the window, but a piece of the drapery had fallen onto my shoulder. My pants caught fire as well as my shirt. I could do nothing except get to the ground as quickly as possible. The men were waiting for me with a bucket of water.

"I don't remember much of what happened after that until I woke up in the hospital. My parents and Marianne were there every day for weeks while I fought to recover. Belinda didn't come once. Her letter did though, with her engagement ring enclosed.

"My mother tried to make the break easier for me, but my sister, told the truth as only the young can do. Belinda had been to see me before I woke up. She was sickened by the extent of my injuries and let it slip to Marianne, just a kid then, that she didn't think she could spend the rest of her life with a man who was so disfigured.

"Don't you suppose most of her feelings were guilt?" Emily asked quietly. "She probably realized that if she hadn't lost her head, you wouldn't have had to go back in there a second time. The ending would have been very different. Every time she'd look at you, she'd remember that."

"That shows how understanding your heart is, but also how little you know Belinda. To her *I* was the one who needed to apologize. She couldn't forgive me for leaving her while I rescued her grandmother. She should have been my first priority. When I took her grandmother first, I told her I didn't truly love her, or so she claimed. Not even my injuries made a difference. I had betrayed her. My scars would always remind her of that betrayal.

"Hmm," Emily hummed, frowning. "It sounds as if she just couldn't face her culpability so she made up her own version. You must have been very disillusioned."

"Disillusioned? Oh, yes. I learned a very bitter lesson, one I don't need repeated."

"Do you want to know how I feel about your

scars?" she said, sidling closer to him. "Now that I know the story of how you came to have them, when I see them, I'll be reassured that I can depend on you to be there if I need you. They are a badge of your selflessness, and your valor. I think I love them."

A deep surge of warmth and tenderness flooded her. She wanted nothing more than to hold him, to erase his inner pain, to bring him joy, if only for a moment.

Impulsively, or perhaps not so impulsively, she stretched upward and touched her lips to his neck. "I think I love you. No, don't say anything. Just kiss me. I'll go in the morning, I promise I will. But let me have one more night in your arms. Let me know your kisses and your arms around me when we don't have an audience."

He wanted that too. His control, already weakened by alcohol, threatened to disintegrate altogether. He wanted, just for a while, to hold her close to him and lose himself in her sweetness. But love? She was so naive, so vulnerable. He hated to be the one to disillusion her. And he couldn't let her leave. Would she be able to live with him after . . . ?

"Emily, we have to talk."

"No. No talking." She clung to him out of a sense of fear and desperation, pressing her womanly body into his. "I don't want to talk anymore."

She slipped the buttons of his shirt open and ran her fingers over the hard masculine contours of his chest. Her head began to spin from the sensations of her flesh against his, and from the whiskey, she realized. But the feelings surging through her body, urging, enervating, weightless yet heavy, were just too compelling sweet and erotic to deny. She wanted to drown in them.

149

She leaned over him and pressed her lips to his skin, brushing against the dark curls that were sprinkled sparsely down his chest. She flicked out her tongue to taste the salty spice of his skin, running the velvet roughness across his chest.

He closed his eyes and groaned in sweet agony, his body coming instantly alive, urgently alive. How could he stop her, how could he put an end to the blissful magic of her shy loving? Instead of pushing her away as his brain commanded, his hands pulled her closer, held her captive so she couldn't escape even if she tried.

He slid down in the bed, taking her with him, pulling her to lie atop him. Surely she was able to feel what she was doing to him, yet even in her innocence, she didn't seem to be frightened by it. Rather, her sinuous movements seemed designed to drive him more out of control.

She tugged his shirt from his pants and slid it off his shoulders and down his arms. Her lips followed its path, covering his shoulder and arm with kisses that came from the depth of her heart.

Seneca flinched at first when her mouth moved to his scars, but she didn't pull away. Finally he relaxed and forced himself to endure her caresses. She wasn't repulsed, but her preoccupation with his disfigurement was equally disturbing.

"Why are you doing that?" he asked tightly after a few minutes.

"To get it out of the way. If you're going to draw back, I want you to do it now, then get used to my touch, because I want to touch you and kiss you and I don't want to have to worry that I'll make you uncomfortable. Let me know you, Seneca. For just this one night, let me know all of you with nothing held back."

"Emily, you don't know what you're asking. A

man can't just hold a woman like, and kiss her, and be kissed by her, especially if he cares for her, and not want . . . more than you're bargaining for."

"Then you do care for me a little bit?"

"Emily," he groaned, "you're the most beautiful woman I've ever known. You're honest, open, sweet, and totally exasperating. You're very special, and very innocent. And I can't . . . Someday the right man will come along and you'll be glad you waited." Those were the hardest words he'd ever said in his life, because the thought of her with any other man sent a violent bolt of possessiveness through him, so that he wanted to throw her down and take her and keep taking her until the world knew she was his and until his child grew inside her to prove it.

His breath caught in his throat, and beads of perspiration formed along his hair line. Even his thoughts frightened him. What kind of a monster was he to even think such thoughts about her? And so strongly appealing were those black thoughts that he had to get away from her before he really did it.

He stirred, intending to leave her, but she buried her face in his neck, nipping the skin with her teeth, licking away the sting. With an instinct born of woman, she teased and lured and seduced. He, mortal that he was, had no strength to fight her.

A very powerful change had taken place in her life since her terrible loss of family and her own brush with death. She had learned how much life meant to her. She had come to realize that she had her own dreams. She had come to see that twenty years of life had passed and that none of her wishes had been fulfilled. She'd done nothing but watch life go on around her. Life could be snatched away in the blink of an eye, she now knew, and in the past weeks she'd almost lost hers any number of times.

Whatever days she had left on this earth she wanted to live to the fullest.

"Don't leave me. Kiss me," she pleaded, sliding up his body, moving her mouth to his.

Her hair fell like a curtain around them. Her hips moved against him, causing his manhood to surge against her, her full breasts teased his chest and made his hands burn and tingle. Her scent, sweet and fresh, touched with the faintest spice of whiskey, filled his head. Her voice, beckoning him, pulling him into her, trapping him, was the call of a Siren. His hands closed around her, one urging her rounded bottom into his hips, the other tunneling under her hair to cup the back of her head. He was lost and he knew it.

"Kiss me like you did in that warehouse," she said against his open lips. She resisted the pull against her head to bind their lips together. Instead she teased more, biting his lips, running her tongue lightly over their sensitive edges. "You made me shiver all the way through. I felt as if I was floating free of my body, held in the hands of a black-eyed pirate, and I wasn't afraid. How did you do that? I want to feel that again."

"Witch. What are you doing to me? I could make you pregnant," he growled in one last burst of effort.

As a deterent it was woefully ineffective. The mere mention of carrying his child in her body made her womb clench deliciously and her body fill with a rush of liquid heat.

"Remember when you undressed me?" she tormented. "Undress me now. Look at me again as you looked at me then."

She was more than any mortal man could resist. She was fire in his hands, fire that drew him, compelled him into its devouring flames. She would burn him and leave behind scars much worse than the ones he already had. He should push her away, he should get up, get away from her. He should run like hell.

"I can't," he cried, anguished. "I just can't."

In a flash of movement he swept her into his embrace and rolled her beneath him. His mouth claimed hers in a savage kiss that swept away the barriers of resistance.

Her mind and her body spun away from her, but not before she'd heard his cry, words that signaled his utter defeat at the same time they rejected her. Seduction was no longer hers, for nothing in the world would stop him now.

Her nightdress was torn away and his fiery black eyes shot to her chest, her shoulders. His head jerked back.

"My God." A long lean finger came up and traced the angry bruised abrasion that ran from shoulder to shoulder.

She glanced down, surprised to see the vivid discoloration. He was staring at her face, silent, still, intent. "How?" was all he said.

She couldn't believe he didn't know, that someone hadn't told him. But who'd want to waste time trying to talk to a sullen and surly bonehead, as Jimbo had called him during one of the times he whirled her around the dance floor.

"The towline hit me. I don't know how it happened. It cleared the top of the cabin then snapped down and caught me."

"You could have been killed," he said starkly. "Your neck broken."

"Not to mention run down by the barge."

"Christ, is that why . . ."

"I hit the tiller when I went over the side. Luckily Cob was watching. He cut the towrope and jumped in to help me out. I didn't mean for all that to happen, and I'm truly sorry Elijah lost the purse. I don't know how I could have prevented it. It happened so fast."

He squeezed his eyes shut and rested his forehead against hers, remembering the ugly accusations he'd thrown at her. And Elijah's warning, ". . . consider how you will feel when you learn you've been wrong." What was it inside him that made him so arrogant and sure he was right all the time? He felt like a jackass now.

"It's all right, Seneca. I meant to explain as soon as your temper cooled." Seeing his contrition was all the apology she needed from her tough abrasive pirate. "Are you going to kiss me or not?"

"Emily," he protested on a fresh wave of conscience. How could he make love to her now, after what . . .

"Seneca Prescott," she screeched, feeling his withdrawal. She shoved him aside and got to her knees. "You disgusting . . . disgusting . . . tease."

He laughed remorselessly. "Men aren't teases," he said, unable to disguise the hunger in his eyes at the sight of her full, hard-tipped breasts.

"You are. You've been teasing me since we met, luring me, seducing me. Did you feel safe playing the swaggering male because you felt sure I'd continue to resist? Maybe deep down you're afraid you're not up to it."

"Now, careful," he said quietly, his eyes flashing a warning that she purposely ignored.

"A kiss here, a kiss there, charm enough when you felt like playing your game. Eyes that looked at me as though you wanted nothing more than to see me naked in your bed. Well, here I am."

She tossed her hair, the motion causing her unfettered breasts to thrust outward. On her knees with her thighs slightly parted and her hands on the gentle flare of her slender hips, her hair tumbling riotously about her face and her mocking eyes flashing him a challenge, she was a bewitching and breathtaking sight.

He felt the heat of desire darken his skin. His body caught flame. "If I change my mind," he said through lips that felt stiff, wooden, "will you run away like a frightened rabbit?"

She was going nowhere now that she'd snared him. She threw back her head and laughed, letting the wondrously wild sensations his burning eyes were causing in her body wash over her. She found she rather enjoyed seducing him, and wondered if he felt the same pleasure when he teased her.

He swung her to the bed and loomed over her. "Let's see how you laugh when I'm finished with you."

He unleashed all his expertise on her then, kissing her until she was breathless and mindless, until she began to writhe with unchecked desire. His lips trailed hot kisses down her sensitive neck, and at the same time his hands roved from her hips up to her waist, to the undersides of her breast.

With no warning his mouth closed over the aching engorged tip of her breast. The shock and unbearable pleasure caused her to cry out his name, clutching at his shoulders.

Her skin tightened into tiny goosebumps and he lifted his head. "You're cold." He put her into bed, covering her naked body with soft blankets. He turned the lamp down, shed his own clothes, and slid in beside her.

"Is it okay if I'm a bit nervous?" she asked, coming shyly into his arms again.

He chuckled low in his throat. "From seductress to timid virgin in one breath. Will I ever know what to expect from you?" He nuzzled the satin skin below her ear, and she began to relax again.

"I don't know what to expect from myself anymore," she said huskily. "I don't know me."

"I'm not surprised. You haven't given yourself a chance. Elijah called you a flower bud. Let's coax those petals open together, one by one. Inside I think we'll find a rose of matchless beauty."

"Seneca, that was lovely."

"Are you feeling better, not so nervous?"

"Not so nervous."

His lips roamed softly across her forehead. "Do you still want to . . ."

"More than ever. I want to spend the whole night in your arms."

She was still a little shy, a little apprehensive. He'd known many women, women who were expert at pleasing a man. What if she failed him? What if she disappointed him? But she wanted to belong to him, to know his unimpeded loving. And she knew instinctively that he would be hers completely when they made love. For a few moments she'd be able to hold his heart in her hands, to cherish it, to shower it with her love. The rest of her life, be it ever so empty and barren, would be made tolerable for the memory of that. Without it she would forever know regret.

His hands, maddeningly knowledgeable, found her secret places and brought to life a fountain of eroticism in her young body. His lips, merciless against her hungry lips, her arched neck, her heavy breasts, overflowed with words of adoration and praise, drowning her in a world of silvery sound and wild sensations so that before long she was wimpering in need.

Her own hands, tingling to grasp and hold on through the firestorm of passion, sought out the long muscles of his shoulders and back, the tight curves of his buttocks. How often, as she'd watched him work, had she longed to run her hands down his body. She pulled him against her. He groaned her name and led her hand to more private parts.

She touched him boldly, stroking and cradling him, longing to incite in him the same fierce need, the same joyous pleasure.

"God, angel, yes. You drive me wild. I can't touch you enough. I need you. I need you."

Of their own accord her thighs parted, her legs bound him to her. "Seneca, please. I ache so."

A fleeting sound of sanity intruded, preventing Seneca from unleashing the full power of his passion on her untutored body. He wanted to drive into her fiercely, to claim her, to become part of her and ease her aching body, and his own, but he gritted his teeth and held back, reminding himself that this was her first time, that she was a innocent woman, and that he would bring her great pain if he were not gentle.

With ironclad resolve, he entered her slowly, letting her become accustomed to the feel of him. She was tense in his arms, and he felt regret at the discomfort to come. For an instant he wanted to quit, to get up and leave. Then her eyes opened and she looked at him with open trust and love.

"It's okay, my darling," she whispered.

His heart melted into a puddle in his chest. He gathered her close, never wanting to let her go, and in a decisive move he took her innocence and made her his woman.

She gave a short gasping cry, surprised at the sharpness of the tearing pain. He soothed her with kisses and gentle words and soft caresses.

"It's done," he crooned. "The hurt will go now. Be still for a moment and let me hold you."

Moving very subtly within her for just a moment, he withdrew and began his campaign of seduction all over again, leading her back into his world of sensation. His hands shaped, molded, caressed, and moved on. His lips, his mouth, tutored and tortured until she was again lost to his mastery, floundering in an unknown world, knowing she needed, but not knowing exactly what. Every little sound, every grasping touch, every seductive twist and turn of her body cried out its plea, and only when he was satisfied with her mindless state did he answer with total masculine aggression.

This time there was no pain when he stormed the citadel of her body and sank into the velvet heat of her, and she flowered for him in joyous welcome.

She said his name in a cry of ecstacy, and he answered, repeating hers in a litany of need. What followed was a storm of madness, fevered and unreal. She felt every vestige of civilization shrivel up and die, and born in her was a creature of desperate need and desire who wanted and demanded that which her mate was providing. And more.

He led her, he followed her, and finally, when his restraint was gone, he propelled her to a world that would forevermore change them both. Their bodies exploded in cataclysmic splendor, first hers, then, before her cries of ecstasy had faded, his.

He collapsed, rolling to her side and pulling her into his arms. She turned her head and kissed the tip of his slightly crooked nose. That was all she could manage, her limbs were without substance. Bit by bit her heart slowed, as did the pounding under her hand that rested on his chest. He was soon asleep, his face relaxed, even boyish. Her great pirate brought low by sheer exhaustion. She moved closer, relishing the soreness that remained from their stormy union. She felt wonderful. She closed her eyes and moved his hand so she could entwine her fingers with his.

A tear rolled down her cheek to her ear and soaked into his pillow. If only she had more time. If only she could love him one more time.

"Thank you, Seneca," she whispered. "I'll always love you."

Chapter 10

Emily woke up with hunger gnawing at her stomach. She looked at the clock on the bureau. It said half past eleven.

"It can't be," she gasped, throwing aside the covers. Her nakedness and the acute soreness of her body reminded her of the night she'd spent in a wild frenzy of passion.

Her cheeks burned at the memory. What must he think of her? She closed her eyes to shut out the pictures of them together, but they only came faster, more vividly. And her body responded accordingly, tingling, aching, yearning.

What had he done to her? What sort of wanton had she become overnight? For she had to admit that even after making love to him three times during the night, she wanted him yet again. She dipped water from the wooden bucket into the wash basin and began her normal daily toilette, wondering how she was going to face Seneca.

It was then she remembered that this was the day she had planned to leave. She winced at the pain that accompanied that thought. How could she leave? But how could she stay? She'd promised him she'd go if he spent the night with her. If she changed her mind now, especially when she'd been foolish enough to admit her love, he'd assume she was hoping to persuade him to marry her. He'd really despise her then. She knew what he thought of women and marriage. How could she hope to change a mind that had been set against her gender for three years? And if she were pregnant she would be guilty of the ultimate deceit. She couldn't bear to see the disdain and contempt *that* would bring to his eyes, not after last night. She must leave. She had no choice.

And so she dressed and fixed her hair, and finished packing her belongings into her trunk. Only then did she leave the cabin, shoring up her courage as she stepped out into the sunshine.

Seneca wasn't on board. Elijah was nowhere to be seen. She was alone, except for her kitten and little Benjie who sat at the end of the dock. Some protection he'd make against the bald attacker.

"Mornin', miss," Benjie called, seeing her up and about. "Mr. Prescott said he'd be back later this afternoon and that you was to stay put till then."

Oh, did he now? "And Elijah?"

"Oh, he done gone till tonight, lookin' for his wife and boy, I reckon."

"I see. Did Mr. Prescott say where he was going?"

"No, miss. But you ain't to worry none. I got my slingshot here in case those men come back."

"Your slingshot."

"I've a good eye. And don't forget David kilt the giant with one."

"No. I'll remember that," she said, suppressing a grin. She turned back to the boat and put another piece of wood in the stove. She was still hungry. She may as well eat before going off to find a room for the night. And the linens needed washing. And she supposed she could find several other chores to use as an excuse to be here when Seneca returned, just in case he wanted to persuade her to stay.

And so she worked the afternoon away, cleaning, cooking, tidying both cabins and the cargo area. The sky overhead was clouding up and the leaves were turning their silvery sides skyward. She made a bed for the kitten in a cave between several crates and put an old pillow in there for her comfort. She had just brought the clean linens in when the first big drops of rain fell. By the time the bed was remade the sky had opened and a torrent had begun to pour from the black boiling clouds. Lightning rent the sky and thunder cracked, rattling the window panes with its furor.

She locked the cabin door, pulled the curtains across the windows, and lit the lamp. Seneca would probably grumble at the waste of fuel, but she needed light to dispel her fear, and not just fear of being alone during a thunderstorm. Benjie would have gone for shelter too. She had not even a boy and a slingshot to protect her now. Anyone could come for her. That would solve her problem of what to do about Seneca.

Another boom of thunder made her jump, and then she realized someone was pounding on the cabin door. Icy fear clutched at the back of her neck. She wanted to call out and ask who it was, but if it wasn't Seneca, she didn't want whoever it was to know she was there. The fist pounded again.

"Emily, open the door! It's Elijah."

She unlocked the door with a rush of relief. Elijah shook off his rain slicker and stepped down into the cabin. His face and the front of his shirt were drenched from blowing rain.

She handed him a towel and searched for dry clothes while he pulled the soggy shirt off and dried himself. She glanced up and stood stunned at the network of scars that crisscrossed his back and chest.

"I have some coffee keeping hot," she offered, looking away.

"Not if I have to go outside to get it," he said, buttoning the dry shirt.

"No, it's here. I put it on a rack over a candle." She poured him a cup, and he wrapped his cold hands around the hot mug and took a tentative sip. "Umm," he sighed. "I'm chilled to the marrow. This is good."

"Benjie said you were looking for your wife?"

"Oh, well, every now and then I'll hear something that makes me believe she's around here somewhere. I have to investigate." He rubbed the bone medallion that hung from his neck. "Sometimes I can feel her close by, but my common sense tells me it's just wishful thinking. Purely imagination." He shrugged off his disappointment and smiled at her. "I half expected you to be gone. Seneca said you were threatening to go back to Albany."

"Seneca? You saw him?"

"I . . . ah . . . yes. He was at the Cork and Bottle a little while ago. He wasn't in a very sociable mood. Did you argue again?"

She blushed and looked away. "No." She poured herself a cup of coffee.

Elijah's head came up and he watched her self-conscious movements. "That bastard," he mumbled under his breath.

"I beg your pardon?" Emily asked, glancing up.

He shook his head. "Nothing, nothing. Come. Bring your coffee over and sit with me. We may as well get comfortable. It looks like we'll be here a while. With the storm and all, we won't head out till morning. Were you really planning to leave?"

"Yes. I think I must."

"So you're giving up?"

Her eyes snapped up. "No. It isn't like that."

"Sure it is. He's beaten you. At least be honest."

"I'm not beat. I'm doing this for him. He told me about his fiancée, and about the fire. I know he can't love me back, so . . ."

"So you're sparing him the embarrassment of seeing your love? How noble. Or are you sparing your own pride?"

"Elijah," she objected. "You know as well as I do that he wants me gone."

"Now more than ever, probably, but why should he always get what he wants, especially if what he thinks he wants is the absolute worst thing for him?"

"But . . ."

"And the worst thing for you. Those men are still out there. Why give up the two best protectors on the canal?"

"Seneca will be furious. He'll think I'm . . ."

"So what do you care what he thinks?"

"He'll hate me."

"Again—so what? It may look like he hates you, but what he'll hate is loving you. I have a feeling that's what has him in such a belligerent state now."

"He'll make my life hell."

"Or heaven," he answered, grinning knowingly. "Reconsider, Emily. He needs you. You need him. Fight for him. Fight with him. He can't resist a good fight, and if he wins, make him win you."

Emily thought about Elijah's advice while she prepared their meal. When the rain let up Elijah took the opportunity to raise an awning so that they could go outside and eat. They talked as evening fell and the storm passed over. When the first stars came out in the purple sky, Elijah stretched and yawned.

164

"I'm really bushed. Would you mind if I turned in early. I didn't get any sleep last night."

"Oh, no. Please go ahead. You don't have to sit with me. I have a book I'll read. Goodnight, and thanks."

"Night. Eh, don't mind if I take the kitten with me, do you?"

She chuckled. "She'll love you forever."

Emily paced the cabin for another hour, waiting for Seneca to return. The longer she waited, the angrier she became. Elijah was right again. Who did Seneca think he was to use her as he had the night before and treat her so cavalierly the next day? Had he no decency at all? If not, perhaps he needed a lesson.

She went outside and continued pacing the deck. The Cork and Bottle? Her eyes narrowed thoughtfully and her lips compressed purposefully. Before she could change her mind she lifted her skirts and stepped over the railing onto the dock.

The Cork and Bottle wasn't too difficult to find. All she had to do was follow the rowdy voices and the discordant singing. The tavern was filled to overflowing with revelers and cloudy with smoke.

She stood outside the door on tiptoes trying to spot Seneca. When that failed, she mustered her courage and elbowed her way into the midst of the rowdy canawllers.

"Hey, sweetheart," one drunk drawled, grabbing her around the waist and swinging her off her feet. "Not so fast there. I'll take a little of what you're offerin'."

She gave his shin the sharp edge of her heel then jammed her elbow into his porky stomach.

"Damn hell, wha'dja do that for?" he sputtered.

"Cause that's all I'm offering," she retorted, breaking away from him. His friends hooted and howled

165

with laughter at the doubled-over fool. She didn't care. She ploughed her way into the center of the room.

"Wonder who she's goin' after," one of them said. "Don't envy the poor bastard."

She didn't stop, nor did she have to. She'd attracted the attention of those around her, and some of them recognized her as Seneca's passenger. Seeing the fierce scowl on her face they stepped aside, and a path open, up directly to his table.

He was drinking again, a half-full bottle at his elbow, playing some card game. A frizzy-haired doxy was sitting on his lap and running one blood-red talon around his ear.

Everyone around the table stopped talking and looked up at her expectantly, everyone except Seneca, who turned his head to whisper in his lady-friend's ear. Emily relieved one of the men of a full tankard of ale and upended it over the lovebirds' heads.

Seneca jumped to his feet, dumping the lady into the next man's lap. "What the friggin' hell . . . ," he roared, spinning around. His rage was choked aborning when he saw who stood there. "Emily." He might have been thirteen for the way his voice changed registers.

She tossed the empty stein to the floor. "You vile snake. You lower than the low. How can you call yourself a man? You're nothing but a rotten coward. You're sick and you're depraved and this . . . this . . . floozie is all you deserve. When I think what I . . . we . . . and then to find you here with . . ."

She swung her hand and for the second time slapped Seneca's face. But this time she felt no fear or remorse for having done it. She stabbed her finger at his stunned face. "You ever come near me again and, so help me, I'll . . . I'll . . . Aaagghhh!"

Unable to think of a dire enough threat, she spun on her heels and shoved her way out. She heard him calling her name, but not for anything did she care to hear what he had to say.

As soon as she cleared the tavern door, she quickened her steps through the busy street back the way she'd come. So she wasn't good enough, huh? He had to go find a more experienced woman, and not even twenty-four hours after holding her. She hated him. And she despised herself for the stupid, naive fool she'd been.

"Emily!"

And she had a thing or two to say to Elijah, as well. All that nonsense about Seneca's sterling character and his poor unfortunate past. And she had swallowed it! She wanted to spit up. Belinda, whoever she was, made the smartest move of her life when she dumped him.

"Goddaaammit, Emileeee! Will you wait a minute?"

She lifted her skirts and ran, angry tears blurring her vision. Pig. Lecher. Slime. User of women. She turned toward the dock and fled down the short flight of stairs. On the bottom step she slipped on the mud and wrenched her ankle. Pain shot up her leg, making her knees buckle. Grabbing the rough railing, she went to the ground. At that same second a shot cracked through the air, and wood splinters flew from the railing by her hand. Had she been standing . . .

She didn't panic, simply threw herself flat against the wet ground. Her heart was beating frantically and her breathing was harsh and ragged. Was this how it would end then, with her looking at the moss-coated face of a rock, smelling the damp pungent earth?

"Emily."

Seneca. "Stay back!" she cried. "Someone just shot at me."

Seneca took the stairs three at a leap and leaned over her. "Are you hurt? Did he hit you?"

"No. I . . . I turned my ankle and fell just when he shot. I'm okay."

"Then let's get the hell out of here." He lifted her and led her back toward the boat. She cried out in pain when she put her weight on her twisted ankle. As if she weighed no more than a child, he scooped her up in his arms and ran for the protection of the nearest building, a small shed that held several rowboats and canoes for excursion use on the canal.

"Wait here. I'm going to see who that is."

"No. Don't go out there," she protested, grabbing his arm.

"Just stay here this time. I'm going to find out why that man is after you. And I don't understand what in hell you're doing out here in the first place."

He stuck his head around the side of the building. Immediately another shot sounded. The bullet ricochetted off a rock close by. He jerked back, scowling at Emily.

"Don't glare at me," she spat at him. "Of all the people in the world, you're the last who should be indignant at my actions. You've the morals of an alley cat. And I didn't ask you to get involved in this, so spare me any lectures."

Whoever was shooting apparently meant to finish the task that night, for Emily heard them coming down the steps and over the wet grass. They spoke in hushed tones. She couldn't make out what they said. She looked at Seneca, his familiar tough features a comfort in the dark.

Seneca whispered for her to follow his lead, and he silently reached up and removed two oars from the overhead rack, one for each of them. She moved to one side of the door, giving him room to move on the other, and when he motioned to her to say something, she gave a little cry.

The two men outside reacted as expected and burst into the shed. Before their eyes could adjust to the darkness, Seneca brought the oar down over one man's arm, and Emily smashed hers over the other's head. The man she hit, the shorter of the two, turned on her, bringing up his pistol.

Seneca dived at the man, catching him at the knees and knocking him over backward and out the door. She heard a snap and winced, knowing the man's knee had given way. The other man stirred, the bald one, reaching for the gun Seneca had knocked from his hand, but Emily was faster. She snatched the weapon from the floor and leveled it at her attacker. Without blinking, he laughed at her then and fled out the door.

"Dammit, Emily," Seneca growled, gaining his feet. "Why'd you let him escape?"

"I couldn't shoot him," she said, giving Seneca the gun.

"Keep it and see if you can get back to the boat in one piece. Send Elijah to me. And for Chrissake, stay there."

"You want me to go all that way by myself?"

Seneca looked from her to the man who was moaning and clutching his broken leg. He sighed in exasperation.

"I suppose he can't get very far. Come on."

Emily watched from the boat as Seneca and Elijah went back to collect the injured man and turn him over to the local police. She snuggled the kitten into her neck, running her chin over its furry little head.

"Looks like I'll be taking you to Rochester myself,

little one. If I live long enough to get there." And if the killers didn't get her, Seneca probably would. She'd never seen him angrier than when he'd deposited her on the deck of the boat. She shook her head in bewilderment. Why was it that his temper seemed to make her own wilt? She had just as much right as he to be annoyed, yet she couldn't hold on to her indignation after he'd risked his own life to save hers.

She put the kitten down and opened her trunk. She took out her nightdress and laid it over the edge of the bed, then stripped off her wet, muddy clothes. She poured water into the wash basin. She'd tolerate his temper until they reached Rochester, she'd put up with his rotten disposition, but if he thought for one minute that she'd welcome his attentions again after what he'd done, he'd very quickly learn differently. She knew what sort of man he was now, and no matter how her heart might be breaking because she still wanted him, he was not going to worm his way back into her life.

"I have to rest, Simon. Jes' for a minute."

"No time now," the guide said. "we're almost there. Another mile, that's all, then we cross the river."

"Hear, Mara? One more mile. You can do it. Give me de babe, I'll carry 'im."

"Oh, Simon, I's so tired."

"Come," the guide urged. "They're not far behind us."

Timothy Dawkins took Mara's hand and kept her with him. It had all gone wrong somewhere along the way. These people should have been safely across the border by now, and here they were instead, struggling to make the last miles into Canada

170

with slavers hot on their trail.

Elijah must have slipped up this time. Elijah, who never made a mistake, had picked up a tail when he delivered these runaways into his hands, a tail Tim hadn't been able to shake off, no matter what he tried.

"As soon as you cross the river," he said, encouraging the young woman at his side, "you'll be safe. You'll all be safe, you, your husband, and your baby. You'll be able to start all over again."

"Can't we please rest," Mara pleaded, so exhausted she couldn't even get excited over freedom.

"Just a little farther, ma-am. You don't want them slavers to latch on to your babe, do you?"

She looked over her shoulder at her husband and son, wondering why the world had to be such an awful place to live in. Would her tiny son, so innocent, so precious to her, have to live with the same anger and fear that was her constant companion?

"Keep going, Mara, keep going," Simon ordered sternly. "You make your feet move."

At Fisher's Point on the St. Lawrence River a lone woman waited. What a wretched week she'd spent. Already she'd dodged three slavers. It seemed some man with a pocket full of money, someone named Ryker, had hired a small army to break the underground system in New York. Slavers were everywhere, and they were some of the nastiest men she'd ever seen.

She shifted her weight and rubbed her arms to warm herself. Albany would have been warmer. How would she survive without Albany, without being able to sneak an occasional look at Elijah? At least seeing him and knowing he was well was a certain amount of comfort. Now she was deprived of even that.

But with the infiltration of slave commissioners

into their network, the entire system had to be reorganized. Old routes were abandoned, some of their best guides retired, at least for a while, others relocated. Everything was different.

The group she worked with had sent her into Canada. They were not about to risk the capture and imprisonment of the Princess. That would set the program back years. She had become too valuable and too much of a heroine. For the time being her responsibility was to escort the crossovers into Canada and set them up in adequate quarters. No mean task, that, when the border was crowded to overflowing with refugees from the south.

An owl hooted, then hooted again in a prearranged signal. Bekka scanned the opposite riverbank, spotting the flicker of light from a match through the wisps of fog rising from the water. She signaled back, then launched the rowboat, pulling the oars in long slow strokes through the water.

On the other bank of the river Tim caught the rope and pulled the boat up onto the sandy bank, helping Bekka onto dry ground.

"We must hurry," he said urgently. "Three men are following not far behind."

"Who do we have?" she asked, nodding her understanding. "A young couple with a baby. Simon and Mara Washington."

Bekka's brows rose in a baffled frown, but she said nothing. Elijah had helped a couple with a baby, but unfortunately, there were dozens of such young families seeking freedom. This family could be any one of them. She'd ask them later.

"Let's get them in the boat."

Mara was weeping quietly, mopping her tears on the baby's blanket. Simon held her close, guiding her down the steep bank and into the boat. He put her in the back of the boat and took his place by the oars.

"Thank you, mister," he said.

Distant voices penetrated the forest. Bekka got in the boat. "Perhaps you better come with us."

Tim shrugged. "They can do nothing to me without proof. You're taking that with you." He shoved the boat into the water, holding up a hand in silent salute. "Stay in the fog."

Bekka sat in the bow, acting as Simon's eyes. As tired as Simon was himself, he put his shoulders into rowing. Soon they were out in the middle of the wide river, surrounded by low-lying ribbons of fog. Safe.

Safe. But the hard part had just begun. "I'll take you to a place where you can rest up for a few days. Do you have any money?"

"We have three dollars," Simon said.

She sighed. It was always the same. But then, where were slaves supposed to get any money? Three dollars. How long could they get by on that?

The long barracks, crudely constructed and fitted out with rows of cots around one coal stove, gave little protection against the cold northern night. Mara's hand went into Simon's.

Children, Bekka thought. "Come, here are two together. Sit down. You've set out on a course that will change your lives forever. But this thing called freedom, it is not easy. You can stay here for two weeks only. That isn't a long time, but we can't support you forever. We expect you to find work and find a place to live." The last she directed at Simon.

"Last year," she went on, "we had a young man here who seemed to feel, after weeks of struggle to get this far, that we were responsible for feeding and housing him. He saw no reason to find work. When his stay at the barracks was terminated he panicked and began stealing from his own people. He went down from there until he was arrested for breaking into a grocery store in town. I tell you this because that sort of behavior does none of us any good, and because your lives will be only as pleasant as you make them. Be ambitious, work hard, go after what you want, but be patient. Success does not come overnight, but with slow and steady work."

"How do I find work?" Simon asked.

Bekka smiled. This one would be all right. "Mrs. Baron, one of our ladies, comes each morning with a list of available positions. She also talks with newcomers about what they are experienced at and what types of employment are available to them, and where. You may need to travel yet farther to find your special place."

"Don't worry about us," Simon said confidently. I'm a free man now, and my wife and son are with me. I'll make a good life for us."

"Yes," Bekka nodded. "I believe you will."

Bekka trudged across the muddy road to the office she used as her bunkhouse during the evenings. The little stove in the corner was still hot and the coffee pot half full. She stoked the fire and warmed the coffee. She poured a mugfull and took it with her to the window.

Clouds covered the sky, hiding the moon, but it was up there somewhere, and perhaps Elijah could see it from where he was.

I'm a free man now, and my wife and son are with me. My wife and son are with me. My wife and son . . .

Copious tears filled her eyes and scorched down her ebony cheeks. She closed her eyes but she couldn't stop their flow. Her fist clenched over the necklace she wore, an unusual disk carved of bone.

The night she received it was the night she had

birthed, through hours of agony, Elijah's son. What joy she'd felt when Hannah had placed the baby in her arms. A fire had flickered in the stone fireplace, bathing the room in warmth and light, and when Elijah had come in to see the baby and her, the flames seemed to leap into his eyes. Never had she seen such love and pride on the face of her man. That was the night he vowed that one day they'd be free, that the child he held in his big capable hands would not know a life of bondage.

That was the night he placed the necklace over her head and an identical one over his. And into her hand he placed a third for the baby when he was older.

"This is a token of my promise to you, Bekka. One day we will live as we were intended to live, in freedom and peace, with pride and dignity. One day soon."

Elijah had been good for his word. He had given them freedom, maybe not as he had intended, maybe not at the same time, but he was free and so was she. And Tyler would be free too, if she hadn't been so irresponsible. If she'd just kept him with her that night instead of hiding him in that building. He was so little then, too young to be able to take care of himself.

He was eight years old now. He'd be taller. She tried to conjure up an image of him, but none would come. Instead she saw the ugly laughing face of the overseer where she'd grown up, she saw him whipping the children who couldn't keep up with their work, she saw their little faces cut and bruised from swift calloused backhands. Was Tyler suffering such brutality even now? The thought was as painful as a hot knife in her heart.

How she longed for the shelter of Elijah's arms! How she wished she could lose herself in his passion and wipe away for just an hour the awful pain she lived with constantly. But as long as Tyler was lost to her, so was Elijah. It would kill her to see his disappointment in her, his pain at losing his son, the hatred that would grow within him for her because she had let him down. She was a coward, but she could not face him without Tyler.

Chapter 11

Smoke curled around his head from the slender cigar. He smoked not so much because he liked smoking but because the smoke tended to repel the mosquitoes. He sat at the tiller, waiting for the long night to pass.

Seneca and Elijah had turned the man with the broken leg over to the local sheriff. Then they had searched the town for the other man, but they had not found him. The man in captivity had refused to talk, insisting that everyone had made a mistake and that he had only been trying to help the woman. The sheriff had promised to hold him for two weeks for disturbing the peace in order to give Seneca time to get Emily away—just in case. And so they had left Syracuse and were on their way to Rochester.

Seneca wasn't sure how he felt about taking Emily home with him. Perhaps he should do as she suggested and get a room for her at the hotel or a boardinghouse. After tonight's calamity she'd hardly be likely to feel friendly toward any family of his.

"Gonna turn in now, bossman," Elijah said, strolling back to stand by his friend. "Wake me if you need be spelled."

"Nah. In ten miles or so we hit fairly straight going. I'll get some shut-eye then."

"Seneca, I . . . ah . . . well, I'd like to know . . ."

"What, Elijah?" he said shortly.

"It's Emily. I mean I . . . I know you and Emily . . . eh . . . last night . . ."

"Yeah, and?" His tone was brusk, impatient.

Elijah stood taller. "I want to ask what your intentions are."

Seneca laughed. "My intentions? My intentions? My God, you sound like her father."

"She doesn't have a father now, does she? She has no one to watch out for her. You've compromised a fine young lady. I want to know what you're going to do about it."

"Why do anything? It's not as if she was opposed to the idea. I didn't take her against her will."

Elijah turned away. "I see. She's in love with you."

"I didn't ask for that. I never wanted it."

"But you have it."

"So what do you want, that I should marry her and make both of us miserable. I'm not a marryin' kind of man."

"Why assume you'll be miserable?"

"Besides, she hates me now. You didn't see her tonight. She was . . ." He shook his head and flicked the cigar into the canal.

"You mean because she found your little girlfriend sitting on your lap? You think her anger was unreasonable?"

"You know Hattie. She was in my lap before I knew it. She'd no more sat down than Emily came storming into the room."

"Nevertheless, you showed remarkably poor manners in avoiding Emily all day. She didn't know what to make of your behavior."

"I needed to think."

"And what have you decided?"

Seneca stood and paced restlessly back and forth

by the tiller, running his fingers agitatedly through his hair. What had he decided?

"I just don't know. Last night was a big mistake. I should never have let it go that far."

Elijah didn't have to ask why he had. He could sense the tension, the sparks of awareness that arced between them whenever they were close. "I suppose you only realized that the first thing this morning."

"I'm just a man, Elijah. Dammit, I'm as susceptible to a beautiful woman as the next man."

"And that's all she is, just a beautiful women?"

"That's all she can be. I don't want this again. I won't permit it. I just can't."

"Okay," Elijah responded, holding up a quieting hand. "No need to blow your stack. I just wanted you to think about what you are doing. Well, I'm off to bed."

Emily rolled over and pulled the pillow over her head. She didn't want to hear anymore. She didn't want to hear what she'd just heard, even though she suspected the truth of it already. Hadn't Elijah said as much? Still, she was surprised at how much it hurt to hear Seneca admit it.

Well, she'd have to be tougher than this if she was to go on with this trip. She couldn't be weeping and wailing because the mean man had broken her heart. That would make everyone uncomfortable, including herself. Besides which, she did have some pride. More pride than to let him think he mattered to her any more than she mattered to him.

A slow feline smile curved the corners of her mouth as a plan took shape. He might not like it, but that was all the better. What was more, he needed it. Finally, with a calmer spirit, she was able to sleep.

Seneca, however, lit another cigar. He was sure he'd be up the rest of the night. He still hadn't

179

calmed down from that little episode with the gunmen. For a moment he had thought Emily had been killed. When he heard that shot and saw her lying in the mud his heart had jumped into his throat, cutting off his breath. It was back where it was supposed to be now, but his nerves were still strung tighter than a banjo string.

What he didn't need right now was Elijah's moralizing. Did the blasted man think he had no feelings? He was as sorry as hell about what had happened the night before. He must have been insane.

Insane? He thought about what she'd looked like in his bed—naked, voluptuous, wanton. Oh yes, he'd been out of his mind, all right. Out of his mind with desire, with a need to possess that beauty, that fire, that passion. The one big problem he had to face now was how to stay away from her. Even now his body was burning and throbbing with the need of her. But stay away from her he must. From now on she was off limits. He must rout those images, those memories, from his mind. Treat her like a sister.

And if that didn't work he'd remember Belinda. Recalling her treachery would cool his ardor, that and remembering the long black months of hell, physical and mental. How he'd hated himself then for the choice he'd made, the ugly scars he was certain to bear all his life, the weakness in his character that still wanted to believe in Belinda's goodness and love.

He'd made a fool of himself, begging her to forgive him, pleading with her to come back to him. Such was his love for her that he would have done anything for her. He just couldn't wipe away his scars. And she couldn't stand them. After six months of humiliating himself trying to win her back he had given up.

He'd given up on love, he'd given up his home, his family, his work. He'd given up his entire life in Rochester. He'd gone to Albany to start over, to build a whole new life.

He had that life now, a life he enjoyed, a successful life, a good life. What an absolute fool he would be to let some woman do again to him what Belinda did. An absolute fool.

He had locked off the tiller and was about to doze off when he heard her cry. He came out of his chair as if he'd been shot. Not a second later Elijah was out the door.

"Another nightmare," Seneca said unnecessarily. "I'll see to her. Go back to bed."

"Seneca, wait," Elijah said quietly but urgently, his eyes squinting to find something he'd spotted on the towpath behind them.

"We aren't alone, I gather," Seneca said, not turning.

"I can't spot him now, but I'm sure he's there. I'm going ashore. Don't let on. Just . . . go see about Emily."

Armed with a knife only, Elijah lowered himself quietly over the canal side of the boat into the dark water where he waited for the boat and its barge to pass.

Seneca let him to it. If anyone could catch the man Elijah could. He turned the knob and stepped down into his cabin. Emily cried out again, thrashing from side to side, unable to wake herself from her nightmare. He sat on the edge of the bunk and shook her shoulders.

"Emily . . ."

"No, don't. No!"

"Emily, wake up. You're dreaming."

She went very still and her eyes snapped open. "Seneca?"

181

"Yes. You're okay. It was all a dream."

She shuddered, staring at him as if she'd never seen him before. He gave her another little shake.

"Emily, are you awake?"

She threw her arms around him and pressed her face into his chest. He could feel her racing heart, her ragged breathing. She'd been terrified, that much was evident. And no wonder she was having nightmares, after all she'd been through.

"Easy, sweetheart."

"He's dead, isn't he? Peter's dead. And Uncle Joe?"

"Yes. They're dead."

"I was too late. I couldn't get to them in time."

"Emily, honey, you were dreaming. Peter's been dead for weeks now."

"Weeks?" She put a hand to her furrowed brow. "Yes, yes, I remember. Just a dream."

She was fully awake, but the reaction set in and she began to shiver and tremble. Seneca pulled a blanket around her shoulders then stood for a minute and poured her a measure of whiskey.

"Drink this. It will calm your nerves."

She took a sip and immediately choked. He kept at her until she'd finished all of it, and only then did he take her back into his arms. She remained there until her shaking subsided, then lifted her head and looked into his eyes.

"Thank you. You always seem to be here when I need you." She closed her eyes and gave a brief shudder. "It was so real this time."

"Do you want to talk about it? Maybe you can remember some details that you couldn't remember before."

She drew a deep breath and exhaled. "Well, this time I do remember one of them spoke with a deep Southern drawl. 'Y'all get back here, now,' he yelled.

Then he ordered the men with him to stop us, and how didn't matter, because he didn't want us blabbing what we heard. One of the men didn't think a woman and a kid could cause them any harm, but the man with the Southern accent insisted. He said he was the one who'd have to face the judge."

"Face the judge? Those were his words?"

"It was only a dream, Seneca."

"But it could have sprung from what you actually heard in Albany. Can you think of anything else?"

"No. I'd rather forget the whole thing."

"Emily . . ." he urged, wanting her to go on, to make herself remember, but he bit back the words. She'd endured enough terror for one night. "It's all right. Go back to sleep."

"Can you stay with me for a little while. Until I fall asleep?"

"I don't know, Emily," he said reluctantly.

"Oh, yes, I forgot. Sorry. I wouldn't want you to make another mistake." She pulled away and lay down. "Goodnight, Seneca."

He stood and returned the empty glass to the bureau. "You'll be okay, then?"

"Certainly. It was only a dream. Goodnight."

She turned away and huddled under the blankets. She looked so small to Seneca, so helpless, so vulnerable. Hell, she *was* vulnerable. Save for that slimy step that caused her to fall, she'd be dead. He'd never have another chance to hold and comfort her, to laugh with her and fight with her, to make love with her.

"Emily," he said huskily, sitting on the side of the bed. "Emily, if you want . . ."

"No, that's all right," she answered, pushing herself up to sit facing him. "Actually I'd prefer to talk for a few minutes. About last night."

"Emily, I didn't . . ."

"No, wait. let me say what I need to say first. You see, I don't know how you feel about me, but the last thing I want is to hurt you. I told you that I care very much for you and I do. And last night was a very special time for me." He was looking distinctly uncomfortable, and she forced back the grin that threatened to ruin her ploy.

"About last night," Seneca interrupted.

"About last night," she interrupted him. "I think we both better try to forget it. It really was a mistake. I'm so sorry if I've led you to believe anything would come of our relationship. I'm just not at all sure that it can work between us. Not sure at all. Please, don't be embarrassed or feel rejected or anything like that. You gave me a beautiful night, one I'll remember with fondness for years. I'm sure very few women have had the privilege of initiation at the hands of so fine a lover."

She could almost feel remorse at the stunned and baffled expression on his face. Almost. "Please, don't look like that," she said sadly, laying her hand along the side of his jaw. "See there, I've already hurt you."

"A night you'll remember with *fondness? Initiation?!*" he spat, slinging her hand away.

"Now Seneca," she placated, backing out of reach. "I know you want to punish me and make me hurt too, but you don't have to save face with me. I think no less of you for last night."

"Save face?" His eyes darkened even more than usual in his anger.

"Can't you calmly accept the way things are without going all . . . male on me." Her voice took on a harder tone. "Why is it men think they own every woman they take to bed. How high would that number be for you, Seneca? I won't be owned. I'm not ready for any permanent commitment."

His expression turned inscrutable. "So you were

184

just spreading your wings, eh? Free of your father's morals and now your uncle's, you've decided to have a taste of the forbidden."

Dirty player. "Why so hostile? Were you expecting me to marry you when we reach Rochester? Is that what last night was? A trap to get me down the aisle? Seneca, I gave you credit for more finesse than that."

"It wasn't like that. I have no intention of marrying you," he blustered.

"Then where's the problem? She smiled coyly. "We agree after all. I was experimenting, and you were just using me."

"Dammit, Emily. You're twisting everything around."

"Then explain it to me," she requested quietly.

"You have it all wrong. I wasn't using you. What happened just happened."

"You lost your head momentarily."

"Yes."

"Three times in a row?"

"No. Emily, what the hell is it with you? You're no tramp who just sleeps around."

"Have I done that?"

"No, but I don't like your attitude."

"It's the same as yours. Are you a tramp?"

"I'm a man. It's different."

"It's the height of hypocracy. Why are we arguing again?"

"Because I don't want you experimenting," he snarled.

"Only with you, you mean."

"You're damn right, that's what I mean. You're my woman and you better remember it." He strode angrily to the door, flung it open, then turned for his parting shot.

"And if I decide you're going to marry me, you

damn well will."

"Never," she shouted back.

"We'll see about that," he growled, slamming the door on her.

Her eyebrows rose in surprise, and a broad grin of delight spread across her lips. That was relatively easy, as first steps went. She wondered how long it would take for him to come back. Five minutes should be enough time for him to pop his cork.

She was brushing her hair when he returned, aware that her raised arms thrust her darker nipples against the fine weave of her nightdress. He glowered at her, although she noticed he didn't deny himself the pleasure of looking at her. She smiled knowingly.

"Excuse me," he snarled, going over to the bureau and grabbing up the bottle.

"Mind if I have just a teensy bit more before you take it away?"

"I thought you didn't drink."

"I find I have several new habits since I met you." She held up a glass, and reluctantly he poured some whiskey into it.

She leaned back against the wall behind the bed. "Um, this is good. Thanks. It's just what I need to relax me." She gave a musical laugh. "And it's just as well you're still angry with me. We both know what happens when I drink. I seem to loose all my inhibitions. Goodnight, Seneca."

She drained her glass, set it aside, then slid down into bed, knowing that his eyes followed her every move. He stood motionless, as if turned to stone, then with a low curse spun around and slammed out the door.

So much for ignoring her all day, so much for floozies on his lap, so much for tearing his precious hair out over what to do about her. And so much for wishing he'd left her in that warehouse in Albany.

Ironically, she didn't get a great deal of pleasure from taunting him, especially when her body still longed for his. But she did have her pride.

He hadn't been all bad, she reminded herself. He had come after her in time to save her life. He had been here for her when her dream returned. Was her pride really that important?

Of course it wasn't, but she couldn't permit Seneca to continue to play loose with her emotions or her body. It would do him a world of good to taste his own bitter tonic, and his character would profit with having to consider the consequences of his actions, just as everyone else must do.

She had the feeling Seneca's life was full of people he'd charmed into doing exactly as he wanted, which might have been good for his ego, but had contributed no little amount to his arrogance.

She turned over and punched her pillow into a more comfortable shape, deciding that her conscience was working overtime. He was a handsome rogue but a rogue just the same, and in a few areas she was determined to succeed with her reformation. So he could just beware.

She didn't hear him return. One minute she was alone, the next he was there, looming over her, unbuttoning his shirt.

"Seneca, what are you doing?"

He grinned out of one side of his mouth. "You're an experienced woman now. Surely you can add two and two."

"We made one mistake. Why compound it?"

"Blame it on the whiskey, blame it on the circumstances that threw us together, blame it on what the hell ever you wish, but I find I cannot stay away from you.

187

"So you're going to use me again?" She should have been infuriated, but how could she be when the sight of his broad, hard-muscled chest sent her pulse racing, when the bold evidence of his desire for her sent heat rushing through her body and settling between her thighs.

His lips tightened in annoyance. "If that's how you want to see it, then fine, but you'll use me, too. I'll show you pleasures you never dreamed of. Before I'm finished with you, you'll be as experienced as the best of them."

"The best of whom?" What an idiotic question, but she couldn't think straight when he was kicking off his boots and unbuckling his belt. "Look, you're going to be sorry about this in the morning."

He nodded agreement. "But you see, it's very late at night, I'm tired, I've had a few drinks, my good sense is gone, and my resistance is at it's lowest. This is not the ideal time to flaunt your delightful attributes in front of insanely hungry eyes."

"Insanely hungry?" she parroted, watching the slow deliberate movement of his hands as he unfastened his trousers. Unconsciously she ran the tip of her tongue over suddenly dry lips.

"Look at you. You are a witch sent to drive me out of my mind, to lure me into your clutches where you'll rob me of my will, where I'll become so addicted to you I won't be able to live without you."

"I think you had better leave."

"You lips say that, but your body, your beautiful body tells me to stay, angel. Your body wants mine as much as mine wants yours. We're captives to our flesh, Emily, you're bound to me, me to you.

"Nonsense. I won't be . . . I won't be owned," she said breathlessly.

"Don't be afraid of it. It's painless, really, as long as we're together."

188

"Like you and your whiskey?"

"You impudent brat," he growled and wrestled her until he captured her beneath him on the bunk. "I don't know about the whiskey, but it is true with you. And if I'm going to suffer, I'll make sure you do too."

"I thought you said it wouldn't hurt."

His lips brushed hers lightly. He inhaled the fresh clean fragrance of her. "No. No pain, just the sweet agony of wanting and the pleasure of having."

His kiss was curiously gently, as if he was intent on persuading her to need him the way that he needed her. She knew that in his own way he was afraid of her, he'd want her commitment before admitting to his. She could understand his reluctance, but she was wary herself after his recent demonstration of fickle-mindedness.

Yet she loved him and she wanted him, and not for any brief and passing relationship. She wanted him for all time. So if a physical bondage was all they could have for now, she'd do her best to make it one neither of them could break free of.

She wrapped her arms around his neck, tunneling her fingers into his thick black hair and holding his lips to hers. She opened her mouth to his questing tongue, joining him in his passionate explorations.

He lifted his head after long moments, his eyes glazed with desire. "Do you really want this? Please say you do, that you're not leading me on."

"I don't want just *this*, I want this with *you*. Make love to me, Seneca. Be my pirate tonight and make me your woman, and don't treat me like glass. I'm no longer a virgin."

"Emily," he groaned, taking her mouth in a savage kiss. "No other woman has ever made me feel like you do. I want to become part of you and make you part of me. Can you feel any of that?"

"Yes, I can. I don't know why you're waiting." But she did. He wanted her to prove she wanted him. He didn't want to be accused of using her. He wanted her active and willing participation.

She propelled him to his back and leaned over him. "You are much too slow," she accused teasingly.

"Are you in a hurry?" he chuckled.

"I think we still have too many clothes on," she drawled, running her fingers under the loosened top of his trousers. "Get rid of these."

"And what of this?" he asked, fingering the mounds under the lace-trimmed gown.

"I do find it stifling. Shall I remove it?"

"Why not permit me," he said silkily.

As before, when they came together, flesh to flesh, their passion for each other exploded into an unbridled frenzy of need. Seneca, a man who took pride in his self-control, was helpless to hold back the tides of his desire for the eager womanly body he held in his arms. Emily, always a proper and demure lady, was stripped of her restraint and a wild wanton whose body arched and writhed in demand of the fulfillment only he could bestow.

"Torment me next time if you must, but not now. Please, Seneca, take me."

He rolled her over until she was stretched out full length on top of him. He cupped her face in his big hands. "You're so fair against my dark skin, your hair golden white against mine. You're so delicate I think I could snap you in two with my bare hands."

"Do you want to?"

"You'd run if you knew what I'd like to do."

"I'm not running anywhere. Please, Seneca," she pleaded, urging him with little movements of her body.

"What is it you want, Emily? Tell me." So slender. His hands almost spanned her waist. He gripped her hard and lifted her until he could bury his face between her full rounded breasts.

"God, Emily, I'm in heaven."

"Please. You're tormenting me."

His tongue and teeth found the dark engorged tip of her breast and teased, then his mouth drew the nipple in and suckled hard on the sensitive bud. She cried out in pleasurable agony, in sweet torment, as he moved from one yearning breast to another.

Her thighs fell apart and she straddled his lean hips. She wanted closer, she wanted to become one with him, but he held back. He wouldn't take her. Why wouldn't he take her? She needed him, her body cried for him, she hurt for him.

Sanity spun away from her. Her fingers closed over his shoulders, leaving tiny curved marks in his skin. He was driving her mad with need until she couldn't wait any longer. She threw all her preconceived ideas to the wind and took him, impaling herself on the proud shaft of his body.

Her head went back at the relief and pleasure of his body within her. How odd, she thought fleetingly, that men and women were created to crave each other so much. Literature was full of references to the unquenchable thirst of some for the act of procreation. Nature's way to insure the future of the species.

As before the mere thought of taking his seed into her body caused a delicious flowering deep inside her, an opening in welcome of his fullness.

Seneca groaned as his own body responded to hers, convulsing and thrusting upward. He clamped his hands on her hips, holding her locked against him, burying himself completely in the hot silken depths of her.

Their gazes met and locked as their bodies had done, and Emily knew how right Seneca's words were. This dark obsession between them was not going to be denied as long as they were together. Their bodies, to spite their minds, knew their mates. Their bodies needed no other reason to seek each other out. Pride, wariness, right or wrong, all ceased to exist in the face of passion's call.

"Seneca, Seneca."

"I know, angel, I know. Me, too."

Their passion rose on a swift moving tide, lifting them, rocking them, and finally engulfing them in the wondrous driving power of that final swell to the crest of fulfillment.

He held her, a precious creature in his arms, as they slowly drifted back to calm waters. He turned his head and looked into her face. Her skin was dewy and touched with vital color, her eyes closed as if unable any longer to bear the weight of her long, thick lashes. They were incredibly dark for one so fair.

Through half-closed eyes he regarded her nose, beautifully formed with just the faintest upward turn at the tip, her high and perfectly rounded cheekbones, her feminine chin that could jut forward with determination, her lips—full, pink, bowed in a perpetual smile except when she was annoyed with him. She was exquisite. She was perfection. She was all that Belinda had been and much more. She was a woman, kind, caring, compassionate, and with a passion that equaled his own.

He had not found that in Belinda. Belinda fussed about her hair, her makeup, her gowns. She preferred not to be touched unless she wanted a favor from him, or some pretty bauble. Then she could play her part well. He had been indulgently amused at her reluctance, so sure he could teach her to be the kind of woman he needed. How arrogant he had been in his youth!

He dropped a kiss onto Emily's head and closed his eyes. He would take her home with him. He could do no less without offending her. How his family would react he had no idea. But he wasn't letting her go. Not now. Not yet.

Chapter 12

By dawn Elijah had still not returned. Seneca prowled the deck of the boat, restless, concerned. Emily brought a cup of freshly brewed coffee.

"Do you think he's in trouble?"

"I think I need to find out." He barked out an order for the hoggee to guide the boat in to the edge of the canal wall. Seneca leaped to the bank and after a brief conference with Cob set off in search of Elijah.

Again she was left alone on the boat. She wondered if they made a habit of deserting ship. And did they expect her to play steerman again? Already Cob was leading the team forward. But apparently the tiller was set to accommodate the straight line of the canal and needed no handling. She would, however, keep her eyes open.

And so she did, for two hours, while she waited and watched for Seneca's return. Finally she spotted the two men making their way toward them. She suspected nothing until they were near the boat, and then she saw the blood-soaked shirt wrapped around Seneca's forearm.

"Now what have you done to yourself?" she exclaimed, helping him over the side and into the boat.

"It's nothing," he groused, giving her supporting

shoulder a brief hug just as his knees started to buckle.

"Huh. A *nothing* doesn't bleed like a stuck pig. What happened?"

"A couple slavers ambushed Elijah, had him tied up in the back of a wagon. I got a little careless when I jumped them."

She led him to the cabin and insisted he sit down on the edge of the bed. He must have been careless. She'd seen him fight before and knew that not many could get the better of him. Very slowly she unwrapped the wound, careful not to start the bleeding all over again.

"Oh, Seneca," she cried mournfully. "This is bad. You'll need a doctor."

"Where do you think I can find one out here?" he replied." Can you fix it?"

"Me?"

"Sure. All woman can sew. It's simple."

"Is it? Seneca, I have to clean this or it will become infected. Do you have any medications?"

"Well, not much if any. Elijah, do you . . "

"I'll get it, bossman, sir."

"What happened out there? Why did he leave the boat in the first place?"

"He saw someone following us last night and went to investigate."

"Oh good. Now I feel responsible."

"So you can pay your debt by sewing my arm together. And be neat about it. I don't relish another scar."

"Then you should be more careful. This is deep. You're lucky you didn't sever an artery."

He laughed humorlessly. "But I got Elijah. Those vermin think they can grab just anybody whose skin is brown. God, now more than ever, I mean to fight them. They didn't even care if he was a free man or not. They wanted him back in chains."

"How can they do that and get away with it? Doesn't the law . . . "

"The law won't interfere. Hell, half those men are duly sworn deputies from the South, just carrying out their orders.

"But some aren't?"

"Some aren't," he agreed, nodding seriously. "Some are men like Ryker, men who trade in human flesh."

"What do you mean?"

"They run breeding farms, they capture these runaways with no interest in returning them to the men who claim to own them. The poor men and women are bred like animals and worked from dawn to dusk in some mill or mine or whatever. Some slavers actually return the slaves for a fat fee; some just keep them; all are parasites who feed on human misery."

"You said once that Ryker was after you."

"No doubt about it. I busted up one of his operations, a big one, and I'll do it again, given any chance at all. At least he has one less man on his payroll."

"Meaning?"

"One less, that's all."

"You killed one of those men?"

"It couldn't be helped."

"But won't the law be after you then?"

"No. The second man never saw my face. He doesn't know what happened."

"So the bald-headed man . . ."

"These men were a different lot."

Elijah returned with an assortment of paraphernalia — scissors, needles and thread, clean bandages.

"No antiseptic or ointment, I'm afraid. Can you do with some whiskey?"

"We'll have to. I'll need a pan of water. It should be hot by now."

Elijah fetched it for her, then stood by and braced Seneca's arm as she cleaned the wound with soap and water then poured a good measure of whiskey over it.

"Jeezzuss, woman. That smarts."

"I have more powders if you'd like some, for the pain . . ."

"Later, if it gets bad."

"You're going to prove how tough you are?" she said, grinning as she threaded the needle with the heaviest thread she had.

"No, I don't expect this is going to be much fun. It hurts like hell already. I'll just put a little of that whiskey on the inside as well as the outside." He tipped the bottle and swallowed three long draughts, wincing as he handed the bottle back to Elijah.

"As I see it, you need at least six stitches, eight to minimize scarring. Which do you want?"

"Eight. I want to be beautiful for you."

By the time four neat little stitches had been tied off, heavy beads of perspiration stood out on his forehead and his skin had taken on a sickly green hue. She stopped and took a deep breath and, noticing his palor, gave him the whiskey bottle again.

"Save me a drink, please," she said dryly. "It won't be long now. I'm getting better with each one."

The remaining four stitches were taken briskly, efficiently, and confidently, Emily having learned that to hesitate, to work slowly, caused him more pain, not less. She gave him a kiss when she finished wrapping a clean bandage over the wound. She pulled off his boots and pushed him back on the bed, draping a quilt over him.

"Sleep now."

"I have work . . ."

"No work. You lift as much as a pan of water with that arm and you'll tear out the stitches. And much as we tried to clean it, you could still end up with an infection, especially if you get it wet in the canal."

"Emily's the boss this time, sir," Elijah concurred. "You have a day to sleep away in bed. Emily and I can handle anything that comes up between here and Rochester."

He seemed to sink into the mattress. "Okay, you win. And thanks. I do seem to be lightheaded."

"Drunk, more than likely," Emily muttered.

He laughed tiredly. "Yes, preacher. Come see me after a while. I'll need some tender loving care, and lunch. And your company."

"And in that order, no doubt."

Rochester came into view the next evening, and for the first time Emily was happy to be getting off the boat. Seneca had proved to be a difficult patient, demanding her constant attention.

She knew he was doing it to goad her. He had no real reason to stay in bed past the first day, so he sat up on deck and ordered her about. *Coffee, please. How soon is lunch? Would you cut my hair? Can you put a coat of oil on my boots?"* It went on and on until she wanted to tip him into the blasted canal, injured arm and all.

Her trunk was packed and waiting when the boat was docked, and Elijah hefted it and Seneca's satchel onto the dock. He swung her over the side and stood her beside her belongings.

"I will see you again?" she asked, realizing he was not coming with them.

"Yes, Miss Emily," he said, clutching his hat at his waist. "I ain't never far from de bossman, usually. But I be gone for a week or two."

"Another quest?"

"Yes'm." His voice dropped. "Down Pennsylvania way into West Virginia. The men that ambushed me mentioned a mine where they have some sort of slave operation going. They made another strange comment that led me to suspect Bekka is there."

"I hope you find her. Does Seneca know where

you'll be, in case."

"He does. You'll stay with him? I'd rest easier if I knew you were with him."

"For his sake or mine?" she teased.

"Both, now I ponder it."

"God go with you, Elijah, and please don't worry about me."

"Do I have your word you won't run out on him?"

"Yes, you have it."

He bowed his head low and backed subserviently away. She turned aside, allowing him the dignity of walking away without playing such a degrading role. She looked around, wondering who was mean enough to expect such behavior of him. She saw Seneca striding toward her.

"Oh, there you are."

"Emily, this is Harley, our butler, handyman, and caretaker. Harley has the buggy across the street. Come along. He'll bring our things."

"I'm pleased to meet you, Harley," Emily offered with a smile.

Harley looked from her to Seneca and back, unable to mask his surprise quickly enough. She saw it. "Yes, miss," he replied lamely.

"Is there anything I should know, Seneca?" she asked as they made their way through the busy waterfront street to their carriage.

"Such as?"

"Such as why folks look at me as if they'd seen a ghost."

He threw her an oblique glance, his jaw muscles teasing. "I don't know why they would either."

"Hmm. For some reason, I don't believe you."

"Now, Emily, are you accusing me of being a liar? You look quite alive to me."

"You're being evasive, but never mind. I'm certain to find out in time, am I not?"

He didn't answer, just guided her into the coach

and climbed in after her, seating himself across from her.

"My family naturally will not be expecting you. Nor do most folks expect to see me with a woman in tow. I suppose it is understandable that they will show a certain amount of curiosity. Don't let it upset you."

"Your mother—will she be annoyed that I'm coming?"

"On the contrary. I think she'll be absolutely thrilled. She'd given up on me, you see?"

"In what respect?"

"Getting married, giving her grandchildren."

"Oh, I see. And she will assume that you and I . . . that we . . ."

"Would it hurt to let her believe that?"

"I don't like to deceive people, Seneca. I'm not going to marry you or anyone for quite some time."

"Even though I've compromised you?"

"In whose eyes?"

"And if you're carrying my child?"

"I'll deal with that if and when it happens."

"So you've become a loose woman? Do you plan to spread your charms near and far?" She could not discern whether he was serious or teasing.

"Haven't you? Yet if I called you a loose man, you'd laugh."

He chuckled. "You have to admit there is a difference."

"In whose eyes? But for the record, I don't intend to do any such thing. Neither do I intend to lie to your parents."

"Then we'll make it official. I am asking you now to marry me."

"And you'd choke if I accepted. It would serve you right . . ."

"Try me."

"No. When I marry, I shall marry a man I can

trust for longer than it takes him to get out of my sight."

His lips compressed. "I told you how that happened."

"And you weren't enjoying it at all?"

"All right. You shook me up. I was trying to prove to myself that I hadn't made the mistake of falling in love again."

"I see. So wanting . . . or rather *asking* me to marry you has nothing to do with that foolish state of love." Hearing it, even from her own lips, left her feeling painfully empty and alone. She might be turning the tables on him by refusing to marry him, but she still had hopes that he would come to care for her. But not for anything would she spend the remainder of her life thinking of herself as another of Seneca's mistakes.

"So you're refusing to marry me?"

"I'll have to think about it, and I won't be rushed. I don't want to make a mistake either."

"A mistake," he barked, glowering.

Oh, how the mighty had fallen. "You don't think marriage to you would be a mistake? Well, I don't care to risk it," she said without waiting for his answer. "I shall require time to make a thoughtful and prudent evaluation."

That set him off. "Fine. That's fine. I'll try to be patient while you balance the matter."

She patted his knee. "I'm sure you will, and I appreciate it." She hid the grin that wanted to pop out at his thoroughly piqued expression.

Harley returned and took his seat up top after loading their luggage in the boot. He snapped the reins and the carriage moved forward. For one brief moment she wanted to tell Seneca to take her to an hotel. The prospect of meeting his family, especially when she wasn't expected, left her feeling anxious and unsure of herself. But she stiffened her resolve.

201

The only way to learn why all Seneca's friends viewed her with such wide-eyed surprise was to look into his past. Perhaps his young sister, if she was still as forthright as she'd been earlier in her life, would reveal that secret.

Besides she wasn't through with Seneca yet. Not by a long way.

Seneca's family home took her breath away. Standing alone on a hill on the outskirts of town, its gray stone front was awash in the last red rays of the setting sun.

"My grandfather had it built when the canal came through. He correctly predicted a sharp increase in his own business."

"It's beautiful, Seneca. The gardens are lovely." Tall evergreens rose in pillars along the drive. Flowers of every hue bloomed in the beds that meandered in a free shape along the stone paths. Azaleas and rhododendron bushes circled the house.

"I'll take you on a tour tomorrow when the sun will show off the colors. Grandfather loved his gardens. There is much more in back."

She could imagine his grandfather walking through these paths with a young boy by his side, a boy whose black hair fell over his forehead, whose black eyes turned up to his as he listened to his stories and his sage advice.

She could also imagine that same man, gray and shrunken in stature, looking up to that same boy, now grown to full manhood.

"When did he die?"

"Two years ago."

"He must have loved you very much."

His black gaze snapped around to pin her with its sharpness. "Why do you say that?"

She frowned, feeling him tense, watching his eyes turn hard and inscrutable again. "What did I say now? Can't I even imagine an old man watching his grandson grow up without being scolded?"

He said nothing, just studied her speculatively in silence, his jaw working, his lips twitching as he scrutinized her discomfort.

"Forget I said that. He must have been thoroughly exasperated with you. You were undoubtedly as wretched then as you are now. We're here. Are we going in or not?" She turned away and waited mutinously for him to help her out of the carriage.

"I'm sorry, Emily. It's just that . . . well, never mind. I'm sorry, that's all. Can we at least appear to be on speaking terms for my mother's sake?"

"Seneca, I'm not totally without manners."

"I didn't mean that. Lord, why am I constantly apologizing to you?" He opened the door and stepped down. She placed her hand in his and threw him an impish grin.

"Because you are beginning to see how utterly deplorable you are? They say that change only comes by recognizing the need for it. I may reform you yet."

He groaned and lifted her down. How could one angelic-looking creature cause such havoc with his peace of mind. He felt totally out of step, yet each time he tried to get into cadence with her she changed the beat.

"Seneca!" The jubilant cry emanated from the open front door, and out hurled a mass of swirling skirts over stocking-covered legs. A wild mane of curly black hair flew out behind her.

"Seneca," she cried again and flung herself into his arms. He laughed, lifting her and swinging her in a circle. Emily couldn't suppress a smile. She had to be Marianne. Her black hair and bright black eyes were a dead giveaway. And her devil-take-appearances attitude proclaimed her Seneca's kin.

Following her out the door were his parents. Mrs. Prescott, a tall, fair woman who moved with wonderful fluid grace, and a man who, except for the gray at his temples, could have been Seneca's brother, stepped out together. Arm in arm, they watched joyously as their children greeted each other.

Emily felt a swift and sharp pang of pure envy and longing at his welcome. How lovely to be part of such a family. Seneca set Marianne on her feet and swept his mother into his arms. He shook hands with his father, but as if neither could help it, their hands pulled each other into an embrace.

Only then did Emily realize she was the object of two pairs of astounded eyes. She smiled self-consciously, vowing that Seneca was going to explain a few things. She was not imagining these looks she was receiving.

"Mother, Father, Marianne, I'd like you to meet Emily Harcourt, a friend of the McMurdies."

"Holy smokes, are we ever gonna see the fur fly," Marianne exclaimed.

"That will be enough from you, young lady," her mother reprimanded. "Welcome to our home, Emily."

"Thank you," she replied, glancing at Seneca's face. His sheepish shrug said his sister was just a crazy kid. Hers said, *Like hell . . .*

"Come into the house. You must be ready for a cup of tea," Mrs. Prescott said. "And after tea you'll have a nice hot bath. I know how restricted that boat is." Her lovely smile turned to a grimace at the thought. "How could you bear it?" She shook her head in bafflement. "Then again, Marianne loves it."

"There is a charm about the canal," she said. "But I'd dearly love a bath."

"I knew it. And I'll have Wanda press your clothes. Marianne, see that the yellow guest room is made up. And tell Wanda to prepare tea and put water to heat. Oh, and . . ."

"Mother!" Marianne complained.

"Oh, all right. I'll see to Wanda. Please, have a seat and make yourself at home. I'll be back in a minute. Oh, here come the men. Good."

Emily selected a chair, high-backed and covered with a lovely rose and beige stripe. The entire room was decorated in shades of pink and beige with accents of pale and deep green, all the shades in the exquisite fringed carpet. Fresh cut flowers were arranged in crystal bowls and vases on glowing tables and reflected in beautifully framed mirrors. A lovely crystal chandelier, suspended from the high gilt ceiling, refracted the colors of the sunset streaming through the tall windows.

"Oh, so we're to be permitted to sit in the parlor, are we?" Mr. Prescott said, laughing as he and Seneca took sets around the tea table. "You are very honored," he said to Emily.

Blue. His eyes were deep blue, not black like Seneca's.

"I . . . ah . . . thank you." She threw Seneca a questioning glance.

"We are seldom permitted to enjoy this room," Seneca explained.

"It is reserved for special occasions and special guests."

Marianne came bounding down the stairs and joined them, sitting on the sofa beside Seneca.

"Emily brought you a present. I imagine Harley has delivered it to the kitchen by now," Seneca said indulgently.

"A present? Whatever is it?"

"Why don't you go and see. You can then help your mother with the tea," Mr. Prescott said. Out she bounded again to her father's amusement.

"So you know Paddie and Margaret. It's been almost a year now since our last visit. How are they?"

Emily looked down at her clenched fingers. "I'm not sure. Paddie was fine, but Maggie was injured

205

just before I left. I only hope she's recovered."

"Emily has acquired an enemy, it appears," Seneca explained, "one who wishes her dead. Margaret intercepted a bullet meant for Emily—a wound to her upper arm."

"Not serious then?"

"No. And Margaret is probably enjoying Paddie's attention. For a change, *she'll* be waited on," Seneca said dryly.

Mr. Prescott laughed. "I remember how he'd sit back and enjoy her indulgences. How did you come to know Paddie?" he asked, turning to Emily. "And why is it we haven't met before?"

"Paddie and my uncle, Joe Harcourt, were friends."

"Joe. I met him. We had a drink together. His wife had just recently died, leaving him with a small son to raise."

"Yes," Emily said, eyes alight that he had known her family. "Peter was his name. He was a wonderful child."

Mr. Prescott's brow furrowed thoughtfully at her use of the past tense. He watched her lovely face lose its radiance and fill with sadness.

"Emily lost both Joe and Peter last month," Seneca said. "They were murdered by the same men who are trying to kill Emily. Paddie took Emily to live with them after the funeral, but when these men began stalking her he asked me to get her out of town. And none too soon."

Emily steadied her nerves and looked up. Very slowly she explained the events that led to her being in his home. "So, Mr. Prescott, I'd be most willing to go to a hotel if you think I might endanger your family."

"I won't hear of it. And please, Emily, you must call me Liam."

"Liam. You're Scottish."

"My father came from Scotland, yes. Any brogue you hear comes from him. I'm purely American."

"How did Seneca get his name?" she asked.

"My mother was French-Indian. Her people were Seneca Indians," he explained. "My father suggested the name when our son was born with black hair and eyes like coal. An unusual name, I know, but Louise, my wife, liked it. She adored my father, you see. Sometimes I think she married me to get him."

"I heard that," Louise Prescott said, coming into the parlor with a large and full tray in her hands. Liam stood immediately and took it from her, setting it on the serving table.

"You've made a friend for life," Louise said to Emily. "Marianne loves the kitten. She's been wanting one for some time, but we hadn't got around to finding one."

"That was a gift from Mrs. Potts, a woman who lives along the canal and who seemed very fond of Marianne."

"Ah. Well it was kind of her. Seneca, you be sure to thank her properly next time you see her." She poured the tea.

"Yes mother." He rolled his eyes upward.

"All right, I won't nag. Ah, Marianne, you decided to join us after all. I wondered if your curiosity would win out over your kitten."

"Mom," she grumbled in a singsong tone. She took the tea her mother handed to her and added an excess of sugar.

"The kitten is a gift from Mrs. Potts," Emily explained. "She chose it especially for you and asked me to deliver it."

"Oh yes, I remember her. I only met her once, but I liked her enormously."

"So did I," Emily agreed.

"Oh, did you win the race, Seneca?" Marianne asked, turning to her brother.

"We had a little trouble this year," he drawled, cocking an accusing brow at Emily.

"Now that's not fair," she protested. "I found your flowers, your gravestone, your kitten. I caught your winning fish."

Seneca laughed and, much to her embarrassment, went on to relate with much drama the disasters that had befallen them at her hand.

When the housekeeper announced that Emily's bath was waiting, the party broke up.

"Never mind them," Louise said, escorting Emily up the wide curving staircase to her room. "I know my son, and I know he undoubtedly had a large hand in everything that happened. I am happy to see that you are not intimidated by him, however. He can be an overbearing tyrant at times, but I get the feeling he treads easy with you."

"Probably because I pushed him in the canal for being just that."

Dinner was a festive occasion for which Wanda outdid herself preparing the meal. After her busy trip across the state, Emily enjoyed every minute of being waited on. Liam Prescott, especially, paid her lavish attention, refilling her wine goblet, including her in their conversation, and relating humorous incidents from Seneca's past, incidents that Seneca would much rather have left untold.

The uncomfortable sense of being stared at, her every movement watched, gradually passed as the family got to know her. Except with Seneca. Seneca watched her always, his black eyes taking in her tiniest response as if gauging her reaction to his family.

At least he didn't torment her as she thought he might. He turned his wit against his young sister instead, teasing her mercilessly about her current suitors.

Only when coffee was served after dinner in the parlor did the atmosphere change, and then only when visitors arrived. Marianne came back from peeking out the front window to announce that the Martins had come to call. All eyes turned to Seneca, who cursed under his breath, and whose eyes then came to rest on her.

Not only were the elder Prescotts and Marianne dismayed, but Seneca looked distinctly uncomfortable. She read a silent apology in his eyes just as Harley announced Mr. and Mrs. Martin and Miss Belinda.

Everything fell into place when Belinda glided into the parlor. Emily employed all her powers of control to keep her shock to herself, even managing to smile graciously in the face of Belinda's obvious hostility.

Seneca, rigid in his stony silence, left introductions to his father, moving to place one of the high-backed chairs between himself and the other people in the room.

Coward, she thought furiously. *Coward and liar.* Her anger began to simmer, brewing itself into a good head of steam. Why hadn't he warned her? What was so difficult about telling her she looked enough like his former fiancée to be her sister? He'd even gone so far as to plead ignorance about all those curious stares she'd been receiving from all his friends along the canal.

So, was he still so much in love with the other woman that he was willing to take a look-alike as a substitute? Was that what she had been—a convenient stand-in until he could get back to his beloved Belinda? Oh, he might have told everyone he hated her, but wasn't that a common cover for hurt pride?

As difficult as it was to accept, it explained much of Seneca's hostility toward her, as well as his attraction, reluctant though it was. And all the time Elijah knew. She found that thought most difficult to take, especially as Elijah had encouraged her to believe in Seneca.

209

Behind her smiles and pleasantries she felt bruised and betrayed. Had no one given any mind to how she would be affected when she finally met the ex-fiancée.

"So you were on the boat with Seneca for nearly a week," Belinda said, looking her over as if she were a lower form of life.

Emily glanced at Seneca to see if he would respond to that innuendo. Or would he duck that the way he dodged telling her about Belinda?

"Yes," she answered baldly when he didn't even look up. "It's been very nearly a week. I had a wonderful time on the canal. I look forward to the trip home."

"You actually liked that boat?" she asked disdainfully.

"Not everyone is afraid to get their fingers dirty," Marianne replied shortly, springing to Emily's defense. "You miss out on half of life when you live like you're above it all."

"Marianne," Mrs. Prescott reprimanded gently.

"That's quite all right, Mrs. Prescott," Belinda said too sweetly. "She's still very young. I take no offense."

"How generous," Marianne bit out. "What brings you out to visit after all this time? You haven't paid us a call in two years now. Hear about our houseguest, did you?"

"Well, yes, of course I did. But there were a few matters of importance I wished to discuss with Seneca

"Really? I can't imagine what."

"I'm sure you can't, but then it really is my business, not yours. Seneca, would you mind a stroll in the gardens?"

Emily watched, fascinated, at the by-play between sister, ex-fiancée, and Seneca. Marianne was fairly bristling with antagonism, Belinda doing remarkably well at controlling her resentment at Marianne's impudence, and Seneca at trying to convey no emotion whatsoever.

Without even a glance her way he nodded at Belinda and escorted her from the room. Emily watched them go, watched Belinda's flirting and acting as if they'd never been parted, watched Seneca's stiff manner and the grim line of his mouth that warned of an explosion to come.

Who would be on the receiving end of his temper this time? Would it be Belinda for daring to reenter his life so suddenly and embarrassingly, or would it be Marianne for daring to criticize the woman he used to love, perhaps still did? Or would it be her for just plain *being?*

Chapter 13

Emily lay awake for a long time, tossing in her soft bed, wondering what she was to do now. Should she stay on, knowing her presence was going to be a disruptive to Seneca's life, or should she just go? But to go was to give Belinda free running for a reconciliation with Seneca, and Emily was stubborn enough not to want to do that.

The Martins had stayed late into the evening. With Seneca and Belinda outside discussing whatever urgent business she had come to discuss, Emily found her nerves and her social graces stretched to their limits, especially when Mrs. Martin made it a point to talk down to her or ignore her existence completely, or to refer to "their children," Seneca and Belinda, as an established couple again.

The longer she remained in the parlor the more she grew to dislike the Martins. They were obnoxious and offensive and completely insensitive. The Prescotts were uncomfortable too, having guests who were unkind to another of their guests and not knowing what to do about it.

Finally she had had enough, and as graciously as she could, she excused herself and went up to bed. Marianne followed, tapping quietly on her door.

"Are you very angry?" she asked anxiously. "I wouldn't blame you if you never wanted to lay eyes on any of us again. I could see right away that you had no idea you and Belinda looked so much alike. And she can be such a bitch. She thinks she's society's darling. If she could see clearly, she'd see people walk the other way when she comes near. She can take the most innocent event and turn it into a scandal."

"Like my trip with Seneca," Emily said, nodding. "I saw how she did that."

"Yes, the lift of a brow, a subtle inflection. Nothing anyone could pin her down for. 'You were on the boat with Seneca for a whole week?' " she mimicked cattily.

"Her parents seem to feel a reunion is a foregone conclusion," Emily said, glancing at Marianne for her reaction.

Marianne shook her head in exasperation. "Belinda was engaged to Gerald van der Zee for three months. Last week he broke their engagement. This is Belinda's way of saving face, of spitting in Gerald's eye, making him look a fool. If she can get Seneca to squire her around or, heaven forbid, agree to marry her again, she can claim she never got over him in the first place and Gerald was an unfortunate mistake. Anything Gerald says then would make him look like a spiteful loser."

"That's rather clever."

"Oh, she's that. Clever, self-centered, spoiled, ambitious. Too bad she never learned how to care about anyone but herself."

"Do you think . . . I mean Seneca did love her. Would he . . ."

"Would he take her back? I don't know. He was really wrecked when she gave his ring back. I didn't think he'd ever get over it. I just can't think what he'd see in her now when he has someone like you."

"Someone who looks like her, you mean, but who isn't."

"Listen, Emily, you can't let the fact that you are both blonde and blue-eyed and beautiful get in the way. Isn't it reasonable for a man to be attracted to the same looks in the women he meets? Some men like short women, some like them tall, some like dark women. Seneca has always had an eye for blondes. And it isn't as if he came looking for you to replace Belinda because of your looks. You sort of fell into his life."

That made sense. Emily felt that tight knot of resentment ease a little. Perhaps Seneca really was attracted to her for herself and not merely as a substitute. It could be as Marianne said. He certainly had never slipped and called her Belinda.

So she would build on that attraction and hope that he could see the difference between her and Belinda. And if he still chose someone as selfish as the other woman, then he was welcome to her. But she was not giving up without her very best effort. Or the toughest war she could wage.

"All right, Marianne. I'll try not to let them get to me."

Marianne sighed in relief. "Good. I wondered if you might take a mind to leave. I'd be sorry if you did. We all would."

"I don't blame any of you for the Martins' manners. Or for what happened in the past or what Seneca will get in his head to do next. Besides, I've nowhere to go. I'm afraid Seneca is stuck with me."

Marianne giggled girlishly. "Boy, Belinda will hate that."

"I'm counting on it," Emily answered with a grin. "Perhaps she'll show her true colors to Seneca."

Hours later Emily decided sleep would elude her for a while to come, so she got up and belted a robe at her waist. She let herself out of her room and

214

found her way down to the kitchen for a glass of milk, her usual cure for insomnia.

She walked into the room without seeing the light under the door, and came face to face with Seneca and Liam Prescott. They were seated across from each other at the kitchen table, each holding a mug of hot cocoa.

Liam stood at seeing her and immediately pulled out a chair for her. Without asking he poured her a cup.

"Seneca was filling me in on the details of how you met and how you came to be traveling with him."

"I see." She overlapped the edges of her robe further and tightened the belt self-consciously. She hadn't expected to see anyone. Her hair fell forward and she brushed it back.

"Drink your hot chocolate and quit fidgeting," Seneca said. "You can't be that nervous around me."

"You?" she huffed. "Don't be absurd. I was embarrassed that your father . . ."

"I think you look enchanting, my dear."

She glowered at Seneca and drank from her cup. She turned back to Mr. Prescott and offered an apologetic smile.

"Please don't involve yourselves in my troubles. I would hate to think I brought danger into your home. I probably shouldn't even be here."

"Oh, I think we Prescotts can handle any trouble you could bring."

"Men are shooting at me. What if they find me here? I can't guarantee no one will be hurt. Margaret's already been shot trying to protect me."

"Then the quicker we get these villains, the better. Would you mind telling your story again to me?"

"All right. If you think it might help." So she related the story of her uncle and her cousin and their deaths from the beginning. "So you see," she said, "these men want me dead, and it appears they will not stop until I am."

Liam sat back and lit his pipe, filling the room with a sweet cherry scent. "So, we have a child and a young woman who overhear a conversation. For that the child is dead, the woman hunted. We're talking about something major here, a conspiracy of sorts, I'd guess."

"Like what?" Seneca asked. "Don't forget the one man spoke with a thick Southern drawl."

"We're sitting on a powder keg right now with the North pitted against the South. If anything, I'd guess this Southern gentleman was attempting to strengthen the position of the Southern states."

"How?" Emily asked. "What have I got to do with any of that?"

"Whatever it is, it has to do with Erie and Lady Chautauqua. And since that is all we have to go on, I think we should leave for Erie immediately," Seneca said.

"Go to Erie?" she asked, perplexed. "You mean face these men? Hunt them down?"

"You do want to be free of them, don't you Liam?" Prescott asked gently.

Yes, she did. And in Erie she wouldn't be endangering Seneca's family. "When shall we leave?" she asked finally, resolved to get to the bottom of it all.

Mrs. Prescott helped Emily pack her things the next morning, making certain she had everything she might need.

"I'm afraid that you're leaving us because of those awful Martins," she said worriedly.

"I'm leaving because Seneca insists on finding the men who are threatening me. Please don't distress yourself over last evening. It was nothing I couldn't handle. And I do hope to be back soon. We'll have some time then to get acquainted," she said.

"You're welcome here any time," she said as Seneca came for her luggage, two pieces borrowed from Marianne's closet. "You see that she comes to no harm, Seneca," she warned. "And try to be civil to her. You were raised to be a gentleman, remember that."

"I'm not in short pants anymore, Mother."

"You just mark my words, young man."

The side-wheeler took them into the big waters of Lake Ontario, where they traveled along the shore line toward Buffalo. After settling into their small cabins they met in the dining room for coffee.

"Aren't you going to ask me?" Seneca prodded at last, annoyed at her deliberate silence.

"Ask you what?"

"What Belinda wanted."

"I would rather ask why you lied to me in saying you had no notion why your friends were looking at me so strangely."

He let out a long sigh. "I should have told you. I didn't want you to think I was interested in you because you looked like her. That is what you thought."

"Yes, because you deceived me."

"I did not deceive you," he said heatedly.

"Keep your voice down. People are staring at us."

His hand sliced through the air. "All right," he replied more quietly. "What should I have done? When you fell off the boat in Albany, should I have told you about Belinda before I saved your life? Women all over the world have blonde hair and blue eyes. Would you have understood if I'd told you I was not kissing you simply because you looked like someone else I knew long ago, someone who possessed the same features? You'd have thought I was as crazy as a loon.

"I kissed you because you were there, you were

beautiful, and I wanted to. I took you with me, in part, because Paddie asked me to, but mostly because I couldn't let you go. I admit I didn't want to want you," he added reluctantly. "I resented the attraction I felt for you. "

"Admit it, you still do."

"Maybe. But the point is it has nothing remotely to do with Belinda."

"What did she want to talk about last evening?"

He grinned smugly at her curiosity. "She realizes now the mistake she made three years ago. She wants us to try again. She says she still loves me." He leaned back in his chair and watched her reaction.

At first she wanted to explode, then she wanted to laugh. She did neither. "Can you believe her?"

"I believe she believes it," he evaded neatly.

"And are you still in love with her?"

"I don't know. You seem to have confounded my mind. I'm in a total muddle."

"Meaning what? Not days ago you were telling me you loved me and wanted to marry me."

"You should have accepted then. Now I'll have to retract the offer until I can think straight again."

"There's no need to retract an offer I declined," she shot back. "Did you kiss her last night?"

"Several times, if memory serves. And you didn't decline. You said you needed time to think."

"So while I was inside suffering an inquisition and beheading at the hands of the Martins, you were outside in the moonlight caressing and kissing your ex-fiancée. Did you talk about me?"

"I can't remember."

"Did you tell her you'd asked me to marry you?"

"Not exactly."

"Well," she said, letting the word drop and die all alone while she returned his scrutiny.

"Well what? Are you jealous?"

"I'm feeling confused myself now. Jealousy is part

218

of it, yes. So is disillusionment, disappointment, self-disgust."

His indolence fell away and he sat up straight. "Why would you feel that?" he demanded.

"You wanted me, a thought that made my heart thrill, but you hated wanting me, which took the joy from the wanting. You made love to me all night long, a golden experience in passion and sharing I'll never forget, but I find you the next day in the company of a whore. That pretty well tarnished the night before and made me see it for what it was for you, a meaningless night of carnal pleasure. Free, at that. You ask me to marry you, and I find my doubts being laid to rest again. But before I can give you an answer, you run into the arms of your ex-fiancée. In my place, what would you think?

"I think I'm being used," she continued. "I think I've been brought here to punish Belinda and to bring her to heel. And any little extras you can get along the way, all the better. And who the blazing hell cares what Emily feels about any of it?"

"That's not true," he hissed, looking away guiltily. He'd never meant for anything he'd done to hurt her or make her hate herself. Hell, he was only goading her to get her dander up.

"Did you tell Belinda you weren't interested in resuming your relationship?"

"I . . . ah . . . No."

She tied her bonnet under her chin and pulled her soft shawl around her shoulders. "I think I'll take the fresh air and sunshine. Excuse me, please."

She was gone before he could react. He sat back down and let her go, wondering if he'd lost her for good. How could he have been so blindly insensitive? That was easily answered. He'd spent the last three years cultivating a selfish and uncaring attitude toward life. Elijah was the only person he considered with any seriousness. Everyone else either fit into his life at his convenience or not at all.

Three years ago his whole life had been changed, torn asunder. He'd been a long time putting it together again. And now he shuddered, for here was Emily threatening to change it all again.

And she could. She could hurt him far worse than Belinda had, because he'd never loved Belinda the way he loved Emily. So why was he playing such hurtful games with her? She was sweet and innocent. Jealousy and doubt could crush her heart. Somehow he'd have to make it right with her. Somehow, before they returned home again, he had to have the promise of her hand in marriage. Otherwise he could lose her forever.

As he'd seen the night before, Belinda was quite capable of plotting the destruction of anyone who got in her way. He couldn't avoid the first meeting of the two women, but he could try like the devil to prevent any in the future.

He shook his head in amazement. Why had he never seen Belinda's selfishness before? Why had he made so many excuses for things she'd said and done.

She'd changed some in three years, but not for the better. Now she could add thoughtless arrogance to her list of attributes.

"Seneca, oh Seneca," she had cried the night before when she'd flung her arms around his neck and pulled his lips to hers. "Seneca, I've been so miserable without you. I know now what a dreadful mistake I made when I broke our engagement. Can you forgive me for being so silly. I was awfully young, you realize, and still in shock over that fire. Please say I'm forgiven."

"You're forgiven," he'd parroted warily, watching and waiting.

"Oh, thank you. I knew you'd be generous with me. We did share something very special once. Remember our picnic at Foster's Lake?"

Of course he remembered that. For all of her supposed strict morality, she'd succeeded in seducing him that day, although she'd been quick to imply that he was the naughty one for leading her astray. *Astray.* She'd been no virgin, but he couldn't bring himself to care how many men she'd had so long as she continued to give herself to him. She'd made his head spin with her praise of his masculinity, his looks, his body, his skill as a lover. She knew all the right words to bewitch a young and vain man.

Within two weeks she had his ring on her finger, where it remained for six months until that perfection of manhood was marred forevermore. Flawed. Scarred. Worthless.

According to Marianne's gossip, Belinda had had five other suitors in the past three years. He thought then of Emily. Sunny, funny, Emily, in whom no artifice existed. He disentangled himself from Belinda's arms.

"I understand you are engaged," he said. The word *again* seemed to hang unspoken in the air. "Congratulations."

"Seneca, you don't understand. That is why I came to see you. I had to break my engagement because of you."

"*Me?* I haven't seen you in three years."

"I can't get past my love for you to truly love someone else. Oh, I've tried. I thought it was what I wanted. But you're always there between me and anyone else. I've finally come to realize that we were always meant to be together. I've wasted so much time. Let's not waste anymore."

"Just what are you saying, Belinda?"

"That I've decided that I want to marry you after all. I know you still love me or else you wouldn't have brought some girl home who looks almost like me. You were trying to make me jealous, and I am jealous, but there's no need. I'll marry you any time you say."

"What if I say never?"

She smiled coyly and let her hands roam expertly over his body. "You won't. I know how to make you feel *sooo* good."

"We aren't the same people, Belinda. I'm not the same man whose head was turned by empty flattery. I want warmth and sincerity and genuine passion in my bed now, not a talented actress." And just the thought of Emily's response sent waves of tight heat through his loins.

"I've changed too. I can give you that." Again her arms circled his waist, pulling his lower body tight to hers. She laughed triumphantly at his arousal. "Let me show you how good it can be again, darling. Don't deny me. It's been so long. Take me to the summer house. We'll be alone there. Hurry, Seneca."

He clapped his hands around her shoulders and leaned away from her. "Belinda."

She covered his hands with hers and drew them down her arms, taking the low-cut bodice of her dress with them, exposing her breasts to his view.

"Now see what you've done, see what you do to me. Touch me, Seneca. Kiss me."

Seneca stepped away and turned his back to her. "Make yourself presentable, Belinda, and stop behaving like a bitch in heat."

"Seneca," she cried in distress. "That's a very cruel remark."

Seneca turned to meet her petulant frown, but at least she'd covered herself again. "I'm sorry it seemed cruel, but I had to stop you before you went any further. I've no intention of making love with you tonight."

"Because of her?" she sneered.

"Maybe, maybe not."

"You can't be serious about her, not when you can

have me. You love me."

"I *did*, much to my regret. I *did* love you."

"You will again. I'll make you love me. We'll have a wonderful marriage."

"Not so fast. I've agreed to nothing."

"You will, won't you? I can depend on you."

"Like I depended on you?"

"Seneca, I was a child."

"A twenty-year-old child. No, Belinda. I'm beyond swallowing your fantasies or falling for your dubious forms of persuasion. If I decide to marry you, it will be after I've proved to myself that you are the kind of woman I can love and respect."

"I am. You know I am."

"That's just the point. I don't know you at all. Whereas Emily is quite a charming young woman."

"I won't give you up without a fight. I warn you."

"Just keep Emily out of your fight. If you harm her by so much as a word, I'll make you sorry."

Pushing away the memory of Belinda, Seneca left the dining room to go in search of Emily. He felt very strongly that he owed her an explanation and an apology. She was right. He'd been behaving worse than Belinda had. It was long past time to take responsibility for his own actions and for his own life and happiness.

They stood side by side as the steamer approached Niagra Falls. Seneca's arm cradled her to his side, protecting her from some of the evening chill.

"This is magnificent," she yelled over the roar of the water. "I can't believe anything so fantastic exists."

"I agree. I'm amazed every time I see it. We'll go around it now through a series of channels and locks. We'll be in Erie before morning."

"We won't be by the falls again?" she asked.

"Not this trip. We'll stop on the way back for as long as you like. Our dinner will be served soon. Shall we find a table and have a glass of sherry beforehand?

Emily couldn't have asked for a more pleasant evening with Seneca. He was charming, witty, attentive, and drew from her laughter and humor of her own. They danced to the music of a small band, swinging from one waltz into another, joining others in learning a folk dance the pianist insisted on teaching them. Finally, as the music became slow and mellow and as the other passengers began to drift sleepily away, Seneca walked Emily to the stern where they could be alone, where they were sheltered from the wind.

He pulled her into his arms and covered her lips with his. Back and forth his mouth moved against hers until her lips opened beneath his. His tongue thrust forward, taking possession in a kiss of such wild and uncontrolled hunger and need that she moaned in mute submission and melted in his arms.

"Emily, oh, my darling Emily. I want you so much."

"I know. I don't want the night to end. I want to stay right here forever."

"Let's go to your cabin, angel. Let me make love to you. Let me love you all night again. Let me hold you in my arms when sleep claims us. I don't want to leave you tonight. I can't, Emily. It's much too late to walk away."

He led her to her cabin and locked them in. The room was lit only by moonlight streaming in the window. Darkness followed when Seneca closed the drapes.

"Shall I light the lamp?" she asked.

"No. I will see you with my hands and my lips, I will drown in the scent of you and be lost in the sound of your sweet cries."

"Oh, Seneca."

"Do you want me?"

"Yes, you know I do."

"And do you love me?"

"I think I shall burst with love for you."

"And I for you, my sweet woman. I want to devour you, to sink into you and become one with you. I'll lose my mind if I can't have you."

Their clothes fell away as swiftly as urgent fingers could manage, until they stood flesh to flesh. She covered his chest with tiny kisses, stopping to tease his flat nipples, to pull gently at the crisp hairs that peppered his chest. She felt his body leap to life in response, and her body answered, arching invitingly into his.

"Patience, sweetheart," he murmured, still removing pins from her hair.

"No," she cried, shaking her hair loose with her own hands. "I've no patience. Take me now. Right now."

In one movement he laid her on the bed and filled her aching body. The moments that followed were wild and tempestuous. Their unbridled passion crested swiftly, sweeping them both into the cataclysmic fulfillment that satisfied their craving bodies and left their souls bound together in sweet unity.

This is love, Emily thought. This is what men and women are about. What life is about. This is what I want in my marriage. And she could have this if she married Seneca. If he ever asked her again.

Erie was just waking up when they arrived at the harbor. Seneca hailed a hansom cab and gave the driver the name of their hotel.

"Yes, Mr. Prescott, your rooms are ready," said the clerk upon their arrival. "I'll have your luggage taken up directly. Rooms 3A and 3B."

"Could you send a porter up with breakfast for two. Eggs, bacon, French rolls, the standard fare. And coffee."

"Yes, sir. Right away. Will your sister require a bath?"

Seneca looked down at her and grinned. "She would love one, thank you. Come along, my dear. Help me find our rooms. You have a busy day ahead of you, buying out the stores."

"Buying out the stores?" she asked humorously when they were alone in her room. "This is lovely."

"I had to say something. If I'd said you were my wife, we would be expected to share a room. I couldn't say you were my fiancée because you turned me down. So you are my sister. And why else would I bring my sister to town except on a buying expedition."

She sat on the edge of the bed and tested its softness, running her hand over the blue satin coverlet. The same blue framed the windows on either side of the bed. On the floor was a carpet in muted shades of blue and yellow. Large yellow pillows were tossed on the blue striped chairs flanking the fireplace. A huge vase of bright daisies was placed on the bedside table.

"I've never done that. Someday I will. When I return to Albany, I shall have to see to Uncle Joe's business affairs. Mr. Petrie is taking over for now, but Uncle Joe left his share in my care. I shall have to become a businesswoman. And then one day, when I've saved enough money, I'll go to New York and I'll see the ballet and the opera and listen to the symphony. And I'll shop at the finest stores and have beautiful gowns sewn for me."

"Do you care so much for finery, then?"

She shrugged. "No, not really. But it would be fun once in my life to get all gussied up and go somewhere elegant."

"Do you know anything about Harcourt's business?"

"Nothing. Uncle Joe never discussed business with me. I'll have to begin at the beginning."

"I could help, if you'd like."

"Yes," she said enthusiastically. "I'd really appreciate your help."

"Ah, here's our luggage. And our breakfast. Shall we eat before you have your bath? Set the table up in my room, please," he directed the waiter. "The chamber maid can unpack and ready my sister's bath in the meanwhile."

"Very good, sir."

Emily grinned. "I knew it. All along I knew it."

He looked askance at her. "Knew what?"

"Look at you." And she did. She looked at the way his dark trousers accentuated the long lines of his thighs, the way his coat was cut to fit the breadth of his shoulders and the slenderness of his waist. In his hands he toyed with the brim of his hat. "No longer a pirate but a noble gentleman," she said laughingly. "I once said you were hiding behind your rough and tumble waterfront manner. Now I see the man I only suspected then."

He took her arm and led her across the hall. "And which do you prefer?"

She had to think about that. She'd grown to love her disreputable pirate. "I think you are both of those men, and one without the other would never work."

After breakfast Emily returned to her room to find her bath waiting, hot and scented with rose petals. Large fluffy towels were piled on the stool by the embroidered bath screen.

"If I may help with your clothes," the chambermaid said, "I'll have them cleaned and pressed. Have you a preference in gowns for today?"

"The green, thank you."

"I'll lay it out for you, then." She helped Emily into the bath and assisted her with washing her hair. Emily permitted that much, but felt too self-conscious in the presence of anyone else while she was in her bath.

"That will be all. I can manage the rest. I'm not

accustomed to being waited on."

"As you wish, miss."

Emily enjoyed her bath, lingering in the scented water until it cooled. Wrapped in her satin robe and brushing her hair dry, she wandered to the window and looked down onto the street below.

Her hand stopped in midair and her whole body tensed. She blinked twice and looked again, pulling back the edge of the lace curtain to see better. It couldn't be. But it was. She couldn't mistake that tall physique, that head of black hair, the way he held his hat in one hand, her arm with the other.

The woman turned her head up and laughed with him. She was lovely, with shiny red hair under a saucy hat, a bright smile, a curvaceous figure beneath her smart two-piece dress. He led her across the street and around the next corner.

Emily let the curtain fall back into place and sat down heavily on the bed.

You have a nice long bath and a nap before lunch. We have much to do this afternoon. His exact words as he walked her to her room. No wonder he wanted her to nap. So he could slink off with another of his ladyfriends, she concluded bitterly.

Well, he could waste his day if he chose. She intended to make use of her time. She didn't need him to find Lady Chautauqua. She'd do it herself.

The nerve. The blasted foul nerve of the man. She'd no sooner turned her head than he was squiring some other lightskirt around. She gritted her teeth and said a word she'd never said before. Then she threw her brush down and began to yank on her clothes. Cursed, fickle rogue.

Chapter 14

"Where in hell have you been?" he roared when she returned at noon. "You were supposed to be in your room."

"No doubt you'd rather see me tucked away in some corner. See no evil, eh?"

"What are you babbling about? You've one of the best rooms in the hotel."

"Although the view is rather restricted to the street below."

"You were sightseeing?" he demanded, angrier still, and missing her point completely. "Have you no sense?"

"My senses are working perfectly, thank you very much."

"Where were you?"

"If you really care, I was at the library trying to determine who or what Lady Chautauqua is."

"There was no need. I already have a few ideas. Why don't you leave this to me," he said patronizingly.

That made her temper flare. "I'm surprised you can find the time between all your other activities."

He muttered an oath. "I don't pretend to know what you're talking about, but let's leave it for now." He checked his pocket watch. "I have an appaintesnt this afternoon. Let's get some lunch."

"I'll come with you this afternoon."

"Emily, I'd rather you didn't."

She huffed. "Sure you would. How inconvenient to have me tagging along. That *would* put a wrench in the works."

"Look, I know you didn't expect to spend your time in an hotel room, but I can work a lot faster if I don't have to keep watching over my shoulder for someone who has a gun pointed at your back. Humor me in this, Emily."

His smile, the questioning tilt of his brows, his persuasive black eyes destroyed her resistance. She nodded once, looking away in disappointment.

Her downcast face tugged at his heart. "We'll do something this evening. Fair enough?"

Fair? "Sure. If you'd like."

"Emily, this is very important this afternoon. The people I have to see will take one look at you and think the worst."

"And what is that?" she asked pointedly.

"We've been discreet. I won't have people talking about you as if you were my mistress. I won't have it."

"And so I must remain out of sight." *Like a mistress.*

"It's for your own protection, angel."

"Mr. Prescott," the *maitre'd* greeted them. "Miss Prescott. A table for lunch? Right this way, sir."

"Thank you, Henri, and a bottle of wine, not too dry."

"Yes, sir. Miss?" he said, holding the chair for Emily.

She thanked him and watched him walk away. "Are we celebrating? A whole bottle of wine? Or are you trying to get me so drunk I'll fall into a stupor and sleep the afternoon away? You've no need to worry. I won't get underfoot."

After a longsuffering sigh he let the subject drop and turned his attention to the menu. Lunch arrived shortly after they had given their orders, and it was only when Seneca caught her eyeing the lovely dresses and hats of the other ladies that the perfect solution came to him.

"Emily, how would you like me to call on Mother's dressmaker and have her come over with her dolls and samples and fit you for some gowns?"

"You mean to order dresses made?"

"Why not? She's an excellent seamstress. Mother and Marianne both have several of her creations."

"You don't have to placate me."

"I'd like to do this for you. I'll arrange it," he said with finality. "You won't have a boring day after all."

It would be fun, she thought, especially as she wasn't to have Seneca's company. "Will she come at such short notice, do you think?"

"I think I can persuade her."

She laughed. "You could persuade the very devil to do your bidding. All right. I'll look forward to it."

Evening came and Emily waited expectantly for his return. She'd dressed in her best dress and had spent an unusually long time fixing her hair. She wanted to look as lovely as the ladies she'd seen in the restaurant.

Each minute that passed increased her excitement for the evening ahead. Where would he take her? What would they do? Finally she could stand waiting no more and she opened her door a crack to see if Seneca had returned.

Just then a porter entered the hallway bearing a tray of covered dishes. He came to her room.

"Miss Prescott? Your dinner, miss. Shall I set it up for you?"

"My dinner?"

"Oh, yes, and your brother sends his regrets that he cannot join you until later."

"I see. When did you receive this message?"

"Twenty minutes ago, miss. Shall I use this table?"

"Oh, yes," she answered distractedly. "Just leave the tray. I'll see to everything."

"If you're sure. I'll be happy . . ."

"No. That will be all."

"Very good, then. Enjoy your meal."

She saw him to the door and was about to close it when Seneca's door opened and the redhead walked into the hall. She turned and leaned back into the room. "Stop by any time. If I'm out, Janie can help you. She's very good. I wish I could stay, but I have to see another client. Maybe after that? Bye, love."

Emily closed her door as if ashamed to be seen by the other woman. *Bye love? Stop by any time? Another client?* "That does it," she growled. "I'm not taking any more of this humiliation."

Balancing the dinner tray on her hip, she flew out of her room and into Seneca's. He was sitting in the long copper tub, scrubbing his legs. His hair was wet, raked back by fingers, his shoulders and chest glistened with drops of water. His jaw was covered with a thick lather of soap in preparation for shaving.

The sight might have been her undoing except for the knowledge that she wasn't the first to see him this way. The redhead had probably scrubbed his back for him.

"Emily . . ." he managed, his eyes growing alarmed as she strode purposefully toward him. "Emily, now hold on. What do you think you're doing."

"Stop by any time, love," she mimicked scornfully. "If I'm out with *another* client, Janie can help you. She's very good."

"Hey, wait," he said, trying to stop her by holding

out a restraining hand. "You don't understand."

"I understand perfectly. Another whore, is she? Is she the business that detained you? Well, I don't want to eat in my room, so have your damn supper."

"Emily!" he howled furiously as the tray tilted in her hand and spilled its contents. The crystal vase and rose, silver, linen, the china cup and teapot, a hefty chunk of bread, and the dinner plate with whatever it held under the silver dome, all slide into the bath water between his knees.

"Emily, are you trying to scald me?!" he shouted, jumping up and looking back at the sickening mess that was his bath.

She tossed the silver tray onto the bed and strode to the door. "I'll have my dinner out tonight. And maybe I won't have it alone."

She slammed his door as she left, collected her handbag from the bureau in her room, and stormed out into the hall, shutting her own door forcefully.

"Emily," Seneca barked, stepping into the corridor with only a towel draped around his hips. His face still bore the white lather. "Get back here this instant. I'm warning you. If you don't get back here this instant . . ."

An elderly woman popped her head out her door at the commotion, giving a gasp of outrage when she saw Seneca garbed in so little.

"Would you go back to that man if he was standing in a towel threatening you with murder," she asked the woman with wide-eyed innocence.

"Emily," he growled, taking a step toward her.

"You leave her alone, you pervert," the older woman ordered.

"Maybe the hotel manager would like to know one of his guests is parading around in an uncouth and offensive manner," she suggested lightly, her eyes sparkling with unholy glee.

"You tell him, dearie," the women advised. "And you, mister, get out of the hall where decent people have to pass."

Emily chuckled all the way to the lobby, where she ordered a cab to go to one of the restaurants the dressmaker had mentioned as being very good. Not for any reason would she stay in the hotel one moment longer.

"You did not like the meal we prepared for you?" the night manager asked.

"Mr. Prescott decided to have that. I prefer to go out this evening. I'm meeting some friends for dinner. Good evening."

Fish, she thought disgustedly as she rode through the streets. He'd ordered *fish* for her dinner. After a week of fish, did he think she'd want *fish* at a restaurant? It looked far better swimming in his bath water, headless though it was.

Seneca's hand shook as he sliced the lather and his whiskers away. A few nicks was little price to pay for the chance to get his hands around her throat. He'd find her if it killed him, and when he did . . .

He was just leaving when a knock sounded at the door.

"Hi, love," Dolores chimed, walking in. "Whoa, you've butchered your chin."

"Not now, Dolly. I have to find her."

"Who? Emily? She's gone?"

"She must have overheard you as you were leaving — something about clients and Janie being real good at what she does, and your promise to return later, all delivered in your usual suggestive manner. That on top of canceling our evening."

"Oh, dear. I take it she didn't like what I ordered for her dinner."

He nodded to the bath, the soggy bread, the teacup, and several pieces of fruit bobbing among the remaining bubbles.

She snickered, then, despite Seneca's warning to the contrary, broke out into deep, throaty laughter.

In for a penny, he thought. "And to top it off, I went after her, clad only in a towel, and ran into a lecture on decency from some busybody down the hall."

Dolly had fallen into gales of laughter, rocking back and forth on the edge of the bed. "How I would . . . love to have . . . seen that," she sputtered, trying to catch her breath and curb her fits of laughter. "You're always so . . . perfect."

"Be serious, Dolly. She's out there somewhere and she's all alone."

Dolly sobered. "You don't know. She may be downstairs at the restaurant."

She wasn't, of course. Neither was she at the restaurant to which she'd asked directions. Seneca stood outside the front door, a fist on one hip, the other hand raking through his hair. He looked up and down the street as if seeking the answer there to where Emily had gone.

"Let's get back to the hotel, Seneca," Dolly suggested. "We'll never find her this way. You may as well wait until she returns. Much as I'd like to stay around and watch, I have some business to tend to, so I'll say goodnight."

"I'll walk you to the cab stand at the corner."

From the corner table across the street in the small Indian restaurant Emily saw them leave the restaurant, the one where she'd hoped to convince Seneca to take her to dine that evening. Instead, he'd ordered her fish and taken his redhead to dine with him on French cuisine.

She fingered up the last crumbs of her honeyed pastry and drank her cooling tea.

Well, never mind. She'd thoroughly enjoyed her

curried chicken. And she'd rather have her own company and that of the lovely family who ran their little restaurant than that of some two-timing blackguard. She allowed the serving girl to refill her tea cup and sat back to enjoy its flavor while she listened to the turbaned old man play the sitar, a haunting lutelike instrument that soothed her nerves the longer she listened.

When Emily finally rose to leave, the owner's wife came out to take her money.

"You are, I think, not so very distressed as when you came to us," she said gently with a wonderful British accent.

"I've had a lovely time, and the food was delicious. Please thank your daughters for cooking for me, and your husband for the music."

"I will do so, thank you," she replied with a stately nod. "And this man who troubles your heart—you must tell him, as I tell my man, that he must be very good to you or he will come back in the next life as a woman and have to suffer life with a man such as himself. That will make him think."

Emily laughed delightedly. "That's wonderful. I'll tell him. Goodnight."

She took her time walking to the corner where a row of cabs waited. Once seated inside, she asked the driver to show her a little of the town, so that the hour was late when she finally entered the hotel.

Surprisingly, Seneca was nowhere about. She collected her key and went up to her room. Maybe he was still with *her*. She glanced at his door, but she wouldn't permit herself to slow her steps enough to listen for voices. She refused to care about him or what he was doing.

Conversely, Seneca was pacing frantically around his room, watching the hands of his clock move at a snail's pace, listening intently for the sound of her footsteps in the hall.

When he heard them, he was out his door and into her room before she could shut him out.

"God, Emily, you took ten years off my life tonight." He pulled her into his arms and just held her tightly for a long quiet moment. Still holding her shoulders, he leaned back and looked into her face.

"Are you all right? Nothing happened?"

"I'm fine, Seneca. I had a lovely meal, met some charming people, went for a short ride, and now I'm back. How was your evening? Did you enjoy yourself?"

He stepped away, ruffling his hair even more than it was ruffled. "Did I enjoy myself?"

She knew she was in for it. Whenever he started repeating her words in that soft tone of voice, the explosion was never far behind. Very deliberately she took the pins from her bonnet and removed it, setting it on the bureau.

"The porter said you were going to be busy this evening. I assume you went out."

"Well, I didn't," he snapped. "I spent my evening searching for you."

"Whatever for? I'm perfectly capable of finding myself a meal in your absence."

"Were you followed?" he demanded. "Did you let the world know where you are?"

"Don't be ridiculous." He was just trying to alarm her, to frighten her into hiding in her room all day. "I'm very tired, Seneca. I'd like to go to bed."

"Let me help you with your dress," he offered, bending over to kiss the side of her neck.

She shivered with pleasure, but she knew what he was doing. She pulled away. "I can manage, thanks," she said stiffly.

"Emily, I'm sorry about tonight. I know you were looking forward to an evening out, but . . ."

"I had an evening out."

"With me, I meant."

"Well, you were otherwise occupied."

"Listen," he coaxed, pulling her into his arms. "I know how it looked, but trust me, it wasn't like that."

"You mean I only imagined she was in your room while you were in the bath? I only imagined I heard her promise to return later tonight?"

"No, but Dolly and I are . . ."

"Dolly?" she shrieked. "Her name is Dolly? How very . . ."

"Dolores. Dolly is short for Dolores." He began to grin crookedly. "You're insane with jealousy, aren't you? Admit it."

"I will not," she denied hotly, struggling to free herself.

"You want to know who Dolly is?" he teased. "I'll tell you for a kiss."

"You think I'm going to kiss some two-timing cheater? Who is she?"

He laughed, brushing her nose with his. She jerked her head aside, but he clamped his hand under her jaw and turned her face back to his.

"I need a kiss," he murmured against her mouth.

"No. I don't want you to kiss me." Her pulse was pounding at her neck, in her fingertips. Her stomach clenched in delicious expectation.

"Yes you do. Open your mouth."

"No, Seneca. Don't do this."

"I want you to trust me."

"Just like that? Just . . . trust you?" That doused her passion.

"Exactly. What do we have if we don't have trust?"

More than once that very question nagged at her. What exactly did they have? "Trust has to be earned," she said resolutely. "Do you trust me the way you want me to trust you? Have you ever trusted me?"

"I trust you now."

"After I proved myself? You've never seen me with another man after being in your arms. I haven't made excuses to you so I could take someone else to dinner. I won't be used like this."

"Used?" he repeated quietly, stepping away. "I think I'm the one being used here. I thought what we shared was special. We played none of the usual games. We knew where we stood with each other. Now you're using your body as a bargaining tool. You're no better than . . . than Belinda." He was out of her room in a few long strides, closing her door with undue force.

"Belinda? Belinda?" she screeched, furious. "How dare he." She marched out her own door, across the hall, and exploded into his room.

"You bastard. How dare you compare me to that supercilious conniving bitch. If anyone in this room bears any resemblance to the real Belinda Martin, it is you. Her fiancée jilts her so she wants to jump back into your bed. For all I know she succeeded. You talk about trust. You tell me, what grounds have you ever given me to trust you? Every time I turn around you're with another woman. If that's what you need, then fine, but I was raised with a different set of morals." She jabbed her finger at him in outrage. "You aren't welcome in my bed after you've had someone else in yours." She snatched up a silk scarf she saw on the end of the bed, held it under his nose, then tossed it in his face. "Trust?" she spat, then stormed out, slamming his door behind her. She slammed her own for good measure.

It burst open right behind her, and she spun around to face an angry giant. A pirate. A rogue. A devil. Her chin came up defiantly. "Get out of my

239

room."

"Not until we get this straightened out once and for all."

"What needs straightened out? It's all perfectly clear to me." She held the door for him.

He gritted his teeth in frustration. Pulling her away from the door, he closed it, turned the lock, and slipped the key into his pocket.

"You have no right to . . ."

"Shut up." He pushed her ahead of him and sat her on the edge of the bed, glowering down at her.

"I was not with another woman," he claimed stubbornly.

"Don't take me for a fool. I know what I heard and what I saw. I saw you coming from that restaurant with her, when you fobbed me off with some excuse."

He took her chin and waved the yellow scarf at her. "This belongs to my cousin. Dolly is my cousin, my mother's brother's eldest daughter. She's been helping me."

"What?" she exploded, jerking away. Was that supposed to make her feel better? "You are too ashamed of me then to introduce me to your cousin? You'd rather let me endure the pain of thinking you . . . That's sadistic. It's almost worse."

"Emily, I was trying to protect you. I wanted you safe. I didn't want you to worry."

"You've been there for me whenever I've needed you in this past month, but that doesn't mean I'm not strong enough to face my own troubles. I'm not Belinda. I'm not afraid of the fire. This is *my* business. *My* life. *My* problem. I won't be shut out while you let your cousin involve herself."

"She's a professional. She knows what she's doing."

"A professional what?"

"She's a . . . an investigator."

240

Emily noted his hesitation. "She's more than that, isn't she?"

"Don't ask questions I can't answer."

"What did you learn today while I was being shut out?"

"Why not let Dolly do her work?" he evaded. "We think this is a matter for specialized personnel."

"You know what it's all about then, don't you? You're not going to tell me," she guessed correctly.

"I'll explain everything when it's over. Until then I can't say anything. Dolly asked me not to."

"So much for trust."

"This has nothing to do with trust. And while we're on the subject, there is nothing between me and Belinda. She kissed me, but that's all. I did not make love to her. How could you believe I'd do that to you?"

Why was it he could take the wind from her sails so easily. How could he look so guilty one minute and be able to turn that guilt back on her the next. So maybe she had jumped to conclusions, but she didn't have far to jump by the looks of things.

"You could have explained to me."

"You didn't give me a chance. You tore into my room, dumped hot tea on me, and ran off."

"You had plenty of time to explain before that, just as you did with Belinda. You do it deliberately, don't you? Is it some sort of test to see how rotten you can be before I'll do anything about it? Don't expect blind faith. I don't know you well enough. Too many secrets keep popping up. And don't expect me to read your mind."

"Yes, dear."

"And don't be flip. I'm serious."

He cocked a brow, grining at her display of indignance. "No, dear."

"Now what are you doing?" she cried as he bore

her backward onto the bed with him. "Seneca, I said no."

"I'm going to kiss you. Then if you say no I'll leave quietly and without a fuss."

"Just a kiss?" she asked warily.

"I promise." He nuzzled her ear, sending shocks of pleasure along her nerve endings.

"And nothing more?" Her head tilted involuntarily, exposing her neck.

"Whatever you want, angel."

His warm breath fanned the sensitive skin at the hollow of neck and shoulder, teasing, promising more, but withholding.

"You've skin like the petals of a pale pink rose, smooth, soft, flawless." He brushed his lips along the length of her neck. "And you smell as sweet. I want to devour you."

His hands were not even touching her, yet she felt herself pulled by the will of her own body into the hardness of his.

"I thought you were going to kiss me," she said, breathlessly.

"I am. Believe me, I am. Sometimes the best part is the waiting. Does this feel good?"

"You know that it does. Touch me," Her own hands were eagerly caressing the masculine contours of shoulders and back.

"Angel. Sweet angel." His lips met hers lightly, once, twice, brushing like the wings of a butterfly. At long last they settled across hers, hard and insisting.

His tongue teased then plundered her mouth, meeting and mating with hers, drinking deeply of her kiss. Emily was lost. She should have known she couldn't withstand even one of his kisses. When had she ever been able to do that? When was there a time when she didn't melt in his arms? And he, black devil that he was, knew it. Was *counting* on it.

He lifted his head. "Well, I must go. Goodnight, sweetheart."

And for good measure she should let him leave. He deserved a good lesson. "Good night."

He walked to the door, taking the knob in his hand. He looked back expectantly.

Smiling to herself, she stood and began to remove her dress, thrusting her breasts forward as she reached for the buttons at her back. Her hair was already beginning to slip free of its pins, and she shook her head, causing its heavy weight to tumble around her shoulders. He wasn't leaving. How could he, after all, until he took the key out of his trousers again?

Her dress fell to her knees, and she stepped out of it and laid it across the chair. She kicked off her slippers and rolled her stockings down, wiggling her toes against the thick nap of the carpet. She looked up enquiringly.

"Was there something you forgot?" she asked sweetly, unlacing her chemise.

He swallowed hard. Black fire burned in his hungry eyes, threatening to scorch her from across the room. His jaw tensed and his nostrils flared.

He withdrew the key and tossed it at her feet. "I'm locked in." He removed his coat, flinging it to the floor. He began to work his necktie loose. "Pick up the key and open the door if you want me to go.

She let her hair cascade forward to hide her grin. "Way over there?" Why didn't you unlock it?" She slid the straps down her shoulders.

"I can't. You'll have to have me carried out now. It will take every man in the hotel to get me out of this room."

"But you said . . . Seneca!" she shrieked when he dived for her and took them both to the bed.

"So call me a liar, hit me, scratch my eyes out. I can stand that. I can stand anything except being without you. God, I want you."

She laughed victoriously as he tore the remainder of their clothes away and covered her with his body.

"Witch. Angel. Sorceress. Damn, I love you."

Chapter 15

Emily stretched lazily, coming awake slowly. She opened her eyes, seeing the sun stream through a crack between the drawn drapes to illuminate a lovely watercolor painting on the opposite wall.

She reached out her hand for Seneca, but found the other side of the bed empty except for a note on the pillow. She picked up the paper and sat up to read it. The warm glow inside her of a woman fully loved turned cold as she read. Nothing had changed. Why had she thought he had heard her? He didn't hear anyone but himself. After all their talking, he and Dolly had gone off without her to follow a lead on the mysterious Lady Chautaqua.

She crumpled the note and threw it across the room. *Be a good girl and stay in the hotel today.* "Aarghhh!" she cried furiously. A pillow followed the note.

With determined movements she went through her morning preparations. Over a scant breakfast in the dining room she pondered how to go about finding answers of her own.

"Peter," she asked the waiter who refilled her coffee cup. "If you wanted to find an answer to an odd question, a piece of trivial information, who would you ask?"

"About the most trivial thing in these parts is the local paper," he answered facetiously. He laughed at his own humor, eliciting a grin from her. "Not really, but I suppose no one knows more nonsense than those men. I mean, well, they have to keep up on things, trivial and important. So I'd say," he answered, curling his lips thoughtfully, "I'd go to old Harv. Harvey Pembroke. We have a saying about town. 'Right from the pen of Pembroke.' "

"Thank you, Peter. Oh, and will you put my breakfast on Mr. Prescott's bill."

She walked briskly through the streets of town, glancing in windows without really seeing as she made her way to the newspaper office. She was hoping to catch Mr. Pembroke before he left on some assignment.

She was shown into his office when she asked for him and was surprised to learn that not only did he write for the paper but that he was an assistant editor.

"What can I do for you, Miss Prescott?" he asked, checking the name his assistant had written down for him. He looked like her uncle. He looked like a man she could trust.

"Actually, Mr. Pemboke, my name is Emily Harcourt. My escort, Seneca Prescott, thought we should pose as siblings for the sake of propriety. We're in Erie on a mission to discover why the name Lady Chautauqua, and the fact that I overheard it from a collection of politicians, some who are from Southern states, should be cause for the murder of my uncle and young cousin and for repeated attempts on my own life."

Mr. Pembroke jumped to his feet. "Can I get you some coffee, Miss Harcourt?"

When she declined he poured himself a mug and sat back down, drawing a tablet of paper in front of him.

"Lady Chautauqua?" he asked, scratching the neatly trimmed beard on his chin. "Let's begin with that, then you can give me the whole story."

"Oh, it wouldn't do to find this in tomorrow's paper." She couldn't imagine Seneca's rage if that were to happen. "Please."

"Look, I'm a newspaper man. If we have a story here, I want it."

"But you won't print it until I say so?"

"I want the story first," he demanded, driving his own terms home. "Exclusively."

"Yes. All right."

"Good. Now, as I see it, Lady Chautauqua could be a woman, a ship, a riverboat, a mine. Down in Titusville they're naming oil wells. Or . . . ," he said, dragging out the word thoughtfully. He tossed his pencil on his desk and sat back. "Or it could be a fancy private railroad car. You know, the kind political candidates use to campaign their way across country."

"Political candidates?" she repeated with a premonition that she wasn't going to like what was coming.

Mr. Pembroke flipped through a daily calender on his desk until he found what he was looking for. He frowned and became very still as he stared at the date. The date was two days hence.

"Let me hear the whole story before I make a complete fool of myself by crying wolf. "

"What do you mean? What is it?"

"Remember, the story is mine. Where you go, I go. I want in on this the whole way."

"What? You want in on what?" She grew impatient.

"Next year is election year, a very crucial election, I might add. One that will determine the way of life in America. Now tell me everything."

Haltingly she went through it again, answering his probing questions as she did.

"So I came to you," she finished. "Now can you tell me what you suspect?"

"Erie is scheduled for a visit by a would-be presidential candidate, a man from Illinois. This man, Abraham Lincoln, has caught the eye of some very influential people who think he's exactly the man to push abolition through. I've yet to hear him speak, but I understand he's quite articulate."

"Where does Lady Chautauqua fit in?"

"It's only a hunch, but . . . Well, why don't we go down to the depot and check it out? Can you spare an hour?"

"Yes," she said eagerly as Harv Pembroke all but dragged her out of the building. "Do you suspect foul play with this Mr. Lincoln? Surely not," she said incredulously. "That can't be possible. Those men were reputable public servants."

Pembroke guffawed. "You are naive, Miss Harcourt, if you believe that. The South will be virtually bankrupt if the wrong man gets into office."

"And they think this Lincoln is the wrong man?" She had to run to keep up with his headlong strides.

"Lincoln is an abolitionist. These men you overheard know what I say is true. They have everything to lose. *Everything.* They'll do whatever is necessary to secure their positions. Whether or not he is ultimately elected, he is still walking around right now with a bull's-eye on his back. And you, my dear, and your family, were expendable since you got in their way."

"How can you be certain?"

"I can't yet. But nothing else of note is happening in Erie in the near future. If Lady Chautauqua also fits the puzzle, we have our answer. We'll know who and we'll know when."

"Maybe we can stop it."

"We'll give it our best shot."

"I can get help. Mr. Prescott's cousin Dolly has some influence with the authorities. I'm not sure what."

"Dolly, the redhead?" At her nod, he whistled through his teeth. "Influence is right. That one is the dragon lady. Influence is an understatement. She's liable to bring the sky down on my head if I interfere with her case. I tangled with her two years ago. My wounds still haven't healed. Why come to me when you have her?"

"I didn't know anything about her or how good she is at investigations."

"Investigations? Who told you she was an investigator? Hell, she's a . . ."

"A what?"

"Better not to say. Here's a cab."

The depot was busy with people boarding and those collecting their belongings from the train that sat by the platform.

"This way," Pembroke directed, pulling her with him through the assembled throng. "John," he called, waving high overhead. "John Burney."

The man turned. "Harv! Hey, good to see you," he said when they shook hands. "It's been too long. How have you been?"

"Great, great," Harv answered, impatient with meaningless prattle. "John, I need a favor. Can you help me?"

"Sure, if it's legal," He gave a horsey laugh.

"I need to know what trains are due in day after tomorrow," he fished.

"There's a schedule posted."

"Special train. And who its passengers are."

John balked, knowing which train Harv was referring to.

"The campaign train? That information is confidential. Sorry, Harv, I can't divulge any more than the public already knows."

"Tell me this, then. Is Lincoln the only presidential hopeful aboard?"

"Yes. Congressional candidates join him in each state."

"And the name of his private car?"

"That I'll have to look up. Why?"

"It's important, that's all I can tell you yet."

John found the information in the log book in his private office. He swung the heavy volume around for Harv and Emily to see.

Lady Chautauqua.

"Jumpin' hellfire," Harv muttered.

Emily found a chair and sat down.

"You better explain, Pembroke. I don't like the feeling I have here."

"Can you contact the engineer of that train?" Emily asked.

"No. No, you can't do that," Pembroke said hurriedly.

"Why not. You can't just let it happen."

"Nor do we want to show our hand."

"For God's sake," John exploded. "What are you going on about?"

"We believe an attempt will be made to kill Lincoln."

"Good God."

"Right," Harv agreed. "But if the assassins know we suspect, they will simply move the event up or back a day, or to another town. He drummed his fingers on the log book, concentrating.

"John, don't say a word to anyone about this yet. I have to turn this information over to a government agency I know. They'll have to handle this. It's too big and too dangerous for us.

"And Miss Harcourt," he went on, "you must keep out of sight. If they think you've put it together, they'll cancel the attempt. And they'll kill you."

Emily felt the blood drain from her skin, leaving her chilled all over. Seneca and Dolly would have reached the same conclusion. No wonder he tried to keep her locked up, out of sight.

Anger brought color rushing back into her cheeks. Trust. She should have trusted him. But so should he have trusted her with an explanation. A few little words. And now what if she'd ruined everything? He'd be furious. He'd be worse than furious.

"Shall we go, Miss Harcourt? Miss Harcourt," he repeated to get her attention. "Time is of the essence."

"Yes. I'm sorry," she offered, rising. "Thank you, Mr. Burney, for your help."

"I'll have a cab brought to the side door. Wait for that, Harv. It wouldn't do for you two to be seen here together."

Emily let herself out of the cab a block from the hotel, giving Harv a brief wave as she walked away. For once she hoped Seneca wouldn't be there when she returned. She was going to have to tell him. Better he find out from her than someone else. But oh, she dreaded it.

She glanced up as two men left the hotel and came down the stairs toward her. Her blood froze. Staring right at her were the same two men who had caught Peter and her spying on them in Albany.

"Hey, that's her!" one said.

The other, the one with the Southern drawl, answered. "I told you we'd have to do it ourselves. One can't trust these matters to the hired help. Get her, and don't make a scene."

She backed away. "Who are you? What do you want? I don't know you."

"Just come along quietly."

"Why should I? What do you want with me?" She waited until they were closer, then with all her strength she shoved one into the other and ran for her life.

Elijah waited patiently as the others in his car gathered their belongings from the racks and aisles and made their way to the doors at either end of the car. Even dressed in the finest clothes and bearing his papers, Elijah was asked, politely but firmly, to ride in the rear of the train with the other servants.

He grinned grimly, knowing change would come slowly and at great cost. He picked up his traveling case and left the train. The sign said Matfield, West Virginia. Matfield, a peaceful little town by all appearances, but home nevertheless of Bristol Quarry and Mines. Bristol was owned in partnership by three individuals: Bristol was one, Carl Sidwell another, and the third, he'd learned, was Ryker.

Elijah was not happy to be south of Pennsylvania, even if West Virginia was predominantly a slave-free state. She was still tied politically and economically to Virginia, a strong advocate of the right to own slaves.

In West Virginia's mountainous terrain, slavery was not the economic advantage it was in states where large plantations required extensive manpower. But some were always around who could find a means to capitalize on free labor. Ryker was one such man.

Ryker and his partners had transported more than two hundred captured slaves to the hills outside of Matfield, where they had put them to work in the mines and the quarries that produced the valuable bituminous coal that was needed for the increasingly

252

industrialized nation.

The irony of that left a bitter taste in Elijah's mouth. That one race of people should live with poverty, pain, and hardship so that another race could live in effortless convenience and comfort was more than he could bear to think about.

Even though some white men and women believed as he did and offered to help at risk to themselves, they could not really know nor understand the awful sense of rage, humiliation, and frustration that ate into a man's soul at being held in bondage and being made to suffer at another's whims. Worst of all was the sense of futility.

Under the guise of overseer for the slaves of one Morris Dryden of Louisiana, Elijah presented himself to the foreman of the Bristol Quarry and Mines. His papers stated that he was traveling under the authority of Mr. Dryden to seek out and bring back three runaway slaves who were rumored to be held at the mines.

Finch was a burly bear of a man with an unruly mane of black hair and a full beard. He had a coarse covering of hair on his thick arms and tufts between the knuckles of his fingers. His narrowed yellow-brown eyes and his permanent thick-lipped sneer declared to Elijah that here was a man who loved his job, that of keeping the slaves in line. Finch fondled the handle of his long leather whip very lovingly as he perused Elijah's papers.

Elijah withstood the scrutiny of those beady eyes as Finch studied him. The hatred coming from the foreman was palpable.

Slowly Finch folded the documents and returned them to Elijah. With a nod and a curious grin he directed Elijah to precede him out the building and along a rough stone path toward the mouth of the mine.

"Down below to your right are the barracks. We'll check them later. The entrance to the mine is just ahead on your left. We run two twelve-hour shifts daily."

"De men go down dere at night?" Elijah asked, uncomfortable at the mere idea of it.

"Day, night, what's the difference down there?" Finch laughed mockingly.

"Only the matter of rescue should an emergency arise," he said under his breath.

"What'd you say, nigger?"

"I says I didn't think of it dat way, sir."

"Yeah, well, that's to be expected. Take a lantern and watch your step. We're working the third level today. The cage is straight ahead."

Elijah held himself stiffly as they descended into the earth. He hated closed-in places. He especially hated dark closed-in spaces.

"Hey, Curly, this here fella's lookin' for some friends of his," Finch said when they exited the elevator. "Let's take him on a tour, what say ya?"

"Right," Curly drawled. "What are you called?" he asked, looking Elijah over head to toe, noting with dislike the fine fabric of his clothes.

"Massa calls me Lije, sir," he answered, nodding a respectful bow. He felt sure these men would expect it. The ring of pickaxes on stone, of iron wheels on an iron track, of muffled voices, the crack of a whip, all these sounds met his ears as they found their way deeper into the hillside.

The tunnel opened into a wide area, all lined with men and women at work digging the black rock from the earth. The men wielded the picks and broke up the rocks. The women, some heavy with child, separated the coal from the rubble, loading it into carts. The carts were rolled to a wooden chute that led out the side of the hill to large shuttle bins.

From there the coal was loaded onto trains. A guard stood by the opening to the chute. His eyes roamed hungrily over each of the young women who emptied their load into the slide.

The women, he noticed then, were all young, and most in one stage of pregnancy or another. Those who were with child were sensibly spared the whips. Not so the men. Any slacking off earned a painful reminder. So this was Ryker's stud farm. No pleasure palace, for sure.

"Do you see any of your niggers?" Finch asked.

Elijah looked around, turning this face or that to the light for a better look. Their eyes were filled with such pathos, begging wordlessly for help. "Pick me," they seemed to cry. "Get me out of here."

Elijah turned away, to all observers oblivious of the suffering of his fellow men and women. "No, Mistah Finch. Day not down here. Mebbe in de bunkhouse."

"Yeah, Mista Finch," Curly mocked, circling Elijah like a predator. He picked at his sleeves, the neat pleats running down the front of his shirt. He pulled the knot free from his neck. "Fancy duds for a nigger." He took Elijah's hat and tried it on, strutting around like a peacock. "How do I look, boss."

"His clothes are mine," Finch said.

"Hey, share the wealth, man."

Elijah's back straightened. This had been a horrid mistake. He should have known better. Never trust a rattlesnake. Or a greedy man.

"Take them clothes off, slave."

"I got a massa already, sir, an' I gots to get back to 'im.'"

"You don't get it, do you? You ain't never goin' back. You belong to us now."

Curly sneered. "He's a fine buck. He'll make good babies."

"Yeah, after some of them uppity ways is beat outa him. Strip out of them clothes now."

Elijah's hands tightened into fists. He could probably take two of them, but not four or five. That old familiar rage churned in his gut. Denial flooded through the marrow of his soul. Not again. Never again.

Finch pulled a pistol from beneath his grimy coat. Elijah released the tension in his hands and let his head fall forward. These men would easily kill him for his clothes alone.

"Yes, bossman, sir," he recited emotionlessly, removing his clothes until he stood before them in what Mother Nature had given him.

Finch kicked off his worn boots and his baggy trousers and tossed them at Elijah, more concerned with the shiny finish on the black shoes he had traded for than the fact that his own boots were too short for Elijah to wear.

"Git to work, before I give you a taste of the whip. Keep a close eye on him, Curly. He's trouble. Look at them scars on his back."

Elijah picked up an axe, suppressing the urge to bury it in Finch's skull. Wait, his mind encouraged. Wait. Your time will come. Seneca will come. Don't do something rash that you'll regret.

Silently he went to work, chipping away at the wall. Behind him Curly laughed a maniacal laugh. Hot, breathtaking pain shot through his back and chest. He knew that pain.

"Put your back into it, nigger. You ain't no fancy man no more. You'll earn your keep here or feel the sting of me whip."

"Holy hell, look at this. He's got hisself a gold watch and a wad o' money. And his papers," Finch said, searching the pockets of his newly acquired trousers. He set his cigar to the corner of the doco-

256

ments and watched the papers curl and burst into flame. Laughing, he dropped them to the dirt floor.

Elijah didn't blink an eye, just struck out at the vein of black rock with all the strength he possessed.

The two men were gaining on her. Emily, her chest burning from the exertion, ran faster toward the busy center of town, away from the quiet streets of hotels and restaurants.

She ran into a bustling market area lined with shops, screaming for help. Several men approached.

"Please, help me! These men are going to kill me! Help me! Get the police. Oh, please!"

The Southern gentleman reached her, holding up a restraining hand to the crowd.

"No need to involve the police. She is my wife."

"It's not true. He's lying."

"I assure you it is true," he claimed as his friend caught up with them. "This is Dr. Wolffe, her psychiatrist."

"This is true," the tall thin man said. "We hoped an outing would be beneficial to her. We did not anticipate it would cause such a violent reaction in her."

"Liar," she screamed. "You can't believe them. I can prove who I am.

"Of course you can, my dear," her supposed husband consoled, moving slowly toward her.

"Keep away from me."

"Here, here, what's going on?" The question came from a man in uniform. A policeman. Thank Cod.

"They're trying to kill me," Emily accused.

The two men held out their empty hands and opened their coats. "We are not armed. We have no intention of hurting her, officer. We simply wish to get her back to the asylum."

"Asylum?" the policeman asked, looking at her.

"These two claim she's a crazy," one of the shop-keepers explained. "This one says she's his wife. She says they're lying. She came running down the street screaming for help."

And just who looked crazy? she thought. The two men stood by calmly, waiting patiently for the officer to turn her over to them. They looked sane. They hadn't come racing through an alley screaming for help in a dead panic. They hadn't grabbed hold of the front of the policeman's uniform. Their hair wasn't flying around their heads like a mad banshee's.

She burst out laughing, but that only made it worse. She could think of only one thing to do. She picked up a mellon from a nearby fruit bin and threw it through a shop window.

She turned a smug smile to the officer. "So now you'll have to put me in jail."

"Now, ma'am control yourself. Your husband only wants to help you."

"He's not my husband, I tell you. I insist. I broke that window. You have to take me to jail."

"I'll pay for the window, of course," said the Southern accent.

"Then pay for this one, too," she retorted and picked up a chair. The policeman restrained her, twisting the chair from her hands before the damage could be done. She kicked out her foot and turned over a crate of apples. A barrel of pickles and tart pickle brine followed, splattering the shoes and hems of all the curious but unhelpful onlookers.

"That will be enough, young woman. You win. Jail it is. Maybe a day in the calaboose will simmer you down some."

"Must you, officer? She's in a very fragile mental state."

Emily broke away and bolted into a china shop, pushing the proprietress out of her way and sweeping a table full of figurines to the floor. She was holding an extremely expensive crystal bowl over her head when the policeman reached her.

"Will you take me to jail?" she threatened.

"You have my word on it, lady," the disgusted man scowled at her, taking the bowl from her and tying her hands behind her back. He led her out of the shop and through the crowd. She looked at the two men and gave them a smug grin.

"Next time find yourself a whore and leave decent women alone. I'd rather go to jail any day than be raped by the likes of you two."

As a parting shot it couldn't have been better. The townsfolk, never sure from the start who to believe, seemed to side with her.

"You'd better pay for that window."

"And my china."

"Forget it," the tall man said snidely. "Take it out of her hide."

Murmurs went through the crowd as the two men turned and strode back the way they had come.

Emily walked proudly into the police station, surprised to find Harv sitting there with his feet up on the edge of the police chief's desk. He was equally surprised to see her, though he covered it quickly.

"I had to bring her in, Chief. She broke up two stores downtown."

The chief looked at her long and hard, then shook his head. Put her in the front cell away from that rabble in the back. Then get the particulars from her."

Pembroke rose at the same time. "Haven't we met?" he asked her, giving her a furtive wink.

"Not likely." She played along.

"What happened downtown?" he asked, pulling

out his pencil and an old envelope.

"Harv, this is not for print. She deserves her privacy in case she has to stand trial."

"I don't mind," she said, smiling at Pembroke. "I'd like him to print how unsafe your city is for decent folks to visit. I was about to enter my hotel when two men accosted me. I ran, naturally, but no one would help me, not even your officer. So I broke a window and a few trinkets in a china shop so I'd be brought to you." She turned big blue eyes to the chief. "I knew you'd help me." She glanced at Harv. He nodded once.

"Sounds to me like you better give your men a few lessons in proper police procedure. Where are these two men? What if she was accosted? You could have let two murderers loose and put the innocent in jail."

"Now, Harv," the chief reasoned. "Ed couldn't be sure. She was destroying property."

"Perhaps her only recourse." He walked to the door, pocketing his paper and pencil. "Well, I have work. I'll be in touch on that other matter."

"I'll be waiting to hear."

Emily sat on the bunk and waited. An hour passed very slowly, during which she imagined every scenario possible that could occur when Seneca came for her. In not one did he welcome her with open arms and a warm smile.

"You let me take care of this," a voice came from outside the high window of her stuffy cell. Seneca's voice. Her pulse leaped.

"Now, Seneca, don't be hard on her. She's . . ." Dolly's voice faded away as they walked past.

She's what? Emily wondered, praying that whatever it was, it would convince Seneca to follow her advice.

She stood up, scrubbed at her face with the hem

of her petticoat, brushed her clothes into order, and combed her hair into a semblance or order with her fingers. She composed herself and stood quietly in front of her cell door waiting for Seneca to come for her.

And she waited.

After twenty minutes she sat back down. He wouldn't, would he? He wouldn't leave her in jail until . . . That was two days away. He wouldn't dare.

She jumped up, grabbed the metal dipper by the water bucket, and began to rake it over the bars. "Seneca!" she screamed. "Seneca, don't you dare leave me in here. Do you hear me? Seneca!"

Chapter 16

Seneca didn't blink an eye, just stood outside her cell, staring at her like a black avenging angel. Perhaps angel was a misnomer.

She lowered the dented dipper she was still holding aloft and hung it back over the water pail.

"I thought you were leaving without me," she said lamely. "I thought you were going to leave me here."

"An intriguing idea." He did not smile.

She did. She tried on her best convincing face. "I can explain everything, Seneca. Really, I can. Can we just go back to the hotel?"

"Eighty-seven dollars. Wasn't a new wardrobe sufficient? Eighty-seven dollars."

"I'll pay you back. Every penny," she vowed bitingly. What a nerve. "Maybe you'd have preferred it if they'd caught me. They were very willing to pay for the damages so they could get their hands on me." She sat down on the edge of the bunk, half angry, half dejected. But then, what did she expect?

"Go away, Seneca. Stop glowering at me."

He began pacing in front of her cell. If she squinted, she could imagine him as a black panther in a zoo. She was rather thankful for the bars at the moment.

"I suppose you have it figured out by now. Your

newspaper friend came to see me."

"We know who they plan to kill," she said hopefully. "We found *Lady Chatauqua.*"

"I know. We've known since last night what was being planned."

"You've known. You knew last night while you were accusing me of a lack of trust?"

"I hoped you would stay out of it. If they suspect you've . . ."

"I know. I realize that," she retorted angrily. "I'm not totally naive. As soon as we discovered what was happening, we knew we had to alert the authorities. And we knew any involvement by me could jeopardize all attempts to capture the assassins before they succeeded in carrying out their task."

"Then, if you're so clever, why did you do just that? And why did you land yourself in jail?"

"Well," she said, drawing out the word. She stood, hands on hips, throwing her own angry daggers. "Had I been informed, had you had even a *little* faith in me . . . But all I got was a nasty little note on my bed with an order I found impossible to obey. So don't stand there looking down your self-righteous nose at me. If anyone is at fault here, it is you."

The police chief, followed by the very lovely Dolly, joined them. He opened Emily's cell door and stood aside for her to exit. With as much dignity as she could muster, she walked past him and past Seneca and Dolly into the station office. She stood by the desk and waited for them to join her.

"It seems we owe you an apology, Miss Harcourt. Dolly explained what . . ."

"It's quite all right. I'm sorry, too. Will you please apologize to the two shopkeepers for me."

"Actually, what you did to protect yourself was very clever," Dolly said, pulling on her gloves.

Emily looked at her, not to be appeased. "I'm happy you think so. I was terrified."

"You're free to go, Miss Harcourt," the chief said, patting her hand. "We'll patrol the area around your hotel until the danger is past. Try to get some rest."

She said nothing on the way to the hotel, letting the effervescent Dolly fill what would have been a long silence with her bright chatter.

She helped herself out of the carriage, striding into the hotel before Seneca and Dolly could follow. With a ramrod-straight back she took her key, ordered lunch and a bath sent to her room, and marched up the stairs.

She slept all afternoon, waking only when a knock sounded at her door. She sat up, pushing the bed-clothes aside. She rubbed her face and shoved her thick hair out of her face, checking the gold clock on her bedside table: nearly half past five.

Seneca stood in the hallway, bearing a silver tea service. "May I come in?"

She stood aside, tying the belt to her dressing gown. While he poured, she sat at her mirror and ran a brush through her tangled hair. Slowly she stood and joined him in the sitting area.

He handed her a delicate china cup and saucer. "Emily, I'd like to apologize. I was very bad-tempered today when I . . . ah . . . should have been there to . . . ah . . . hold you. And comfort you. When you told Dolly how terrified you were . . ." He took a long painful breath. "You've been right all along. From now on you stay at my side. Those men were here in this very hotel. In truth you were no safer here than on the street. And you were right about needing to know what we've been learning. Dolly said from the beginning that you should be included. But I was honestly trying to protect you."

She put her cup down. "I know you were. And I

264

have to share the blame. I was determined to learn the truth on my own just to spite you because you were shutting me out. Your note made me furious, and I acted without thinking."

Their gazes met and slowly they both relaxed and smiled. Seneca's brows rose inquiringly and his lips pursed.

"Did you really throw a melon through a window?"

She laughed. "Such a fuss over a piece of glass."

"But I had to pay to have all that lettering done again. And I don't think I'll tell my mother about the china figurines. She'd be heartsick."

"That was a terrible waste. But I was quite desperate by then. The people were convinced I was running from my husband and my doctor, who wanted to take me back to the asylum. They thought I was insane."

"And you thought to prove them wrong by your genteel manner?"

She made a face at him. "I *am* insane. How else have I ended up in this predicament? Why else would I let you convince me to forgive you time after time?" She raised her hands in bafflement.

"Come over here," he said, setting his cup down with a solid clunk.

"Unh-unh." She shook her head slowly.

"Are you going to make me come get you? Haven't I humbled myself sufficiently yet?"

She laughed at the mere thought. "On your knees you would still carry that mantle of arrogance."

"Emily," he protested. He stood and took her hand, pulling her into his arms. She felt so good. All afternoon he'd wanted to hold her, to prove to himself that she was really all right. She came willingly into his embrace, and he buried his face in her fragrant hair.

He hadn't been able to believe what the reporter Pembroke had told them when the man finally tracked them to Dolly's office. Speechless, he'd listened as Pembroke laid out the puzzle, piece by piece. He and Dolly had only reached their conclusions late the previous evening. And Dolly was good. But so was this Harv Pembroke, apparently. And he was smart enough to come directly to Dolly with his suppositions.

He had started for the door, eager to get back to the hotel to check on Emily, when Pembroke stopped him. "She isn't there," he said laconically, accusingly.

"Where is she," he'd demanded.

"In jail." Very deliberately he kept his answer to those two words.

"In jail? You said she was in jail?"

"The officer had to arrest her because she wrecked a couple of shops downtown."

"What?" he'd asked dumbly, unable to make any sense at all of his words.

"What happened, Harv?" Dolly asked sharply. "Stop playing games."

"Games? No, I know I'm partially responsible for what happened. I should have escorted her to her room, however that could have backfired by leading her attackers directly to her. It also could have shown our hand. What puzzles me is how you could have left her alone when you knew someone was hunting her. She's at police headquarters. I'll turn this matter over to you, Dolly, my dear. I claim exclusive rights to this story. And unless you want your identity revealed, and your incompetence disclosed, you'll see that I get it."

"Unscrupulous rat," she muttered as they hurried to the police station. She did not appear to bear him a grudge, however. Rather, she seemed to regard him with humor and respect.

"He is right, though," she said. "You've treated her abominably since you've been here. Were I in her place I would demand to know what is going on. I'd probably do just as she has done and strike out on my own too."

"She's a total innocent, Dolly. She's been sheltered all her life. She can't take care of herself. I only wanted to insulate her from all this."

"Right. Admit it, Seneca. You get a charge out of playing her knight in shining armor. You want her to turn her big blue eyes up to you in blind adoration and gratitude."

"Has anyone ever told you how exasperating you can be? Whatever you think, keep it to yourself. You let me take care of this."

"Now, Seneca," she tried to calm him. "Don't be hard on her. She's young and impetuous."

"The age I can't change. Her impetuosity must come to an end."

"It's too bad someone didn't teach her that lesson before she impetuously succumbed to your dubious charms. It's rather too late now, I suspect."

But he hadn't been able to take it easy on her. His heart had been in his throat when he'd heard how close she'd come to falling into the hands of those who wanted her silenced. Then to see her in that dingy jail cell . . . He'd been furious with her, with them, with the entire situation. Now he could only hold her close and thank his lucky stars that she was alive and safe. He scooped her up and sat down with her in his lap.

"I need to hold you, to have you right here in my arms."

"You are the most changeable man," she said, looking up at him curiously.

"You just make me crazy, that's all," he said, tracing the curved brush of her brow, the perfect line of

267

her nose, the gentle bow of her soft full lips. Her skin was like the purest silk, her eyes the color of the clear summer sky touched by tiny bursts of sunlight.

Silver-gold waves framed her face and cascaded over the sleeve of his coat. He crushed a lock in his hand, sliding it through his fingers when he opened his fist.

"I would suffer a thousand deaths if anything happened to you," he said fervently. "I cannot bear to think of it, I adore you so completely. You are my heart. I have never felt so intensely about anyone in my whole life."

Her chin trembled and hot tears rushed to her eyes and rolled down her cheeks. She turned her face into his hand, planting kisses there.

"I know. I love you the same way. I might get angry and rebellious, and I might say things I regret, but it's because I've been hurt or I feel pushed away. I think I've always loved you."

"Even as a pirate?"

"Ooohh, especially as a pirate."

"Aarraghh, lassie, you like the dark and dangerous type?"

"You're always dark and dangerous."

He gave her a narrow-eyed look. "And you like that? I don't frighten you?"

"I wouldn't say you frighten me. You make my nerves spring to life and my heart race and my stomach leap in wild anticipation. Sometimes it feels like fear when I get near you, but I can't stay away from you. You're too compelling."

"Obsessive."

"Addicting."

"Essential. As necessary as breathing," he said.

"Feel how my heart is pounding now," she said, placing his hand over her heart.

His hand held her breast, shaped it, teased it until

the nipple pressed hard into his palm.

"I want you, Seneca. I want you to make love to me."

He kissed her, a brief but thorough kiss. "I will, you can bank on it, but not just yet. I have reserved us a table at the finest establishment in town. After dinner we shall attend a play." He gave her backside a playful slap. "Now I shall leave you to make yourself ready. I shall call for you, milady, in thirty minutes."

"Can I believe this? Will you really come?" she asked, excited yet wary.

"Nothing and no one shall interfere in our evening of decadent pleasure. I promise you."

Two days later they were waiting in the stationmaster's upstairs office, concealed behind lightweight curtains. Outside was a crowd of people numbering in the hundreds, awaiting the arrival of the campaign train. A small ensemble of instrumentalists struck up a rousing off-key version of "Yankee Doodle." She looked down the track and saw the gaily painted locomotive approaching the depot.

Her heart beat heavily and erratically, and her stomach twisted in an anxious knot.

"What if, after all this, they succeed in killing him? What if . . . What's to stop them from shooting him? It would be over so quickly."

"They wouldn't have spent so much effort on you if they planned an outright attack and didn't mind the risk of being found out. They want this to look like an accident, something disassociated from the South. My guess is they wanted you dead because you could point a finger to them, not because you could stop them. Oh, and by the way, Dolly has some photographs she wants you to look at. She hopes you'll be able to identify the two men from yesterday."

"Where is she? Shouldn't she be here?"

"Look down there. See the lady with the baby pram, the one with the striped bonnet? That's our Dolly. Her men are stationed throughout the crowd, in one guise or another."

The crowd cheered and chanted his name as the very tall and thin man was escorted to the colorful platform that had been hastily constructed that morning. Emily found herself entranced by his kind face, his slow and deliberate manner, his total lack of pretense.

After several other congressional candidates had been introduced and had spoken a few words to the crowd, Abe Lincoln was introduced. He took his place at the podium. The crowd hushed expectantly.

They were not disappointed. Mr. Lincoln spoke in a deep, resonant voice that carried easily across the audience. His words, carefully chosen, beautifully delivered, wove a spell over the listeners, painting an eloquent picture of what life could and should be like in a land such as America, a land founded on personal choice and liberty. He continued with a glimpse of some of the atrocities being perpetrated on fellow human beings of a varying color of skin.

Emily could sense the outrage of the people, for she felt it in herself. The unfair and inhuman practice of subjugating a man of color must be halted before the entire fabric of our personal liberty was rotted and rent in two.

The crowd cheered wildly when Mr. Lincoln concluded his thirty-minute speech and returned safely to his car, the *Lady Chautauqua*. Emily released a long sigh and let the curtain fall back into place.

"He certainly can influence a crowd," Seneca commented. "No wonder some of our Southern states are alarmed at the prospect of his becoming president."

"He was wonderful," she said in awe. "I wish I could vote. I'd vote for him."

Another half hour passed before Dolly arrived. "We did it," she said with pride and satisfaction. "They were attempting to sabotage the trolly of Lincoln's car. When my men spotted them and closed in they had already cut halfway through one front and one rear axle. Hard to tell what else they would have done. My guess is that the car was intended to break up at about the time the train reached the steep grade outside Erie. If not that one, quite a few more grades followed. One or both axles could have snapped, derailing the car, twisting the whole train over the edge of some hillside."

"So the train can be repaired?" she asked.

"Most certainly. The arrangements have already been made for Mr. Lincoln to spend the night at your hotel. He has asked specifically for you and your escort to dine with him in his suite."

"Me," she croaked. "But I . . . Me?"

"But before that you must come with me to identify the two men we arrested."

Her greeting at the police station was quite different from the first time she'd been there. The police chief, Mr. Wallace, rose, took her hand, and very gallantly kissed her fingers. The mayor and several councilmen crowded around her.

Reluctantly she accompanied Dolly to the cell where the two men sat. But only one was known to her.

"That is one of the men whom I overheard in Albany. He is also one of the two who accosted me two days ago. The other man I have never seen before."

"He is a professional killer. I know who he is. His

271

killing days are over."

"The man with the Southern drawl?" she asked.

"We have not located him yet," Dolly said, "but my men are searching the town."

A file folder of photographs did not turn up the gentleman's name either. "A new face," Dolly had surmised. "A young, greedy, newcomer. We'll have a file on him before long."

A special edition of the paper hit the streets that afternoon, featuring a story guaranteed to win Harvey Pembroke another award. Her name was printed prominently under the headline alongside Seneca's. Dolly's was omitted in lieu of the reference to an official government agent on leave in Erie.

"It is with deepest regret that I learn of the loss of your family," Lincoln said in greeting her that evening. "And of my part, however unwitting."

"Thank you, Mr. Lincoln," she replied, "but you must carry no blame for the ill works of others."

"Nevertheless, you have my condolences. And now may I present my wife?"

And so the evening passed with much good food and wine, with serious conversations and amusing antecdotes.

When Emily's yawns of exhaustion refused to be suppressed, Mrs. Lincoln wisely suggested an end to the evening, escorting her guests to the door.

"Thank you, my dear," Mrs. Lincoln said to Emily. "These trips can be tiring when we meet only ambitious politicians. It was a pleasure to chat about ordinary things for a change. I wish you well in your life and in the pursuit of your young man," she added for Emily's ears alone. "He is quite dashing."

Emily grinned, glancing at Seneca. "Yes. He is that."

"I am also compelled to thank you for disrupting your life on our behalf. You need not have followed your leads as you did, and we most assuredly would have perished."

"And what a sad, sad loss that would have been for this country. We need men with your husband's vision and conviction. Good night, ma'am." She received a kiss on the cheek from Mr. Lincoln.

The next morning Seneca escorted Emily to the hotel dining room for breakfast. On the way he stopped at the front desk and inquired if any messages had been delivered for him.

"Are you expecting a telegram?" Emily asked. "From Dolly? Or your father?"

"From Elijah. We've had an understanding this last year because of the slavers that he is never to be gone from me for more than a few days without sending me a telegram to let me know he is safe."

"Perhaps he notified your father."

He nodded. "Who was then to notify me here. I'll contact Father after breakfast just to check."

"What if there is no line where he went?"

"His destiny was Matfield, West Virginia. A line was run to that town two months ago."

"So you suspect he's in trouble."

"I don't like to borrow trouble. I'll wait until I hear from Father."

As they were finishing their meal the police chief and Dolly entered the dining room and came directly to their table. Seneca ordered more coffee.

"Those two men we arrested," Wallace said grimly, "were murdered last night. Poisoned."

"Poisoned? But how?" Seneca asked.

Wallace shrugged. With all the commotion last evening, their dinner trays sat on the desk unattended for who knows how long. Someone apparently got to them."

"In the police station?" Emily asked.

"Or where the food was prepared," Dolly suggested. "Your Southern friend did not wish to be identified."

"So he's out there and he's safe," Emily said grimly. "What's to stop him from trying again?"

"Security has been tripled around Mr. Lincoln. No one will be able to reach him."

"What about Emily?" Seneca asked.

"We've no reason to believe she's still a target," Wallace explained. "Whatever she knew is of no consequence now."

"Except as a witness that this man was indeed part of the conspiracy," Seneca said. "If he killed his own partners to silence them, how can he let Emily live?"

"Because she has no idea who he is, and he knows it. Otherwise he'd have been arrested. Identified in the newspaper, at least," Wallace explained.

"However, we do feel that the two of you should . . . ah . . ." Dolly, for once, was not her usual articulate self. "Should resume your travels elsewhere."

"Get out of town," Seneca said dryly.

"For you own welfare, you understand. Not because you are not welcome here."

Seneca sat back, crossing his arms and pursing his lips in thought. "Give, Dolly. What's happened?"

"Seneca, dear, what makes you think. . ."

"I'm no fool. You're speaking with a decidedly forked tongue."

Dolly sighed and shrugged. "I told you it wouldn't work," she said to Chief Wallace. "A brick came through the police station window."

"I swear I didn't do it," Emily jumped in, attempting to ease the tension she saw growing around the table.

They all looked at her as if she'd grown a second nose. She drank her coffee.

"A note was attached to the brick." Dolly continued. "It warned of reprisal for those who stand in the way of Southern justice."

"Meaning?"

She shrugged. "It could mean we're to stay out of it if they come after you and Emily."

"Or it may mean nothing," Wallace said.

"A means of getting even with us?" Seneca asked. "Scare tactics."

"Possibly. In any event you will be safer away from here." Wallace shook his head in disgust.

Seneca relaxed and shrugged his brows. "We were planning to leave anyway. I have a good friend, an ex-slave, who went south in search of his missing family. He usually contacts me at regular intervals, at my insistence."

"He hasn't done so?" Dolly asked.

"I'm going to look for him. Dolly, I wonder if I might impose on you to take Emily back to Rochester."

Emily let her cup clatter into her saucer. Flinging down her napkin, she rose and stormed out.

Seneca caught her in the lobby, grabbing her by the arm and spinning her around to face him.

"What the hell's got into you now?"

"Absolutely nothing. I'm going to my room to pack my belongings. I'm taking the next train back to the East Coast."

"You're going to Rochester."

"No, I'm not," she said calmly but resolutely. She glanced sideways at the arrival of Dolly and Chief Wallace, then turned back to Seneca. "You've been sitting in there discussing my life as if I were not there. I was there. I am here. What happened to staying by your side from now on?"

"I'll be traveling and it won't be easy."

"I've been traveling with you. Was I a hindrance? Seneca, I want to come with you."

"Emily, I . . ."

"I'm coming with you, or I'm going to Albany alone. Without Dolly. And if I may remind you, two men are still out there who want me dead." She met his stare head on.

"Two?" Dolly asked.

Emily turned to her. "I mean no offense, Dolly, but I won't go with you. "

"Who's this other man you're talking about?"

"We don't know who he is," Seneca answered irritably. He spun around to glare at Emily. "That's a dirty low-down, mean thing to say."

"What other man?" Dolly persisted.

Seneca ran his fingers through his hair. "Two men were trailing us across the canal. We caught one of them, but the other, a large baldheaded man with a broom beneath his nose, escaped. We haven't seen him since—I don't know—Syracuse."

"I'm going with you, Seneca."

"For God's sake, take her with you," Dolly said finally. "I can't keep track of the people gunning for you."

Elijah walked stiffly behind the other workers toward the barracks. Two guards followed. Every muscle ached, but not for anything would he let them see it. His head was held proudly high, his shoulders unbent. He knew quite well that his very posture was an irritant to the guards.

"Look at the damn bastard," one of the men behind them said. "See how uppity he is. He thinks he's some kinda king."

The guards' words he could ignore, considering the source. But when one of them tripped him and shoved him down into the slimy mud surrounding the barracks, that he could not tolerate.

He got back to his feet, wiping the putrid slime

from his hands onto his pants. He squared his shoulders and turned to the two men.

"The basic difference between you and me," he said, tossing his earlier pretense aside, "is not the color of our skin. The difference is that I know and respect myself, whereas you are so afraid you don't measure up as men that you attempt to bolster your confidence by destroying others. But in fact all you do is foul the air."

The two guards flew into him, throwing punches and kicks. Elijah was able to hold his own until two more guards came running to the scene. With two men holding him and two beating on him, Elijah finally crumpled to his knees in agonizing defeat.

His face was swollen, mushy from the beating he'd taken. His eyes opened only to very narrow slits between puffy lids. Blood ran from his nose and lips. Pride made him stiffen his back and stand again.

Other men, men who had worked along side Elijah all afternoon, urged him to repeat what the guards demanded he say. "It don't do no good, man, to hold out on 'em. De jes keep on beatin' on ya till ya ain't got no sense no more."

"That or you're dead," another said. "It ain't no big thing to call you'sef a nigger. We all done it. We growed up hearin' it."

Elijah stood firm, his resentment, his rage, his frustration congealing into a tight frozen knot of absolute denial. He would not. He would not. The pain didn't matter.

His mind spun. His legs still worked, at least they seemed to, but not by any mental direction on his part. He was moving, going somewhere. Where was he going? Where were they taking him? He tried to stop, to resist them, but he had no strength left at all.

Metal hinges squeaked and he was being shoved

down onto hands and knees and into a long, low box. The door closed with a clang and the loud click of a lock. A sweatbox, his mind registered. Tomorrow would be hell. But right now any flat place was welcome. He laid his head down and let the sweet, painless dark steal over him.

Chapter 17

The best course of action for finding Elijah, Seneca decided, would be to trace as closely as possible the route he had taken, or had been planning to take.

"He would have come through Erie," Seneca said, referring to a map of the area. "Several canawllers on the Erie Extension, the canal that runs down to Pittsburgh," he explained, showing her on the map, "are Friends of Liberty. Elijah will have checked in with the agents to see if anyone has seen Bekka."

"So we'll travel on this canal?" Emily asked.

Seneca glanced out at the passing scenery. "Not all the way, no. Elijah will trace a freedom road. I'll have to try and guess which one."

"You mean we might never find him?"

"He'll be all right in Pennsylvania, for the most part, unless Ryker gets to him. But if something happens to him in a slave state, we may *not* find him. We'll have to trust him to get word to us."

"They won't believe that he's a free man?"

"They won't care. Once they've got him, they'll keep him."

Presque Isle was the head of the Erie Extension

canal. Seneca knew several of the captains who were waiting to retrieve their boats at the weighlock. George Heath was one of them. George, a spry man not much larger than Emily, slapped Seneca on the shoulder and shook his hand.

"What brings you down this way? Just saw your man Elijah nigh on a week past now. And who is this lovely little lass?"

"This is Emily, my . . . my wife. Emily, this old reprobate is George."

"How do, ma'am. So you finally tied the knot, did you?" he said laughingly. "Glad to hear it. It ain't right that a man be by hisself."

"George, how would you like a couple stowaways just down to the French Creek Feeder?"

"Sure, sure. Be a pleasure."

"Did you happen to overhear which road Elijah was taking?"

"He mentioned a conductor in Kennerdell. That's all he said."

"He'll have gone through Franklin then. Well, I guessed right. We'll take the French Creek Feeder to Meadville, then the Franklin line to the Allegheny River."

"I reckon that would be best considerin' you got a woman along. Elijah was makin' inquiries about buying a canoe. He wanted to make faster time once he reached French Creek."

Seneca looked at Emily thoughtfully, then made up his mind. "We'll stick to the canal, I think."

"Don't let me hold you back," she said to him when they had a few minutes alone. "If you think we should take the creek, then let's do it. I can manage. The Indians did."

"The Indians didn't wear lace and petticoats."

"That may be all I have at the moment, but surely I can find more suitable apparel at any general mercantile."

"Emily, it's out of the question. We'll take the canal. The discussion is closed."

The French Creek Feeder intersected with the Erie Extension northeast of Meadville. Seneca bought them passage for the twenty some miles into Meadville with a small packet that had a few places open.

Packet travel lacked the casual friendliness she found on both Seneca's and George's boats. The other passengers were aloof and tended to stay with their own set of friends, excluding Emily and Seneca. From the scattered bits of conversation she heard she gathered the groups had been to Erie for a weekend of theater and shopping.

Seneca didn't seem to mind being ignored. He found them two chairs on deck and settled himself in for a nap. When he wasn't asleep he was back at the tiller with the captain.

"Captain Dave seems to be of the same mind as George. Seems they've had heavy rain this spring and summer, and French Creek is moving good. He says he'd rather be on the river any day than running a packet down the canal."

"Are you trying to punish me for insisting on coming with you?" she asked, throwing him an oblique look.

"No," he answered sincerely. "I was just thinking out loud."

"You want to take the creek, don't you? Tell me what it would be like."

"It would be rough. We'll be out in the middle of nowhere with no one to help should one of us get hurt. The wildlife can be . . . "

"What wildlife?"

"Deer, raccoons, beavers, panthers, bears, snakes." The last three he glossed over quickly.

"Ahh. *That* wildlife."

281

"We won't have a roof over our heads if it begins to rain. Thunderstorms can be fierce. If we can't make it into town, we may have to sleep out."

"In the woods," she said flatly.

"Yes. "And if it's hot and sunny you could be sunburned. So you see, all the way around, the canal is a better choice."

"Yes. I think it is. Panthers?" she asked, staring into the heavy forest on either side of the canal. Snakes?

She'd almost convinced herself about the advisability of staying with the canal system when they hit the last stretch of canal into Meadville. Traffic was so slow and congested that what should have taken minutes to cover took hours. Seneca's impatience was a living, finger-drumming presence.

Finally they docked and Seneca grabbed their bags and elbowed his way off the boat. "I cannot abide conditions such as these. Let's find a restaurant and a hotel. In that order. I'm famished."

She agreed. She was hungry herself, having had only an apple and a cup of coffee for lunch.

After dinner he escorted her toward the nicest looking hotel in town. Emily carried her own valise so that she could hold on to Seneca's hand.

"You know something odd? I've only lived in two homes in my life, yet I've always felt at home with you, no matter where we've been."

He looked down at her, brows raised. "Really? What a nice compliment."

They walked in silence until they came to the hotel. He stopped and looked into her upturned eyes. "Shall I order one room or two?"

"Oh, I think it would look curious for a husband and wife to order separate rooms."

He grinned and chucked her chin. "You are a shameless woman."

"All right. Order two rooms. Sleep all alone in your own big cold bed . . . while I toss and turn in the restless frustration of unfulfilled desire."

He threw his head back and laughed. "Good grief, that sounds too painful to say, let alone experience. I shall rescue you from such a dreadful fate and order one room."

"My hero," she sighed, dropping her head to his upper arm.

He led her up the wide steps to the front door and reached out to pull it open. The window pane by his head shattered into a thousand pieces, as did a long framed mirror opposite the front door inside the hotel.

Seneca yanked open the door and shoved her inside and to the floor. "Stay here," he ordered when no other shots followed.

"What was that? What have you done?" shrieked the night clerk, coming from the room behind the desk. "What is going on here?"

"Stay down. Someone took a shot at us." Seneca crawled to the door and leaned out far enough to see the street outside. No one was there at first, then curious men began to investigate the obvious gunshot in the middle of a quiet business district. Seneca ran several blocks in either direction before he returned to the hotel.

The sheriff was sitting with Emily, each holding a cup of coffee. The desk clerk stood nearby. When Seneca strode through the door, Emily ran to meet him, a question blazing from her eyes.

"Sorry," he answered. "I didn't find anything or anyone."

"Tarnation. I thought we were all through with that," she muttered into his chest.

"I know, angel. I know. Let's try to get by here without an extended interrogation. What have you

283

told him?"

"I didn't say anything except that someone shot at us."

"Good girl. Let me get us out of this."

Another fifteen minutes passed before the sheriff was satisfied with their answers.

"It appears that you have picked up an enemy somewhere along your journey, or someone mistook you for someone else."

"That must be it, sheriff. Look, my wife's exhausted. Could we go now? We'll be on the first boat out in the morning, so we won't be any more of a problem to you."

"I'll show you to your room," the clerk said. I'm so sorry this happened at our hotel. I hope you won't bear any ill will against us."

"Now what do we do?" Emily asked, flinging herself onto the wide bed. "Who do you think it was who shot at us?"

He sighed and slumped into an overstuffed armchair, staring off into space at nothing. "Well, we're back to our original supposition, only now we're *both* objects of revenge. It could be one of Ryker's men, or your friend is following us still, bent on evening the score."

"Seems rather pointless, doesn't it?" she asked wearily. "Who is this Ryker and why is he after you?"

"Ryker is an entrepreneur of the South. He has holdings in the cotton industry, tobacco, horses . . . He has gambling houses and places of ill repute in Natchez. He also is involved in several plantations in the West Indies. Sugar, I believe. Anyway, his entire wealth depends on slave labor, save his casino and brothels. And even there . . . His latest venture involved breeding slaves. He captured fugitives and held them for his own purposes, with no idea to whom they supposedly belonged. I set the Federal men on him. I threatened to expose the whole operation if Ryker wasn't stopped, thereby making the Fugitive Slave Law look like a government endorsement of cruelty, human indignity, suffering, and the corruption of human life and morality. I promised that when I got finished, not one of them would still be in office.

"He was shut down overnight, and the slaves who had suffered at Ryker's hand were given safe transport into upper New York, where they could choose to go into Canada or stay."

"What happened to Ryker?"

"He was arrested; he paid a fine; and he went free. He swore he'd get me."

"Could I ask one more question? Was Dolly involved in Ryker's arrest?"

"She was instrumental in the entire affair."

Very much later that night he tried again to convince her. "Emily, we can't go on like this. I can't stay away from you, but we're taking an awful chance. I think we should be married. And the sooner the better. It isn't as if we don't love each other, is it?" He planted kisses along her brow, down her nose to her love-bruised lips. "What do you say, Emily?"

"Seneca, my love, you'd hate me for taking away your freedom. And much as you might think you can get around me, I'd put an end to your drinking and carousing. I won't be Mrs. Prescott and tolerate some floozie on your knee. So be reasonable. I can't see . . . "

"I thought we'd settled that. Are you still worrying because of that?"

"Oh, that and what I overheard you say to Elijah—that you didn't want to get married and that you resented what you felt for me."

"You heard that, did you? That was all a very

285

long time ago. Can't a man have an honest change of heart?"

"How can I be sure? What if you'd heard me say such a thing about you? Wouldn't you wonder? Wouldn't a question remain in the back of your mind?"

"Okay. I'll give you more time. But one of these days you'll believe me." And if they kept on as they were, one of these days she'd have to give in to him. Mother Nature could be very unforgiving. Except for the reproach she would be forced to face, should that happen, he almost hoped it would. He had never experienced any kind of desire to impregnate a woman before. On the contrary, he had been careful in that regard, as careful as he could manage to be, even going so far as suggesting certain methods of preventing pregnancy to his partners.

With Emily, innocent Emily, a young woman he knew to be unschooled in such matters, he hadn't done so. His conscience had prodded him, he had had the means, but he had not done it. Instead he had taken her time and again, knowing full well what he was doing and what the outcome might be.

She snuggled into his arms again and laid her face against his chest. He ran his hand over her golden hair, imagining a young daughter with the same gold locks and big blue eyes. Or a son like himself with dark hair falling across his forehead, a son to tag along with him as he'd done with his father and grandfather.

His body stirred with urgent desire. "Emily," he murmured into her hair.

"Hmm," she answered in a purr.

"I'm not letting you go, Emily. I'm never letting you go, so you might as well marry me."

She chuckled sleepily and tugged playfully at the black curls under her fingers.

286

He rolled her to her back, pinning her hands over her head.

"You don't believe me?" he said threateningly. "A young lady in your position shouldn't antagonize. I might be tempted to . . . "

She twisted wantonly beneath him, feeling her breasts, already sensitive from his previous ardent loving, grow heavy and tight with renewed desire. She was amazed at how soon she could want him again after having been so completely and satisfyingly ravished, but she did. And she was in no mood to be denied.

Nor was he.

He woke her the next morning by dumping several packages on the mound of her nicely rounded backside.

"Get up, sleepyhead. We have a hundred things to do today."

"What time is it?" she muttered, rolling over. "What is all this?" And why was he dressed like that?

"It is eight o'clock and these are clothes. Now get your tempting little body out of that bed before we lose more of the morning."

He tore the paper off the packages, laying out several pairs of trousers, a pair of soft leather boots, shirts, a jacket, a wide-brimmed hat, woolen blankets, two waterproof tarps, and an oilcloth bag.

"I'll get food and a few other provisions while you get into some clothes. I'll be back in half an hour. Be ready, and pack what you need and what you think I'll need into that duffel bag. Go easy. You might have to carry it."

"We're taking the river," she guessed accurately. She nodded, knowing that whatever his reasons, they were good ones. He left and she got to work, taking care of her morning ablutions, weaving her hair into a convenient braid that hung heavily between her shoulders, and dressing in her newly purchased apparel.

Thinking ahead, she selected a set of dress clothes for each of them and tucked them into the bottom of the bag. She followed that with their outdoor clothes, their river clothes, she thought of them, and their personal articles. She'd managed to get quite a bit into the bag and still feel she could carry it. At the last minute she spread one tarp out and rolled the other one and the blankets into a tight roll, securing it with the ropes at the ends of the tarp.

She'd never done anything like this before, but she remembered a hunting expedition her father had made once before he became ill, and how he had packed his gear to keep it dry. She sat down and waited, unable to think of anything else to do.

"Good girl," Seneca said approvingly when he returned. "We'll store our other things here at the hotel for when we return. I've arranged for everything else to be delivered to the boat. But before that we have one stop to make. Ready?"

He hefted the bag and bedding roll as if they were weightless, and escorted her from the hotel, using a back entrance. They left town and hiked across a meadow full of grazing cows to a farmhouse.

"Mr. Brown, Mrs. Brown, this is Emily. Emily, Mr. Brown is the local justice of the peace. He has agreed to marry us."

"Seneca," she said, her grip tightening on his hand. "Could I speak to you, please?"

"Excuse us, your honor," he said, winking. The judge grinned in response.

"What do you think you're doing?" she demanded.

He pulled her into his arms and kissed her. She fought him at first, but as usual, she lost the fight to her own wayward body.

"Now, is that answer enough? Or do I have to

remind you of last night?"

Whether he needed to or not, he had reminded her, and she had to face the fact that he was right. Her submission to his male aggression and dominance had been utterly complete, her response shamelessly unbridled, to the point she had begged him to take her.

And there was that moment when she had dug her nails into his shoulders in a desperate cry for his seed to fill her and find her and burst to new and wondrous life within her, and a moment before ecstasy exploded in them both when she'd seen that same desperate intent mirrored in his own black eyes.

And that moment, she knew, was what he meant now. They could both fight and kick and scream mentally about outward and public vows, but their bodies and their souls had already recognized each other as mates and had made that commitment.

"It's only a formality now. We both know that," he said, seeming to read her mind.

"Your mother will be hurt."

"We'll do it again when we get home. We don't have to tell her about this. But I need it, angel. Guilt, my conscience, a fear of losing you . . ."

"Shh. It's all right. I would be honored to be your wife. I've always wanted it. I just needed to be sure of you."

"Then put your mind at ease, my darling girl. I couldn't love you more."

They were married at fifteen minutes past nine on that Saturday morning in early June. By ten o'clock they were paddling down the rain-swollen French Creek toward a town Emily had never heard of, and she had never been happier in her life.

He stood in the telegraph office in Albany, reading and rereading the telegram he'd received and trying to formulate a response. If he called it all off now, no one could connect him with any crime. He was tempted to wire back that the hunt should be terminated. The men he'd hired had been incompetent fools, anyway.

But the thought of what he stood to lose if she returned and began snooping into things better left as they were made his gut twist in fear and anger. He thought of his family and what would happen to them if what he had done were discovered and he were arrested. It was too much to bear. His wife would never forgive him either if they had to move back out of the big house. She loved the prestige she'd gained with her new furniture and her new wardrobe, her new place in society.

Slowly he began to write, hoping the big son-of-a-bitch would be successful this time. She could never come back. He would be safe, he could guarantee their newfound wealth, if only she were dead.

A. Affirmative. One more week. Do not fail or deal is off. P.

In Meadville, Pennsylvania, the man stubbed out one cigarette and lit another, pacing impatiently outside the telegraph office. His time had run out, but if he could get the bastard to give him just a few more days he could get her. He was so close. Five hundred dollars. He wasn't giving up five hundred dollars. But why worry? Even if the deal was terminated he could still get the girl, he thought. With her, he could get whatever he wanted from that damned weasel in New York.

"Yeah, maybe that's the way to do it," he muttered, grinning beneath the heavy brush of his mustache. "Get rid of the guy and take the girl." That had infinitely more appeal.

Suddenly he didn't care what the answer was. He pulled his cap on, adjusting the brim to shade his eyes against the morning sun. Fondling the butt of his rifle, he hoisted the leather strap over his shoulder and strode away.

The clerk came out, flapping a pink paper in his hand. "Mister, hey mister, your answer. Mister?" The man didn't stop, didn't even turn. The clerk shrugged his shoulders and went back inside.

From a safe distance the man watched them walk hand in hand across the field to the small dock constructed beside the creek. Tied to the dock was a canoe, long, shiny, and loaded with gear.

His lips curled cynically and he shook his head. How easy this would be. On the river they would be as exposed as apples in a barrel. His yellowed teeth showed in a crooked grin. He'd enjoy putting a bullet through that bastard Prescott after the way he busted up Jack's leg. And when he got his hands on that pretty little gal . . . Yes, this was going to be fun.

After two hours Emily begged for shore leave. Seneca helped her from the canoe and pulled the boat well into the bushes. While she took care of nature's call he dug out a couple of fat cookies full of nuts and raisins and poured two tin mugs of sweet tea from a canteen.

Emily rinsed her hands and face from a small stream that burbled into the creek from the hillside above. She stood and rotated her head and shoulders, loosening cramped and burning muscles.

"Let me help," Seneca offered when she sat down beside him in the mossy clearing.

His fingers worked on her strained muscles, kneading out knots, working out the tension. She leaned into his hands and let her head fall backward.

"That's wonderful."

"You're wonderful. You're handling the paddle beautifully. My own squaw."

"Ha-ha. I'm a babe in the woods. I'd be totally at a loss without you. Some squaw."

He pulled her backward and pinned her to the ground. "I'll teach you everything you need to know, wife."

"You mean what berries to eat, how to trap a rabbit, that sort of thing?"

"That too, but I had something much more basic in mind."

"Like how to build a fire?"

"Now you're getting warmer."

"So tell me, will it be difficult coaxing these flames to life?"

"Oh, I think the embers will always be hot enough so that a brief whisper will cause them to flare."

"Let's test your theory," she said seductively. She pulled his head down and whispered a naughty suggestion in his ear.

He groaned. "Wicked woman." His lips claimed hers in a sudden and devastating kiss that was intended to arouse her as much as her words had aroused him. He unbuttoned her blouse and pulled the bows free on the bodice of her chemise. His lips left a hot moist trail from her tempting mouth down the column of her neck, to the soft curves of her bosom.

"Oh, Seneca, you make me melt inside and make my head spin so that I can't even think."

"Good. You aren't supposed to think. Just feel."

His kiss, as effective as always with her, was cut abruptly short. He lifted his head, motioning her to silence. It took her a few seconds to realize that he was listening for something. Something specific.

Quietly they rolled to their hands and knees and crept to the edge of the clearing, peering through the brush that concealed both them and their canoe.

She heard it then, the slap and the splash of a paddle being thrust into the water. They watched, barely breathing, as his boat passed within feet of them. Seneca's arm tightened around her and his fingers came to rest against her lips, stilling the gasp that nearly escaped.

In silent stillness they watched him go, his broad shoulders working, his muscular arms pulling the canoe across the water with long even strokes. He was moving along at a fair rate of speed.

"He's trying to catch up with us," Seneca whispered as the other canoe passed out of sight.

Emily pounded the ground. "How does he do it? How does he keep finding us?"

Seneca's lips tightened. "He's good, all right. We'll keep well behind him." He didn't mention that he'd have to readjust his entire attitude. What had begun as a simple challenge in outsmarting a tenacious politician had turned into a very real struggle to escape with their lives. This man, though he wasn't the best of shots, or hadn't been thus far, was a man used to the chase. A man wise to the ways of the wilderness.

Undoubtedly very experienced in tracking and returning slaves for a fee, as were most bounty hunters, this man had turned his skills to tracking them. And the rifle at his side, the repeated attempts on their lives, told him he was not fussy about what condition his quarry was in when he delivered it. And no doubt the man who hired him wasn't too concerned either.

He took a bracing breath and dug into the food pack, producing a long-barreled pistol and a box of ammunition. He emptied a handful of bullets into

293

his pocket and tucked the long barrel under the belt at his back. He glanced at Emily's worried face.

No one was going to harm his woman, not as long as he could draw breath. She was his wife now and could very well be carrying his child. He had every right to kill to keep her safe. And he would. Whoever that man was, he'd just turned this river trip into a deadly game to survive.

Chapter 18

Seneca bypassed the main French Creek dock in Franklin and went on around the bend to the junction of the Allegheny River. The river was high, almost covering the marker he was searching for, a signal to the conductors that here was a safe waystation. Seneca swung the canoe into shore and guided it into a clump of trees that was already two feet deep in water.

The boat came to rest where a sidewalk covered with a trellis of ivy extended to the river. Somewhere beneath the water must be a dock, she thought. She got out and helped pull the canoe to shore.

They concealed the boat inside the trellis, their whereabouts now a mystery. Frenchie couldn't have caught up with them this soon, but even if he had, he'd never find them here.

She grinned as she thought about their day. "Do you think he's in town by now?" she asked, knowing Seneca would follow her thoughts.

"Quite probably. He'll be searching for us, never doubt it."

They made their way to the basement door of the tall narrow house and rapped out a brisk code.

"The cows are loose," a voice came from inside.

"They're on the courthouse lawn," Seneca answered.

The door opened, and they were welcomed into the dim room. The man looked behind them, expecting cargo to arrive. He turned back to Seneca questioningly.

"We are alone, my friend. We come seeking sanctuary and information." Seneca extended a hand of friendship. "Seneca Prescott, of Rochester, New York, and my wife Emily."

Mr. McDowell showed them around the comfortable room with whitewashed walls and thick braided rugs on the stone floor. A separate area for privacy behind a tall screen that stood beyond the long rows of bunks. One double bed stood in the corner. Emily and Seneca both looked at it.

Mr. McDowell lit the fire in the fireplace and set two buckets of water to heating. "The rain barrel is just outside the door if you need more water. Missus will have dinner on in an hour. We'd be pleased to have your company upstairs."

He left them alone then to bathe and change for dinner. "I'm almost sorry to see you back in a dress after enjoying the sight of your little bum in pants all day," Seneca said as she shook wrinkles from their good clothes.

She made a face at him and began to undress. She threw the soggy trousers at him, followed by her soggy socks. He hung them beside the fireplace to dry. She stepped behind the screen to bathe herself. He laughed at her modesty.

She emerged in several minutes dressed in clean clothes, if a bit wrinkled. "Would you help me with my buttons?" she asked.

"That was quick." He kissed her bare back. "You smell good. Can I use your bath water?"

"It's awfully soapy. I'll come rinse you."

"No fair. You hid behind the screen."

"Nobody kept you out."

"Now she tells me. Just for that, you can scrub my back."

Mrs. McDowell was a rosy-cheeked lady with a ready smile of welcome for her guests.

"Presbyterians," she answered when Emily asked if they were affiliated with a particular church. "Many of our congregation are staunch abolitionists, though few are active in the road. Always, though, we find food or other contributions on our doorstep."

"Aren't you afraid when other people know about your work?" she asked.

"Slavehunters would be run out of this town," Mr. McDowell said. "Been done before."

"Folks can be pretty tight-lipped in these parts. Nobody talks about it except to folks they know real good."

"You say you're seekin' information," McDowell reminded him.

"Yes. A friend of mine, a slave whose freedom I bought, who goes by the name of Elijah, came through here last week. I'm trying to trace his steps. He was following a lead to his family who disappeared, and now it seems he has also. He was heading into West Virginia, so he and I had an arrangement for him to wire me every few days to let me know he was safe."

"And you haven't heard?"

"He's very tall, and handsome," Emily said, "and speaks with a West Indian accent."

"I haven't seen . . ."

"He was here, Charles, when you were at the mill. He came with Josiah, asking about a woman and a boy. I forgot about it. I'm sorry."

"No harm done," Mr. McDowell said, patting his wife's arm. "At least we now know he was here. I have a son in Kennerdell, down the river. He runs a station. If your man Elijah was searching the road, he'd certainly go there. Josiah would have suggested it to him."

"Do you know a couple of men who trap along French Creek, have a laquered wooden canoe with a red rose on the bow?" Like theirs, he thought, but he didn't mention it.

"Ah, that'd be Reynolds' boats, out of Meadville. Makes a good boat, he does. Describe the men."

"One was tall, real thin, wore a ragged leather hat and a red plaid shirt. Carried a double-barrel. The other was no more than a kid, but had a nasty look to him."

"Yeah, I know 'em. Come down from Saegertown," he said disgustedly. "I'd avoid them, if possible."

Seneca grinned and nodded. "We had a man tailing us. He bears a grudge against my wife for thwarting an assassination attempt against Mr. Lincoln. He passed us on the river when we stopped for a rest. I fully expected to be ambushed when he realized what happened. But instead, he ambushed the other two men, who were not too happy about it. When we passed them, the man chasing us was tied to a tree and spouting a stream of not terribly friendly French at the other two men."

The McDowells enjoyed a good laugh at Seneca's tale and at others about his new wife and the Erie Canal. At the end of the evening Emily and Seneca took their leave of the McDowells, stopping to say good-bye before going down to the basement.

"We shall leave very early," Seneca told them. "We'll try not to disturb you. And thank you for your hospitality." He took a bill from his wallet and passed it to McDowell. "I'm sure you can find a use for this. Please accept it as a contribution for the cause."

"Very well, for the cause I will. Good night, and God go with you."

Heavy fog lay in a blanket over the river the next morning when Seneca and Emily prepared to leave. Mr. McDowell arrived as they were loading their belongings into the boat. He passed Emily a small box.

"Food. Mrs. McDowell insisted. And a letter, if you would be good enough to deliver it to our son."

"A pleasure," Seneca said, shaking the man's hand.

"Good. And mind the rapids."

"Rapids?" Emily asked around a mouthful of warm bread and jelly. "Did he say rapids?" She handed Seneca a piece which he tucked into his mouth.

"Yup."

"Are they dangerous?"

He swallowed and took a drink of his cooling coffee. He grimaced and dumped the rest into the river, tossing his cup into the food sack. Emily repacked the bag, securing it against water.

"Answer my question," she prodded.

"They could be. The high water will be fast, but at the same time the rocks will be covered. There is risk, but perhaps not as much as there would be at normal water levels. I will need help to keep the nose off the rocks if the boat gets away from me."

"Wow. So much for easing my apprehensions."

He grinned that heartstopping smile. "No need to fear. Sit back and relax while you have the chance."

She looked up and around at the hazy outline of the high hills on either side of the Allegheny River. "It's warm for so early in the morning."

"Better get your hat on. You can be burned through the haze."

"What do you think Frenchie will do today? Will

he be on the river?"

"We'll have to assume he already is, which means we must be ready at any moment to defend ourselves."

"How can you be so calm?" she demanded, sitting up. She turned and faced the front, picking up her paddle. "How can you say to sit back and relax when that man could be . . . anywhere."

"Panic won't help."

"I'm not panicked, but for goodness sake, shouldn't we both be on the alert? He has a gun."

"So do we. Look, Emily, would you rather get off the river? Would you feel safer if we waited for the steamboat? What would you like to do?"

She placed her paddle over the bow and leaned her elbows on it. What did she want? He could ambush them on a road as easily as on the river. Add to that the inconvenience of a rough and tiresome ride. And bears and snakes.

And on a commercial vehicle they were only safe as long as they hid inside, and as long as Frenchie didn't manage to get aboard also. The idea of hiding for the rest of her life did not appeal. Wouldn't facing him now be far better?

"I'd rather stick to your original plan," she said. "At least there aren't snakes in the river."

He said nothing, and she turned to see why. "Isn't that what you wanted me to say? Don't you want to stay on the river?"

"Yes. Yes, I do. It's just that . . . nothing."

"What? Don't *nothing* me."

"Now don't get alarmed, but you must be careful in these waters. They're home to the cottonmouth."

"Now what's that? You didn't mention that animal in your inventory of wildlife." Her voice rose.

"It's just a snake, for Chrissake."

"Oh," she said, more quietly. "Harmless, then?"

300

"Hell, no. One of the deadliest in the east."

"Lord," she groaned, searching the depths of the water around them. She picked up her paddle and instantly imagined the slimy beast slithering its way up the handle to her white fingers. The paddle fell into the water with a splash.

"Jeez, what the hell . . ." He reached out and caught the end of the paddle, returning it to the boat.

She turned to apologize, a blush staining her cheeks. "That was foolish. Sorry."

"What happened?"

"Runaway imagination." She shook her head dismissively. "I don't like snakes."

"I know. I don't either."

"So we're agreed then?"

"On the snakes? You bet."

She gave him an exasperated glare. "On the river."

"Whatever you say, Emily."

"Why do I get the impression this entire conversation was wasted breath. You never intended to do anything else, did you?"

"No."

"Hmph."

The river narrowed in places, pushing the canoe between sheer granite walls at a swifter rate, and widened in others, requiring that they paddle. High hills rose sharply on either side of the river, lending a sense of prehistoric wonder to the ride.

At first she didn't notice the change in the sounds around her. The breeze rushed past her ears, leaves rustled overhead, water gurgled in shallow riffles nearby. Seneca spoke to her, and she had to ask him to repeat what he'd said. She knew then what the sound meant.

"Get set, brace your feet, and be ready to paddle on whichever side I tell you. Backpaddle right. I want to take a look at this."

"It looks big. Are you sure?"

"Right hard. We'll go ashore and have a proper look."

They tied up and climbed the high outcropping of rocks on the south side of the river. From there they could see the length of the rapids plus a fair distance in the opposite direction.

"Seneca, look. Upriver. Is that Frenchie?"

He swore. "All right, now look. See the place where the water runs smooth. We take that channel then cut a hard right past the big rocks to the channel on the other side. If we make that, the rest isn't too bad. Let's get down there before he sees the boat. All we need is a bullet hole in the bottom. And I don't want him ahead of us where he can ambush us."

Without a second thought to what she was doing, she scrambled down the steep rocky incline and helped Seneca get the boat launched again. They had only brief seconds to get organized before they were pushed over the edge of the first drop.

Water swept over the bow, soaking her to the skin. She gasped and screamed at the sudden cold drenching, then she was too busy to think about it. When she wasn't following Seneca's orders she was bailing water or holding on for dear life.

When they reached calm waters again she turned to him and laughed. "That was fantastic."

"Not bad," he agreed, mopping his face with his sleeve. "Let's take a minute on this sand bar ahead to dump the water from the boat. Our packs are supposedly waterproof, but I don't know how they'll fare sitting in a puddle for hours."

They both jumped out at the same time, each swinging some of their belongings onto the sand. They took the ends of the boat and rolled it over, draining it. Then just as quickly they reloaded and pushed off.

Emily looked back. "There he is. He's missed the turn. Oh, my God, he's fallen out of the boat."

They watched as the canoe was spun like a toothpick this way and that until it smashed into the rocks and splintered under the force of the water. The Frenchman, after tumbling down the first set of steps, managed to make his way to the rocks on the side. He would be all right, but he would be on foot.

Seneca paddled into the river where Frenchie's pack was floating. He scooped it up. The walnut butt of the rifle floated past. He grinned and let it go. Looking back once, he guided the canoe to the sand bar and tossed the pack ashore. He gave the Frenchman a wave and turned the canoe downriver, back to the route he was convinced Elijah had taken.

Kennerdell, a town in a deep valley of the mountains, gave little more information than they had found in Franklin. Elijah had been there, but no one had seen or heard of a lone woman and a child traveling the road.

"What was it that sent Elijah to West Virginia in the first place?" Emily asked.

"He was vague about it, but he said one of the passengers on the freedom road mentioned a child. For some reason Elijah was convinced the boy was his son."

"He'll be so disheartened if he can't find him. Or if it is some other boy."

They did not stay long in Kennerdell but continued down the river toward Pittsburgh. They passed several larger craft coming upriver, all steam powered.

"How do they navigate the rapids we came

303

through?" she asked incredulously.

"They make a run for them. The captains know every rock in the river. If they get the speed they need, they twist those boats right through the channels. Once in a while they have to back up and start again."

"I can't imagine it when we went hurdling toward disaster."

"Don't forget they can reverse the motion of the paddlewheels down the rapids. They don't hurdle anywhere."

Once in camp after an arduous day on the river Seneca set about building a fire and preparing a hot meal. Emily found a flat place and stretched out, relieving her sore muscles.

"What can I do?" she asked, rolling to lean on one elbow.

He looked up and smiled. "Just relax."

"No, I want to help."

"Okay. Take this knife and gather some soft branches of pine needles for our bed. Or moss. Moss is good, too."

By the time she had fashioned a soft pallet of both moss and pine needles, laid out one tarp as a ground cloth and rolled out their blankets to make a bed, Seneca had their meal prepared—a feast of grilled fish, potatoes baked in their skins, and apples cooked in sugar and spices. Nothing in her life had tasted as good.

"It's the fresh air and all that hard work. It improves the appetite."

"I'm not a stranger to hard work, Seneca," she retorted, hearing a hint of patronizing in his tone.

He looked at her consideringly. "No, I don't think you are. You're a good sport and you've a good sense of humor. Let's hope it's there in the morning," he added, turning back to his meal.

She couldn't imagine why he would say that until the first drop of rain fell. With lightening speed Seneca flung the second tarp protectively over their bedding and clothes. Gathering a few fallen branches from the dense forest surrounding the camp, he lashed together a tent frame. She helped him set it in place and drape the tarp over it, securing the corners with rocks. His last act before finding shelter in the tent was to hang the food bag from a high branch of a tree. While he did that she cleaned their dishes and stacked them under the tent.

They were definitely damp but laughing when they finally finished their frantic preparations. They kicked off their wet boots and tugged off their damp outer clothes. She found her brush and began to tug her long braid free.

"Let me do that," Seneca said, sitting behind her with his knees raised on either side of her.

She gave up the brush, clamped her arms around his knee, and leaned her head back to enjoy his ministrations.

"This is very cozy. You have quite a bit of experience as an outdoorsman?" she asked.

"Average," he said, offhandedly.

"It isn't even dark yet. What shall we do until bedtime?"

In long slow strokes the brush ran through her pale hair. He marveled anew at the beauty of contrast, her fairness against his sunbronzed skin, her white-gold locks against his black, her soft femininity against his taut-muscled masculinity.

A quick stab of fear shot through him, as had happened frequently of late when he thought he might lose her. But this time, instead of lingering to torment him, the fear gave way to relief and joy. She was his finally. His wife.

He had wondered once if the driving need to possess her would ease once he'd made her his wife. It hadn't. He wanted her more now than ever before.

"I'll tell you a bedtime story," he murmured in her ear. "I'll tell you about a beautiful angel who came to earth on a silver moonbeam. And there was this lonely mortal man who lived in the cold darkness all alone until quite by the hand of fate he reached out and touched the angel. And he found, once having gazed upon her beauty, once having felt the warmth of her light, that he could not go from her."

She turned, gazing up into his dark eyes, her lips moist and parted. "Tell me more," she invited seductively.

He swallowed visibly and took a ragged breath. "Well, ah," he continued, staring at her mouth. "He . . . she . . . oh, hell."

He pulled her into his arms and rolled backward, taking her with him. He tunneled his hands into her hair and pulled her mouth to his.

He kissed her deeply, needing more and more of her, as if his hunger and thirst would never be satisfied.

His tongue was swollen, his mouth dry, spitless. His lips were cracked and painful. Pain. He could barely isolate one pain amidst all the rest. He pulled his knees up to help the pain in his stomach, but that only stretched the raw and bleeding skin on his back.

"Water," he whispered, but he knew no one heard. No one was out there. No one cared.

"Hey mister," a voice whispered outside. A child's voice. "Mister."

Elijah fought to hold on to his consciousness. He bit his sore lip. "Help me," he croaked. "Water."

"Listen, mister, I can't get you out, but I can pour

water in the air holes. Can you hear me? Move your head over here."

Elijah struggled frantically to do as the boy said even though every movement caused more pain. Water came in a slow dribble through one of the holes, then through one of the others. He drank until he thought he would vomit, and still he kept his face and neck under the steady drip.

The cold water was heaven on his hot and blistered skin. His sanity began to return as the temperature inside the box cooled.

"I have to go, mister. I'm sorry I can't do more for you."

He tried to thank him but his voice wouldn't work. And that made him want to cry, only he had no tears.

The boy stood beside the sweatbox, wondering if the man inside was alive or dead. He'd watched the guards strip the man to nakedness and take the whip to him, and that was after they'd beat his face to a grotesque, bloody mask.

But the man wouldn't stay down. He'd never seen a man with so much pride. He admired him for that, and he felt profoundly sorry when the man's knees had finally buckled and he'd cried out in pain.

That should have been enough. They should have let the women nurse him, but they didn't. They took him to the sweatbox. He shook his young head. The man was probably dead.

That was too bad, and he was sorry, and he was also unreasonably angry at the guards for doing this. Even though he stood a good chance of being caught and punished, he drew bucket after bucket of water from the well and poured it over the hot metal box until it was cool to the touch.

Emily's eyes opened. At first she was disoriented, then she remembered where she was and closed her eyes again, snuggling into Seneca's side. It was not yet morning.

A low snuff had her eyes popping open again. A faint odor reached her nostrils, an odor that grew more distasteful by the second. The snuff sounded again.

"Don't be alarmed," Seneca whispered in her ear. "We have a visitor."

She grew stiff with fright. "What visitor?"

"A bear. Stay here. I'll see to it."

"No, don't go out there," she said, grabbing his arm.

"Emily, she could smash up the canoe."

"What about you?"

He turned and threw her an incredulous frown. "Why would I want to break up our only boat?"

"Seneca!" she screamed when he began yelling and cussing at the bear outside. She crawled to the end of the tent and looked out. The bear on hind legs stood as tall as Seneca, nearly tall enough to reach the food pouch. She took a threatening step his way.

Emily screamed, grabbing the pots and tin plates and throwing them toward the bear.

Two crazy screaming humans were too much for her. She dropped to all fours and scuttled back up the hill behind the camp.

Emily sat down shakily on a log Seneca had pulled up to the fire the evening before. She fought to catch her breath and calm her racing pulse.

"I thought you were going to be killed."

His eyes were remorseful. "I'm sorry you had to experience that. I know how frightening it can be."

She waved her hand dismissively. "It wasn't your fault."

He sat beside her and took her hand. "Yes, it

was. You see, these bears aren't aggressive, not like the grizzlies. They require a fair amount of respect but they're easily frightened off. I should have explained, but I had too much fun teasing you. Look, I'll make a fire and put some coffee on. If I can find the coffee pot. Why don't you get dressed. You'll feel better."

"I'd like a bath. How much were you teasing me about those snakes?"

"Tell you what. I'll check the water first, and if you'd like," he said with a leer, "I'll stand watch."

"Would you? Yes, I'd appreciate it." And at the same time get a little of her own back.

"Hey, I was teasing again."

"I wasn't. I'll get my soap and towel." She turned her back to him as she unfastened her undergarments and stepped out of them. She didn't have to look at him to know his eyes were glued to her. She could feel the heat from them burning into her skin.

She-devil. She knew exactly what she was doing, standing hip deep, sliding her hands over soapy limbs, splashing water over her face and shoulders, tantalizing, teasing.

It was all he could do to stay where he'd promised to stay. She must think he was made of stone.

She waded from the water and reached for her towel, staying just beyond his reach. When she reached for her clean clothes he took a step toward her.

"Oh, no you don't," she said, dodging his hands. "I just got all cleaned up. I'm not rolling on the wet moss. Is the coffee made yet?" She grinned as he muttered an oath.

"All right. I'm going to call this even for teasing you," he said, pointing a warning finger her way. "But don't push your luck."

"Yes, sir. But in the future, think twice before

withholding the bare essentials."

"Very funny. I'm going for a swim."

They dallied over their early morning coffee and breakfast, waiting for the sun to rise over the hills. She was excited to get back on the water.

They had gone only a few miles when a small town came into view. As they approached, Emily saw a sign for a hotel and eatery. One more hour last evening and they could have slept indoors in a bed.

"Hey, I didn't know. I've never been on this river before."

"Tell the truth. It's on the map, right? But you were happy camping in the woods. And you wanted to see what my reaction would be."

He looked sheepishly guilty. "I'm glad you didn't fuss about it. It's awfully nice to know I can depend on you to be a partner anytime, not just when things are easy and comfortable."

"When are you going to be satisfied that you've tested me enough?"

"Look at it from my point of view. I get to show off all my manly skills to you in the process."

She splashed him with a paddleful of water.

Chapter 19

Matfield, West Virginia, was a ramshackle collection of ill-constructed buildings, some better, some worse than others, all radiating a feeling of poverty and neglect. Yet for all that, a few newer homes stood on the hills outside town, testament to the fact that revenue was filtering into Matfield and reaching the hands of the townsfolk.

Seneca and Emily arrived by buggy after spending the night in a little town in Pennsylvania. The proprietress of their boarding house there was eager for the opportunity to spread the gossip she had collected.

"That's Mort Bristol's operation down there. He's a mean one, that. You ain't goin' in there, are you? That wouldn't be wise, Mr. Prescott, not with a woman what got the looks o' your wife here."

"Mrs. Bradford, we must. We believe Bristol, if that is his name, has a man imprisoned there, a man who was freed many years ago."

The old lady shook her head. "You won't get him back. A man went in there in April lookin' for his slaves. He ain't been seen since."

"What does the local sheriff have to say about that?" Emily asked.

"The sheriff just moved into a new house. Answer your question?"

"Does Mort Bristol live in Matfield?"

"Yeah, he does. Them other two don't, though. They got mansions somewhere else. They just take the money from Matfield."

"What other two men? Do you know what their names are?"

"Sidwell and Ryker," she said disgustedly, pouring more tea for each of them. "They're just as bad as Bristol, even though they are only investors. They're three of a kind."

"Ryker. Does he come to visit often?"

She shrugged. "I wouldn't know. He don't come here. Unless Mrs. Bristol's maid tells my niece about it, I don't have no way of knowing."

Seneca stopped the buggy in front of the general store and stepped down. He looked up at Emily with very ambivalent feelings. He wanted her with him so he could protect her, but he wanted her safe at Mrs. Bradford's boarding house also.

"Let me do the talking, sweetheart. Remember we're on a search mission for my father who wants his three slaves returned. We are also interested in possibly purchasing two more."

He lifted her down and waited until she adjusted her dress. He took her arm and led her up the steps. Taking his tall hat in his hand, he approached the shopkeeper.

"We are looking for a Mr. Bristol. Could you direct us to his place of business?" He used an accent much like that of the southern man who was chasing her, and she shivered inside.

The shopkeeper looked them over, then with a disgruntled snort pointed toward a road leading into the woods. "Down there. Can't miss it. No one else in Matfield lives so grand."

"Does he have an office in town?"

"What fer? He don't do business with none of us townfolk, 'ceptin' for the elite few."

Emily glanced sideways at Seneca as they returned to their buggy. "Mr. Bristol hasn't exactly endeared himself to the people of Matfield."

"Think about it. Here, under the town, is a means of livelihood. These men you see sitting around doing nothing should be paid to mine that coal. Instead, Bristol brings in slaves. Very little of the money from this coal stays in Matfield. I might be resentful too."

"The town must profit some. These are new houses," she observed as they drove down a bumpy lane.

"Bristol has some men on his payroll who have to live somewhere. But think how the long-time residents must feel, seeing all that wealth just beyond their grasp, wealth that should be theirs. They profit, yes, but it's nothing to what they see down this road. There. That must be Bristol's house."

A housekeeper in a plain black dress answered the door. The woman had flaming red hair that stuck out at odd angles from her white cap.

"Mrs. Bradford's source," Emily guessed when they had been shown into the large sunny parlor.

Mrs. Bristol arrived shortly, a surprise to both Emily and Seneca.

"Please call me Constance," the very young and diminutive figure said. She was clad in the latest fashion and the finest of silk, and her hair was coiffed magnificently, but still there was a aura of pitifulness about her.

"I have sent word for my husband to return. Will you join me in tea? Melba?"

"Yes, ma'am," the Negro serving girl said, bobbing a curtsy as she left.

Melba was quite advanced in her pregnancy. At least she had a decent place to work and, hopefully, live. What would happen to her, Emily wondered, after her baby was born.

Constance Bristol's hands shook slightly as she served the tea. When she handed Emily a cup, their

313

eyes met. Emily was shaken at the fear and despair she saw in Mrs. Bristol's dark eyes. And she could guess why when Constance reached across the table with Seneca's tea. The lace ruffle at her neck pulled aside, revealing livid purple marks.

"You have a lovely home," Emily said brightly. "Perhaps while the gentlemen discuss business you could show me around."

"Yes. I'd like that," Constance answered eagerly.

"Good. You're not from the South?" she asked, making conversation. She sensed that Constance rarely had visitors and wasn't exactly sure what to do with her and Seneca.

"No. I'm from Ohio. My family had a farm there. They're all gone now." She took a quick sip of tea, lowering her eyes.

Emily exchanged a glance with Seneca. "I'm sorry to hear that."

"My wife just recently lost her family too," Seneca said sympathetically.

"Yes, I did," Emily concurred. "Just before we were married."

"You are newlywed, then?" Constance asked, glancing shyly at Seneca.

"Yes, we are. We are on our wedding trip, a gift from my father. He asked if we'd make this detour and see if . . . Well, I shall not bore you with business."

At that point the front door opened and in strode a man dressed as well as his wife. Suspecting what she did about him, Emily searched his rather homely face for signs of cruelty. They were not hard to find.

He stepped into the parlor, ignoring his young wife, and held out a very brief hand of welcome to his male visitor. He turned then to Emily, as if he was testing Seneca's character, and took her hand in his own, raising her fingers to his lips for a long slow kiss. His eyes roved over her, lingering on her bosom far too long before returning to stop at her mouth.

314

"A pleasure to have such beauty in my home, Mrs. Rand," he said, using the name Seneca had decided on.

"Thank you, Mr. Bristol, but you must be quite used to beauty with your own wife."

"Wife?" he asked, pausing disdainfully. "Yes, I suppose she is my wife."

Emily glanced at the young girl, could see her humiliation and at the same time her hatred.

"You are from the North?" he asked Emily, separating her from Seneca by sitting between them. "Yet I detect a slight accent."

"As a child I lived in Virginia. Later my father and I lived in Philadelphia. I met my husband in New York."

He turned finally to Seneca. "And you are from?"

Seneca's grin was sardonic. "I am from Louisiana, where *my wife* and I reside with my family. And where we shall return forthwith." He stood, and with his most arrogant expression held out his hand to Emily. "My dear?"

Surprised, Bristol stood as well. "It was my understanding you were searching for lost slaves."

"That is true. I am not prepared, however, to submit my wife to lechery in order to find them. Slaves come and slaves go."

"We have some fine flesh. Some from Louisiana, too. I could offer you a more than fair deal."

"Of course you could. You know as I do that I've only to seek out the state attorney general to have your establishment searched and my slaves returned at absolutely no cost to me."

"But you needn't go to that trouble, now," Bristol said jovially, slapping Seneca on the back.

"No?" he asked, turning a black challenging glare his way.

Bristol looked between Seneca and Emily, his brow cocked. Finally he nodded in acceptance. "No need at all," he assured him.

"Your wife has graciously agreed to show my wife around your home while we conduct our business. Shall we go?"

Bristol looked back at Emily and his wife, his eyes resting on Emily's bodice. He laughed a very disquieting laugh and escorted Seneca out the front door.

"You should not have come," Constance said quietly as they strolled through the well-tended gardens behind the house. "Can you return to your home this afternoon? It would be best to go quickly."

"What is it, Constance?" She turned to the other girl and reached out to pull the concealing lace away from her neck. Constance tried to stop her, but Emily persisted. "Did he do this?" she asked, frowning as she placed her fingers on the four distinct marks. If she did not miss her guess, there would be a thumbprint on the other side of her neck.

"Please, you mustn't say anything. You'll only make everything worse. Just . . . go."

"Why don't you come with us?"

She looked at Emily with a mixture of horror and hope, both of which died to be replaced by dead apathy. "No. It would do no good. He'd find me. We'd all suffer."

"How did you meet him?"

"He got my father involved in a business deal that went bad. When Father couldn't repay what he'd borrowed from him, he threatened to take the farm. My mother wasn't well, and it would have killed her to lose the house. Mr. Bristol suggested another deal."

"You in exchange for the debt?"

Constance nodded. "And then my parents were both killed in an accident anyway."

"And the farm?"

"My husband owns it." Her dark head dropped, her chestnut curls catching the rays of the morning sun. Dark eyes looked out from a delicate pale face.

316

"You can't stay here," Emily said. "He'll end up killing you."

"I know. I'm not strong like you. I'm afraid. What would I do? I'd have nothing."

"You'd have yourself and you'd have freedom. That's all the slaves have when they escape."

"I . . . No, I can't. Just get out yourself, while you can. My husband can be very vindictive, and your husband has angered him."

A small boy made his way up the hill, jumping over the gate into the garden. He was surprised to see that his mistress was not alone.

"Sorry, missus. I come back later."

"T.J., come over and meet Mrs. Rand. Emily, this is a young man who comes by each morning to weed the flowers and keep me company." She ruffled his curly head fondly. His pure childish skin was the color of coffee and cream, a mixture of heritages, she thought. His hair was the color of ripe chestnuts. He was a beautiful boy. And around his neck . . .

T.J. bobbed his head courteously. "How do, ma'am."

Emily expelled her breath and drew another, hoping she wouldn't faint dead away. The boy was clad only in a pair of baggy trousers, and a white bone medallion.

"Goodness, you look suddenly pale," Constance said, supporting Emily's arm and leading her to a stone bench in the shade. Go, T.J., and bring a tray of lemonade. And cookies."

"Yes, ma'am," he said, beaming widely.

When he returned he served them each a tall frosty glass with a linen napkin. Just like a little butler, he passed the plate of cookies.

"Thank you, T.J.," Emily said, playing along with the game she could see that the boy and Constance played. "That is a very unusual charm you are wearing."

T.J. held the medallion in his hand and looked away.

"Did someone make it for you?"

317

Again he wouldn't respond, and Constance intervened gently. "T.J., Mrs. Rand asked you a question. It is rude not to answer her."

T.J. looked up at Constance, and Emily could see he adored her. "Yes, ma'am," he said, turning to Emily. "I suppose someone did make it, ma'am, but I don't remember."

Emily didn't press. "Thank you, T.J., I didn't mean to make you uncomfortable. I think it's a lovely charm."

T.J. looked warily at her but seemed to see her sincerity, for he gave her a heartbreaking smile. The young maid who had served them tea earlier came out to the gardens, looking decidedly uncomfortable.

"Mrs. Rand, Mr. Bristol would like you to join him in the library."

Emily looked from the maid to Constance, and back to the maid. "Is my husband with Mr. Bristol?"

"No, ma'am. Mr. Bristol returned from the mines alone, asking to see you."

"Thank you, Melba, we'll be in presently," Constance answered, placing a restraining hand on Emily's arm. Melba returned to the house, and very slowly Constance stood.

"Don't let him near you," she said calmly, taking T.J.'s hand. "I wish I could help you."

Seneca looked from one guard to the other, catching an odd expression in their eyes. They'd been down three dark tunnels, all lined with men and women extracting the coal from the veins and carrying it to the outside.

Not one of the men was Elijah. And Seneca had the gut impression that the two guards knew he wouldn't find the man he was looking for. He also had the feeling that he was the one being guarded.

"I've seen enough here," he said turning to retrace

his steps.

"We've been ordered to take you through the barracks after you've been in the mines. There's also the pit."

"What pit?" he asked disdainfully.

"The quarry. About twenty men work down there," the man called Finch said.

"I'd like to speak to Bristol."

"He's busy right now. He'll see you after the tour," the big, hairy ape of a guard said, crowding him toward yet another tunnel.

Seneca stood his ground until they were nose to nose. "Where is Bristol?"

"Taking care of business for one of his partners. A Mr. Ryker."

"What business?" he demanded, recalling the way Bristol had looked at Emily.

"Personal business, Mr. Seneca Prescott."

The two men laughed. Seneca made the first move, counting on surprise to give him the advantage. He went for the big one first, bringing his knee up sharply into Finch's groin. The man let out a howl of outrage, but was too disabled by pain to do much else.

Seneca's fist connected sharply with the chin of the thinner man, sending him reeling back into the hard rock wall. He hit his head on the wall and slumped to the ground.

A growl came from behind him, and Seneca dodged to the side, catching one of Finch's shoulders in his side as the other man threw himself at Seneca. Both men went to the hard earth, wrestling in a battle for supremacy.

Seneca forgot all his more civilized characteristics and fought to kill. They had called him by his name; they knew who he was, and they would kill him. But they were not about to let him die without inflicting their own form of retribution, and how better than through Emily? And another thought spurred him on.

319

Only one man knew he would be coming, and if Elijah were even remotely in control of his mind, he'd never have told. Elijah was either seriously hurt or dead.

Seneca felt the man's weight crush him into the rocky ground, knocking the air from his lungs. He tried to twist away to catch a breath, but the meaty hands digging into his throat cut off his air supply before he could fill his lungs again.

Seneca dug his thumbs into the man's eyes until the hands at his throat relaxed. A fist slammed into his jaw, but not before Seneca pounded his opponent's ears with the heels of his hands.

Both men were temporarily stunned, each crawling off to gather his wits. Seneca turned as the beast of a man doved at him again. He grabbed a chunk of rock, sharp edged, and swung it at Finch's head. He caught his upper arm instead, piercing the fabric of his shirt and gashing the man's arm.

Finch swore a vulgar oath, promising unspeakable horrors for Emily. Seneca lost his head and launched himself wildly at Finch, taking several successive blows before falling backward into the dirt. He rolled deftly out of the way as Finch landed heavily where he had been. Seneca brought the side of his hand down on the back of Finch's neck, but it did not seem to faze him. He turned and swung at Seneca, catching his eye.

Never had Seneca met a man who could throw a punch like this one, not even on the canal, and he'd been in his share of fights. He hit the dirt like a rag doll. Immediately Finch was on his back, threatening to snap his spine. Finch's hands clamped around his throat again. No matter how hard he tried, he couldn't loosen them.

For the first time in his life, Seneca faced his own death. Always before he'd seen avenues of escape. Now there was none. He fought for air. None would come. He was losing consciousness, and all he could think of was Emily and what they'd do to her.

He gave one last effort to dislodge Finch. The hands tightened painfully. Blackness spiraled inward, inward. *Emily!* his mind screamed.

And then air. Cool, blessed air.

He dragged it deep into his lungs, coughing to clear his pinched windpipe.

"You okay, mister?"

Seneca turned his head to see a small boy standing over him with the broken handle of a shovel still in his hand. He sat up and spun around defensively. The other part of the shovel lay beside Finch's head. Seneca crawled over and checked the man.

"He's dead. They're both dead," the boy said expressionlessly. "Mrs. Bristol sent me to fetch you. Your lady, she needs . . ."

"Get me out of this hellhole," he croaked hoarsely, holding out his hand. They ran together, hand in hand, through the maze of tunnels until they came to the elevator. It had been raised, and ringing the bell repeatedly did no good.

"Come," the boy said, leading Seneca back into the mine. They came to a dead end, a tunnel that had been boarded up. "In here," the young man said, prying loose one of the boards. "Hope you got a strong stomach."

Seneca understood what he meant when, holding the lantern overhead, he saw several shallow graves. Not all the extremities had been covered. The stench was sickening.

"Whoever dies, from one cause or another, gets buried in one of these old shafts. This way."

Two more boards were loosened, letting in a dim shaft of light. The boy crawled in feet first, lowering himself down the steep incline. Seneca followed.

At the bottom of the shaft the opening was covered by overgrown brush, which at least concealed their presence from the guards on the opposite side of the ravine where the entrance to the mine was located.

Below them was a track for the coal shuttles. Seneca counted four guards armed with whips and heavy clubs.

"Stay down low."

Emily watched Constance take T.J. away. She turned apprehensively toward the house where Melba waited on the veranda. She took a long breath and slowly started to walk.

Why would Bristol want to see her? She could guess at one reason from the way he had looked at her earlier. But what if it was about Seneca? What if Seneca had found Elijah and needed her help? What if something had happened to Seneca?

Her heart began to pound frantically. Butterflies jumped wildly about in her stomach.

"There you are, my dear," Bristol said smoothly when Melba showed her into the library and closed the door.

"Mr. Bristol," she said icily. "You wish to speak with me? Has it to do with my husband?"

Bristol gave a low sinister chuckle, turning Emily's blood cold. "Has it to do with Seneca Prescott, you mean? Yes, my dear. It has very much to do with your husband. And with a friend of mine. A Mr. Ryker. Have you heard of him?"

She considered lying and denying all he'd said, but she could see it was futile. "Yes, I've heard of him." She moved to put the desk between them.

"Then you must understand why this must be done."

"Why what must be done? Mr. Bristol, we are supposed to be civilized people."

"You are quite beautiful, much too beautiful to scar." He moved toward the desk and picked up a silver letter opener.

She backed away. "Are you threatening me with violence, Mr. Bristol?"

"Violence? Not if you cooperate, my dear. Just a few of us, you understand."

She understood perfectly. "That is despicable. What would your wife say?"

"She'll say nothing, I guarantee it."

"Well, I assume you intend to kill me," she said, nodding insightfully. "Of course. And my husband. Revenge because Seneca bested you once before."

"Quite right, and we don't intend for it to happen again."

"How many people are you prepared to murder? Seneca's family knows where he is. His father will come looking for him. And a very dear friend of mine is a policeman in New York. He won't let my death go uninvestigated."

"They can investigate all they want. You will have come and gone. What happened after you left here we couldn't possibly know."

"Unless someone here decides to talk."

"And risk the same fate as you and your husband? And your husband's nigger friend?" He shook his head and grinned nastily.

"Elijah? Is he here?"

"For as long as he lives."

"I see," she said, meandering toward the fireplace. She made a quick lunge, grabbed the sharp poker, and swung around just as he reached for her. She swung wildly, just missing his eyes. She cut his face. He jumped back, cursing her as blood soaked into his white linen handkerchief.

"You bitch. You'll regret that."

"How so? I would regret doing nothing. You may succeed in raping me, but it will never be while I live, for I shall fight you to the death first. And you will not emerge without marks you will stare at in the mirror for the rest of your life. If your eyesight is still intact."

"Brave words," he taunted.

She shrugged, keeping her eyes on him. "What have

I to lose? You've taken away every reason for me to exercise any caution."

He backed away from her and reached for the drawer of his desk, snatching up a short silver pistol. At the same moment, guessing what he was after, she swung the poker, bringing it down on his right arm.

He dropped the gun, and she kicked it into the corner. He was enraged, his gray hair seemed to stand on end, his eyes bulged, his face turned purple. She ran.

She made it to the doors only to find they had been locked. He grabbed her hair and twisted her around, pinning her to the doors. With his bruised arm he clamped her throat to the panel. With his other hand he twisted the poker from her fingers.

She raked her nails down his face and pulled his hair when he tried to force her head to his. And when he did grind his mouth against hers, she bit his lip until her teeth met.

He pulled back with a howl and slammed his fist into the side of her face. She went sprawling onto the floor, but she wasn't down long. She scrambled to her feet, grabbed an expensive-looking vase, and threw it at him. He lunged for her, and she threw the table the vase had been sitting on. It missed, and he caught her wrist.

The library doors exploded open, and Seneca, his face bruised and bleeding, stood there like a demon from hell. In his hand was his pistol. Bristol swore and pulled Emily in front of him like a shield, clamping his hand around her throat.

"I'll kill her, Prescott. Drop the gun," he threatened.

Seneca laughed sardonically. "I'm a crack shot. I can put your eye out at fifty paces. If your fingers tighten even a fraction on her throat, I'll drop you."

"And if he doesn't, I will." The voice came from the side doors. Constance's voice.

Bristol twisted around in surprise at her daring. She too held a gun. A rifle. She hadn't lived on a farm and

324

skipped those lessons.

Emily took the moment. She drove her heel hard into his shin. When he yelped and released his hold on her, she threw herself to the floor.

The room vibrated with the deafening thunder of gunfire.

A small hand smoothed the hair back from her face. "You okay, lady?"

She lifted her head. The bone medallion hung in front of her face. She took it in her hand and studied it. It wasn't the same. It wasn't Elijah's.

She put her head down and wept. Seneca took her in his arms. He rocked her back and forth, soothing her, letting her cry. From somewhere he produced a cool cloth for her face and hot tea for her nerves.

When her head cleared, she began to think again. T.J.'s medallion wasn't Elijah's. That didn't mean Elijah wasn't here. Bristol had mentioned Elijah. Elijah was somewhere. Dying.

She pushed Seneca's hand away and took T.J.'s shoulders, forcing him to look at her.

"T.J., you said you didn't know who made your medallion. Have you had it a long time?"

"As long as I can remember."

"Have you ever seen a man here with one like it?"

"No. Only three were ever made. One for each of us."

"T.J., is your name really Tyler?" Seneca asked. T.J. stiffened and looked to Constance for help.

"You can't take him back," Constance said. "He belongs to me now."

"Constance, we came here looking for a man who might be T.J.'s father. His name is Elijah. He is a free man."

"He's here, Seneca," Emily said. "Bristol admitted it. We have to find him. "

"I looked everywhere today, Emily. Except the barracks. We'll start there."

325

"A man came three days ago," T.J. said, his eyes big with anxiety. "He was beaten very much and they put him in the sweatbox."

"Oh, no," Constance groaned.

"I've been giving him water and cooling the box when they don't watch. He used to call out. He doesn't now. You think he's my father?" Tears gathered in his big dark eyes.

"Take us there," Seneca said stonily.

Chapter 20

For three days T.J. sat by his father's bed, praying that he wouldn't die. Seneca brought a doctor from Morgantown to tend to Elijah's worst injuries. The doctor had gone; all they could do now was wait. And pray.

"From all that I've seen, he should be dead," the doctor had said. "He must have a very powerful reason for clinging to life."

"Will he be all right?" Emily asked, twisting the handkerchief in her hands.

"Only time will tell. He's in bad shape, but his burns and lacerations aren't as infected as I expected they would be. He has three broken ribs, but they'll heal in time, too. I've cleaned the cut by his eye and put three stitches in it. Keep a watch on that. I'll be back in three days to check on him."

"What can we do?" Seneca asked.

"Keep him clean, cool, and dry. Force him to take liquids. He is still badly dehydrated. If his temperature rises, bathe him in cool water and give him willow bark tea. Apply the herb solution to his cuts and burns three times a day. That's all anyone can do for him. He'll come out of it or he won't."

Constance had proved to be a blessing to everyone. With the fear of her husband erased from her life, she blossomed into the woman she should have been all along. She went to the mines, eliminated all the opposition, and hired men from town to work in their places. Then she ordered massive changes in working and living conditions. All the women were housed in one of the barracks and given the chore of cleaning the camp and putting in a garden. The men were to continue at the mines, but for eight hour shifts only. On their spare time they were to repair the barracks and dig a new well.

With the government officials watching her, those officials whom Seneca had notified, she could make only a few of the changes she wished to, but she did improve the way of life for those forced to remain in West Virginia. About those few who were claimed by former masters she could do nothing. About those who chose to sneak off in the night, she elected to say nothing. To those who chose to stay, she offered the hand of friendship and help.

"Will *you* stay on here, then?" Emily asked her.

"Yes. I must stay for the time being. Eventually the slaves will go. The mines hold no importance to me, but the town needs them. Run by the right men, they could be profitable for this town and its people."

Constance had opened her house to Seneca, Emily, and Elijah, The servants, having seen the torment Constance had suffered at Bristol's hands, went out of their way to see that those who had rescued her and their own friends and family from Bristol's tyranny were treated like royalty.

The sheriff, seeing the influence Seneca had with certain political figures, backed down on his threat to have Seneca and Mrs. Bristol arrested for murder, especially as a number of people were willing to testify that Bristol was the murderer and that the sheriff had covered for him on more than one occasion in return for his fancy new house.

On the fourth morning Elijah opened his eyes. T.J. was sitting on the edge of the bed when it happened. He called for Seneca and Emily.

"Are you my father?" he asked the man beside him.

Elijah's hand came up, turned the medallion over, turned the boy's face this way and that.

"You've grown. Tyler? Is it really you? You gave me water."

Tyler held back, still uncertain, unable to pull from his memory the picture of his father. Not that it would have done any good. Elijah's face was not the same face as when he had arrived in West Virginia.

In a voice that sounded painfully hoarse, Elijah sang, "Come wif me to de freedom tree where de night done turn to day . . ."

"Where de music rings and de angel sings, an' de chains done fly away. *Papa!*"

"Come here, boy."

Elijah held his child for a long time, tears streaming from his eyes. Finally he let the boy up.

"Your mother?" he asked, braced for the worst. "Where is she?"

T.J. shook his head. "I don't know. I haven't seen her for over two years. She told me to stay at our hiding place until she returned, but she was gone for so long. I got scared, and I went to look for her. Two men found me and brought me here."

"You work in the mines?"

"No, sir. Miss Constance, I mean Mrs. Bristol, she needs me in her garden. Mr. Bristol gave me to her. She treats me nice. She taught me to talk right and do sums and to read, but I ain't to tell anyone that."

Elijah's eyes dropped, then closed. He did not sleep, but he didn't want to cry in front of the boy. Poor, poor Bekka. What horror she must have faced when she found her baby gone. She loved him so much. And where was she now, still out there searching, all alone?

I have him, Bekka, his heart cried out to her. *I have him. He's safe.*

"Come, T.J., he must rest if he's to get well," said a gentle voice.

Through his lowered lashes Elijah could see a pretty young woman take his son's hand and lead him to the door. Her arms were bare, and he could see the purple and yellow stains of some nasty bruises on her pale skin. Miss Constance, or Mrs. Bristol, had not fared well at her husband's hand either.

At the door Emily and Seneca waited. Seneca looked like he'd been caught in a stampede. Emily herself sported a humdinger of a black eye.

"He's just gone back to sleep," Mrs. Bristol said to them.

"But he was awake? Did he know who you were, T.J.?" Seneca asked.

"Yes, he knew. He sang a song he used to sing with me."

"Ah. Good. That's good. I think he'll be fine now. Come, let's have some of those strawberry tarts to celebrate."

"Strawberry tarts?" Elijah croaked, needing their company. "I love strawberry tarts."

Emily's heart rejoiced for Elijah that night, but still the tears fell. Seneca came up behind her and wrapped her in his arms, swaying gently as they both looked out over the moonlit garden.

"Is this just reaction, or is it something else?" he asked.

More tears came, clogging her throat. He turned her around and lifted her chin. "What are the tears for, sweetheart?"

She shook her head. "You'll think I'm crazy."

"Try me."

She sniffed and blinked to clear her vision. "I . . .

ah . . . I'm not pregnant." Her tears started again.

He took her shoulders and looked into her face. "You wanted to be?" he asked, amazed.

She looked up defiantly through her tears. "Yes. I wanted your baby."

He laughed and hugged her, swinging her off her feet. "I wanted it too, Emily, but we have time. There's no need to cry. Think instead of the pleasure we'll have trying again."

He coaxed a weak smile from his young and eager bride. She was a treasure, the one and only treasure he had. And his breath caught in his chest at how much love he felt for her.

"Bed for you, darling. I'll bring you some milk and brandy." He stopped at the door and looked back. "I love you, Emily."

Five days of bed rest was all Elijah could tolerate. Against advice he got up and made his way slowly to the dining room, where the others were breakfasting.

"Elijah, my goodness, should you be up?" Constance exclaimed. She had taken over Elijah's nursing and had come to care greatly for him as both T.J.'s father and as a friend of her own.

"If I don't move around I will become permanently shaped like that bed and as plump and soft as a pillow."

T.J. snickered behind his hand and Elijah turned. "You think that's funny? You would! Whenever I sent you to bed, you'd just crawl up in my lap and you'd be there."

T.J. laughed. Emily felt her smile widen. Just looking at them together made her heart sing. She wondered why she hadn't seen the resemblance before, in their eyes and noses.

Despite his present rough condition, Elijah looked

happier than she'd ever seen him. Some of the haunted quality was gone from his eyes. Now if he could only find his wife or, if she were dead, learn that and get on with his life. But perhaps T.J. would force him out of the personal limbo he'd been living in.

"Miss Constance has given me a gift," T.J. said, holding a brightly wrapped parcel up to his father. "She said you must help me open it."

Elijah looked from his son to the delicate looking dark-haired woman at the head of the table. Elijah's gaze met hers and he nodded in respect and gratitude.

"You have my deepest thanks for taking care of my son. And for this." His voice cracked with emotion.

"But, Papa, you don't know what it is yet."

"Then open it. See for yourself."

The boy tore at the paper until the box was bare. He lifted the lid, baffled by the contents. Pulling the piece of parchment out, he read the words for himself.

"It says you are making me free," he read to Constance. "I am not to be a slave." He turned and beamed at his father. "I am not to be a slave," he repeated proudly.

"Which does not mean you will not have work to do, young man. You have much to learn, although you must thank Miss Constance for the fine beginning you have had with numbers and letters, and for teaching you manners."

"But can't she go on teaching me?"

Constance answered. "Even with proper papers, you are not safe in the South. Look what happened to your father. You must go north, and you must help your father search for your mother. Think how lonely she must be. Now finish your breakfast."

"We should head back north," Elijah agreed, glancing up at Seneca.

"No rush. Take some time to recuperate."

"I've had time. I'm well enough to travel. Nothing hard about that."

"In a couple days then. Give yourself that much time."

They decided to take the same route north; the canal to Pittsburgh, the Allegheny River up to Franklin, and the canals to Erie. Seneca hired a private packet for the canals and two of the best cabins for the paddlewheel on the Allegheny River and through the lakes to Rochester. The trip was accomplished in seven days, with no effort required on their parts. They ate, played games, fished, toured the towns, and slept. And Elijah grew stronger.

A few days of Mrs. Prescott's care and Wanda's cooking would only add to Elijah's general well-being. Since they had found him in the sweatbox his face had returned to normal and his skin was almost healed. He'd gained back some of the weight he had lost and he was very nearly recovered.

What no one could touch, though, was the memory of what he had endured. Emily could see his mind drift back to those darker days, days in the long ago past as well as the recent past. She knew he was seeing the squalor his people had been forced to live in, the exhaustion that etched their faces and the scars that etched their backs. He was seeing the pathos and misery of mothers whose babies were wrenched away from them and sold. And he was seeing for the first time his beloved Bekka without Tyler.

T.J. A grown-up name for a grown-up boy. And Bekka had been almost three years without him. What had she done in those lonely years? Where had she been? Had she tried to find Elijah? Had she searched for their son? Those were the same questions

Elijah must be asking himself. His whole perception of her must be shifting and changing shape. Would he end up loving her more or hating her? Emily wondered . . .

Louise and Liam Prescott were exemplary hosts, and Emily felt openly welcomed back into their home. Her only disappointment was in being shown to the same guest room she'd occupied before. Not that the room was uncomfortable, but Emily knew she would miss the arms of her husband terribly, and she wondered how she could bear to sleep without him. But they had agreed to wait a few days before discussing plans for a wedding.

Marianne was thrilled with the little boy who turned out to be Elijah's son. They immediately raided the kitchen, whence came the delicious aromas of baking. Also, the kitchen was home to the kitten, which Marianne had named, appropriately, Spitz.

Dinner that evening was a festive occasion, well deserved and thoroughly enjoyed. Emily and Seneca were household names in Rochester for what they had done in Erie, and the Prescotts wanted to acknowledge them, too. Also, the reunion of father and son was cause for celebration.

"My friends at school think you're dreamy," Marianne said to her brother. "They want to know all about you."

"Yeah, well don't give away my deep, dark secrets, young lady. A man needs an air of mystery about him."

"The only mystery to me is why you haven't married Emily already."

Out of the mouths, Emily thought, giving Seneca a sidelong glance.

"My marital status is not your concern," he answered, scowling playfully at his sister who plainly worshiped him.

"All right. Just promise me you won't go crazy and marry Belinda Martin."

"Now how do you think that sounds," Liam Prescott rebuked softly. "Is Seneca to marry Emily only to prevent any possibility of his being ensnared by Belinda?"

"That's not what I meant," Marianne cried, turning apologetic eyes to Emily. "Truly. I only . . . Well, we all know she's going to show up on our doorstep now that Seneca's back. Just wait and see. And she's very tricky."

Emily patted her hand. "Don't worry about Belinda. She'll have to go through me to get to Seneca."

"So fierce," Seneca teased, cocking a brow at her. "Are you jealous?"

She stabbed her fork into a potato, glaring at him. "No," she said threateningly. "I have utmost confidence in your good judgment."

"Oooh," Marianne said, laughing. "Better watch your step, big brother."

Marianne's prediction proved true. Belinda and her mother came to call the next morning. This time, though, Emily was not about to be shunted aside.

"How nice to see you again," Belinda said, barely taking the time to look at her. "Seneca, welcome home. Not a day went by I didn't think about you. I've missed you." She stood on tiptoe and waited for the customary kiss.

"Oh, you don't want to kiss her, Seneca," Emily said abruptly. "I mean . . ." She cleared her throat delicately. "Do you think it wise to take the chance? The doctor said . . . Oh, but of course you know best. Don't mind me."

Mrs. Martin's ears perked up. "What, my dear? What doctor? Have you been ill, Seneca?"

"Oh, it's probably nothing," Emily said. "Something he picked up from the canal water. It's just that . . ."

"Something contagious?" she asked, wide-eyed.

Emily hesitated just enough. "I'm sure we'll all be fine."

"Is this true, darling?" Belinda asked Seneca.

Seneca bit the inside of his lip, pulling a straight face even though his family were hiding their grins inside their tea cups.

"I didn't hear what the doctor told Emily. I must have been unconscious. Come in. We're having tea. You know Elijah, don't you? This is his son, T.J."

Elijah, already standing, prodded T.J. to his feet.

"Pleased to meet you ma'am, and ma'am."

"Yes, I'm sure," Mrs. Martin dismissed. She turned to Louise. "You haven't forgotten the hospital social next week, have you, with all the excitement of having Seneca home?"

"No, I haven't forgotten, but we haven't discussed it yet."

Mrs. Martin's face lit up. "Oh. I'm sure everyone would love to see you there," she commented, prodding her daughter forward.

"I'm being very bold, Seneca, but I would be honored if you would go to the social with me." She fluttered her lashes demurely, knowing Seneca would appear quite boorish to embarrass her in public by refusing her.

"How kind of you to think of us, Belinda, and to include my guests in your invitation. We'd all be delighted to go with you."

"Oh, but . . . " She bit her lip. Seneca had done her one better. How could she correct his mistaken inference without appearing an ingracious brat. "Wonderful. I'll look forward to it." She threw daggers at Emily when their glances happened to collide.

Emily stood to help Mrs. Prescott refill the tea table. Belinda stood and took the tray from Louise. "Sit down and visit with Mommie. I'll get this."

Emily knew a confrontation was coming, but she

was ready. She almost felt pity for Belinda. She moved confidently into the kitchen and set the big kettle on the cookstove. She took down the tea jar.

"I'll get this," Belinda said, rinsing the teapot of the dregs. "I know my way around the kitchen. This is practically my second home. It will be soon, you know."

"Oh? I'm not sure I do know. Are you trying to tell me something?"

"I think you know what I'm trying to say. You're a novelty now, and you must realize he's using you to make me jealous. But I'm part of his past; I'm part of his life. Underneath all this . . . pretense," she said patronizingly, "he loves me. He always will. Just as I love him. When he marries, he'll marry me. I don't mean to hurt you, only to prevent you from hurting yourself. Young girls have a way of developing infatuations with older, sophistocated men."

All the while she mechanically prepared the tea she recited her words, as if she had rehearsed this speech and now was simply delivering it as best she could.

"I don't mind your coming along to the social, since Seneca feels responsible for you, but you would be wise to consider returning to Albany after that. You have your own life to lead, Seneca has his."

"With you?" Emily asked archly.

"Yes, I'm afraid so," Belinda replied consolingly. "Surely you can see how much more compatible Seneca and I will be."

"Not really, no. How is it you see yourself as compatible?"

"Why, socially, educationally, physically. In every way."

"So you would be willing to canoe down the rapids with him, sleep out in a tent, fight off the bears? He really enjoys the outdoors. And he loves the canal. Will you go with him there?"

"Oh, come, now. Seneca doesn't need to work at all. He's a very wealthy man now. Why should he want to do any of that? You'll see. He'll change his mind."

"You mean you'll change his mind."

Belinda became thoroughly annoyed with Emily's unruffled calm. "Look, let's cut through this nonsense. I intend to have him and I'm warning you to stay out of my way. If you know what's good for you, you will."

Emily grinned. "I must stay to look after T.J. and Elijah. So sorry. Is the tea ready?" She turned her back on the other woman and carried her silver plate of cakes and cookies into the parlor.

She grinned as Belinda slammed the lid shut on the teapot and plunked it on the tray.

Three days after their arrival Louise Prescott came into Seneca's bedroom carrying an armful of clean linens. She dropped the sheets and towels with a gasp when she found Emily in Seneca's arms. That wouldn't have been so bad except that they were lying together on Seneca's bed—fully clothed, but . . .

With as much dignity as she could rouse under the circumstances, she excused herself and backed out of the room, but not before Emily saw her accute disappointment.

Emily struggled out of Seneca's embrace. "We have to tell her," she demanded. "Oh, Seneca, she was hurt. Did you see her face?"

Seneca grinned crookedly and shook his head. "I suppose, if I want my wife back in the near future, and I do, that we must."

She slugged him with a pillow. "I'm thinking of your mother's feelings. I've offended her in taking advantage of her hospitality. And what if your sister had stumbled onto us?"

He thought for a moment then sighed. "She might

still be disappointed, even after you explain."

"There is a difference, Seneca."

"All right," he said, standing and straightening his clothes. "But this means you move into my room tonight."

"Yes, sir." That suited her just fine.

Seneca knocked on the older Prescotts' suite. "Mother," he called.

Louise answered the door. Emily could see she'd been crying.

"Mrs. Prescott . . . Louise," she amended, "may we come in? We must talk to you."

"Why . . . ah . . . yes, of course. Come in." She hid her feelings well.

Emily handed her an envelope. Mrs. Prescott slid the document out and opened it. She looked at her son in confusion.

"Mother, we wanted to come home and let you give us a proper wedding. I wanted that for Emily, anyway, since she has no family. But I . . . we . . ." For once his glib tongue deserted him.

"And being the honorable son that you raised, he asked me to marry him. Actually I found myself in front of the judge before I suspected what Seneca was planning."

A watery smile peeked through Louise's confused expression. The older woman nodded once, but Emily wanted more than forced acceptance. She wanted her approval and her blessing.

"We hoped to keep our marriage a secret until we could have a church wedding here, but I thought you might like to know, in light of what you saw." Emily bit her lip and looked worriedly at Seneca.

"Mother?" he coaxed. "Are you terribly upset with me? Please don't blame Emily for this. She wanted to wait. She knew you'd be hurt."

"But you knew you were not going to leave her

alone?" Mrs. Prescott guessed, nodding. Her eyes began to sparkle again.

"Yes, I knew. And I didn't want to risk losing her. Nor did I want to risk . . . anything else. Mother, I love her."

She raised a skeptical brow. "No one watching you would have guessed. You've kept your feelings quite hidden."

"It has been extremely difficult to do so, too," he grumbled.

Emily glanced at him and laughed. He scowled at her.

"You have been a grumpy bear at times," Louise recalled, grinning. "I guess it all makes sense now." She smiled at them both then kissed Emily. "I welcome you to the family, my dear. May I tell Liam, or would you prefer the secret to remain?"

"No, go ahead. But I'm serious about the wedding. Do you think we could arrange it for two weeks from Saturday?"

"I'm sure we can. Oh dear, have you any idea how angry Belinda is going to be? She had her cap set for you."

"Poor Belinda," Seneca said. "She always did try to fool everyone, even herself. I never encouraged her."

"I know, dear. Your money did that. Her father has fallen on bad times of late, you see."

"So that's why her mother has been so pushy."

"I'm afraid so. Now, my dears," she said brightly, "I am going to take Wanda and Marianne to the market with me. We'll have lunch in town. The men are not expected home until later today. You have this house to yourselves." She walked out of her bedroom with a bright smile and a definite lilt to her step.

Chapter 21

The day of the hospital social arrived, and Emily donned one of the gowns she'd had made for her in Erie. It was a lovely creation in blues and gold and was the perfect accompaniment to her coloring.

A knock sounded at her door just as she finished adjusting her skirt over her hoop and petticoats.

"Come in." Expecting Seneca, she was surprised to see Louise and Liam enter her room.

"You look beautiful, my dear," Louise said fondly.

"Indeed, I cannot blame my son for rushing you to the magistrate. You are a pearl of great price."

"And as a wedding gift we would like you to have these. They were my mother's," Louise said.

Emily gasped at the perfect pearls nestled on a bed of black velvet. She looked up, astonished. "Oh, I . . . Surely, Marianne should have these."

"She has my mother's," Liam said. "These were intended for Seneca's wife."

"And they will be lovely with that gown. They match the lace madame put at your elbows and at your hem perfectly. Oh, yes," she said enthusiastically as Liam draped them around her neck and fastened the clasp.

Emily attached the earbobs then went to the mirror. They're beautiful," she sighed.

"Not half as beautiful as you are," came another voice from the doorway. Her husband walked toward her and lifted her fingers to his lips. "And these are from me."

She took the jeweler's box and opened it. Inside was a set of combs for her hair, studded with clusters of pearls and diamonds.

"Oh, Seneca," she cried, looking into his black eyes. "I . . ." Her voice choked off.

"Now, now, none of that," he reproved, chucking her chin. "You'll make your eyes red." With sure fingers he attached the combs to her hair and handed her a mirror for her inspection.

She felt like a princess, and she looked like one when she turned her shining eyes up to Seneca. He was so handsome and she loved him so much.

Louise looked up at her husband and they shared a smile at the picture their son and new daughter made together. If they had not been able to see their love before, they could see it now. It shone like a bright light around them.

"Everybody ready?" Marianne asked, bounding into the room. "Holy smokes, you both look great," she said to Emily and Seneca. "There's gonna be fireworks tonight."

"Marianne, control your imagination," Seneca said with fond exasperation. "Fireworks, indeed."

"Go ahead. Make fun of me. You'll see."

The social was the annual fund-raiser for the hospital, and all monies raised went toward improvements and expansion of the facility. Everyone went to the yearly community affair, which crossed the lines of social or racial distinction. Elijah and T.J. were as welcome as were Louise and Liam, the poor as well as the wealthy, the very young as well as the very old.

Because of their number, the older Prescotts and the household staff took one carriage; Elijah and T.J. escorted Marianne in the other. Seneca and Emily went with the Martins.

Emily knew the evening ahead would be difficult as soon as she left the house on Seneca's arm. Mrs. Martin looked thunderous, Belinda's eyes promised retribution.

"Seneca, how splendid you look this evening," Belinda cooed. "Hello, Emily."

"Good evening Belinda, Mr. and Mrs. Martin. It's nice to see you again." The lie came easily, and she was almost ashamed of herself.

"Thank you," was Mrs. Martin's rather curt response. "Where are your friends, Elijah and his son?" she asked, looking toward the house.

"Oh, they decided to take a separate conveyance, to accommodate Marianne's hoops, I think."

"Yes, well, it is a shame to be so squashed in," she said, throwing Emily a pointed glare.

"Oh, are you crowded, Belinda?" Emily asked, feigning concern. "Come, Seneca, you can move closer to me. I don't have as many underskirts, so I don't need as much room as Belinda. There, snuggle right up."

Anger blazed from Belinda's eyes. "I never said I was crowded. In fact, I enjoyed sitting close to Seneca. It brought back so many memories. Do you remember our ride up to the lake in that little one-horse buggy? Why, there was barely room enough for one in that. And remember, it rained, and we had to stop and wait inside the covered bridge until the storm was over? That was cozy. Do you remember that?"

"Yes. I recall," Seneca said.

"You must have hundreds of pleasant memories

of your time with Belinda," Mrs. Martin said, turning to look back at them.

"Yes, I suppose I do," he answered noncommit-
tally.

"Do you remember the night you asked me to
marry you?"

He turned his head, raising a quizzical brow. She
had that a little backward, but he didn't correct her.
He had been foolish enough to think it an absolutely marvelous idea.

"I remember," he said, wondering where she was
going with all these reminiscences.

"We were so happy then. If only . . ."

"Now Belinda, darling," crooned her mother,
"don't torment yourself over the past. You were very
young and you'd just had a frightful experience.
Seneca understands that now, don't you, dear?"

Seneca looked from Mrs. Martin to Belinda. Yes,
he understood perfectly well. "Of course, I do."

"Then you forgive me?" Belinda asked and pouted
prettily.

"Belinda, I never think about it. Why rake it up
after all this time? Three years."

"Because I can't stand thinking you may still hold
a grudge against me for the silly things I did. And
I've never told you how sorry I am that I hurt you.
How sorry I've always been that I broke our engagement."

"Why did you?" Emily couldn't help asking. She'd
had to sit through that pathetic attempt at an apology. She wanted to know what reason Belinda
would use to absolve herself of guilt.

Belinda and Mrs. Martin swung around to stare
at her with astonishment, as if they had forgotten
she was even there, or more likely, couldn't believe
she would have the audacity to inject herself into

their conversation.

"That's a rather impertinent question," Mrs. Martin said in velvet tones that couldn't quite conceal the acid beneath. "My daughter is finding this difficult enough without . . ."

"Mrs. Martin, may I remind you that Emily is my guest? She is here in the carriage with us, therefore any conversation taking place also involves her."

"I meant no disrespect," Emily said. "I was simply curious to know what was behind the dissolution of their engagement."

"Well, it is rather private," Belinda said shortly.

"Really? I had the impression that you were trying to point out to me exactly how close you had once been to Seneca."

"We were close," she said, looking at him longingly. "Weren't we?"

"At one time, yes. But we aren't the same people, Belinda," he said gently, "and this is not the time."

"Will you talk to me later, then? When we can have our privacy? Please, Seneca?"

Seneca hesitated, glancing at Emily. He dreaded any such confrontation, but he knew he'd have to speak to her sometime. He had to explain about Emily.

"We'll talk."

"Tonight?"

"Yes, if you wish."

"Oh, thank you, Seneca. I have so much to tell you, to explain. I want you to understand. Truly I do."

"All right, Belinda. I said we'd talk. Phillip, how is the mill doing?" he asked to change the subject. But that question didn't seem to lessen the tension any.

"You aren't going to discuss business, are you, dear?" Mrs. Martin said, scowling at her husband.

"I'm going to answer the man's question, Geraldine. We've had a touch of bad luck, lately, Seneca, but we'll pull through it. We have in the past, I imagine we will this time, too."

"What kind of bad luck?" Seneca asked, admiring the man enormously for being willing to admit to trouble, especially with the conniving he must see going on beneath his nose.

"We lost several important contracts lately because of some nasty rumors that have been going—"

"Phillip, that's enough," Geraldine snapped. "I don't want our private business disclosed to all and sundry."

Meaning her, Emily thought. "Perhaps Mrs. Martin has a point," she said. "Seneca, why don't you visit with Mr. Martin sometime this week. Perhaps you can offer some advice."

"I'd appreciate that," Phillip Martin said eagerly. "You've always had a keen business head. What about Monday morning, my office?"

Seneca looked at Emily, pride and love in his eyes. "Yes. I can be there. I'll do what I can to help out. My pleasure."

"We'd also like you to come for dinner one night this week," Mrs. Martin said.

"I appreciate your invitation, but I'll have to leave that for another time, what with my guests. You understand."

"Well, I . . . I suppose, if you can't get away . . ."

"It isn't a matter of getting away, it is a matter of courtesy."

Seneca was beginning to lose patience, Emily could feel it in the way his body was tensing. She tried to think of something to lighten the atmo-

346

sphere, but she was certain anything she said would only be taken the wrong way, so she sat in the corner of the seat and held her breath.

Mr. Martin was the one to change topics. Unfortunately, he chose her. "Tell us again what brought you to Rochester, Miss Harcourt. And all those stories in the newspapers, were they true?"

"Yes, I'm afraid they were. I had some frightening moments through it all, but it's over now, and thanks to Seneca, I'm still alive."

"And so is Abraham Lincoln, I understand. He has more than a good chance for election next year."

"We heard him speak. He was marvelous," she said animatedly. "I wish I could vote."

Belinda chuckled. "Come now, what would a girl like you know about politics?"

"More than I know about silly fashions and frippery," Emily retorted, aggravated into snapping back.

Belinda eyed her dress disdainfully. "That doesn't mean much. Did you get that little frock from the rack at Donnigan's?"

Seneca swallowed a grin and sat back to watch Emily duke it out with Belinda. He'd learned to his own detriment that his wife was quite capable of holding her own.

"This dress? No. I picked it up in Erie. Some lady designed it for me—a Madame . . . eh . . . Rogers? Was that her name, Seneca?"

"Roget. Madame Roget," he corrected, pronouncing the very French name with a very French accent.

Both Martin women gave a gasp. Emily smiled questioningly. "Is it absolutely horrid then? Did Seneca pay for nothing?"

"You paid for her dress?" Belinda demanded,

scandalized. "It must have cost a fortune."

"Yes, she's cost me quite a pretty penny since I've known her," Seneca teased.

Emily blushed, but threw him a look that promised he had yet something else to pay for now.

Thankfully, they arrived at the park before any more could be said. Already a large crowd had gathered. Colorful banners and streamers were strung from the bandstand out to lampposts throughout the area. Additional lamps were suspended from branches in the trees, making the park sparkle and come alive. An orchestra was playing a lively tune that set a festive mood for the gala event.

"Finally," Marianne exclaimed, rushing to meet them. "I was beginning to think you'd all got lost."

Emily heard Belinda mutter something that could have been a wish for Marianne to do just that. She wondered what Marianne had ever done to antagonize Belinda so, besides being her perceptive and outspoken self. Maybe that was enough, if Belinda preferred to live in a world of make-believe.

"Come on," Marianne enthused, grabbing Emily's hand and Seneca's arm. "Excuse us, please, but my friends have been dying to meet these two," she threw over her shoulder to the Martins.

"Don't forget our talk," Belinda reminded him as they were hurried away.

Marianne rushed them through the dozens of booths that had been set up to sell food and goods for the hospital auxiliary fund. Finally she came to a breathless halt, turned toward them, and laughed.

"There. You're rescued. I thought you might need an excuse to break away for a while."

"You little scamp," Seneca laughed. "Thanks."

"Well, I'll see you both later. I'm off to find

348

Darlene."

"What about Freddie and Tom?"

She twirled back around, showing a flash of white pantaloons. "Oh, they'll find me." With a swish of black curls she was gone.

"I don't remember ever having that much energy," Emily said, watching her dance away. "She's incredible."

"That she is. She's almost eighteen. That's hard to believe."

"I suppose so, when you used to bounce her on your knee."

"It won't be long until she's planning a wedding. She has enough suitors to choose from."

"I hope she waits until she finds a man who makes her feel the way you make me feel."

"Mmm. And how is that?" he asked, lowering his head to hers.

She threw him a provocative look. "Well, let's see. First, my heart begins to pound, and . . ."

"No, never mind. I don't think this is the time or place to hear this."

She laughed at him. "I'll tell you later, when we're alone in the candlelight with our soft bed behind us. I'll tell you then."

"You little witch. You had to say that, didn't you?"

"Let's go find your parents. And Belinda, poor darling, will be looking for you."

"Don't be too hard on her. I never realized before how narrow her world is. Not that she isn't intelligent, she's just so preoccupied with what she thinks she wants."

"She wants you. She's convinced herself she'll have you. She even warned me off."

"You've been remarkably tolerant. I don't recall

349

seeing that side of your nature before."

"Now Seneca, that just isn't true. I only pushed you in the canal once. Do you know how many times I walked past you that I was tempted to shove? I was extremely tolerant."

Elijah and T.J., escorted by Marianne, wandered through the booths, filling themselves with the sugary goodies for sale. Marianne introduced T.J. to all their friends, most of whom had know Elijah since Seneca first brought him north. T.J., in his own charming way, stole their hearts, and their faces reflected their pleasure at seeing father and son reunited after such a long time.

It wasn't long before the tables of food were set up and lines began to form for dinner. Several young boys approached T.J. and asked him to eat with them and play a game of ball afterwards.

"Papa?" he asked, looking up at Elijah.

Elijah laughed. "Yes, of course. You're here to enjoy yourself too. Go have fun with your new friends."

Elijah watched the lot of them bound away toward the tables. He suspected the other boys were as eager to hear the tales T.J. had to tell as to have another player for their games.

"He's so amazing, that he could come through what he has without becoming withdrawn and hateful," Marianne observed.

Elijah nodded, watching his son. He knew how it was done. Always a part of the heart was reserved so that when others let you down, you weren't completely devastated. One learned how to be selective with friends and how to be protective with others. It was unfortunate, but often necessary. Only with Seneca and his family had he been able to relax and be himself and *feel* again. Luckily, T.J. had formed a close bond with a white woman, through whom he had learned that love and trust between races was indeed possible.

Elijah looked down at Marianne's sparkling eyes and gave her shoulders a brief hug. "Thanks for taking him under your wing. You've helped him get over leaving Mrs. Bristol."

She scowled and punched his arm playfully. "You don't need to thank me for loving your son. How could I help but love him?"

Elijah caught sight of two young men approaching with a purposeful stride. "Your swains are coming this way. I don't think you're going to escape this time."

"Oh, dear. Well, I guess I can spare them a few minutes," she said haughtily.

He tweaked her cheek. "So you can, mademoiselle." He laughed at her and she danced off.

As he straightened and looked toward where T.J. had gone, he noticed another figure moving furtively in the outlying trees. Without drawing attention to himself, he began to make his way in that direction.

He walked almost the whole perimeter of the park before he caught another glimpse of the bald head. Once he was certain of what he saw, he went in search of Seneca.

Before he could find Seneca he came upon Mrs. Martin and Belinda. Their heated exchange caused him to halt in his tracks and move out of their view. Their words kept him listening .

"I told you this was no good. Seneca is not a man to be manipulated," Belinda said.

"If you had a brain in your head, you'd know how to do it," her mother shot back. "It isn't as if you're saving yourself."

"Don't you think I tried that?"

"Not hard enough. All it would take is one time, then you could claim you were pregnant."

"How am I supposed to get near him with her around all the time. Did you see them earlier? I tell you she has him bewitched."

"We need to get her away. Or discredit her, or something."

"She won't leave. She said she had to take care of Elijah's boy."

"Belinda, if we don't do something, we're going to be in the poorhouse."

"Seneca said he'd help," she argued.

"He can't help. Don't be stupid. Nobody's going to hand us the money we need this time, not unless he's part of the family. If only Mr. van der Zee hadn't learned about our problems."

"That wasn't my fault. And this isn't getting us anywhere."

"All right. You say she's staying because of those coloreds, then let's get rid of them."

"What do you mean? Mother, you can't . . ."

"It's them or us, Belinda."

"No, mother. Not that."

"Now you listen to me. You owe us this. We've lavished you with everything you've ever wanted. We're in trouble now. Your father needs your help, and you aren't going to disappoint him."

They walked away, and Elijah heard no more. What he'd heard was ample, though. Seneca suspected Belinda might try something. He needed to be forewarned that they were plotting against Emily. And himself and T.J. as well.

Seneca grinned and shook his head when Elijah told him what he'd overheard. "They can plot all they want. What can they actually do? I mean besides irritating the hell out of us?" He sighed and rubbed the back of his neck. "But I better go talk to her. I guess she should know the facts before she embarrasses herself any more than she has already. Keep an eye on Emily while I'm gone. This might take a while if I know Belinda."

"Histrionics?"

"Buckets full." Seneca had gone before Elijah remembered the bald man. He moved to Emily's side.

When Seneca returned shortly thereafter, Elijah raised a curious brow. "That was quick. Painless, I hope."

"I couldn't find her. I looked all over the fairgrounds."

"What about her parents?"

"They thought she was with me. Phillip suggested that she might have gone off with young Gerald van der Zee, but Mrs. Martin was certain she'd have nothing to do with him."

"So where is she?"

He shrugged. "I have no idea. Let's get some dinner and enjoy ourselves before she shows up again."

"You're convinced she will."

"I'd stake the boat on it."

She did return some time later that evening, and after a few dances with several of the eligible men in town she came over to Seneca.

"Hello, I haven't seen much of you this evening. Would you care to go for a stroll around the park?"

Seneca put aside his glass of ale and glanced at Emily. "Yes, I would. We could have that long talk you wanted."

"Yes. Elijah can keep your friend company. She won't miss you."

"Her name is Emily," Seneca prompted.

353

Belinda smiled at him, then threw Emily a look of pure venom.

"That is one nasty lady," Elijah said to Emily a moment later. "But still the same, I feel sorry for her—having the mother she does."

Seneca escorted Belinda down a dimly lit path and found a bench for them to share.

"Doesn't this bring back memories, darling?"

"Belinda, we really do need to talk."

"I know. I have so much to say."

"No. Let me say what I have to say first," Seneca asked.

"No. Not yet. Give me a chance. You can do that. I have to say this to you. I love you. I've never stopped loving you. No matter who I was with, I imagined you, your lips, your arms. I haven't made love to anyone since you. I haven't been able to bear the thought of it. Please, Seneca, please believe me."

He tried to be compassionate. "That's all very flattering, but the past is the past. You must see that we can't go back. What we had then we don't have anymore."

"We can get it back. It's still there for me. I can make you happy, sweetheart. Can't you give me a chance?"

"No, Belinda. I've tried to make you see. It's been over between us for a long time."

"It was a mistake. I made a mistake. Haven't you ever done anything you regretted later?"

"Of course I have, Belinda, but please, accept it. I'm not in love with you."

"I don't care about that. I love you enough for both of us."

"Well I do care. I'd like to think I loved my wife."

"People don't always have love when they marry.

Love can grow."

He let out a long slow breath. "Marry? Why are you talking about marriage? Belinda, I love someone else."

"It's her, isn't it? That girl you brought with you. She's not right for you, Seneca. Can't you see that?"

"She's very right for me. Belinda, she's the one I'm going to marry. As a matter of fact, the wedding is scheduled for next week. The pastor will announce it tomorrow in church."

"No!" she cried in real distress. "No. You can't do this to me. I've told everyone we're getting back together again. I'll be made to look an absolute fool. I'll never be able to show my face again."

"You had no right to say any such thing," he said crossly. "It's time you learned to take the consequences of your thoughtless actions. I'm sorry, Belinda, but you've been trying to manipulate me ever since I came back with Emily. I've tried to make you see sense, but as usual, all you see is what you want to see. Open your eyes, woman. I'm not going to marry you."

"You'll ruin everything. I can't let you ruin all our lives. My life. You don't have to live in this town, but I do. Be reasonable. If you have to have her, set her up as your mistress. I'll be understanding."

"No, Belinda. She's going to be my wife and we're going to be married in our church. This is special to my parents and it's special to Emily. I won't change even one of my plans just because you continue to act like a spoiled brat."

She stood up, flounced away, then spun back around. Her eyes were a cold, steely gray.

"You'll regret this. You'll see," she said threateningly.

"What I regret is ever thinking you could be sensible to begin with."

"You're getting even with me, aren't you? You're being purely vindictive. I must have hurt you very much to make you so cruel."

"Don't go on deceiving yourself."

"I'm not. You're using her to hurt me back. Well, I hope you're satisfied, because you've succeeded."

The tears started, and then the deep wrenching sobs. Even though he knew he was being manipulated again, he put his arms around her. She curled up into his embrace and wept as one lost. She sounded so pitiful he felt like a heel. He led her to the bench again.

"Don't, Belinda. You'll make yourself ill."

"What am I supposed to do? For years I've been hoping you'd come back to me. For years. And now I'll spend the rest of my life regretting one impetuous decision. I just can't bear it, Seneca. I just can't."

He mopped her face and tried to calm her. "Let's walk some more. It will calm you. Come on, up you go."

"I'm so sorry. I didn't mean to cry all over you."

"Never mind that. Take a deep breath now. Feeling better?"

"I think I'd like to go home. Can you take me to my parents? You don't mind finding another ride home, do you? Under the circumstances . . ."

"We'll be fine. We could take a short cut this way."

"That's all right. I'd rather . . ."

Somehow she slipped from his grip and fell onto the dusty ground.

"Belinda? Are you hurt?"

She made her way to her feet, leaning heavily

against Seneca. "Oh, no. I've torn my dress." She pulled her hand away to reveal a glimpse of her well-rounded breast. "What shall I do?"

"Well, I guess we better get you home."

"Let's hurry. I think I'm going to cry again."

She did cry. She fell sobbing into her mother's arms. "Oh, Mommie, it was awful. I was so humiliated. Please don't let him hurt me again."

For a moment he couldn't make sense of what she said, then it all began to make a sick sort of sense. A crowd of curious onlookers seemed to think so too.

"Hurt you? What did he do? Why, look at your dress. My God, you've been . . ." She pulled herself upright and glared at Seneca. "I never thought you would stoop so low as to inflict your unwanted attentions on a young lady of good breeding. Why, the poor thing is scared to death, and look at you. You look as if you'd like to kill her. Phillip, do something."

"Well . . . ah . . . What is it I should do?"

"Go get the constable, dolt. Our darling girl has been attacked."

"You have it all wrong, Mrs. Martin. Your darling daughter fell down. Tell her, Belinda."

Belinda cried harder. "Stay away from me. You're despicable."

She was putting on quite an act for the assembled crowd. He knew she was trying to save face, but he couldn't let her do it this way. His family would be humiliated.

Phillip Martin looked from his daughter to Seneca. His eyes narrowed.

"Daughter, look at me. Do as I say," he barked when she hesitated. "Now, did this man attack you, or did you fall as he said?"

"Papa, he said he's marrying that girl," she whispered harshly.

"Answer my question this instant, and it better be the truth, or you'll no longer be welcome under my roof."

"Phillip," Mrs. Martin gasped.

"Papa, you can't mean it."

"Every word. Now what happened?"

Belinda looked at her father's set face then turned furiously to Seneca. "I never said he attacked me. Mother said that. You know how over the top she goes all the time. I fell down."

She glared at her father. He raised his chin and sent both his wife and daughter to their carriage.

"I apologize, Seneca. She's always been impulsive and unpredictable. I don't know what gets into her."

In the shadows of the trees stood a tall figure, listening intently to the confrontation. As soon as the two women huffed away, he pushed himself away from the tree trunk, spit out the toothpick he was chewing, and followed them.

Chapter 22

Monday morning breakfast at the Prescott house was interrupted by an imperious knock at the front door. The housekeeper was led by the sheriff into the dining room, where the family was seated around the table. Two unkempt men followed. Liam Prescott stood.

"Sheriff, what brings you out this morning, and why have you made so free with my home? Release my housekeeper, if you please."

Sheriff Dwyer looked from Seneca to Elijah. "Seneca," he said, coming directly to the point. "These gentlemen claim you're harboring fugitive slaves that belong to their employer."

"Then they are liars," he ground out coming to his feet. "Elijah is a free man, and were he not, he would belong to me. I hold his original papers, plus his grant to freedom, as well as the boy's."

"I'm afraid I'll have to ask you to produce those papers."

"Sheriff, Seneca will get the documents you want," Liam said, "but get this scum out of my home. You had no business bringing them in here."

"Liam, the law says . . ."

"The law protects my right to choose who will or will not be permitted in my home. Do you think I

359

want my wife, my daughter, my guests, and my staff submitted to the stench of bounty hunters."

"Now, Liam . . ."

"No, Dwyer, get them out. Now."

"All right, all right. Let's go, boys."

"We want the two nig . . . coloreds," one of the two men insisted. "The law says . . ."

"This situation is not governed by any law because these two are free," Seneca insisted.

"Says who? You?"

"Yes, me. And my word is worth a damn sight more than yours. You'd sell you own mother into slavery if you could earn two bits to buy a beer."

The bounty hunter lunged toward Seneca. Louise Prescott stood, dashing her glass of water into the man's face. He jerked to a halt and swore at the cold surprise. The sheriff stepped forward and took the man's arm firmly.

"Get out, Hank. Come on. You're not in some drinking hall here. This is the lady's home. I shouldn't have brought them, Mrs. Prescott," he said ruefully. "Sorry, ma'am." He turned to Seneca. "If you could . . ."

"I'll get them," Seneca said, moving toward the library. "But before I do, I want to know who told you I was harboring fugitives, because no employer of these men sent them. It's obvious they're common flesh peddlers."

"You know I don't have to tell you that," Dwyer said.

"Yes, you do. Because I intend to make certain my friends end up where you say they belong." He stopped in the foyer by the doors to the library and turned to face the slavers. His eyes were like chunks of coal—hard, cold, implacable. "I also require identification from these two men. And an affidavit from their employer, stating the identities of his slaves."

"We don't have to do that."

"This time you do." He turned to the sheriff. "This is becoming a witch hunt," he said. "If someone comes to you and claims Marianne is a witch, are you going to burn her at the stake?"

"Hell, no, Seneca, but . . ."

"It's the same thing here. I just returned with Elijah. He went to West Virginia with several documents in his possession declaring him to be a free man. I found him near death, stuffed into a sweatbox."

"I know that the law isn't always perfect, nor are the ways of enforcing it, but I have to do my duty. These men have a valid claim."

"Fine. Let them produce their documents as well."

"Hank, Flynn? Do you have any?"

"Well, no. Not with us."

"Then let us meet tomorrow morning at the police station. You bring your papers, I'll bring mine," Seneca said.

"Fair enough," the sheriff said.

"Wait on, here," said the man called Flynn. "We don't got to do that. Them is niggers in there."

Sheriff Dwyer's nostrils flared. "That man you call a nigger in there is more of a man than you'll ever be. Now move. I've made my decision."

"We don't like your decision," the one called Hank said. "The law says you got to turn them over to us."

"If they are runaways," Dwyer said, nodding. "The law don't say I have to give you free men."

Seneca went into the library as soon as the sheriff and the slavers were gone. He went directly to the lower right drawer of the desk where his folio of private papers was kept.

Elijah's papers weren't there. Neither were those given to T.J. by Constance Bristol. He jerked open the other drawers. The more he looked, the more he was certain that someone had been rifling through the desk.

361

"Something wrong?" Liam asked, coming to join Seneca.

"Someone's been in here. All my papers have been disturbed, and Elijah's and T.J.'s are gone."

Around the table they discussed what could be done.

"I don't see the problem," Emily said. "I've seen the papers, you've seen them, why can't our word be enough?"

"That might work," Liam said, "if we can get Judge Morris to sign an affidavit for us to that effect. That might appease the sheriff."

"But where are the originals?" Louise asked. "I don't like the thought that someone invaded our home unbeknownst to us."

"Nor do I," Liam agreed. "I aim to learn who that was."

"I think T.J. and I should disappear. We'll go north into Canada. I won't risk my son being enslaved."

"But you can't go," Marianne cried. "You can't let them win."

"They won't win, not if I have to go to the president with this. This sort of thing cannot be permitted to continue," Seneca fumed.

Liam and Seneca left to find Judge Morris. Elijah and T.J. went to their room to pack, in case Seneca couldn't get a voucher.

Emily and Louise went to the kitchen to help Wanda with the chores. "I can't imagine how anyone could get in. I'm sure we locked the doors," Wanda said.

"Do you keep a key outside somewhere?"

"Yes, we hide one in back, but only the family knows," Louise said.

Emily's eyes narrowed thoughtfully. Why, after three years, has someone come for Elijah? All the slavers along the canal knew Elijah was free. Everyone in town knows it. These two slavers must come from somewhere else, they were brought here. But why? And then she thought she knew.

"Louise. I told Belinda I couldn't leave here as long as T.J. and Elijah remained. Is there any possibility she knew where the key was kept?"

"Yes, I suppose so. We've kept it in the same place for years. When she and Seneca . . ."

"She warned me not to get in her way. She said I'd be sorry if I tried to interfere with her plans for Seneca. Do you think she's capable of this?"

"I don't know."

Marianne walked into the room. She'd overheard enough to answer. "You know she is, Mother. Remember what she did to Ralph Kyper, one of her old beaux," she explained for Emily's sake. "She started a terrible rumor about how he had this unspeakable disease from being with a prostitute. He couldn't get a girl to speak to him for a year after that, even when the doctor verified that he was in excellent health. What would she have to gain, though, by setting slavers onto Elijah?"

"Time," Emily answered. "Saturday evening Seneca told her we were getting married next week. She went over the edge, almost to the point of accusing Seneca of attacking her."

"Her father made her tell the truth," Louise explained, shaking her head.

"Where was I?"

"Off with your friends. You didn't miss much, dear."

"I think she came over here. Seneca tried to find her earlier in the evening, but he couldn't. She wanted Elijah and T.J. out of the picture, because with them gone I had no reason to stay. Or I let her think that."

"But after she learned you were getting married why would she go through with it?"

"If anyone takes Elijah away, is Seneca going to hang around for a wedding?"

"She's trying to prevent the wedding, then," Marianne said.

"We mustn't jump to conclusions, girls," Mrs. Prescott said. "We would be just as mean as Belinda if we started rumors that were not true."

"Could you loan me Harley and a buggy? I think I'll drop in on the Martins and have a talk with Belinda."

"I'll come along," Mrs. Prescott said.

"Me, too," Marianne said with determination. "We'll present a united front that will intimidate her into telling the truth."

Mrs. Martin was reading a book in the parlor when the three Prescott ladies were shown in. Upon hearing that they had come to speak with Belinda she sent the maid upstairs to fetch her.

"I presume this is not a social call," she said haughtily, marking her book and setting it aside.

"We have some questions we think Belinda might be able to answer," Mrs. Prescott said. "It's very important."

"I don't know why you should expect her to help you when you've managed to ruin her life."

Belinda walked into the room. If her life had been ruined, it was not evident on her smugly satisfied face.

"How nice," she trilled falsely. "Visitors."

"Hello, Belinda," Louise offered. "We wondered if we could speak to you for a few minutes."

"Certainly, Mrs. Prescott. I always have time for you."

"Actually, it was my idea that we come here," Emily said, taking hold of the conversation. "This morning two men came to the house trying to take Elijah and T.J. from us."

"Yes?"

"Yes? Is that all you can say? I'm referring to slavers," she said, irritated at her blasé attitude.

"I understand. What has it to do with me?"

"That's precisely what we came to ask. What part did you play in this?"

"Whatever makes you think I played a part in anything?" Her brows rose indignantly.

"Frankly, because you want me gone, and I once claimed I was staying because of T.J. and Elijah. I think you were hoping to eliminate me by eliminating them."

"Really, now," she scoffed. "You place far too much importance on yourself. Why should I care whether you go or stay?"

"That's a different story from earlier," she replied, knowing Belinda would recall their discussion in the kitchen.

"Well, it's as Seneca said. We're different people now. He isn't what I want anymore, no offense meant, Mrs. Prescott."

"That's funny. Seneca said you bawled your eyes out when he told you he was marrying Emily," Marianne taunted.

"Yes, I was upset. He was quite brutal when he told me."

"You left the social. Seneca looked for you for half an hour and couldn't find you. Where were you?"

"Just because Seneca couldn't find her doesn't mean my daughter left the grounds."

"Maybe if I explain," Louise said sedately. "There is a chance that two people very dear to us might be endangered."

"You mean those coloreds," Mrs. Martin asked. "It escapes me how you could risk your good name by taking them into your home."

"But if they were servants, would it be different?" Marianne demanded.

"Well, of course. This whole slavery issue has been

so exaggerated. It's ridiculous."

What could be said to that? Emily knew it was pointless to argue the matter. Mrs. Martin was so locked into herself she couldn't see past her own lashes. Her world did indeed revolve around her. No wonder Belinda was manipulative. She'd learned at her mother's knee how to shape her world.

She decided to be more aggressive. "We believe Belinda went to the Prescotts' home, let herself in, and took the papers Seneca kept on Elijah and T.J. We think she notified two bounty hunters to come and take them away so Seneca would have to go after them."

She watched Belinda's reaction the entire time she spoke, hoping to invoke a response. But there was nothing in her expression to indicate she knew anything at all about a break-in or papers.

"Are you saying that Seneca can't find the proof of Elijah's independence? That's what this visit is all about? You are accusing me of stealing papers so a man and a child can be sent back into bondage?"

"Except that it wouldn't be just bondage. Elijah nearly died in West Virginia. He won't live through another beating like he received there." And just to drive home her point, she went on to relate some of the horrors she had seen in Matfield.

"Oh, my, must you be so graphic?" Mrs. Martin objected. "I don't care to hear this."

"I know. Most folks prefer to surround themselves with pleasantness. Some are not so fortunate," Louise said.

"Belinda, did you take the papers?" Emily asked directly. "If not, I apologize from the bottom of my heart. If you did, please, please return them."

"And if I did take them, why should I want to give them back?"

"Because you didn't know what pain and misery you would be sentencing Elijah to."

"What has Elijah done for me that I should be so concerned for him, saying, of course, I had the papers."

"All right. I'll concede you've no reason to be especially concerned about any of us, maybe you even think you've reason to be vindictive, but common decency demands you prevent suffering whenever you can."

"I'm sorry, I can't help you. Oh, Mommie, aren't we expected at the dressmaker soon?"

"One more thing," Emily said. "You may not think you know Seneca anymore. I can guarantee you won't want to know him if he learns you pulled a stunt like this."

At that Belinda did react. She turned away very suddenly, then spun back around, pure hatred seething inside her.

"You're going to tell him that, aren't you? It's not enough you're going to marry him, you want him to hate me. You'll say anything, do anything to ruin me in his eyes and the eyes of everyone in this town."

"I think you had better go," Mrs. Martin said irritably. "You've upset her now. Don't cry, my darling," she crooned, wrapping arms around her weeping daughter.

"We'll see ourselves out," Mrs. Prescott said.

"She's lying. I'm positive of that," Marianne declared on the way home.

"Maybe we shouldn't have come," Emily said softly.

"Oh, pooh. I told you she's tricky. We did nothing but ask questions she could have answered with a yes or no. *No, I did not take your papers.* Seven words. Did you hear them? Did you hear any outright denial? No, you did not. Instead you got recriminations and tears, so that you're beginning to doubt yourself. She's very good at it."

"Marianne's right, dear. That girl has some very real problems. She's always been like that."

"Perhaps, but we're no closer to finding those papers. And maybe we've driven them further underground. She may never give them up now, out of pure spite."

"If she has them, Seneca will get them," Marianne said confidently. "She doesn't know brutal yet."

Emily had never felt the full force of Seneca's anger, but she'd been close and she'd seen it in his eyes. Poor Belinda.

"Now, Emily, let's wait and see," Louise advised, patting her hand. "If we wronged her, we'll offer our apologies. But don't be too quick to discount your instincts. Marianne is right."

Judge Morris was sympathetic, but unable to help them. "All I would be doing is affirming what you said. That is no proof at all. I'm sorry, Seneca."

The men returned and found the ladies in the kitchen, busy preparing morning tea. From Marianne Seneca learned that they had just returned from Belinda's, and why. After what Belinda had almost done to him the night before, he could well imagine her striking back at him through Elijah.

"Are you going to go over there and shake the truth out of her?" Marianne asked avidly.

"She'll be expecting that. No. I'll go over to see Phillip at work. Besides, I promised I'd go over today."

"Yes, and you have music lessons today, Marianne."

"Ah, Mother can't I miss today?"

"No, you may not. You missed last week. Now get your books together. Seneca can drop you on his way downtown. Your father and I have errands to run. We'll stop and pick you up."

After lunch Emily, Elijah, and T.J. strolled through the garden. Elijah rested his arm around

368

her shoulders as they walked.

"Wouldn't you like to be back on the canal right now?" Emily asked. "Peace, quiet, and a certain amount of solitude."

"T.J. and I are leaving tonight if the papers aren't found. I hope you understand. And I appreciate what you've done to help us."

"Don't talk like that. I can't bear the thought of you two spending your lives on the run. I was hoping you'd come to Albany and help me run Uncle Joe's business. He has a factory where they build carriages. It seems I own it now, only I don't know what to do with it."

"Seneca will help you."

"Yes, but he has his own business interests. Oh, all I'm saying is that we want you with us."

His eyes misted as he watched his young son bound ahead to the bench swing. A boy should have a home, friends, a mother. Elijah would love to accept Emily's offer, but he couldn't. No use dreaming. He had to keep on the go until he found his wife, until he gave T.J. his mother again. To do that, he had to be free.

"In time perhaps I can come back."

She turned her face into his chest, wrapping her arms around his waist. "Sometimes I want to scream at the whole world. Why is it that the voice of fairness and reason is a gentle whisper when greed and fanaticism scream to get what they want?"

"It seems that way at times, sweet lady, but it is not always so."

She shook her head. "This time it is. She won. She'll drive you away. Seneca will come to realize that she did it because of me and he'll resent me. Life will become intolerable."

He chuckled. "You're feeling down right now. I don't see you ever permitting Seneca to blame you for anything Belinda does."

She smiled reluctantly. "No. I won't. Oh, Elijah, I know she's involved. Do you think you could convince her?"

"Good grief, all she'd have to do is say one word and I'd be in prison for attacking her. No, thanks. I'll take my chances in Canada."

"You ain't goin' to Canada, nigger," said a voice behind them. Elijah and Emily turned to face the two slavers, both holding rifles trained on them. "Get the kid and let's go. And don't try nothin' funny or I'll kill the pretty lady."

Emily placed a warning hand on Elijah's forearm. "Don't be foolish. Do as he says."

"Leave her. I'll go along with you quietly, but leave her out of it."

"Sorry. She comes with us. We get a tidy little sum for bringin' her along."

T.J. ran up to them, and Elijah put a protective arm around him. "Who's paying you to do this?" He stalled for time, hoping Wanda would see what was happening.

The man she remembered as Hank jabbed his gun into her side. "Go, lady, through them bushes and over the fence." Flynn prodded Elijah to follow. They had walked only a short distance before they came to a wagon. Flynn motioned them aboard then tied their hands behind their backs.

Emily hadn't experienced such indignities before, but the rage in Elijah's eyes told her this was not a new experience for him.

"Emily," he said evenly, his voice at odds with his eyes. "I want you to do whatever I tell you without questions. Will you do that?"

"Yes. What can we do?"

"For now we wait."

"No talkin' back there or we'll gag you."

Emily glared at the men in the seat of the buckboard. She'd wait, but she'd do whatever was necessary to protect herself and her dear friends. She could almost feel Seneca's strength surge into her.

Seneca began to fidget. He tried to pay attention to Phillip but his mind kept straying to Emily. And he found he was becoming increasingly nervous.

"Philip, I'm going to have to go home and check on Emily. I have an uneasy feeling about leaving her and Elijah there alone."

"Oh? I'm not sure I understand. Elijah wouldn't . . ."

"No. Nothing like that." He went on to explain what had happened that morning, including Emily's suspicions about Belinda's involvement.

"Phil, I don't know where this idea started that she and I would reconcile. I'm going to be honest with you. Emily and I are already married. We're having a ceremony for my parents' sake, but . . ."

"Did you tell Belinda?"

"No. I told her about the wedding, though."

Phillip rubbed the back of his neck. "Do you know how many times she's been engaged to be married? Four times. I'm sorry you won't be my son-in-law, but I can't blame you for marrying Emily. She's a lovely woman."

"Yes, and I have an odd feeling that she needs me, so if you don't mind . . ."

"By all means. I'll keep your marriage a secret and I'll do what I can to learn the truth about Elijah's papers."

Seneca's buggy was just outside, and he quickly climbed aboard and turned the horse homeward. He had no explanation for the urgency he felt, and he'd probably feel a fool when he reached home to find her safe and sound. Nevertheless, he slapped the reins against the horse's rump.

He strode into the house, letting the front door

slam back against the hinges. "Emily," he bellowed.

Wanda came down the stairs. "Seneca. My word, what is it?"

"Where's Emily. I need to see her."

"She's out back with Elijah and T.J."

He began to relax and breathe easier. "Thanks," He strode through the house and out the back door. Not seeing them right away he walked down the path to the swing. The gazebo was empty as well. "Emily," he called repeatedly. "Elijah." Where had they gone? He was feeling that sick dread again.

"Wanda! Wanda, come down here. Wanda, they aren't out there," he shouted. She rushed back down the stairs. "Where else could they have gone? Both buggies were being used. Was anyone here?"

"No. No one."

He paced the foyer, running fingers through his hair.

"Dammit! I knew something had happened. I had this feeling. Wanda," he said, taking her shoulders, "tell Father I've gone to the Martins. If that witch is behind this, she might know where they are."

T.J. snuggled into his father's side. "Are they going to take us back to West Virginia? Will I be a slave after all?"

"No," Emily said sharply. "You will not be a slave."

"Why can't I get another paper from Miss Constance?"

"You can, don't worry. But we don't have time right now," Emily whispered. "Seneca will know what to do."

"I told you to be quiet back there," Flynn scowled. "Now, shut up."

"Emily's right," Elijah said in hushed tones, hugging his son. "Seneca's never let me down yet."

T.J. nodded, accepting his father's word. He

wasn't as frightened as Emily thought he'd be, or as frightened as she was. He was either very stoic or a tough little character indeed.

They were taken to a small house outside of town, back a long and very overgrown lane, and led down into a dark cellar. The ladder was drawn up and the door overhead was lowered and locked.

"Emily, turn around, I'll try to get you untied."

Freed of their bonds, they began to search the damp and musty room. Emily found a lantern, but the matches beside it were so damp she tried five before she got one that burned.

Elijah moved a barrel so that he could stand on it and get closer to the overhead door to listen for voices. It wasn't necessary. Their voices carried well enough through the planking.

"You have the girl as well?" asked a voice above them.

"Oh, no," she gasped. "It's him."

"Him who?" Elijah asked.

"The Frenchman. The bald man."

"You got our money?" They recognized Flynn's voice.

"I'll pay you, I said I would."

"Fifty dollars."

"*Oui*, fifty. It is all there. Now bring up the woman."

The door opened. Three men looked down at them. The Frenchman laughed. "So finally I have you. You have caused me much trouble, woman."

Elijah pulled Emily behind him. "You have no one. Flynn, what am I worth? And T.J.?"

"Well, I . . . What can we get Hank?"

"You'll get nothing, because no one will pay for a dead man. You'll have to kill me to get this woman."

"And me," T.J. said bravely, stepping up beside his father.

"Get her up here," Frenchie demanded. "Where's

373

the ladder?"

"Hold on, now," Flynn stated. "We got us a problem here."

Frenchie pulled a revolver from beneath his shirt. "I do not see a problem. Stand aside." He kicked the ladder to the edge of the opening and slid it down. Before the ladder reached the ground, Elijah grabbed it and pulled it out of Frenchie's hands, letting it fall with a heavy thud to the dirt floor.

"Now, which one of you is brave enough to come down here and get it?"

The revolver clicked, then exploded. It fell to the plank floor, and Frenchie swore.

"You ain't killin' our slaves," Flynn growled. "Not unless you pay for 'em first."

"Yeah," Hank agreed. "A hundred dollars for each of them."

"Done," Frenchie said.

"Wait a minute," Emily cried. "I'll give you two hundred for each."

Flynn laughed. Frenchie swore again.

Chapter 23

"Face it, Flynn," Emily said after a long argument. "Neither Frenchie nor I have the cash with us, but which do you think can get it? If you send a message to the Prescotts, they'll pay anything you want for our return. On the other hand, if any of us is hurt, your life won't be worth one cent. Seneca will hunt you down and cut out your heart. You know Seneca, don't you, Frenchie?"

"Shut up, bitch."

"Tell them how he outsmarted you time after time. Then tell them what a bungler you are. You've been trailing us for over a month and you haven't caught us yet."

"I've got you now," he gloated.

"Actually, Flynn and Hank have me. And from what we heard up there, they have you, too. What are you going to do, Flynn? Are you throwing in with a man who ambushes the wrong people and gets himself tied to a dead tree hanging out over the river?" She laughed mockingly.

"We gotta think about this," Flynn said. "Tie him up," he ordered his friend. "And shut that damn door. I heard enough for now. I gotta think."

The door overhead thudded shut, sending a shower of dust and dirt down on them.

"Well, well, well," Elijah said, chuckling. "The little kitten has claws."

"Oh, stop," she whispered huskily. "I only did what makes any sense at all. We have to alert Seneca. He'll take it from there."

Seneca knocked on the front door and waited, trying to calm his temper. When Mrs. Martin opened the door, he strode in without invitation.

"Seneca," she gasped.

"Seneca," Belinda cried, coming to the parlor doors. She took one look at his thunderous face and backed away.

"Where are they?"

"Who? Seneca, what are you doing here?"

"I'm not in the mood, Belinda, for any more theatrics. Where are Emily, Elijah, and the boy?"

"Well, how should I know?" she huffed.

"Because you arranged this little disappearance, didn't you? *Didn't you?*" he thundered.

She sat down on the nearest chair, her eyes wide with shock and fear. He didn't back off at her show of feminine vulnerability. He strode into the room and towered over her.

"I'm waiting. And I'm warning you. And you, too," he threatened, jabbing a finger in Mrs. Martin's direction when she took exception to Seneca's tone. "You have exactly one minute to tell me where they are. After that I go to the sheriff. He'll have men out here in minutes to tear your house apart searching for my documents. And if Emily or Elijah or that little boy are hurt, or God forbid, killed, you will stand trial as an accomplice to murder. *Murder*, Belinda! Has your greed and jealousy taken you that low?"

"Don't, Seneca. Don't be so cruel," she cried, breaking into a torrent of tears.

"You're time is running out. If you think my wedding would be cause for humiliation, wait until the papers get hold of this story. You'll never live it down. "Woman murders ex-lover's wife.""

"She's not your wife, and I don't know where she is."

"Fine," he said furiously. "Have it your way." He strode toward the door.

"Wait," she cried. "Damn you. I only did it because I love you."

"If this is a sample of your love, it's no wonder your men jilt you. It's a cold and sick thing, what you call love. Where is my wife?"

"Why do you call her that?" Belinda screamed. "She isn't. She never will be. I'll make sure of it."

"Belinda," Mrs. Martin cried, aghast at her daughter's venomous outburst. "Belinda, what are you saying?"

"She is my wife. I love her, Belinda. I married her two weeks ago. *She is my wife*. Now where is she?"

"No! You'll never have her. He'll kill her, then you'll come back to me."

"If I come back, it will be to strangle you."

"Belinda, dear, calm yourself. You aren't making any sense. Have you done something? It was that man. You went back to see him, didn't you? After you brought me home, you went back."

Belinda jumped to her feet in agitation as Mrs. Martin slumped into a chair. "I only wanted to stop the wedding. You wanted it too. You said we had to stop Seneca from marrying that girl."

"But not by harming her. Where is she?"

"I don't know. I don't know where he took her."

"What about Elijah and T.J.," she asked.

"Oh, what about them? I don't know."

"Who was this man you spoke to?" Seneca demanded.

377

"I don't know that either. He was French."

"Bald, with a moustache?"

"Yes." She stood with her rigid back to him, staring out the window. "I hope he kills her."

"Belinda," her mother cried in horror.

She spun around. "I do. I hate her. Because of her everything is ruined. We're ruined. I want her dead." She glared, wild-eyed, at Seneca. "I want you to suffer."

"If she dies, I promise you you'll never see the outside of a prison cell again. Your life will be spent thinking about what you did and how little it gained you. You'll have nothing but rags to wear, disgusting food to eat; you'll work your fingers to the bone so that you'll age twenty years in five. Is that what you want?"

"Mother," she wailed. "Make him go away. I don't want to hear this."

Mrs. Martin wrapped her arms around her daughter, her face scored with lines of distress and worry. She turned beseeching eyes to Seneca.

"Belinda," Seneca said more gently. "Think what you're doing. Three people may die. You don't want to live with that."

"I want you."

"No, you don't. Not really. You knew that when you broke our engagement three years ago. Belinda, help me. Please. Where was he taking her?"

"I don't know."

"Belinda!"

"I don't know, I tell you. I don't know."

He believed her. Whatever she had done had been a momentary bit of malice that had somehow gone beyond her control.

"What did you say to the Frenchman?"

"I told him you'd be away this morning and that your parents and Marianne would be busy as well."

"Making it easy to kidnap my wife. Mrs. Martin, if she says anything else that might help, would you let me know. Oh, and the papers."

Belinda went to the library and extracted a book. Inside was an envelope. She brought it into the foyer where Seneca stood waiting and handed it to him. Without another word she walked up the stairs.

Seneca returned home feeling flat and sick with worry. "She couldn't tell me anything," he said to Wanda. "I got the papers back, but even though she set the whole thing up, she didn't know where the men had taken them."

"Emily was right. She could sense that girl meant no good. Come, have a cup of tea, then take another look around the garden. You might find a clue."

Within the hour Louise and Liam came home and found him in the library. Marianne had decided to spend the afternoon at her girlfriend's home, they explained at his alarmed question. He nodded and poured himself a whiskey.

"What is it, son? Where is everyone?"

"They've been kidnapped. They're gone. Oh, God, I feel so helpless."

"Now, take it easy," Liam said. "Have you sent for Dwyer?"

"Dwyer," he spat. "After what he did? No, I didn't want to leave in case . . ."

"Louise, send Harley, would you."

"I shouldn't have left them. I should have guessed he'd find us."

"The same man? The Frenchman?"

"I should have killed him when I had the chance. Instead, I keep letting him go." He slammed his fist down on the mantle. "Why is that?"

"Because you're not a barbarian. Seneca, don't browbeat yourself."

Louise came back into the room, towing a little boy

with her. "Seneca, this lad has a message for you."

Seneca hurried across the room and bent down. "What is it?"

"Mr. Seneca Prescott?"

"Yes. Yes."

He took out a folded paper and handed it to Seneca. "Can I go now?"

"Just a minute. Who gave this to you?"

"A man. He paid me twenty-five whole cents to bring it here."

Seneca's obvious bad temper scared the boy, and Liam led the child aside and knelt down beside him. "What did this man look like. Was he bald?"

"I don't know. He had a hat on. A dirty old hat with snake around it."

"That's the man the sheriff brought here. Flynn," Louise said.

"Dear God," Seneca groaned. He sat down heavily. "They're in this together, all three of them. He says he wants five thousand dollars for their return, and he wants it by tomorrow or he'll let the Frenchman have Emily and we'll never see the . . . Elijah and T.J. again."

"I'll go down to the bank," Liam said. "How do we get the money to him?"

"From what I can tell from this scribbling, we're to make an exchange on the footbridge in the little park west of town. Tomorrow at six o'clock. He says to come alone."

Seneca let the hand holding the note drop into his lap. Such a long time to wait. He didn't know if he could bear it.

"Seneca," Louise said, placing a comforting hand on his knee as she knelt in front of him. "She's with Elijah. You know Elijah. He's not going to let them hurt her."

"Elijah's recovering from near death."

"Sure he is. But he's strong. And don't you think he'll be on his guard all the more for what he went through in West Virginia. Think, Seneca. Elijah's not going back there. He'll do something."

"There are three of them, Mother."

"Don't be silly," Liam said. "I saw the two who were here. Elijah can take them easily."

"Then why hasn't he. Why aren't they back?"

"Because he'll wait to learn the best way to handle the Frenchman. Emily's going to be fine."

Seneca finished off his drink. They were right. He was overreacting. He had to calm down and begin to think. What would Elijah do?

"Should I get the sheriff?" Louise asked.

"No," Seneca said gruffly. "No. I'll handle this." He found a couple of coins in his trousers and tossed them to the boy. "You go home now and forget all about this. And if you see that man again, stay away from him."

"Yes, sir."

The lantern flickered against the stone walls. Somehow she knew it was dark outside. One root had grown in through the crack between the stones. It looked like a snake crawling up the wall. She looked away, back at the lantern. T.J. snuggled into Elijah's arms. Emily hugged her arms to her chest.

"We're getting cold air from outside," Elijah said, looking around the root cellar. He stood, transferring T.J. to Emily's arms. Very slowly he walked the perimeter, feeling for drafts of air.

"Ah, here," he said, lifting the lantern high against the back wall. His hand roved over the stones, then he tested one or two. He sat back down.

"Emily, see the moisture line around the top. The stones above that line are above ground."

"Are they loose?"

"Not yet. They wiggle, but I can't get them to move without making a racket that would alert them to what we're doing."

"What if I distract them with a little racket of my own while you do what you must."

"Worth a try. Let me get the barrel over where I can stand on it."

When he was set with part of a barrel hoop to pry at the stones, Emily set up a ruckus. She stood the ladder up and hammered it into the floor boards overhead.

"Open up this door, you animals. We've been in here most of the day without a thing to eat or drink. I'm hungry. You can't do this to me. I'm a friend of the Prescott's. You'll be sorry if you don't treat me right. And that means food and water." All the while she beat rhythmically on the floor. Every time she beat, so did Elijah.

"Shut up, down there. You'll get food when your lover boy comes across with the money."

"I can't sleep when I'm hungry and thirsty. I demand food. Do you hear me?" She looked at Elijah, whose muscles were bulging from his exertions. She beat on the floor harder.

"Damn you, how do you expect us to sleep with that racket? Cut it out."

"If I can't sleep, neither will you. I demand food! Food, food, food," she began to chant at the top of her lungs. A loud crack sounded at the back, and Emily turned quickly. "We want food." She banged the ladder from one end of the cellar to the other. The iron barrel hoop had snapped, but Elijah was grinning. He gave a mighty shove and the big stone tumbled out.

The trap door opened and Elijah froze. Emily moved into the light, glaring up. "You can't leave us down here without water and food. And we're cold.

382

Don't you have blankets?"

"Lady, you're one baggage I'll be well rid of." He threw down a tin canteen and several apples. The blanket followed. "Now shut the hell up."

"Yes, sir," she said meekly as the door slammed shut.

"Brat," Elijah teased, propping the ladder up against the wall. "Eat your apples. We'll wait for a while until they settle down again. And Emily, you'll have to leave your petticoats."

She rustled out of them and tossed them on top of the barrel. Elijah tore the blanket in two, handing part to T.J. and part to Emily. He rolled his own heavy cotton sleeves down. The wool blanket was scratchy, but it felt good against her bare arms.

T.J. was quiet but fully awake. He watched the two adults with amused curiosity. He'd never seen a white lady and a Negro man get along so well before. Miss Constance had liked him, of course, but he was a kid. Most white women would be offended or afraid to be alone with a Negro man like his father. At least, that was the case with most of the white women he had known. Miss Emily wasn't, though. She wasn't afraid to be touched, she even hugged his dad. And she wasn't offended when he told her what to do. She trusted him, like a friend trusts a friend. She was pretty, too. He liked to look at her.

Emily must have dozed off, for she awoke with a start, her heart beating frantically from some forgotten dream. Elijah's arm rested around her shoulders. T.J. was across their laps.

"Elijah," she whispered. His eyes blinked open instantly.

He cussed and looked at his pocket watch. "Good, only two hours. I thought we'd slept the night away. T.J., wake up, son. It's time to go."

"Where are we going?" Emily asked. "Do you know

383

where we are?"

"We came west, so we'll go east. We'll eventually come to town or the waterway to Lake Ontario. We have to get back to town before they realize we've gone. We'll have to move fast."

"Yes, I want to go home. Seneca will be frantic. Somehow we have to stop him from paying all that money. I shouldn't have told Flynn he would."

"Why? It bought us time. I couldn't have done half as well. I'll go first. We can't take the lantern. They might see it through the floorboards. T.J. will follow me. You bring up the rear, and don't lose touch with each other. Remember, they're right above us. You ready, son?"

"I can do it, Pa. I'm good at sneakin'."

"I'll have to bear that in mind, then." He climbed the ladder and wedged his broad shoulders and chest into the hole he had made. He scanned the darkness, then heaved a sigh of relief. He could see moonlight not too far away.

Emily climbed the ladder, following T.J., and peered into the darkness under the house. She reached out and brushed aside some cobwebs. She took a breath and pushed herself up. She was almost through when her skirt caught on the ladder. She couldn't reach back, so she gave it a yank. It tore free, but dislodged the ladder. It slid down the wall, clattering against a row of empty shelves.

She closed her eyes in exasperation, but what was done was done. She followed T.J. Above her head she heard voices and footsteps.

Elijah was there to help her up when she reached the outside. "What happened?" he whispered.

"My skirt caught on the ladder and I . . . I'm sorry, Elijah. I heard them, they're awake."

"I know. Let's get out of here."

Loud shouting erupted from the house behind

them, and they knew their escape had been discovered.

Elijah changed directions. They were running outright across a field, only instead of going toward town they were going south of the house to skirt around the long way. He found them a thick clump of bushes to hide in. "We'll wait here and see which way they go. Be as quiet as possible."

Except for Frenchie, Elijah's plan would have worked. "They ain't dumb enough to go that way," he predicted, leading the other two men in the chase. "They'll try to throw us off."

Emily looked at Elijah, who motioned both her and T.J. to silence. He pulled them close and covered Emily's fair head with the blanket.

The three men came within feet of their hiding place, the light from their lantern bouncing off the branches overhead. Elijah's arms tightened around them. Emily was thankful for that much security.

As soon as they had passed, Elijah led them south. For hours they ran, putting as much distance as possible between them and the kidnappers. Were it not for the woman and the boy, he would have doubled back and dealt with the kidnappers one by one. But he wouldn't risk any harm to Emily and T.J.

"I'm tired, Pa. Can't we stop?"

Emily sank to her knees, taking the decision from Elijah. She sat back on her heels, exhausted.

"We'll rest a while, but we have to move on soon. Come dawn, and that's not long from now, that Frenchman will find our trail."

"Do you know where we are?" Emily asked.

"In these hills? Sorry. And with this cloud cover I can't even be positive which direction we're going. When the sun rises, we'll know."

"Then we could be minutes from town?"

"Or minutes from the cabin."

"You mean we've been going in circles?" T.J. asked.

"I mean I don't know. Try and get some sleep. I'll stand watch."

Seneca strolled up and down the paths of the garden, a glass of brandy in one hand, a cigar in the other. He put the slim cigar between his teeth and checked his watch. Three o'clock in the morning.

"Damn, and damn," he cussed. If Emily suffered at all, he'd make that witch pay. "Elijah, keep her safe for me," he said aloud.

The rest of the night passed in a blur of anger, fear, recrimination, and desperate hope. He was sitting in the kitchen when Wanda came in to start breakfast.

"So you've learned know to make a decent cup of coffee, have you?" she asked, helping herself to the last of it. She set a fresh pot of it on to brew. "You're up early."

"I'm up late, Wanda."

"Couldn't sleep, huh?"

"How could I, wondering where she is and if she's all right? I did finally go to bed, but every time I shut my eyes I saw her face. I finally gave up."

"You'll get one of your headaches if you aren't careful."

"I'm fine," he said, rubbing his temples.

"Sure you are. Well, if you don't sleep, you have to eat. I'll fix you some pancakes."

"That sounds good, Wanda. Thanks."

The day passed more slowly than any Christmas Eve Seneca could remember as a boy. Liam was able to get the money needed from his banker, although the banker suspected what he needed it for and urged him to go to the sheriff.

Seneca refused to involve Dwyer in case Dwyer came up with some other reason to use the law against them.

"He's a good sheriff for the most part," Liam said in Dwyer's defense. "Just a bit zealous at times. He goes by the letter of the law rather than the intent."

"Yes, and I'm not letting him spout some reason why I can't deal with these kidnappers in my own way. It used to be a man had a right to protect home and family. Now it seems the law thinks it has a right to come into a man's home and take his wife and friends away."

"Dwyer didn't do that, exactly."

"As good as. Do you think he'll do anything to those bastards for kidnapping Elijah and T.J.?"

"Maybe not, but he'll see they go to prison for taking Emily."

"And you don't see the injustice in that?"

"Of course I do," Liam said, holding up his hands in surrender.

"Sorry. I guess I'm beat."

"Son, it's only three o'clock. Go up and catch a nap for a couple of hours. I'll wake you at five. Go on. In your state, you won't do anyone any good."

He went.

Emily awoke with a start to find Elijah's hand on her shoulder. His other hand came over her mouth.

"Shh. We have company," he whispered, barely speaking at all. He nodded at the direction of the footsteps he'd heard. She heard them too. "Let's go."

She grabbed T.J. 's hand and followed Elijah through the trees. The afternoon sun was beginning to burn through the trees, the heat was growing unbearable. How could he have found them? He must be part hound dog. Or Indian. Damn the man.

The longer they ran the more certain Emily became that they couldn't outrun him. The man could track a

387

crow. Of course they couldn't do much to cover three sets of footprints in the soft ground cover, especially with scrambling uphill and sliding down.

"Elijah, why not just fight the man?"

"I think I'm going to have to. We can't shake him." He found a crevice between two large boulders. "You two stay put right here. No matter what you hear outside, don't move."

"Papa, we can help," T.J. said.

"No. Let me handle this devil."

Emily backed into the crevice, taking T.J. with her. "Be careful, Elijah. We're lost without you."

"Don't worry. And if by chance I don't come back, go east. Can you do that?"

"I know how, Pa."

"Good. I know I can count on you."

He was gone then, and an ominous silence descended on the forest, as if the animals, the birds, even the insects knew trouble was coming. T.J. looked up at her with big frightened eyes. She held him close, too frightened herself to do more.

They waited.

A sudden rustle and thud sounded to their left, followed by a shot. Emily clapped her mouth shut and buried T.J.'s face in her bosom to muffle his cry.

A loud grunt followed, and then the sounds of a real fight. Anger boiled up in her, hot and unstoppable. Elijah could not suffer again.

"Stay here," she said to T.J.

"No. I'm coming too."

Together they peeked out of their hiding place. They saw Elijah slam the Frenchman's hand against a boulder until his gun went flying behind him and down a ravine.

"Try and find the gun, T.J. Go on."

Emily looked around until she found a short thick branch she could use as a club. She danced around

388

the two struggling men, wincing as the Frenchman's fist connected repeatedly with parts of Elijah's face and body. But they were so close she couldn't help.

"Get out of here, Emily. Take T.J. and run."

"No. He wants me. Come on, Frenchie, come get me, you bungling idiot."

The Frenchman growled and lurched toward her. Elijah dived for his legs and brought him crashing to the ground at Emily's feet. Frenchie reached out and grabbed her ankle.

She fell on her bottom. His hand on her leg made her skin crawl, and the sinister leer on his face made her want to vomit. She beat his arm with her club until he let go. And all the while Elijah was smashing his head into the ground.

With a mighty growl, Frenchie rolled over, dislodging Elijah and rolling on top of him. When he came up, he held a rock between his hands to smash into Elijah's face.

At that moment Emily saw the face of a truly evil man. The Frenchman wanted to kill Elijah, would kill Elijah to get to her. He would kill, and it would never cross his mind again. And he would kill T.J. and he would kill her. Or she would wish he would.

His arms began their downward descent. She made her move. With all her strength she swung her club. She hit him across the side of his face. The rock he held slipped from his hands, but Elijah lurched out of the way as it fell heavily onto the ground.

She hit him again and again. She hit him as he fell back against the boulder. She hit him as his head lolled to the side. She hit him for all the times he had terrified her, for the times he had tried to kill her. He had no right. *He had no right.*

"Emily, stop. Emily."

Elijah wrapped an arm around her waist and lifted her back. He wrenched the bloody club from her hands.

"Enough, Emily. Enough."

She came out of a hazy red mist of rage to see the Frenchman, his face half destroyed, slumped inertly against the rock. Her own hands were bloodied by her grip on the rough club. She looked from the Frenchman, up to Elijah, down to her hands. She twisted herself out of his arms, running away from him. Frantically she wiped her hands on her dress, trying to rid them of the crimson stains. She felt hot; she felt cold; she felt violently ill. Wrenching spasms hit her stomach and she fell to her knees, vomiting until all that remained were painful dry heaves.

"I found it, Emily. I found the gun," T.J. cried.

Elijah lifted her and turned her into his chest, rocking her, soothing her. He took possession of the gun and led his son and Emily away from the Frenchman's body.

"Come. A good long walk will do us all good." And the sound of the gunshot would bring the others. He didn't have the strength to fight anymore.

Behind them the Frenchman's hand twitched and opened.

Chapter 24

Seneca checked his watch for the fifth time in as many minutes. The money was in the satchel he held at his side. In his coat pocket was a small silver pistol. In his mind and heart were thoughts of Emily.

The footbridge where he was to meet the kidnappers was just ahead of him. Shadows from the tall trees fell across the slender neck of the duck pond, turning the water a deep green color. He took a long breath and exhaled slowly. Under different circumstances this would be a lovely spot.

He didn't turn to look at them in case he was being observed, but his father and Harley were behind him, hidden just off the footpath. He hoped he'd have no need of their support.

At five minutes past six a man walked toward him. Flynn. He had his hands in the pockets of his jacket, and Seneca knew he also was holding a weapon.

"Is that the money?"

"Yes. Five thousand dollars."

His eyes moved to the satchel, flashing greed. "Throw it over."

"Where is my wife? And Elijah and the boy?

Our deal was an exchange, five thousand for the three of them. I don't see them."

"Your wife, huh? Well, we ain't given' them over till we have a chance to check that there money."

Seneca opened the satchel and took out a few bundles of bills. "It's here, all of it. More money than you'll see in your lifetime. And you can have it all when my wife and friends walk across that bridge."

"I don't know, Prescott. There's this man who wants the woman real bad. I might have to give her to him, unless I have the money to give him instead."

Seneca closed the satchel and casually placed his hand in his pocket. "A deal is a deal. Sorry. You know, I don't think you've got them anymore. I think they'd be here if you did. No one would give you this amount of money for fugitive slaves, so I was your best deal. But I'm no fool."

Flynn pulled his gun. "I'll take that money, Prescott."

"Okay, don't get crazy. You can have the money. Just tell me where they are."

"Hank, get out here. Go over there and get that satchel." Hank appeared from behind a tree and moved haltingly toward the bridge.

"Hank," Seneca said calmly. "If you know what's good for you, you'll stay right where you are."

"I'll kill you," Flynn said.

"Maybe. But I also have a gun pointed at you. I guarantee you'll fall the same time I do. And my father is behind me with his hunting rifle pointed at Hank. If you're smart you'll disappear. And I mean out of New York State. I can have you arrested for what you've done, and I won't hesitate if

I ever see you again." Seneca hoped they'd buy that. They were too skittish to be handling weapons. He didn't want to be shot before he could help Emily and Elijah.

"What's it worth to know where they were?"

"Nothing if they aren't there now."

"Look, we need that money. That lady told us she'd pay us for the slaves. Five hundred each, she said."

"Sorry. I have in my pocket the papers proving they are free men and cannot be sold."

"Dammit, Flynn. I'm gettin' out of here. You've involved me in your last harebrained scheme."

"Hank, come back here." But Hank was gone.

"So now what will you do, Flynn? Kill me? My father would drop you before you could blink again."

"Damn you, Prescott. Damn you to hell. I hope he catches her." He spun on his heels and ran after his pal.

"You gonna let them go?" Harley asked, rushing out to Seneca's side.

Seneca shrugged. "They're no use to me. They don't have them. They were counting on fear, hoping to get the money anyway."

"Then where are they?" Liam asked.

"Out there somewhere. Frenchie's trackin' them. If I know Elijah, he'll head for north country. He has no way of knowing I have the papers back. He's not going to risk capture, either theirs or Emily's. He'll travel the road. He knows I'll follow."

"But should you let Flynn and Hank go?"

"Oh, them. The sheriff is waiting for them down the lane."

* * *

Emily understood why they weren't returning to Rochester immediately. If Hank and Flynn were still around, and if Seneca hadn't recovered the documents the sheriff required, then Elijah and T.J. risked capture. And if the slavers had attempted to extort money from the Prescotts and failed, they could very well come back for revenge. Elijah's way was best for the time being, until they received word that a return was safe. She leaned back against the cool stone wall, so much like the walls of the root cellar, and closed her eyes.

"Emily, here. Eat something, then get some sleep," Elijah said gently.

The station master of that particular station had offered to let Emily have a bed in his home instead of in the backroom of his mill, but Emily wouldn't leave Elijah. Even now she held onto T.J.'s small hand.

When the mill owner looked uneasy at the thought, Elijah tried to explain. "She had to kill a man this morning, a man who's been trying to kill her for months now. She's still in shock. She needs to be with friends."

The man nodded. "Yes. I remember."

Elijah frowned. "I beg your pardon?"

"I once took a life. Like her, I was defending myself and my family, but still . . . I'll bring a bath and some of my wife's clothes," he said sympathetically, looking at her blood-stained gown. "She'll feel better once she's clean." The man's brows drew together, puzzled. "If you don't mind my saying, you don't look nor act like no slave I ever met."

"No, sir. My son and I are legally free." Briefly he explained their circumstances.

394

"I'll do my best to pass a message along the grapevine. Seneca Prescott, that's her husband's name? Yes, sir, I'll do my best."

That night Emily dreamed again, only this time she reached Peter in time to see him killed. But it was wrong. All wrong. Frenchie was there. She beat him with a stick until his face was gone. Still he came after her. She ran and ran, but each time she turned he was there. Laughing. Leering.

"No. No!" she screamed. "Get away, get away."

Elijah called to her, trying to wake her. He held her shoulders and gently shook her. "Emily, you're having a nightmare. Wake up."

"Let me go!" she screamed. "Get away, get away! Help me, someone! Help me!"

So deep was she into sleep and into her dream that the station master and his wife arrived before Elijah could rouse her.

"Let me try," the woman said softly. "Perhaps a different voice will help." She called to Emily in gentle tones, soothing tones. "Emily, it's all right. You're safe now. He's gone. He can't hurt you. Emily, you can wake up now."

Emily grew still, then blinked suddenly awake, jerking back from the strange woman. Her eyes scanned the room until they latched onto Elijah.

"Elijah," she cried, tears coursing down her cheeks. She held out her arms for him. "It was so awful. I was so frightened. I want to go home, Elijah. I want Seneca."

"I know, sweetheart, I know. Soon, I promise. Very soon."

T.J. came over to her and climbed up beside her. He stroked her long hair. "We'll keep you safe, Emily. We won't let anyone hurt you. It was just a dream. I used to have them, too, when I got lost."

"Oh, T.J.," she said, pulling him into her arms. "Thank you. I'm so glad I have you with me."

She looked up self-consciously. "I'm so sorry. I got you all up."

"It's only half past ten. We hadn't gone to bed yet," the other woman said. "I have some powders that will help you sleep. Would you like me to make you a drink?"

"Thank you," Elijah answered for her. "I'll see she drinks it. She needs some rest."

After a little while, Emily settled back down in her warm bed, the sweet tea and powders beginning to take effect. "Elijah, I killed a man today."

"Don't worry about it. There are times when we do what we have to do. How many chances did you give that snake to back off? Good grief, you could have killed him several times over, but you didn't. It was us or him, Emily. He would have killed T.J. and me, and you know what he'd have done with you."

"But you would have been able to best him. We could have taken him to the sheriff."

"He was a madman, and he fought with the strength of a madman. I don't know if I could have taken him without help. He tossed me around as if I was nothing. I'm very grateful for your help, Emily."

"Really? Then you don't think I'm a murderess?"

"Good heavens, you're a saint, Emily. An angel. Why would you think that? You get that idea out of your head this instant."

She grinned sleepily. "All right. I think I can sleep now. Could you sing one of your songs for me?"

396

"Come wif me to 'de freedom tree, where 'de night done turn to day . . ." She hummed the rest of the song as she rocked the infant to sleep. She ran a finger over the little face, tracing the tiny features. His little fist searched for his seeking mouth, she helped him find his thumb. Silky black curls hugged her fingers. How she remembered those days when Tyler was just a baby. She and Elijah had been so happy then.

She lifted the fretful babe to her shoulder and closed her eyes, remembering so clearly the feeling of cuddling her newborn. He smelled so sweet, so warm and new.

She blocked out the other thoughts that always seemed to plague her these days, thoughts that left her depressed and wondering at the futility of working so hard to bring young couples from one bondage to another. A bondage that might be worse.

Were they doing these people a disservice, taking them from secure homes and turning them loose in a vast country that was either untamed wilderness or overcrowed with people just like themselves? Perhaps escape was the answer for people who were beaten, treated like animals or worse. But others . . .

Hattie, the baby's mother, had been a lady's maid in a huge plantation house. Her mistress had wed a man and moved away, so Hattie decided time had come to go after her own freedom. She and her young man had fled. And here they were, naive, unskilled, penniless, and with a brand new baby to care for. They were completely disillusioned.

Bekka was beginning to have serious doubts about her work.

"You're tired, Bekka," Charley had told her when she confided her feelings to her friend. Charlaine had run the shelter for two years. She'd seen them all come and go.

"I miss my son," Bekka had admitted. "I lost him, Charley. I lost my baby."

"Lots of children die, honey chile. You an' your man can have more."

"No. I mean I lost him. I left him alone for an hour, and when I went back for him he was gone. He's out there somewhere. They have him. I used to be able to search for him, but since being sent here . . ."

Charley nodded her understanding. "Tell you what, girl, you need to get back on de road. If'n you don't, you gonna lose your mind. It's sittin' 'round here what's gettin' you down. Ain't I right, now?" Just the thought of traveling lightened her spirits and lifted a heavy yoke of oppression from her shoulders. To travel again. To search again. To catch a brief glimpse of Elijah again. Yes, she wanted that.

"When can I leave?"

Seneca reckoned he was little more than a day behind them, but what with having to convince the station masters and agents at each stop he made that he was on Elijah's side lost him precious time.

For whatever reason, perhaps having Emily with him, Elijah was traveling fast. He rode a wagon one day, caught a steamer up the lake the next. But Seneca understood and was grateful for the care and caution the road keepers took with his friends and his wife. If they were being followed by the slavers or the Frenchman, he wanted them protected, even if it meant he was extra days in locating them.

On his third night out he rode up to a farmhouse outside Oswego. The farm was owned by a very reserved gentleman, who, because of Seneca's gun, didn't want to open his doors to him at all. Eventually Seneca gained entrance and was led to a long narrow room where eight Negroes were gathered for supper.

All of them tensed at his arrival. "Relax. This man is a Friend of Liberty," the station master said, passing Seneca the bowl of beef stew. "He has brought fifty-three across the canal in two years. He means no one here any harm."

That met with shy smiles and nods of approval, except for one woman at the far end of the table. Seneca found her reserve captivating yet irritating. She was an extraordinarily beautiful Negress with raven hair pulled straight back into a chignon that accented her exotic eyes, her queenly profile, and her sensuous lips. She was tall and lithe, and her movements were graceful and fluid. And she played on his memory.

Names were rarely exchanged, nor were friendships formed at the stations, so neither he nor the others were introduced. Passengers were cordial, but kept to themselves unless they were traveling together. Too much sorrow lay in parting from new friends. They spoke to each other, instead, of dreams and goals and the bright future that lay in store for them in Canada. And sometimes, like that night, they sang together.

Seneca helped clear the supper dishes, then strolled to where the enchantress stood at the window. He had learned nothing about her except that she had been a conductor on the road for several years. She was not with a group now.

"Are you going to collect your passengers?" he asked, lighting up a thin cigar.

"Not just yet. I'm changing assignments. I want to find a busy route to work." Her voice was as musical as her movements.

"Are you legally free?"

"No. You are wondering if I would travel the canal?"

He nodded. "We're very visible, though. I have a friend, a man whose papers I bought, who works with me as my partner. We are often stopped by slavers trying to take him."

"He is not your slave? Your possession?" she asked, sliding him a sidelong look.

"It has been his wish to work to pay for his freedom. He is a proud man. It is not my wish to make him less. His debt is paid as of two weeks ago."

"I have seen him with you," she admitted, hoping for more information from him. "I have heard him say 'Yes, sir, bossman, sir.' Do you ask him to humble himself so?"

Seneca chuckled. "That was Elijah's way. If he thought he'd avoid trouble for us, he'd do it. It's amazing how many folks resent an articulate Negro."

"Elijah? That is his name?"

"Yes. He's been my partner for three years now."

"Tell me about him."

"Well," he said with a twinkle in his eye, "he's

400

married. Don't be too interested."

"I see. And are you?" she asked. "Married?"

"As a matter of fact, I am. I married just recently. She's beautiful. She's as fair as you are dark."

Bekka remembered the woman. "Congratulations. I hope you have a happy life."

Seneca sobered. "Yes. So do I. Excuse me. I think I'll turn in now. I want to get an early start in the morning."

"Are you going far?"

"As far as I have to," he said enigmatically.

She asked no more, just turned back to the moonlit night. A dozen questions buzzed in her head. She could ask none of them without revealing who she was.

So what would be the harm? Hadn't she suffered enough in three years. How long must she endure the awful loneliness of being separated from a loved one. From her family. How she longed to walk into Elijah's arms and let him bear some of her burden of guilt. Would he be able to do that? Or would he hate her, push her away?

That thought was so painful her breath caught in the throat. And suddenly she wanted Seneca's company, she wanted to be near the man who was part of Elijah's life. She turned toward him, but already he had found a bunk and was stretched out with his head pillowed on interlocked fingers. His thoughts were elsewhere, far away.

She turned back to her midnight moon. Her hand went automatically to the medallion at her neck. She lifted it from beneath her blouse and pressed it to her lips.

Seneca watched her proud back from beneath

lowered lashes, wondering why such an elegant creature would spend her life trekking across the country in all kinds of weather, living in hideaways tucked behind the world, risking her life for people whose names she did not know. What drove her? What demon was she exorcising? For what foul deed was she punishing herself?

He could see it in her, because he'd seen it in himself so often. He'd run too. He'd embarked on a course of self-destruction that shamed him to remember now. And all because he held himself responsible for what he saw as the end of his life.

Not until Emily burst into his world did he begin to see himself clearly. He'd been beating himself up for nothing. He'd found himself in a position where he had to make a life-and-death decision. He made the best decision he could at the time. His life had turned around because of that decision, that was true, but he saw now how his physical pain, his heartache and depression, his anger, had all conspired to send him into a dark tunnel of self-doubt, self-derision, and guilt, until he saw himself as unworthy of anything good. And that's how he'd lived. Until Emily.

He closed his eyes and rolled to his side. He'd like to go and talk to her, learn her name, a little about her, but he knew he wouldn't. He knew from experience that if she was running from herself and her pain, no amount of well-intentioned interference would change her attitudes.

Seneca packed his belongings onto the back of his saddle the next morning. He thanked the farmer for giving him shelter and for what information he was able to acquire from him. He slipped him a bill to help with expenses.

As he was mounting he asked one more question. About the woman. The farmer hesitated, but finally he answered.

"She's a special woman. Some call her the Princess."

"She's the Princess?"

"That's what folks call her. No one knows her given name. A real mystery, that one. And she's always fingering that white necklace she wears. Like it's some magic charm."

Seneca dismounted. "White necklace? About this big? With carving on it?" he demanded.

"Ah, yeah, that's right. I seen it last night."

"Where is she now?"

"Why, gone. She left nigh on to an hour ago."

"This is urgent. Did she say where she was going?"

"Hey, you some kind of slaver?"

"No. God, no. But I have to find her."

"She was going to the lake to find a conductor who'd take her to Buffalo. She wanted to go to Buffalo."

Seneca was torn. Emily was less than a day away if the station master's information was correct. And if the woman he'd met last night was who he suspected, then Bekka was only an hour away.

Emily was with Elijah. She was safe. Could he do less for Elijah's wife? Her demeanor, the look in her eye when she spoke to him last evening, made sense now. She had recognized him. She had been reaching out to touch Elijah through him.

Why was she running? Why hadn't she come to them earlier if she knew where they were? Because of T.J.? Because she had lost the boy? Did she think Elijah would hate her for that?

403

And then he remembered what he had thought about her, how she seemed so much like him, and he understood. She felt that as long as T.J. was still gone, she could never give herself to Elijah, was unworthy of him.

She didn't know T.J. was home.

He mounted. "Give me directions, the fastest way to intercept her. Believe me, this is important. What I have to tell her will make her the happiest woman in the world."

Seneca rode like the very devil, crossing meadows, streams, jumping fences that were in his way. He saw her ahead of him, and then he didn't.

He rode to where she had last been and dismounted. He'd hunt her down on foot if he had to. He stood perfectly still, listening.

"It's no use, I know you're in here," he said, tying his horse to a low branch and strolling into a thickly wooded glen. She bolted and ran deeper into the woods. He dived after her, slashing the branches aside.

She was sliding carefully down a ravine when he caught up with her. He went after her, his long legs closing the distance between them. He clamped an arm around her waist. She fought, throwing them off balance. They slipped, fell, and rolled together down the hill.

Seneca caught her wrists and pinned her to the ground.

"You," she gasped, when she looked up into his face.

"Yes, me."

She closed her eyes and tears squeezed their way between long curled lashes. Seneca released her wrists and rolled to his side, pulling her into his arms. This is where she had wanted to be last night. He had felt it. That was why he'd left her so suddenly? But now he could hold her, and it was all right.

"Hush," he soothed, but no words he could find could stem the flow of her tears. All her grief and pain spilled forth in deep anguished sobs.

"Don't, Bekka. Don't punish yourself anymore. It does no good. No one expects it of you. Look at me."

She turned tear-filled eyes up to his. "You know." She would have looked away, but Seneca wouldn't permit it.

"Yes, I know. Oh, woman, don't you realize that Elijah's been looking for you all these years?"

"I can't see him. You must promise not to tell him."

"Nonsense. You're coming with me to find him right now."

She shied away and sat up. "I can't. I can't."

"Because of T.J.?" Seneca sat up, facing her.

"Who?" She shook a baffled head.

"Tyler. He calls himself T.J. now. He's quite a young man, your son."

"You've seen him? Where is he? I must get him."

"No need. He is with Elijah."

Her shoulders sagged and her head dropped. "Then I can never go back. But I'm so happy for Tyler. I was so worried for him. I knew Elijah had you, you see. But Tyler . . ."

"Bekka, don't torture yourself. What happened wasn't anyone's fault. It just happened."

"I lost my son. I lost Elijah's son."

"T.J. didn't stay where you put him. He went looking for you. He couldn't have understood the

405

dangers."

"All the more reason why I should never have left him."

"Right. And you're a rotten mother, a horrid wife. You don't deserve Elijah, or T.J. Certainly not happiness in any form. And you'll do penance for the rest of your life by leading slaves into Canada in the dead of winter or the killing heat of summer, and by shutting yourself off from any relationship that might bring you joy. And no risk is too great to take, because if anything happened to you, it would be no less than you deserved. Am I close, Bekka?"

She took a shuddering breath and stared at him, appalled that he had come so close to the center of her heart.

"I've been there, sweetheart. I'd be there still if Emily hadn't come along. She forced me to see myself as I'd become, and as I was becoming. It was pretty much of a shock. Don't turn yourself into a hard, cold, lonely woman, when you can have all the love and happiness in the world. You've done your penance, if you must look at it in that way. No one could have done more than the Princess. Now it's time for you and your family. They need you. And like it or not, I'm taking you to them."

He helped her to her feet and pulled the leaves from her hair. He tipped her chin up and wiped away her tears with his thumbs.

"Elijah was right. You're beautiful. I should have known you just to look at you, but I confess, I thought he was exaggerating. We're fortunate men, Elijah and I. Emily is an absolute angel. You'll like her."

"Yes. I met her once. I didn't want to get involved, but she was in trouble. It was in Albany, on the docks. Her friend had been hurt and I went for help. I had a man find you. You helped her, didn't you?"

"That was you!"

"I used to sit up in one of the empty attics and watch Elijah."

He groaned and gathered her close. "No more dark attics for you, young lady."

"I'm so scared."

Emily watched as Elijah shifted T.J. to his other arm.

"That's enough Elijah. You can't carry him all night. Let's make camp here."

"No. Just one more mile. Not even a mile. Look, you can see the light through the trees. It's a safehouse, Emily. Can you make it that far?"

"Yes, but can you?"

Emily rapped on the door when they finally arrived at their destination.

"The lawn needs cutting," said a voice from inside. A woman's voice.

"Turn the cows loose," Emily replied.

The door opened. "Who have you there?" she asked, not even blinking at Emily's presence.

"A man and a boy."

"One minute." She closed the door and returned shortly after with a basket and a lantern. "This way please. My cellar is full. You'll have to use the barn."

"That's fine. Anywhere."

"I'll show you a back room where you'll be safe

enough. And I've brought you some food. Leave the basket here when you leave in the morning. I'll get it later."

Elijah followed them into the back room of the barn and laid T.J. on the corner cot. He took off the child's shoes and unwound the old woolen blanket he'd been wearing as a wrap.

The woman set the lantern down and tucked one of the blankets around him. "He's a beautiful child," she said. She lifted the medalion and looked at it carefully. "Does this have some special significance?" She looked at Elijah. "I see you have one also."

"No, no special meaning."

"I'm sorry if I'm prying. It's just that I saw another one just two days ago. A woman traveling alone wore it. A very sad woman."

Chapter 25

Elijah sat down on the edge of the bunk. He looked winded. Shocked.

"Ma-am, do you know this woman's name?" Emily asked. "Can you describe her?"

"I don't remember her name. She kept to herself. She was very attractive though. I remember that much."

"Bekka," Elijah said, dumbfounded.

"Yes, that was it." The woman nodded toward the basket. "There is a flask of coffee in there. I'll see you in the morning."

"Wait," Elijah said, suddenly coming to life. "Where did she go. Which direction?"

"I can't tell you that. You know the rules."

"She's my wife. She's my wife and I haven't seen her for three years.

"They each had a medallion when they were separated," Emily explained. "We want their family back together, that's all. We wouldn't ask otherwise."

"She was going south. That's all I can say. Good night."

Emily turned hopefully to Elijah. "Do you think she's your wife? Oh, that would be wonderful!"

He took a long breath. "I'm afraid to let myself believe. I feel as if I'm on the edge of a precipice, and if I jump off I'll either fly like an eagle or I'll crash like a rock to the ground."

"It will be all right, Elijah. It will. If she is Bekka or if she isn't, you still have T.J. and us. We consider ourselves your family."

"Thanks, Emily."

"Hey, come on, let's eat. Should we wake T.J.?"

Like Pennsylvania, New York, had an impressive network of underground railroads, but because of the threat of legal action against the operators by commissioners of the Fugitive Slave Law, they were altered frequently. Only two ran up the western side, both crossing over at Buffalo into Canada. Further east quite a few routes were in use. Two of those ran through Syracuse, one connecting to the railroad north, the other going up the shore of Lake Ontario.

Elijah decided to take the shore road. "She'll go that way. She always loved the water. It's in her soul. Her mother came from an island in the Pacific Ocean."

Emily prepared for their departure in silence. She was afraid for him, afraid he would be devastated if he found his wife's medallion on another woman. Afraid he would go just a little bit insane if he knew how close he'd been to her without finding her.

"Where would she be going? Does she have passengers to conduct? Who would know?" she asked.

"If she is a conductor, the logical place to meet passengers would be near the safehouse in Oswego. Agents might change conductors there."

"Would she go to Buffalo? Would she go to the

canal?"

"I don't know why. Buffalo is crawling with slavers. They try to get the slaves before they cross the channel into Canada."

They walked for hours along the dusty lakeside road. Elijah was loathe to stop even for the briefest periods. But at least they were not being pursued. Their haste was due to eagerness, not fear.

Emily began to understand, to experience how refugees must feel to be homeless and penniless and at the mercy of other folks, to be beholden and know there would never be a chance to repay their debt.

That evening they were given directions to a station house run by a widower, Mr. Archer, where they were offered a hot meal and board. Halfway through the meal a rider approached. The stationmaster left the table and went outside to greet his visitor.

They were out there a long time. Elijah looked at Emily, both knowing that if slave commissioners found them, Elijah and T.J. would be taken away. She would be left alone. Just the previous month one of the station masters had turned over a slave for a large reward. Not everyone could be trusted, unfortunately.

"I'm going out there," she said. "Go into the back room and wait."

She opened the door and strolled onto the porch, draping a shawl over her shoulders. "What is it, dear?" she asked sweetly, moving to stand at Mr. Archer's side.

"Why, there you are, darling," he said with a suspicious twitch to his lips. "I believe it's your husband come to call."

411

"Wha . . ." With mouth agape she spun around to look at the bearded stranger beside his horse. His white teeth peeked out of his crooked grin.

"Seneca!" she cried, running down the steps and into his open arms. "Oh, Seneca." She planted noisy kisses all over his face as he swung her around.

Finally he set her on her feet and turned to face Archer. "My wife, Emily. She can be a bit over-emotional at times."

Emily poked his rib. "You were gone so long," she said to Mr. Archer. "We began to worry."

"Emily, I brought someone with me."

Emily turned back and looked up at the rider seated on the horse. Solemn and apprehensive eyes looked back.

"You," Emily said. "It's you! You're Bekka! But why?"

"Because of T.J.," Seneca answered, understanding her question.

She had no chance to react to that for just then the front door burst open and T.J. bounded out, followed by Elijah. Both stopped at the top of the steps, caught by the sight of Bekka on the horse.

Seneca helped her down. "Go on. Don't be afraid."

Bekka walked nervously toward the stairs and the two people who had been denied her for so long.

"Mama? Mama!" He ran down the steps and into her open arms. She went to her knees and held his face between her hands, looking, loving, kissing, crying.

"Ty, oh Ty, my baby. I have you back. Thank you, God. Oh, I've missed you so much."

Her arms were full of her child, yet she couldn't

412

seem to get enough of him as she held him to her bosom. Long legs walked into her line of vision. Elijah. She had to face him. Now was the time, but she was so afraid.

She set T.J. away from her and slowly came to her feet. "Can you forgive me?" she asked, looking at her entwined fingers.

"Can you forgive me?" he asked in return.

She looked up at last. He was the same, yet not the same. But her love for him was stronger than ever. "For what? You haven't done anything," she said.

"I'm to blame. I made mistakes. I got caught. I left you to fight for your lives on your own. I wasn't there for you."

"But I lost Tyler. You didn't do anything. It's my fault."

"No, Mama, I didn't stay where you said to stay. It's my fault. You didn't do anything either."

"Stop it," Emily said crossly. *"Blame, fault.* Are you all crazy?"

They all turned to look at her. Seneca and Archer stared at her too.

"What I mean is . . . Well, who's to blame here, really? Did you ask to be made slaves? Don't you believe you had a right to fight for your freedom? So something went wrong. It happens. You didn't leave T.J. alone because you were tired of having him with you. You did it for a good reason. And he can't be blamed for worrying about you. None of this is anybody's fault. There is no blame to be had. And I don't want to hear anymore about it. Come along, T.J. Finish your supper while your mother and father get reacquainted. Gentlemen."

"Bossy, isn't she," Seneca said, laughing. But he

and Archer followed her and T.J. into the house.

Elijah opened his arms and Bekka rushed into them. For a long time they just held each other. Finally he leaned back and tilted her face up to the moonlight.

"As beautiful as ever. More beautiful. I've never forgotten your face. It's been in my dreams constantly."

She fingered the line by his eye. "You've a few more scars than before. Oh, Elijah, I have another confession to make. I've known where to find you for a year now."

His head tilted in puzzlement. "You were afraid of me?"

"Not that way. Had you scorned me, I would have died. I had to wait until . . . "

He understood. "We could have searched together."

"I wanted to spare you that pain. You thought he was with me. That's how I wanted it to stay. There was no comfort to be had for what horrors I imagined."

"You would have had the comfort of my love. You thought I would hate you? I could never hate you. You are my heart. Let's go for a walk. Away from here," he said, lifting Seneca's bedroll from the back of his horse. "They won't miss us for a while. And, oh God, how I need to love you."

"I'm very proud of you and what you've been doing, Lije."

"Not for one minute did I stop looking for you. And you? I'm told you're a conductor, too."

"I've done my share."

He laughed. "Yes, you have."

She sobered. "Seneca told me about West Virginia. I'm sorry you had to endure that."

"I'd go through it again to have my family back. I can't believe the long years of waiting are over at last."

"It seems like an eternity," she said, "yet when I look into your eyes, I feel as if we've never been parted."

"Where did Seneca find you?"

She explained how he'd tracked her down because of the medallion. He told her how he was coming back to look for her because the woman noticed their medallions.

"They were given to us with a blessing, and blessed they have been," Elijah said. He spread out the bedroll and sat down, holding out a hand for Bekka to join him.

"It's been a long time, Elijah."

"I'm not in any hurry, and to tell the truth, I'd like to just hold you close for a while. The nights were the worst, when my arms ached for you."

She nodded and snuggled into his side. Very slowly he lowered them both to the ground until they lay facing each other in the moonlight.

Elijah smoothed her hair back and loosened it from its confinement, spreading the long black tresses over her shoulder.

"I'm glad you didn't cut it," he said. "It's so silky and smooth. I remember the feel of it against my skin."

"Touch my face like you used to do. Oh, Elijah, I have missed you so much. I used to go to towns where you'd be just so I could see you for a minute or two. I would ache for you for weeks after, wanting to feel your arms around me, hear your voice in my ear."

"Shh. No more talk now of the past. We will put it to rest. We have a future to build."

"What will we do, Elijah? Will we go into Canada?"

"No. No more running for us. We are going to Albany. I have work there if I want it. If you want to go there."

"Baby, I can't go there. I'm not free. They can take me back if they find me. And they will. I've become somewhat notorious."

"T.J. and I both have our papers. We'll get yours."

"They won't sell you mine. I've caused them too much trouble."

"Oh, I think Seneca can manage it. He has a considerable amount of leverage now after what happened in West Virginia. If that story were published, especially in connection with the assassination attempt on Abraham Lincoln, the Southern cause would suffer a stunning blow."

"Then why not just do it?" she asked, her interest piqued.

"Politics. Peaceful negotiations. The governor of West Virginia has promised to clean up his state. The other states are now undergoing an examination by Federal investigators on how they're handling the Fugitive Slave Law. Politicians want the whole issue hushed. The South is afraid they're going to lose the law, the North regrets very much having passed it in the first place. They're very nervous."

"I bet they are."

"But it works to our advantage. Seneca can twist a few arms to get what he wants."

"He'd do that for me?"

"Hell, yes. I'll tell you sometime what he did for me."

"Yes, I'd like to hear it. Sometime. But not just this minute. Look, the moon's out. I used to stand outside at night and imagine what you were doing under the same moon as I was under."

"I can answer that tonight. I'm making love to my wife."

His dark head lowered, his lips brushed her forehead, her eyes, her exotic cheekbones, her wonderfully tempting lips. "Bekka, Bekka, tell me I'm not dreaming."

"I can't. I'm afraid I'll wake up. It's just the same, isn't it? You still leave me breathless."

"I love you more than ever."

Her arms wound around his neck, pulling his lips to hers. She kissed him, and for some reason tears came to her eyes. How silly, she thought, and then she was weeping openly, clutching at Elijah, crying his name over and over.

"Ah, sugar cakes, don't weep." But he held her and he comforted her, and her copious tears seemed to cleanse and heal not only her afflicted soul, but his, as well.

The barriers between them, fear and uncertainty, fell away. She was still his Bekka; he was still her man. And the desire that had always been a living part of their lives together was alive again and growing.

She kissed every new mark on his chest, his shoulders, his back. He learned again the sleek lines of her supple body, her womanly curves.

She stood beside him and slowly unbuttoned her blouse. Elijah knelt in front of her and buried his face between her breasts, inhaling the sweet wom-

417

anly scent of her. Her head fell back at the sensations she'd long denied herself.

He found the dark swollen tips of her breasts, lavishing attention on each until Bekka was weak and wild and trembling with desire.

Elijah remembered how it had been with Bekka, how they had always loved coming together in the past. Bekka was a creature of nature, a child of the earth, a woman of intense passion. What she felt she felt deeply and completely. And when she made love, she gave totally of herself.

He felt himself being wrapped in that wonderful blanket of sensuality. Her fingers, long and graceful, and talented in the art of love, played across the planes and valleys of his body, uncovering and seeking out those places that drove him mad with wanting her. Her mouth, hot and moist, was against his skin, biting, kissing, laving. Coherent thought was lost in a mist of sensations, the scent of her, the sultry sound of her throaty cries, the feel of her silken body swaying and undulating naked against his, the heat, the scorching heat of her, burning into his mind, his body, his soul.

He took them to the blanket, covering her lithe body with his. He took her quickly, forcefully, unable to hold back, and she gave an exultant cry of pleasure, of feminine victory.

Their loving was unrestrained even after years of abstinence. They came together wildly, as if to obliterate the past pain and loneliness. Their bodies craved each other and found joy in the having. When fulfillment came it was tumultuous, sending them both into a wild paroxysm of ecstasy. And when the delightful storm had passed they looked at each other and laughed with joy at being together again.

They were welcomed with a grand feast when they returned to Rochester. Wanda couldn't do enough for Emily.

"I'm so sorry I didn't see those men take you away. They didn't hurt you, did they? I could live with myself thinking that."

"Wanda, Wanda," Emily interrupted her. "I was with Elijah and T.J. They wouldn't let those men near me, would you, champ?" she said, smiling down at T.J. and giving him a hug.

"I'm glad you had two such men to protect you then. I was worried, I can tell you."

"We took good care of her," T.J. boasted importantly. "Just like Seneca took care of my Mama."

The next few days were busy days full of laughter and fun. They took an excursion to the beach for Bekka, they picnicked for T.J., they went out dining for Emily.

Bekka, at Louise's insistence, had a completely new wardrobe fashioned for her. And Emily's wedding gown was still waiting to be worn.

Once the ladies were busy finalizing the plans for the wedding and the party to follow, Elijah and Seneca slipped away to tend to some unfinished business.

Seneca wired Dolly in Erie, inviting her to the wedding and asking a couple favors of her. Next they went to the sheriff's office and checked on the two kidnappers. The men had been transported to a prison facility where they would spend two years at hard labor. Elijah gave a full report of what happened in the woods with the Frenchman. The sheriff promised to check into it, but saw no problem with Emily defending her own life as well as Elijah's and the boy's.

Elijah then went to the county clerk's office to register his and T.J.'s emancipation papers, to have copies made and stamped with a court seal and duly recorded in that office so that he need never be without proof again.

Seneca had one more stop to make on his way home. He visited Phillip Martin at his place of business.

"Seneca," Phillip greeted him seriously, offering his hand. "Come in, have a seat. I can't begin to apologize for the pain and distress my family has caused yours. I am deeply ashamed and sorry."

"You were not to know what they were doing."

"But I should have. I, more than anyone, know what they are both capable of. I just didn't want to see it. And when I did, the damage had already been done. If there is any way I can make amends . . ."

"There is no need. In a way, it was all a blessing. Elijah found his wife. We are all fine. The wedding is to be this Saturday. We're going ahead with it even though we've been married for nearly a month now."

"For Louise, I suppose," he said, smiling for the first time.

"And Emily. Every girl has her dreams. How is Belinda?"

He shook his head. "How you could even care I don't understand. We've sent Belinda to my sister in Harrisburg, Pennsylvania. Angela is a nurse in the hospital there. She knows a man who can help Belinda."

420

"But surely . . . "

"We have to do something before she kills some-
ne. She's always been obsessed with having what
he wanted at any cost. She's been worse of late.
And this thing with Emily . . ."

"I feel responsible in a way. Maybe if I had
otten her out of that fire sooner . . ."

"No, Seneca. I don't know what my wife told
ou, but you did the right thing. Did you know
ny mother's will stated that Belinda was to receive
 sizable amount of money at her death?"

"Are you saying . . . ? No."

"Yes. Belinda started that fire, hoping her grand-
nother would die. Why do you think she was so
ngry with you? She wanted that money. And who
lid you save first?"

Seneca shook his head, remembering all the tor-
nent he'd gone through because of that fire. He
ulled a bank draft from his coat pocket. "I'd still
ike you to accept this."

Phillip Martin looked at the draft and handed it
ack. "I can't accept it."

"Then consider it a loan, payable when you can
nanage it. Use it to implement those new ideas we
liscussed."

"A loan, then. Thank you, Seneca. Thank you
ery much. You won't be sorry.

The wedding day dawned bright and sunny. Em-
ly stretched and yawned, waking when Wanda
rought her breakfast in bed.

"Is everyone else up?" she asked. "Where is Sen-
ca?"

"Yes, everyone else is awake, and Seneca and
Elijah have gone to collect the flowers. Eat your
reakfast now. I'll have a bath ready for you in half

an hour."

"Am I being waited on today?" she asked, laughing.

"You bet you are. You're the bride."

"But you've so much else to do."

"Ah, Mrs. Johnson and her daughters have come over to help. We've everything under control. You don't think I'd miss the fun on the day my little Seneca gets married, do you?"

"Oh, Wanda, I love you all so much. You're the family I always wanted."

"Well, for better or worse, you're stuck with us now."

"Do you think we're being silly, having this wedding?"

"Oh, no. Everyone there will be taking their vows all over again, too. And Louise is so excited about it. It would be a shame to deprive her."

"I'll tell you a secret. I'm excited, too."

"Course you are. Now eat up. I'll be up to help you do your hair after your bath."

The pearls Louise and Liam had given her were the perfect compliment to the tiny pearls sewn into the lace on the bodice of her gown. Wanda had used the combs Seneca had given her to secure her headpiece and veil to her hair.

Marianne, in a pale pink gown, and Bekka in one of her new two-piece dresses in pale gold, came in to wish Emily well. They were going on to the church to see that the men were ready.

"Daddy will be up in a minute. You look fantastic, Emily. I'm so glad you're my sister."

"Seneca couldn't have found anyone more lovely," Bekka said. "I wish you all the happiness in the world."

Two days later their party of five boarded Seneca's boat for a trip back down the Erie Canal. New lives awaited them, and new challenges. And some old and dear friends.

"Emily and I will be living at my home," Seneca explained.

"But Uncle Joe's house is empty now. If you like it, you can live there."

"A whole house just for us?" T.J. asked, amazed. "Does it have a back yard and a swing?"

"Yes," Emily said. "And a treehouse you and your friends can use as a clubhouse."

"But it's your home," Bekka said reservedly. "We couldn't."

"I have no use for it now. It will be included as a benefit of Elijah's employment. It won't be easy running the business."

"What of the man who's overseeing it now?" Elijah asked.

"He's just the bookkeeper. He can't manage the men at the factory. He can't get parts or promote sales," Seneca explained. "He'll be happy to have the responsibility lifted from his shoulders."

They remembered those words later when they arrived in Albany and took a cab to Emily's former home. It was early morning, and the sun glistened on the cobbled streets. Memories came flooding back. The carriage came to a stop at the front door, and everyone climbed down from the cab.

"Please, wait for us," Seneca asked the driver. He followed Emily up the steps. She stopped and moved a brick beside the front door, extracting a key.

Full of excitement and enthusiasm, she led everyone into the foyer, into the parlor. They all came to a halt at the startled gasps from their left.

"What is the meaning of this," huffed a very indignant man who stood up from the dining table.

"Mr. Petrie," she said, dumbfounded. "What are you doing here?"

"Me?" he spat angrily. His glare took her in, head to toe, and went to those with her. "What are *you* doing here?"

Chapter 26

"That house belongs to us. Uncle Joe left it to me in his will. I may not remember much of what was in that will, but I remember that."

"Don't worry about it now, sweetheart," Seneca said, unloading cases from the boot of the carriage. "My—our home is big enough for all of us. After we're settled in, we'll go over to see Paddie and your lawyer."

Paddie opened the door with a scowl for having been wakened. "What the devil do you . . ." His eyes widened. "Seneca! Emily! Good Lord, come in." He gave Emily one of his monstrous bear hugs and slapped Seneca's shoulder as he pumped his hand up and down. "Good to see you. Good to see you. So, you're back. Maggie's kept your room ready for ya, gal. She'll be tickled pink you're home."

"Oh, Paddie, didn't you get our wire?"

"Wire? No. What's wrong?"

"That explains it. I wired the police station. I thought that would be the surest way to reach you," Seneca explained.

"When? I'm on two-week leave. Maggie and I just returned to town."

Emily grinned. "Paddie, Seneca and I are married."

"Married. Well, you ol' son-of-a-gun. I knew you couldn't resist her. I'll be damned. Is he treating you good, lass? If he don't, you come to me."

Emily and Seneca both laughed, and Seneca hugged Emily's shoulders. "She's led me a merry chase. It's a three-beer story."

"Where is Margaret?" Emily asked.

"This is her morning to work at the hospital. She'll be back after she feeds her patients their lunch. Married, eh?" He shook his head, beaming ear to ear.

"Paddie, Elijah has his family back together," Seneca said.

"This has been a trip to remember then. I knew Emily would bring you luck."

"But we have a problem. Emily offered Elijah the position of foreman at the factory."

"That's great. Don't see any problem in the long run. Might have a bit of resistance from some until he proves himself, being a stranger, you understand. But once they know him . . ."

"That's not it. As part of the deal, she offered him use of Joe's house. Her house."

"And?"

"And Petrie has moved his family into it."

"He *what?* Did he know you were married, that you wouldn't be living there?"

"I guess he expected me to live with you and Maggie for the rest of my life."

"Paddie, can you arrange a meeting with her lawyer for later today?"

"Hell, let's go over there now. He'll see us."

Mr. Stevens greeted Emily warmly, patting her

shoulder, then touching her hand when she was seated beside his desk.

"Congratulations, my dear. Mr. Prescott, I've heard good things about you."

"And some not so good, I'm sure."

Stevens chuckled and pulled on his earlobe. "Well, yes. You have developed a reputation of sorts."

Emily laughed. "He's a pirate and a rogue, Mr. Stevens. Don't let these trappings of civilization fool you."

"Well, I can see he's been good for you. Now what can I do for you."

"We would like you to read Joe's will for us," Paddie said. "That Petrie's up to no good. He's gone and moved his family into Emily's house."

"Do tell. That *is* curious. Had you given him reason to believe he was at liberty to do so?" he asked, turning to Emily.

"I haven't spoken to him since before Uncle Joe died."

Stevens pulled Emily's file from his cabinet and sat down with it. "I'm glad you asked to go over this. You weren't paying much attention last time."

"Does Petrie know what it says?" Seneca asked.

"Of course. As a partner in the business, he was mentioned in the will."

They all listened attentively as Stevens read what Joe Harcourt had wanted done with his worldly possessions. When he finished, Seneca and Emily could only stare at each other.

"Nothing in there that says Petrie can just take her house from her." Paddie was getting angry.

"No. Not unless she dies, at which time he gets it all," Seneca said viciously. "He knew about that clause all along?"

"What are you getting at?" Paddie asked.

"Consider this. He knew Joe and Peter were murdered. Accident or not, someone killed them, and someone tried to kill Emily. If you knew what could be yours if that someone succeeded, wouldn't you try to help them along?"

"Are you saying he moved into that house because he never intended for her to return at all?" Paddie asked thunderously. "I'll damn well kill the bastard."

"Now hold on here," Stevens said calmly. "No going off half-cocked. Let's have a closer look here."

"No," Seneca said. "I'm convinced. Petrie was not only annoyed to see Emily, he was surprised. And you have to admit, Emily, that that damned Frenchman showed up at every turn. Remember how odd we thought it that he'd still be after us when Lincoln was safely on his way."

"Yes, and we thought he might be one of Ryker's men who was after you."

"We've had entirely too many bastards trying to kill us. Who has copies of the books that Petrie keeps on the buggy works? I'd like to go over them. Let's see what he's been up to before we accuse him."

Paddie and Seneca carried armloads of books and records from Mr. Stevens's storage room out to the carriage. After delivering Emily and the books back to the Prescott home, they went to the factory to collect the current records and to notify Petrie that they were investigating the business.

"You might see if your previous home is still available, because Emily has plans for her house," Seneca told Petrie after he'd explained the reason

430

for their visit.

"Emily," Petrie scoffed. "What does she know of business?"

"Perhaps nothing yet, but as her husband, the business becomes my responsibility. I assure you I am capable of adding up your figures to see how you're handling her affairs."

He blanched and began to sweat. "I've worked for Joe for ten years. I got ten percent of the company. Ten lousy percent. He left the rest of it to her."

"She's family. He left the business in Emily's trust for his son. He wouldn't have expected Peter to die with him. But none of that is reason to play squatter with her home."

"Look, Mr. Prescott, she doesn't need that house. She's married to you."

"Nevertheless, we shall require you to vacate. And we require that all furnishings, down to the smallest item, be replaced. We would appreciate your attending to that with all due haste."

"I'll need two weeks," Petrie said stubbornly.

"You have *one*. And should you entertain any more ideas of getting rid of my wife and me, let me warn you that several people already know about the numerous attempts on our lives and what you have to gain. If we turn up dead, you'll be the first person Paddie comes after."

"What makes you think . . ." His voice trailed off in the face of Seneca's black look, but he glared back with stubborn defiance as Seneca helped himself to the books and walked out the door.

That evening Seneca, Elijah, Paddie, and Stevens shut themselves in the library and began going over the logs. Emily and Bekka had a chance to visit

431

with Margaret.

"I couldn't be more pleased for both Seneca and Elijah. I've been feeding those two for years now, whenever they were in town. They were both miserable under their tough facades. And Bekka, you're just as lovely as Elijah said. You wouldn't consider . . ."

"Wouldn't consider what?"

"Oh, nothing. I'm being presumptuous. It's just that the ladies of our church are having a fund raiser tomorrow to aid the refugees who come through Albany."

"How might I help, Margaret?"

"I'm sure we could double our yearly contribution if you would come and speak to us, tell us what is needed. We want to help, but we really have no idea what it's like for the runaways. To be very honest, we don't really know what slavery is like. We've all been insulated from any of that sort of thing. It's a different world to us, which does not excuse our years of indifference, mind you. But now . . ."

"I think I understand. We have momentum going now."

"Yes, and it has given us a chance to become involved where we didn't know how to do so before."

Emily stood and began to pace thoughtfully. "Why stop with fundraisers. Why not arrange a lecture tour to raise the public awareness of the plight of the slaves and those seeking freedom. We have a golden opportunity. If we can help to get Mr. Lincoln elected, the slaves will be freed within years. What do you think, Bekka? Could you do it?"